MOBBED UP II

RETURN TO NEW YORK

A Novel by Stephanie Baldi

ISBN: 978-1-951543-34-1—Print

ISBN: 978-1-951543-35-8—eBook

Library of Congress Control Number: 2023900382.

Front Cover Art by Mary Rogers
Cover Design and Layout by Colin Wheeler, PhD, MFA

Printed in
The United States of America

Dedication

Dr. Margaret Elyse Wheeler, without whose hard work, friendship and guidance I could not do this.

Dr. Colin Wheeler, for his time and expertise in completing the cover.

To all my fans who enjoy reading my stories. You inspire me to keep writing and creating the characters who have forever become a part of my life.

Acknowledgments

To all my dear friends at Fairfield, whose continued love and support enables me to write down the stories in my head.

My Brooklyn gals, as always, Doreen, Marianne & Pat.

To the talented Mary Rogers, who designed and painted a canvas for the cover.

The Carrollton Writers Guild, whose members continue to encourage me.

Chapter 1 — Tony
Contemplating Revenge

Tony Morello traced his fingertip along the faded scar circling his neck. It was a reminder, an indelible mark that matched the one running down the center of his naked chest. Laser resurfacing treatments, steroid injections, and surgery made both scars much less visible. But Tony could never erase the memory of how those scars came to be.

He went to the window, pulled back the edge of the heavy drape, and peered out. Rays of sun blazed hot and quick outside his Palm Springs Desert hotel room. Clusters of succulents dotted the landscape under several tall palm trees. The barrel cactus had lost their yellow and red blooms for the winter. All remained quiet except for the cawing of a California quail in the distance.

"Come to bed, baby."

Her sweet, sleepy tone beckoned to him, and he turned. Kai's raven hair splayed over the pillow, her ebony eyes and sensual lips tempting him. One of her shapely legs had freed itself from underneath the rumpled sheets. He grinned as he made his way towards her. Reaching down, he swept his palm along her thighs, smooth, light, mocha-colored skin.

"Good morning, beautiful," he said. "Did you sleep okay?"

"You know I did." She stretched cat-like and yawned, a soft sigh escaping her mouth. "How about you? Any more nightmares?" she asked.

"No time for nightmares last night," he teased, remembering the feel of her body beneath his.

Kai Nez. As far as Tony was concerned, the sound of her name floated in the air like the touch of a gentle breeze. Her first, Kai, meant

Willow Tree in Navajo. How did a former mobster from New Jersey end up with this gorgeous American Indian girl? The answer to him was simple. He willed it from the moment he caught sight of her.

Refusing to enter the Government Witness Protection Program after his release from the hospital, he fled New Jersey and traveled to Washington, D.C., with a purpose. He needed to find Eddie Marconi. The only problem was finding a person in witness protection proved nearly impossible unless you knew someone inside the FBI who could get the information for you.

Tony was no fool. Monica Cappelino would never reveal Eddie's whereabouts. But as they say in Italian, *probabilità a tuo favore.* The odds were in his favor when he watched from across the street one night as Kai walked into FBI headquarters.

Later that same evening, he followed her into The Willard InterContinental Hotel a few blocks away. An all too familiar place where he had booked a room a few days prior. It didn't matter that her hand wrapped around another man's arm. When they seated themselves at the well-known Round Robin Bar, he took a seat in a dark corner. A few customers sat scattered about chewing the fat over their workday.

Nicknamed the Oval Office of Bars, the surface of the circular mahogany bar top gleamed in the dimly lit room. Portraits of famous previous guests hanging on the forest green wood-framed walls included Walt Whitman, Mark Twain, Nathaniel Hawthorne, and President Abraham Lincoln.

He observed the two while pretending to text on his cell phone. The smartly attired bartender mixed and served them their drinks. Tony was surprised when he noted she ordered the bar's signature cocktail— a Mint Julep, something unexpected. When the waiter took his order, he asked for a scotch, neat.

The man she was with wore a business suit and was good-looking in a commanding sort of way. Tony could see what attracted her to him. His chiseled features, strong jawline, and thick salt-and-pepper hair made him appear handsome.

His stomach had dipped for a moment. The man looked familiar. Then it came to him. It was that Acosta guy from the FBI in New York. Lying in a hospital bed, still groggy after his altercation with Frank Uzelli, the man's face was a bit fuzzy and out of focus. But seeing him again in the bar, Tony remembered he was the one who tried to persuade him to go into witness protection.

But Tony knew what he wanted even back then, and it wasn't protection. While Frank Uzelli was still in custody, he headed for his secret safe house as soon as he was released. Retrieving the cash hidden in the floorboards, he filled a duffle bag and then went after the overseas accounts, hoping the FBI had not gotten their hands on that information yet. Over the years, Frank, under an assumed name, transferred millions. Not computer savvy, he needed Tony's help.

But getting Frank's money was not enough. He wanted Frank, the slippery snake who, with a high-priced lawyer, avoided doing prison time—the man who had sliced his body with a razor without so much as a second thought.

Helping Eddie rescue Ann Walsh made him refocus. No more preying on some poor slob who owed some dough to the mob. His only prey now was Frank.

Withdrawing farther into the dark corner, he waited until they were gone. Biding his time, it was two months until he spotted Kai again. She was alone at the same bar, the brightness in her face dimmed. Tony figured it could only mean one thing. Acosta was in her past, and he was about to step into her future.

Things became serious between them after several dates, including lies about his last name and his reason for being in Washington on business. He didn't expect that part to happen, but it did.

One night, after they finished making love, Kai spoke about growing up on the Rez, as she called the Reservation in Arizona. "When the Spaniards came here, they named us Navajo, but we are Diné," she said. "It means an all-surface being. Up where there is no surface and down where we walk on Mother Earth." She let out a slight laugh. "It does not mean 'the people' as believed by others outside the Indian Nation.

"Where I come from isn't just about my name or where I grew up," she continued. "What defines me is my clan."

Tony raised an eyebrow. "Clan?"

"Yes." Her eyes had misted a little. "Navajo people are born into one of four clans. Each clan comes from a distinct part of the Navajo Nation, and like spokes inside a wheel, many other clans spin off from these."

"Oh, I get it," Tony said. "The same as the Italians. Some are Napoletana from Naples or Sicilian from Sicily."

She shook her head. "No, not really. You see, my mother's clan is the first, my father's is the second, my maternal grandfather is the third, and my paternal grandfather the fourth. But my father's clan recedes after two generations. It's structured, so my mother's clan always carries forward."

"Seems unfair to your father," Tony mused. At his remark, she poked him playfully on the arm before continuing.

"When I was born and handed to my mother for the first time, she whispered her maternal clan into my ear. '*Kinyaa'áanii.*' which means towering house. Then, my paternal clan, *Tódich'ii'nii,* or Bitter Water clan. She said, 'In this way, you are my baby.'" She pointed her finger at Tony. "You have relatives related by blood, while ours are related not only by blood but by clan, too."

Tony tried to take in everything she told him. "Clan or blood relative? Are both equally important, then?"

"Yes, my love," she purred, wrapping her arms around his neck. "I'll tell you more in the future about my life on the Rez, my culture, and long-standing traditions. Those things will never leave me, no matter how far away I am from my clan."

After she finished speaking, Tony caught the expectant look in her eyes that said, 'I told you something about my life. Now it's your turn.' But at this point, he didn't have a taste for ripping open old wounds. Taking a chance she would help him, despite it placing her job as a Special Agent for the FBI in jeopardy, was a big ask. He needed to ensure their relationship was solid before letting that one out of the bag.

When he remained silent, she said. "What about you? You've told me so little. Where did you grow up?"

"New Jersey. Ordinary, nothing unusual," he lied. "I think you would find the details boring." Pulling her closer, he swept back her long hair. He breathed in and trailed soft kisses along her neck.

She melted into him and sighed. "The scars on your body and the nightmares tell a different story."

"Yes," Tony murmured. "A story for another time."

He told himself he would confess everything when he was ready. Kai was special, and he didn't want to drive her away. She could be gentle and sweet at times, but he had witnessed her fiery temper, which more than made up for her soft side.

Leaving L.A. several days ago with Kai behind the wheel was nothing short of eye-opening when some guy cut her off on the freeway. Enraged, she punched the gas pedal and chased after him.

"Whoa!" Tony said. "Leave it alone, Kai. It's not that serious." The last thing he wanted was some type of altercation with the man.

She never took her eyes off the road while replying. "He wouldn't have done that if you were behind the wheel."

Catching up, she pulled alongside him. She slid the window down and proceeded to shout obscenities some of which even he never heard before. Tony could see he was only a mere teenager. The young man was about to say something when Tony leaned forward, formed the shape of a gun with his hand, and pointed it at him while shaking no with his head—a warning the boy heeded by speeding off the freeway at the next exit.

Without seeing Tony's action, Kai turned to him, a satisfied look on her face. "See, he'll think twice before he does that again."

Tony laughed. "Yeah, maybe. But it would be best if you didn't let something so trivial get to you. It's not worth it."

Kai had cut her eyes at him. How quickly storm clouds could brew inside them.

"People like that need to know there are consequences for their actions."

"People like that," Tony quipped. "He was just a young kid."

Now, feeling her body so close to his, he wondered what her reaction would be when he asked her to help him. They made love again, and after Kai had fallen asleep, Tony crept over to the dresser. Beneath a pile of shirts, although he was no longer a smoker, he dug out his gold Zippo Lighter. Padding into the bathroom, he closed the door and sat on the bathtub's rim.

He studied his initials engraved on one side of the lighter. Once a prized possession, a gift from Frank Uzelli, it now signified his burning hate. His finger flipped open the top. His thumb pressed against the flint wheel, sparking a flame. His eyes captured the flickering light. How foolish to even think Frank cared anything about him. He closed the lid and heard the familiar click. For three years now, he had run. It was time to stop running and put an end to Frank.

Soon, their short vacation in Palm Springs would be over, and the serious business of finding Eddie Marconi needed to begin.

Chapter 2 — Monica
All In a Day's Work

Monica swelled with pride when three-year-old Andrew's hand slipped from her own, and he jetted away, his tiny legs pumping fast toward the classroom. No fear, just like his mother and father, she thought. Their little boy was growing up. A tingling sensation hit the pit of her stomach. Almost involuntarily, she unbuttoned her heavy navy-blue blazer and patted her middle, remembering how, not so long ago, Andrew nested inside her.

Going through pregnancy and Andrew's birth without Eddie was almost unbearable. She always envisioned the two of them raising their child together. Her pulse jumped at the prospect. Would the nagging ache ever go away?

Taking a deep breath, she swept back the dark curls framing her face and got into her car. She insisted on dropping Andrew off at preschool each morning whenever possible. Lisa, his nanny, picked him up in the afternoon.

Her job on the FBI's Joint Terrorism Task Force turned out to be both a blessing and a curse. Chasing down leads, gathering evidence, and making arrests, sometimes overseas, took its toll. The six-month maternity leave after the birth wasn't enough to make up for the times she needed to be away from Andrew. Lately, she questioned the wisdom of her decision to join the JTTF.

Arriving at the J. Edgar Hoover Building Headquarters, she parked and went inside. Bob Acosta had called and asked to meet. Though primarily based in the New York office, he traveled to Washington sporadically for meetings.

Taking the elevator to the 9th floor, Monica reminisced about her additional training at Quantico before joining the JTTF. Time spent learning valuable procedures for collecting and sharing intelligence in order to respond to threats and incidents at a moment's notice was all a part of her new job.

Once again, she found herself in the fictional Hogan's Alley, the mock town at the FBI Academy in Quantico. Tactical Instructors developed scripts based on real cases regarding terrorist attacks and cybercrimes. Immersed in realistic, stressful scenarios, she was expected to utilize firearms skills and defensive tactics to aid in her decision-making under duress.

Determined to stay in shape, Monica was thankful for all her hours at the gym after her pregnancy. Otherwise, the physical demands on her body at Hogan's Alley might have drained her.

The elevator doors slid open, and she strode up the hall to a conference room where Bob waited inside, his handsome features unchanged since she first met him at the Bureau in New York. He got to his feet as she entered and held out his hand. "It's good to see you again, Monica."

"Same here, sir," she said, extending her own. The scent of his cologne drifted by. Strange how it elicited certain memories of working together in the past.

Bob pointed to a chair at the long conference table. "Please sit." He sat across from her and rested his elbows on top. "I guess you're wondering why I wanted to see you. But before we go any further, I need to ask you something. Are you happy here in Washington?"

Caught off guard, she paused. What *did* happiness mean to her? She had a lovely apartment, a beautiful little boy, a job she loved, and...

Bob's grey eyes darted over her. "I notice there is some hesitation on your end."

"No, it's just that I wasn't expecting the question."

"It's a simple question, really. You are either happy or not."

For some reason, the tone of his voice and his last statement rankled her. "No disrespect, sir, but it's not simple for me. You know what I went through before I left New York. It's taken me a while to get used to things here in Washington."

"Sorry if I ruffled you," Bob said, his face softening a bit. "Look, you should be proud of the work you did in New York. You shook up Organized Crime, and as a result, some bad people were either given prison time or, like Salvatore Marconi, eliminated by their organization."

"I am proud, it's just that—"

"Monica, you need to forget Eddie Marconi," Bob cut in. "He's out of the picture, and rightly so. Regardless of how you once felt about him, don't second guess the choice you made. It was the right one."

She wanted to say, the right one for whom? But she didn't because he was correct. She needed to move on. It was the only way to heal.

"Look," Bob continued. "I wanted to see you because I'm putting together a special unit, and I think you would be a good fit."

"What kind of unit?"

"Charged with investigating money laundering and racketeering. It means dealing with Organized Crime again. Not only the American Mafia but the ROC also. We are well aware that the two have become intertwined." Bob leaned forward and clasped his hands. "And ... it means returning to headquarters in New York."

"Oh, I see," Monica said, her interest piqued. Investigating Russian Organized Crime might prove challenging, and if nothing else, she loved a challenge.

Going back to New York wouldn't be easy. There were so many memories of Eddie and her there. She had rented out her townhome, and her best friend, Cookie Asante, ran the florist shop she owned as an equal partner. Her tension eased with thoughts of her. They communicated by phone, and Cookie had visited her several times in Washington. It would be nice to be close to her again.

"Well, Monica. Do you think you might want to join the task force?"

"Can I have time to think about it?"

"Sure, but don't take too long. I'll be here in Washington for the remainder of the week. I'm pulling some additional agents interested in making the move."

She got up, and they shook hands again. "I appreciate your thinking of me, sir."

Later, finished with the workday, she drove home as thoughts of Bob Acosta's offer buzzed in her mind. Since moving to Washington, happiness had eluded her. No, that wasn't true. Losing Eddie was the root cause, not the move.

She never imagined missing someone so much, especially after Andrew was born. Every time she looked at her little boy and caught Eddie's face reflected in his, tears would well up for a moment, her world upended once again.

That evening, with Lisa gone, she fed and bathed Andrew, putting him down for the night. Sitting with a glass of wine in her living room, she contemplated what the move back to New York would mean. It was critical she face her emotions head-on and deal with them.

Her relationship with Eddie was over. She chose the Bureau. Eddie needed to grow up and become the man she knew he could be all those years ago if not for his Uncle Sal. Tucked safely away in Arizona and far from a life of crime gave him plenty of room to reflect and hopefully change. Lucky for her, she had a friend or two in the U.S. Marshal's Office. Since they handle all those who enter witness protection, she could never have gotten the information on Eddie's whereabouts without them.

Leaving Andrew's picture in his mailbox was all part of her plan, a nudge, so to speak. See, she wanted to say, now you have a son. Be a better man so you can meet him someday and be proud of your life.

Monica finished her wine and padded to the kitchen, where she placed the empty glass in the sink. In the window above, her reflection stared back at her, and for a moment, she saw Eddie there, too. His handsome, smiling face beckoned to her.

She quickly turned away and shut off the light. You must let go, she told herself. Maybe taking this position in New York would help her to do just that.

Grabbing her cell phone, she dialed Bob Acosta's number. "Sorry it's so late," she said. "I wanted you to know I'm in. I'll join the task force."

Chapter 3 – Alexei
The Wolf

The black Chevy Suburban cruised down Manhattan's West Side, its heavily tinted windows concealing the powerful men inside. Alexei Volkov glanced out as the overcast January sky let loose a volley of dense white flurries. Saddened by the sight, he sighed. Too many things reminded him of Russia and his boyhood home. Gritting his teeth, he raked his hand through thick dark brown hair streaked with gray.

A cell phone buzzed. His thoughts interrupted, Alexei jerked his head toward Leonid behind the wheel. The phone continued to ring. "Are you going to answer the damn thing or not?" Alexei demanded.

Leonid Rabinovich sucked in his protruding belly and reached into the pocket of his suit jacket. His gray eyes squinted at the screen. *"Nyet, ni nada,"* he said, tucking the phone back into his pocket.

Flustered, Alexei eyed him. "What do you mean, no need? Who's calling?"

"Sergey," Leonid grumbled. "The bum is always second-guessing everything I tell him to do. It has become tiring. When I give an order, he needs to follow it."

"You complain about him all the time," Alexei groused. "Just get rid of him."

"It is easier said than done. So far, he keeps the money flowing and his men in line."

"Sometimes it is better to let go of someone regardless of how good a job they do," Alexei scoffed. Leonid was his Brigadier, the one he should trust, but as of late, Alexei questioned some of his actions. On several occasions, he suspected Leonid of skimming some of the profit belonging to him.

Alexei needed proof. So far, none had materialized. However, Leonid was directly responsible for brokering his current working relationship with the Italian Mafia. A relationship that was critical to his operations.

The Suburban picked up speed as it approached the Hugh L. Carey Tunnel entrance to Brooklyn. Alexei sighed. "I will never understand the citizens of New York changing the name of this tunnel to honor a dead Governor. No, it will always be the Brooklyn Battery Tunnel to me."

Leonid nodded but remained silent.

"I remember riding through this tunnel many years ago," he continued. "One of my first impressions regarding my new home here in America." His emotions rising at the memories, he breathed deep and collected his thoughts.

"When are we meeting with Enzo Carbone?" Alexei asked. "We need to straighten this business out with the shipments."

"I will set it up," Leonid said.

Alexei could feel his angst rising. Dealing with the Italians was never easy. They made a point of ensuring you always recognized that *they* were here first. "I don't want things getting out of hand like the last time. People ended up dead."

Leonid shook his head. "No one ever found out we were working with Salvatore Marconi. The women were only a small part. We weren't involved with his drug operation."

"Yes, but I'm not sure this thing with Frank Uzelli is a good idea. The Five Families are still at odds with him. Even though he's been paying them back big time out of his current operations, you can't just make a contract disappear."

"So, you think they still might pull the trigger on Frank?"

"Maybe. So, we don't mention Frank. Let's see how things go when we meet with Carbone."

The car emerged from the tunnel and traveled down the Brooklyn Queens Expressway toward the Belt Parkway. Thirty minutes later, they drove into a gated community of condominiums nestled by the waterfront in Brighton Beach.

Leonid parked in the underground garage, and the two men exited the vehicle. They stepped into an empty elevator and rode in silence until it reached Leonid's floor.

"Don't worry so much," Leonid said as he got off. "Everything will work out."

The elevator doors closed, and Alexei continued to his Penthouse Apartment. Once inside, his body relaxed. He removed his shoes and put on his slippers, which always rested by the front door next to the ones belonging to the rest of the household. Removing one's shoes was a Russian tradition his family always abided by.

Gleaming hardwood floors greeted him in the large living room with floor-to-ceiling windows and ocean views. He went into the kitchen. Opening the Subzero Freezer, he removed a bottle of Beluga Premium Vodka and set it on the marble countertop. After pouring a glass, he raised it to his lips and stopped.

He lowered his drink, his eyes focused on the bottle's label. The premium Russian brand of vodka made in western Siberia was his favorite, but it also forced him to remember what happened all those years ago.

Alexei was fourteen years old on that snowy evening in Russia when they arrested his father, Radimir, sending him to the renowned Black Dolphin Prison—a place reserved for those who commit the most heinous crimes. Prisoners remain isolated within cells containing three sets of steel doors and are allowed only 90 minutes a day of exercise inside a large cage.

Of course, his mother insisted his father was innocent. It was just a simple accident that caused the death of some man acquainted with his father.

But there were many reasons not to believe her. Radimir Volkov had been a member of *Solntsevskaya Bratva*, Russia's most feared criminal gang. Alexei would sneak and follow him when he left the house late at night. He witnessed first-hand some of the brutality dished out by Radimir. To him, the murder charge against his father wasn't surprising.

After they took him away, he never saw his father again. Later, he came to despise his mother when she took up with another man who treated him like nothing more than a stray dog. At seventeen, he left home and joined a gang. He was determined to come to America and forget Russia.

Alexei lifted the glass and swallowed the vodka. He heard the front door close. A female voice called out. "Alexei, are you home?"

"Da," he answered. "In the kitchen."

Darya strode in carrying several packages. She placed them on the counter and then pushed the hood of her long fur coat away from her face. "Good to see you are early for a change."

Alexei never tired of looking at her. They had been together over thirty years, and yet, at times, she still resembled the nineteen-year-old girl he married in Moscow. Every movement of her tall, slim body exuded grace and poise. Full lips complemented her heart-shaped face. Shoulder-length sun-kissed blonde hair framed sultry amber eyes capturing the innocence of her youth.

"What have you been up to?" he asked.

"Just arranging a few things for the party."

Alexei bristled for a moment. "Please, Darya, don't make a fuss. Our son is not a little boy anymore."

Her lips brushed his cheek. "That is the whole point, my *malysh*." She set about putting groceries away.

Alexei eyed her. "When you call me baby, I am sure you are planning something I am not going to agree with," he scolded.

Her laughter, like the tinkling of chimes, filled the kitchen. "You know me so well." She turned toward him, hands gripping her waist. "Look, let me do this for him. Becoming twenty-one years old is a big deal. Especially here in America. Besides, I did it for Damien. It would be unfair not to do it for his little brother, too."

"Did you ever stop to think Roman may have plans of his own?"

"No, I forbid him," she said sternly. "He is very clear on that. The party will be at the River Café in the Terrace Room. He is a good boy and deserves the best we can offer him."

Alexei shook his head. Of course, she had picked the most expensive place in all of Brooklyn. "Darya, really!" he exclaimed.

Darya swept past him. The patter of her slippers could be heard as the bottoms kissed the tile. Her fingertips brushed his cheek. "Yes, really. You must make a list of who you would want me to invite from your circle. We will talk more later. Now, go get ready for dinner."

Knowing it was useless to try and change her mind, Alexei headed for the master bathroom. Besides, he could never deny her anything. It had always been this way from the very beginning. He faced the vanity, turned on the faucet, and soaped his hands, letting the warm water pour over them. Studying his face in the mirror, he thought about his two sons.

They were polar opposites. When he first met Darya, Damien was already three years old, the product of Darya's out-of-wedlock mistake. After they married, he adopted the boy and raised him as his own.

He pushed Damien to become better. Better educated, better behaved, and most of all, a better human being. Growing up, he never caused trouble, his head always inside his books, a son any father would be proud of.

It wasn't until fourteen long years later, and after six miscarriages, that Darya gave birth to Roman. Only Roman was *not* a good boy. Numerous times he had saved the boy from some foolishness and kept it from Darya, which made him feel guilty. Roman was determined to follow in his father's footsteps, no matter how hard Alexei tried to dissuade him. The potential danger of doing so did not faze him in the least. Admittingly, he himself had done the same thing by following in Radimir's footsteps.

He sighed and then rinsed his hands. Grabbing a towel, he glanced into the mirror again. His age was beginning to show. Several worry lines marked his face. He recalled his discussion with Leonid earlier. This thing with Frank Uzelli could mean trouble. They should offer to do the contract and rid the Italians of him. But then they would stand to lose much in the way of cash.

Alexei studied his blue eyes. Eyes that witnessed so many horrible things in Russia and in this country, some of which he had played a major role in orchestrating. Maybe that is why he inherited his father's nickname —a name that struck terror in Russians here in America. They needed to fear the *Volk*. A smile crept across his lips. Yes, he was the Volk, the Wolf. And no one had better ever forget it.

Chapter 4 — Eddie
Lost In Protection

Eddie Marconi slipped on his navy suit jacket, straightened his tie, and checked the full-length mirror. He smoothed his thick, dark hair and grinned. "Not bad," he murmured.

Picking up his wallet, he glanced at the driver's license before tucking it inside his pocket. For Eddie, the hardest thing to handle living in witness protection was getting used to his new name, address, and birth certificate, courtesy of the United States Government. He was now Jack Ricci, born and raised in Seattle, Washington.

He headed for the garage, pressed a button, and watched the door rise. Sunlight beamed across the silver Audi A5 Cabriolet. Eddie climbed in and let the top slide down. He loved the weather here in early January. With daytime temperatures reaching the high 60s to low 70s, Scottsdale, Arizona, offered a stark contrast to the biting cold winters of New York.

He pulled out and drove toward Desert Sanctuary at Camelback Mountain. The luxury resort where he worked presented the best of everything in rooms, opulent villas, spas, and restaurants. Overlooking Paradise Valley, it was a short drive from Old Town Scottsdale. The minimalist décor and private outdoor spaces let guests focus on the gorgeous scenery, including Praying Monk Rock, a rite of passage for Phoenix rock climbers.

Twenty minutes later, Eddie parked in his designated spot. He grinned as he exited the car and glanced at the Hospitality Manager Sign with the name Jack Ricci printed in red below it. Who would have ever thought he could come this far?

Determined to turn his life around and one day prove to Monica what kind of man he could become gave him the drive to succeed. Working nights at the front desk at the resort was the catalyst for furthering his education. He studied hard until he could attend Arizona State, where he took an Accelerated Degree Program.

Living alone allowed him ample time to excel and graduate sooner with a Bachelor of Business Degree in Hospitality Management.

Eddie wanted—no, needed respect. He received his first dose from the Resort Manager, John Campos, who took a liking to him. He complimented him on his ability to tackle problems with difficult guests and handle emergencies.

After Eddie received his degree and the previous Hospitality Manager quit for greener pastures in California, he offered him the position. Of course, there were rumblings among the staff. Who the hell was this guy to jump ahead of some of the others waiting in line for the position? But Eddie didn't care. The job was his, and he intended to keep it.

Inside, he crossed the vast lobby with its wood-beamed ceiling and stone walls, which provided instant relief from the bright Arizona sun. Sofas in cool beige tones next to small, round glass tables were strategically placed throughout the room. The polished tile floors gleamed.

"Hey, Jack," Amelia Ford called from behind the large circular desk. "You're just in time."

"In time for what?" Eddie said, his good mood fading as he approached the front desk.

Amelia leaned forward, a conspiratorial look on her face. The white shirt of her uniform had the two top buttons undone, revealing ample cleavage. Her bobbed red hair showed a glint of gold while her bright blue eyes focused on him.

Eddie nodded toward her. "Amelia, please fix your blouse."

She glanced down, a slight blush sweeping her cheeks. "Oh, sorry."

Eddie sighed. It was no secret she had a thing for him. She probably undid those buttons when she spotted him pull into the parking lot. Management had warned her numerous times about the exposure. Amelia wasn't bad-looking, but she was just not his type.

She redid the buttons, and although there was no one else in the lobby, she lowered her voice and said, "Remember the couple that checked into the Mountain Suite yesterday?"

"Do you mean the Saunders?" he asked.

"Yeah. They're causing a commotion. They showed up at the pool stark naked, wanting to go for a swim."

"Seriously?"

"Yup. The other guests are livid. One lady has her little boy with her."

"Who's on shift?"

"Monty," she said. "But he just stood there gawking at them for over five minutes before asking them to vacate the area."

Eddie shook his head. "It figures." Monty Campos was an idiot, but he was also the Resort Manager's son. "Did they go?"

"No. They're refusing to leave."

He quickly made his way to the pool, where shouting could be heard above the surrounding fountains. Several guests huddled together at the other end of the pool deck while Monty stood in front of an irate, naked, middle-aged couple.

Mr. Saunders was pointing his finger inches from Monty's face. Mrs. Saunders, hands clamped on her waist, looked on defiantly.

Eddie's eyes swept over them. The woman's breasts drooped, nipples facing downward. The guy lacked muscle tone, and his middle carried an extra layer of fat that spanned the top of his stomach.

Monty, short and slim, was almost a head shorter than the man, but Eddie could see neither one was going to back down. He hoped he could squash this whole thing without calling security. He approached the group and focused his attention on Mr. Saunders.

"Mr. Saunders, Jack Ricci. Can we all please take things down a notch?"

Monty glared at Eddie. "I was about to tell these two they need to pack up and check out immediately."

"Let me handle this, Monty. You're needed up front, right away," Eddie lied.

"What's going on?"

"Not sure, but Amelia was looking for you. She said it was urgent."

Monty gave the couple one last dirty look before stalking off.

Eddie knew the Saunders were at fault, but they were important, wealthy, well-connected guests. He always made it his business to research people who reserved the most expensive villas on the property.

"Look," Eddie said. "Could we continue this conversation away from the pool? Let's talk, and you can tell me your side of things."

The couple hesitated before following him out into a small, empty courtyard.

"I don't see what the big deal is," Mr. Saunders snapped. "People act like they've never seen a naked body before. We just wanted to take a quick dip."

Eddie experienced a momentary flashback of earlier days when he would have taken a baseball bat to this guy's legs. *Let's see you take a dip now, asshole.* He reeled himself back in and took a deep breath. "Listen, I get where you're coming from, but would you agree not everyone is as comfortable with the naked body as you two are?"

"Not our problem," Mrs. Saunders piped in.

"Well, I could quote you resort policy, call security, and have you escorted off the property, but because we value you as guests, I really don't want to do that. I would rather offer you a free night's stay with dinner on the house. I'm sure you're familiar with Elements, our five-star restaurant."

Eddie observed their change in body language, the tension evaporating out of the air. This is how you deal with people of their caliber. It was the same way in the mob. Offer something to put a stop to the drama. The only difference is that it might cost you later on.

Mr. Saunders glanced at his wife. She nodded as if giving him permission. "Okay," he said. "I think that's acceptable."

"Can we agree on one thing? No more coming to the pool naked," Eddie implored.

"Sure. We'll do that," Mr. Saunders said.

"Great. I'll arrange the extra free night and alert the restaurant."

Eddie watched them walk away, their wrinkled butts reminding him of dried-up prunes. He strode up the path toward the pool. The other guests were now settled on lounge chairs. "Sorry, folks," Eddie said. "The situation has been handled. Please enjoy the rest of your day."

He was about to return to the lobby when he spotted a little boy, about two years old, splashing in the water at the other end of the pool in his mother's arms. Eddie's breath caught. He thought about Andrew, who would be three by now. Every morning before getting dressed, he would study the photo on his fridge that Monica had left inside his mailbox. It was both a blessing and a curse.

The heavy longing inside to see them never grew any lighter. He would give anything to hold his little boy and gaze into Monica's green eyes again. So often, temptation beckoned, and he wanted to take his chances and come out of witness protection.

But Monica's words haunted him. "You need time to find yourself and begin a new life. One you can be proud of." So, here he was. He had done what she asked and was confident Monica would agree with the changes he made. But he wasn't sure how long he could live here without her and his son.

Deep down inside, this new life fit him like the wrong size pair of shoes. Way too tight.

Chapter 5 — Kai
A New Assignment

Kai studied the paperwork spread out on her desk. The words, New York, screamed out at her. She never thought Bob Acosta would choose her to be on his task force, especially since they shared a history together.

Their relationship lasted a little over a year. He gave no hint of breaking things off, at least not one she saw coming. After all, his office was in New York, and she worked at the FBI Headquarters in Washington. They met on his frequent trips in, and at his request, she never traveled there to see him. In retrospect, she should have questioned this.

Bob said he still cared for her but felt their relationship wasn't progressing as he would have liked. He wanted things to remain amicable between them. A stinging remark that sent her into an angry rant. Was he playing with her feelings all along?

Kai could tell there was no changing his decision, and after a twenty-minute argument, she stormed out—something she still regretted to this day. Taught to maintain balance in mind, body, and spirit, she had shamed herself by her display of weakness.

Her bad temper was another issue. No matter how hard she tried, she couldn't control it and always regretted her outbursts later on.

Ultimately, they parted as friends, but her heart was wounded. To forget the hurt, she focused on her job in the Cyber Crimes Unit, excelling and gaining several accolades.

Still mending from the breakup, she had no desire to enter into another relationship. Then Tony Rossi entered her life, his persistence wearing her down until she agreed to go out with him. His good looks and charm drew her in until she fell for him in a big way. Her feelings for Tony outweighed anything she experienced with Bob or any of the others that came before him.

Their first date at the Capital Grill on Pennsylvania Avenue was nothing short of amazing. Sculpted life-sized lions flanked the entrance. Colored inverted pendant lights hung from the ceiling, giving the interior a cozy vibe. A long, sleek, glass-topped mahogany bar ran down one side of the room while dark brown leather booths hugged the opposite wall. White-linen tablecloths covered the tables lining the center.

They savored fresh oysters on the half shell, followed by lettuce wedges with smoked bacon. Seared tenderloin with butter-poached lobster tails completed their dinner. After polishing off a bottle of Cabernet Sauvignon, they shared a slice of house-made coconut cream pie.

Though tempted at the end of that first date, Kai refused his invitation to return to his hotel room. It took three more dates before she finally agreed. She admired Tony's patience and calm demeanor but thought it odd that he always wore a dark turtleneck underneath his suit jacket.

The night they finally slept together, Kai could hardly contain herself. Soft kisses turned into parted lips with tongues probing and Tony's hands tracing the curves of her body. Their clothes tumbled to the floor, and she almost gasped when she saw his scars, but still, she couldn't stop herself from pulling him even closer until they lay naked on his bed.

They enjoyed sex three times that night, with Kai amazed by his thirst for her and hers for him. Like two empty wells, they filled each other up over and over again. When morning light shone across the room, she studied a sleeping Tony, his angry scars almost making her cry.

His eyes opened, and he gave her a lazy smile. "So, now you know," he said.

"But how?" she asked.

He rolled away from her onto his side. Kai swept her hand up and down his shoulder. She kissed the nape of his neck and sighed. "It's okay. You can tell me when you're ready," she said.

Tony turned, resting on his back, hands behind his head. "What if I'm never ready?"

His words sent a slight chill through her body. Whatever happened to him must have been awful. The moans slipping from his mouth as he slept told its own story. Something deep inside her flashed a warning that she chose to ignore. It doesn't matter, she convinced herself. At least not yet.

She pushed up and leaned on one elbow. Her fingers brushed back the strands of dark hair that lay across his forehead. "You will be, someday. But let's not dwell on it." She leaned and kissed his lips.

His arms came around her, pulling her down on top of him. She felt the heat of their bodies. Hungry all over again, she melded into him.

Later, she thought about running his name through the NCIC Criminal Data Base System, but with the deep connection between them growing, she refused to ruin it.

As she reviewed the paperwork, she wondered how to tell Tony about her move to New York. She sucked in a breath and reprimanded herself for knowing so little about him. He told her he was a Finance Analyst and traveled a lot for work. But where was home? New Jersey, perhaps? He mentioned growing up there.

Kai believed that any relationship that held secrets was doomed to fail. But she kept her own secrets. Secrets too painful to reveal.

Her thoughts were interrupted by the buzzing of her cell phone. She glanced at the number, deciding whether or not to take the call. Having declined it several times this past week, she forced herself to answer.

"*Yá'át'ééh,* Mother," Kai said. "How are you?"

"Finally!" Her mother's voice held that familiar, menacing tone. "Do you know how long I've tried to reach you?"

"*Shoohá,*" Kai responded in almost a whisper. "I've been busy."

"*Atsé,*" Don't say sorry and don't make excuses. You need to come home for a visit. Your *shimá sání,* Aponti, is not well."

Kai's breath caught. She loved her grandmother more than anything. She was the only one who tried to save her all those years ago and sought to convince the others. "What's wrong with her?"

A long-winded sigh came through the line. "She's getting old, Kai. She won't live forever."

"I'll book a flight."

"Okay then. Be a good *ach'é'é.*"

A good daughter? How many times had she heard that? Only every time she told her mother what he did — how he hurt her. Being a good daughter meant staying quiet.

Lightheaded and hyperventilating, Kai ended the call and bolted straight for the restroom. Glad it was empty, she went to the sink and splashed cold water onto her face.

Only one person could cause this reaction. She had told Tony so little about her time on the Rez and nothing about the man who almost ruined her all those years ago. He was the reason she never wanted to return home to see her family. Like Tony's scars, this man left scars on her, too. Only hers were invisible.

Kai dried her face and leaned against the sink. She understood more than anyone else why Tony refused to talk about his past and why she didn't push the issue. Maybe his hurt was as deep as hers. Kai returned to her desk and picked up her cell. She punched in Tony's number.

"Hello, beautiful," he said. "Are we still getting together tonight?"

"Of course. But I have some news to tell you."

"Good news, I hope,"

"That depends. We'll talk about it when I see you."

"You sound a little strange. It's not fair to leave me hanging like this, Kai. Why can't you tell me now?"

"Please don't push," she said. "I'll see you later." She hung up, logged onto her computer, and reserved a flight to Arizona for tomorrow afternoon.

First, she would tell Tony about New York and then about needing to go home to see her grandmother, but that was all she would say. For now, she would let his past and hers remain unspoken.

Chapter 6 — Cookie
The Surgeon

Carlotta "Cookie" Asante raised the sheet and stared at her left ankle. It appeared to be twice its normal size. A dark, angry, deep purple bruise, the color of eggplant, formed a ring around it.

"So stupid," she hissed under her breath. How did she not spot the water that had spilled from a vase onto the floor of the florist shop? Her legs flew out from under her, and she was barely able to stop the back of her head from slamming onto the wet tiled floor. But her left foot wasn't so lucky.

Removing and tossing her heels aside, she had eased up, steadying herself against the edge of the counter, her breath catching as she watched the swelling in her ankle accelerate with each passing minute. Hopping over to the register, she grabbed her coat and purse and, by the grace of God, drove barefoot to the Staten Island Hospital Emergency Room.

Now, two hours later, she was still waiting for the results of her X-rays. A strong antiseptic smell and the glare of overhead fluorescent lights contributed to her restlessness. Not wanting to see or listen anymore to the moans and complaints of the other patients nearby, she asked a nurse to pull the curtains closed around her bed.

Reaching for her purse on the small bedside table, she pulled out her cell phone. She reread the text message from Monica. *'We're coming home. I'll call you tomorrow to explain everything.'*

Despite her pain, her spirits lifted a bit. She hadn't seen Monica or Andrew in a good while. It was just the thing she needed. Digging inside her purse again, she drew out a compact and held it out at arm's length. Smoothing her tousled dark auburn hair, she noticed the corner of one of her false eyelashes lifting. "Darn it. I don't have any glue with me," she huffed.

Removing both lashes from her eyes, she placed them into a tissue and put them into her purse along with the compact. Her ankle pulsed with pain. "Damn it. I wish someone would tell me what the hell happened to my foot," she grumbled.

Fingers pulled the curtain back. "I guess that would be me," a voice said. A tall, good-looking man with shaggy hair the color of butterscotch and amber eyes, stood next to the bed smiling. He wore a grey polo shirt and a pair of dark jeans and held a clipboard in his hand. "You sure did a number on that ankle. Your x-rays show a fracture."

"A fracture?" Cookie shook her head. "No, it's only a little swollen. I just need to ice it. Or maybe you could give me one of those boot thingies to wear."

"Boot thingy?" He threw back his head and laughed.

Cookie wanted to reach up and smack him. "Look," she said. "Just send in the doctor so I can talk to him."

He cleared his throat, and she could see he was trying not to laugh again. He glanced at the clipboard. "Ms. Asante, I am your doctor. Dr. Damien Volkov. I'm the Orthopedic Trauma Surgeon on call, and I can assure you icing your ankle or wearing a boot thingy is not going to help it heal. You have a displaced ankle fracture, meaning you have broken bone fragments that are separated. You'll require surgical treatment."

Cookie studied him for a moment. How could he be a doctor? For one thing, he was too handsome and appeared to be way too young. She eyed her cell phone. Maybe she should call Monica for advice before she let someone inexperienced mess with her ankle. "I think I want someone older," she said. "I'm sure you're a very good doctor, but ..."

"But what?"

She surveyed his polo shirt and jeans. "I mean, you're not even wearing a white coat."

He blew out a long breath. "I guess a total of thirteen years of school and well over 1200 surgeries is not enough to qualify me to repair your ankle. I've worked with some of the major sports teams in the New York area. If you think a white coat makes someone a good surgeon, I'll go get you a doctor whose wearing one."

Cookie could feel the color rising in her cheeks. Her ankle throbbed, and all she wanted was for it to stop.

"Would you at least let me take a look?" he said.

Nodding yes, she tugged the sheet away, exposing her injury. She gasped at the sight of the bruise which had traveled down toward her toes. His fingers probed the swelling, and she winced.

"I'll have them give you something for the pain, and if you agree, I'll find out if there is an O.R. available. I really need to get in there. The longer you wait, the more damage will be done. Screws, or pins, and a plate will probably be necessary for a good outcome. And you'll have to stay off the ankle for several weeks after surgery. Then I would recommend physical therapy."

The more he spoke, the more frightened she became. "What do you mean by screws and pins?"

"It's the only way to repair your type of fracture. I assume you do want to walk on it again."

At his last remark, her anger overrode her fear. "Listen, Doctor—whatever you said your name was."

"Volkov. Damien Volkov."

"Yeah, well, I don't like the idea of a bunch of nuts and bolts inside my ankle. Can't you fix it another way?"

"I'm afraid not. The intake sheet says you fell. I'm curious as to how many feet."

"Feet?" What the hell was this guy talking about? "I slipped in some water on the floor of my florist shop."

"Oh, I see." A smile creased his lean cheek. "What kind of shoes were you wearing?"

"Okay, buddy, listen. I'm not sure what you're getting at, and I'm not too fond of your bedside manner right now."

Ignoring her remark, he continued, "Heels, I'm guessing. Very high ones at that."

"So, what if I was," she shot back, knowing her three-inch heels were most likely an accessory to the mishap.

"The number of injuries I see each year from women wearing those things is astonishing."

"Yeah, but I bet you like looking at women who wear them." She watched his face flush a bright pink. Score one for her.

"Okay, Ms. Asante. Is there anyone you need to talk to before you decide on the surgery? Your husband or a relative, maybe?"

"No," Cookie said. "There is no husband, but I can call my father. He needs to know where I am."

"Good. In the meantime, I'll check on the O.R. in case you agree to have the surgery done. I'll be back in about fifteen minutes."

He stepped away, and she heard him speaking to one of the nurses. It wasn't long before medication flowed through an I.V. line inserted into her right arm. She dialed her father and let him know what happened. Of course, even though she protested, he said he was on his way.

Her head felt lighter, and her pain eased. Whatever was in that I.V. was working. She pictured the doctor's face. She thought he was somewhat of a smartass, but she got the feeling he would take good care of her.

He reappeared just as she was basking in the comfort of the pain medication.

"Well," he said. "There's an O.R. available. I need to know your decision."

Cookie tried to focus on his amber eyes, drinking them in. Her muscles relaxed, and she felt herself floating. "You can do the surgery on one condition," she mumbled.

"What's that?"

"That you take me out to dinner after." Her eyes closed and didn't open again until six hours later in the recovery room.

Chapter 7 — Tony
Losing Kai

Tony waited in a booth at the Capital Grille, now their favorite restaurant, and checked his cell phone for the tenth time. Kai was punctual to a fault, and he had assumed she would be here first. But she was late.

He needed to tell Kai the truth about his past, and he must do it tonight. But it would be risky revealing his deception. Kai had a fierce temper.

Watching the dinner crowd rush in, he sucked in a deep breath. Surely, she wouldn't lose her temper right here in this crowd. But what if she did? The waiter approached, and Tony ordered a bottle of wine.

Before Kai, he wouldn't have cared about what his woman thought. He said and did whatever he wanted, indifferent to how it affected them. But then again, he had never been in love.

He caught sight of her approaching, and his angst increased. A wide grin spread across her full lips as she removed her coat. Stunning in a burgundy cocktail dress with intricate lace sleeves and bodice, she slid into the booth, unaware of the many eyes on her.

"Sorry," she said, smoothing her long hair. "I got held up with stuff."

Tony reached for her hand across the table. "You look gorgeous. I've missed you." She gave his hand a little squeeze and then withdrew. Tony poured them each a glass of wine before continuing. He recalled how she sounded so peculiar on the phone earlier. "What's going on, Kai?"

Her gaze focused on him momentarily before she lifted her glass and sipped. "I told you I had some news. I've been selected to join a new task force."

"Is it something you want?" he asked.

"Yes, but it means a transfer to the New York office. I wasn't sure if this would be an issue for you. I mean, you're here in Washington, and whether I like it or not, I'll be working with Bob Acosta—"

"Listen," Tony cut in. "If this is good for your career, I'm all for it. We can figure things out." He wanted to be supportive, but her working in New York with Bob Acosta didn't sit right with him.

Rethinking his decision to come clean here, he signaled the waiter. "Let's order and continue this conversation later at my hotel. I just want to enjoy our time together right now."

Kai winked at him. "You're aware of what typically occurs when we visit your hotel room. Only I can't stay over. I'm leaving for Arizona tomorrow. I need to see my grandmother. She's not doing well."

"Sorry," Tony said. "I understand. Family's important."

"Which reminds me of how little I know about yours."

Tony's pulse raced like an approaching freight train. He steadied himself before saying, "Tonight could be the night I finally tell you."

"Tell me what?"

Tony drank in every detail of the woman sitting across from him, her sensual lips, magnetic dark eyes, perfect nose, and high cheekbones. He didn't want to lose her, but couldn't let go of what he needed from her. "Let's order," he said softly.

An hour and a half later, Tony closed the door to his suite while Kai slipped off her coat and settled herself on the edge of the bed. He watched as she kicked off her black suede heels and stretched. "Thanks for the wonderful dinner. You spoil me too much."

Tony tossed his suit jacket aside and sat beside her. "Can I ask you something?"

She bumped her body against his. "Of course."

"How important is our relationship to you?"

She shifted her gaze toward him, reached up, and cradled his face in her hands. "I've never had feelings this strong for anyone. I love you, Tony." Her lips found his, her tongue probing. She kissed him long and deep.

Making their way around the bed, they soon lay next to each other, her head nestled in the crook of his arm. "I need to talk to you," Tony said. "I'll understand if you don't want to see me anymore."

Kai pushed up and leaned on one elbow. She gazed down at him and ran her finger across his cheek. "You're scaring me."

Tony brushed back a lock of hair from her forehead. "You wanted to know about my past." He reached down and unbuttoned his shirt. Pointing to his scars, he said, "These are a part of my past, Kai, and it's not a pretty one." Moving farther from her, he got to his feet and paced.

Slowly rising from the bed, she went to him. "You don't have to do this. I'll be patient until you're ready."

Tony stopped and locked eyes with her. "I'm more than ready." He guided her over to the bed again. "Please sit down and let me finish."

He told her his real last name and talked about his boyhood home in New Jersey, where his brother and sister still lived. He explained how the Little Italy neighborhood in Downtown Paterson had shaped his life. When he reached the part about joining the Mob, Kai jumped up from the bed.

"No!" she cried. "Stop. I don't want to hear anymore."

Tony's eyes watered, blurring her face for a moment. He turned away and continued. "I'm sorry, but you need to know. These are the things that made me who I was back then. Confessing some of the terrible deeds he carried out at the behest of his boss, Frank Uzelli, he burned with shame.

He included the initial razor cut down the center of his chest when he refused to kill his best friend who had betrayed Frank. He ended with the rescue of Ann in New York with Eddie Marconi, and pointing to his neck, he revealed what Frank did to him for the second time.

She was slipping into her high heels when he mustered the courage to face her. She glared at him, and he caught the trembling on her bottom lip. "Kai, please wait," he begged.

"Wait for what? How could you do this to me? Why would you..." Her voice faded in mid-sentence. Her eyes wide, she stepped back. "You want something from me, don't you?"

"Yes, but it has nothing to do with my feelings for you. Those are real."

"Real? None of this is real, Tony. You lied to me about everything."

"No, not everything. I love you more than you could ever imagine. That will never change even if you hate me after what I've done."

Hands balled into fists, she charged at him, her breath coming in uneven gasps. Tony ducked just in time to avoid a wallop to his jaw. "Kai, stop! Calm down."

She lunged at him again, but he grabbed her wrists and yanked her body forward. They stood chest to chest. A gnawing dread surged through him as he stared into her storm-filled eyes. He was losing her for sure. "Please, don't do this to us. I need you to understand."

Her knee jerked up. Searing pain struck his groin, forcing him to let go. Tony doubled over while trying to gulp air.

"Understand what, you son of a bitch! You played me."

Straightening up, the throbbing palpable but receding, he hobbled over to the bed and collapsed onto it. Head down, he couldn't bring himself to look at her. His voice, low, scarcely a whisper, he said, "You're right. At first, I did. But I never expected to fall in love with you, Kai. So, I'm not sorry for the lies because they gave me you."

The room fell silent. Seconds ticked by before she said, "What is it you want from me?"

He raised his head. "I need to find Eddie Marconi."

"Why?" she asked, quickly adding, "No, don't answer that. Once you do, I'm obligated to take matters further." She retrieved her coat and purse and stomped to the door. Yanking it open, she stopped and turned. "That's twice," she said. "First Bob, now you. I can't believe how stupid I am, always falling for the wrong man."

"Tell me something before you go," Tony pleaded. "Did you love him the way you loved me?"

Tears spilled down her cheeks. "After all the time we spent together, how in the hell can you ask me that?" She stormed out, slamming the door behind her.

Leaning over, he dropped his head into his hands and stared at the grey carpet. What had he done? For the first time, he found someone he genuinely cared about and who loved him in return.

His heart wrenched, and he searched his mind for a way to mend what he had torn apart. But no answers came. He wounded Kai by betraying her trust, something he knew all too well from being in the Mob. *Fiducia.* Trust was all that mattered.

This drive within him to get to Frank Uzelli came at a high cost. How much would he be willing to lose before his entire life fell apart? Picking up the pieces would become harder and harder. Kai was gone, but his need to reach Eddie and hunt for Frank did not lessen. Somehow, he would find them, with or without her help. Tony went to the window and glanced upwards. Stars scattered across a black velvet sky flashed like warning lights as he turned away.

Chapter 8 — Roman
Death of a Grocer

Roman Volkov frowned at Artyom Popov. Why did they always have to make threats to get the money? This impish little man knew the deal. You pay for protection, or your business gets vandalized. The damage would be enough to force someone to think twice before refusing to cooperate again. Roman turned up the collar of his brown leather jacket, letting it brush the tips of his blond hair.

Colorful mounds of fresh fruits and vegetables in baskets lined the center aisle. Their scent mingled with the odor of deli meats arranged in a long glass case. Roman plucked a ripe Mcintosh apple from a basket and sank his teeth into it. He chewed and then spat the pieces out onto the floor. One of the overhead fluorescent lights buzzed and blinked.

He glanced over at his best friend, Emil. "What are we going to do with this guy?"

Emil puffed out his chest. He swiped a hand through his dark hair and gave Roman a crooked smile. "Teach him a lesson." He signaled to Luka, standing watch at the door, holding a baseball bat.

Luka, round as he was tall, drew up his six-foot-four frame. Old floorboards creaked beneath his weight as he lumbered over to a refrigerated case. He swung the bat, stopping short of the glass front.

"No!" Artyom shouted. "I'll pay. Please don't cause me any trouble."

Roman nodded at Luka, who promptly lowered the bat and returned to his position by the door. "That's more like it, Artyom. You should know better by now," Roman chided.

Hands shaking, Artyom reached toward the cash register. Roman pounded his fist on the counter. "The cashbox," he said.

Artyom eyed him for a moment, then dropped below the counter, coming back up with a handgun. Trembling, his finger on the trigger, he pointed it directly at Roman.

Roman's heart lurched. His pulse slammed in his neck. Before he could react, Emil let loose two rounds from his 9mm, hitting Artyom dead center in his chest.

The gun dropped from Artyom's hand. His eyes bulged as he clutched at the wound. "Please," he croaked before collapsing onto the floor.

Emil sprung over the counter and back again with the cash box. He grabbed Roman by the arm. "Let's go."

They hurried through a rear door and exited into the alleyway. All three broke out into a run, scrambling up the alley and onto a back street. Sirens wailed in the distance when they reached the end.

Roman stopped short. Gasping for air, he said, "Wait…wait. We need to catch our breath so we can walk normally."

Emil opened the cash box, pulled out a stack of bills, and stuffed them into the pockets of his heavy wool coat. He caught sight of a dumpster, opened it, and retrieved a rag. After wiping the metal box, he tossed it inside. Stuffing the rag into his coat pocket, Emil caught up to Roman and Luka. They stepped onto the bustling sidewalks of Brighton Beach Avenue.

Luka turned to Emil and frowned. "What about my car?"

Emil shook his head. "Don't worry, you can go back for it later. We parked quite a ways down from the market."

Luka constantly glanced over his shoulder until they crossed the street and onto the Brighton Beach Boardwalk.

"Would you stop that," Roman snapped. "We're fine. No need to act suspicious." After walking a bit farther, they sat on one of the many benches overlooking the ocean.

"You didn't have to kill him," Luka said, his stormy eyes fixed on Emil.

Emil shot him a venomous look. "Are you kidding me right now? Would you rather have him shoot Roman? I did what was necessary." He pulled out a pack of cigarettes and lit one. Smoke billowed from his mouth. "Stop being such a *trusiška!*" he snapped.

"Coward? I'm no coward, Emil. Just smarter than you. This whole thing could come down on us."

Roman, silent, listened to them argue back and forth. Unable to digest what transpired, his thoughts immediately went to his father. He would never approve of their minor shakedown operation. Things had gone smoothly until now.

The fifteen or so store owners they coerced into paying protection money always cooperated. Under the mistaken impression this was authorized by Alexei, the Wolf, their fear was greater than their desire not to pay.

The memory of Artyom falling onto the floor flashed before Roman. He curled his hands into fists to stop them from shaking. A flock of squawking seagulls soared above the foamy waves crashing onto the shore. He inhaled the calming scent of sea spray while he tried to clear his mind. "We must stick together on this," he said. "When the others find out, they might point the police in our direction."

Emil shook his head. "No. They'll be too scared. And on our next visits, we will make them understand they might suffer the same fate if they talk to the cops."

"Our next visits?" Luka said. "You want to continue this craziness?"

Emil shrugged. "Sure, why not? They all believe we have orders from the Wolf." He winked at Roman.

Roman tried to ease the angst roiling inside him. He ignored the warning bells raging through his mind. "Yes, they would never go against my father."

"What about Artyom?" Luka asked. "Even though he pulled a gun, I think he just wanted to scare us."

Emil gave him a dirty look. "I couldn't take the chance he would hurt Roman. You have to—"

"Enough, you two," Roman snapped. "It's done. No more talking about it. Emil, you need to get rid of your gun."

"It's untraceable, but I'll walk out onto the pier. It won't be found."

Luka got up from the bench. He went to the railing and stared out at the ocean. His bulk cast a shadow across the wooden planks in the fading sunlight. Without turning to them, he mumbled, "You did not have to kill him."

Emil let out a sigh and leaned back against the bench. "Are we still going to Tatiana tonight?"

Tatiana, a nightclub and waterfront restaurant owned by Roman's father, Alexei, where Vegas-style floor shows paired with authentic Russian Cuisine, was their favorite place to hang out.

"Yes," Roman replied. "Nothing changes. The more we act as usual, the better." He got up and stationed himself next to Luka. Squeezing one of his enormous shoulders, he said. "Please put this behind you, Luka. We are brothers, and brothers look out for each other. What's done is done."

"Yes, brothers," Luka answered without looking at him.

Roman glanced over his shoulder and nodded at Emil. "Come and see how beautiful the sunset is."

Emil joined them, and then the three watched a blood-red sun dip below the horizon.

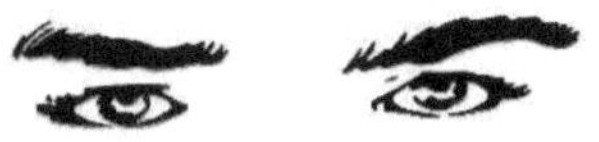

Chapter 9 — Kai
Leaving For Home

Hours had passed since Kai walked out on Tony. Trying to erase him from her mind was much more challenging than she anticipated. She had fallen for him hard and fast. Now, here she was, picking up the pieces once again. After Bob, she promised herself that she would take things slower.

She rummaged through closets and drawers, deciding what to take on her trip to the Navajo Reservation.

Tossing several items of clothing into her overnight bag, she sighed and sat on the bed. Eyeing her cell phone, she picked it up and scrolled through all the text messages Tony had sent and, up until an hour ago, was still sending.

'I love you, baby,' she read. *'Please call me. I'm so sorry. I never meant to hurt you.'* All followed by broken heart emojis.

Why did she fall for a former criminal? But *former* didn't exactly fit. Tony planned on committing some type of crime. His facial expressions and voice gave away his deep anger towards Frank Uzelli. But why pull Eddie Marconi into all of that?

It made no sense. After hearing about Ann Walsh's rescue, she figured he'd formed a bond with Eddie. But Tony couldn't possibly understand the ramifications of what he was asking her to do. She could lose her job if someone in the FBI discovered she had revealed Eddie Marconi's location.

Her cell buzzed. Tony was calling for the hundredth time. Why hadn't she blocked his number? It continued to ring as she stared at it. Unable to resist anymore, she swiped and said, "Hello."

"Kai, baby, thank God you answered."

"I shouldn't have," she replied dully. "What do you want, Tony?"

"I want you to forget about everything and for us to start over."

The pit of her stomach aching, she replied, "I think that ship has sailed. How can I ever trust you again?"

"I know, I know," he moaned. "I fucked up. But you have to believe, that no matter what, I do love you. I love you with all my heart, Kai."

His words almost broke down her resolve. She sucked in a long breath. "Look, I need time. I'm leaving for the Rez to go visit my grandmother."

"When are you coming back?" he asked, the sadness in his voice washing over her like an ocean wave.

"In a few days. I'll try to call you when I get home."

"Promise?"

How could he expect her to do that? It almost made her angry. "No, Tony, I can't. I'll see how I feel when I return." She ended the call, knowing that if she stayed on the phone any longer, she might cave in and make that promise.

The next afternoon, Kai boarded a flight to Arizona. Outside the plane window, she studied blue skies holding whisps of white clouds. The closer it came to her arrival time, the more her anxiety grew. She had not visited home for over two years.

Later, after changing planes in Phoenix, she touched down at the Gallup Airport. Settled in her rental car, she steeled herself for the forty-five-mile drive to the Navajo Reservation. Traveling down I-40, she kept telling herself to remain calm. What happened on the Rez was in the past and couldn't be changed. When she reached the sign reading 'Entering Navajo Nation,' her hands gripped the wheel tighter, and she took a deep breath.

Kai concentrated on the beauty of the land, twenty-seven thousand square miles filled with deserts, grasslands, forests, plateaus, mesas, and canyons. As a child, she played in its twisted, meandering streams, feeling safe, comforted by domes of red and orange rocks that formed mountains in the distance. Until that safety was ripped away.

After a while, she turned down a winding dirt road leading to her mother's house. A simple one-story ranch with tan siding came into view. A grey Ford pick-up truck sat out front. More fortunate than some other families who lived in different parts of the Reservation, she had grown up in a home with running water, sewage disposal, and electricity.

Kai got out, her eyes searching. A little over one hundred yards to the left stood her grandmother's hogan. A sudden urge swept through her, and she wanted to run toward it, but instead, she took out her overnight bag and went up the few wooden steps to the front door.

Before she could knock, it opened. Her mother, Secoya, appeared dressed in jeans and a maroon sweater. Silver and turquoise earrings peeked through her shoulder-length dark hair. She remained as beautiful as ever except for a few faint lines on her forehead.

A broad grin lit up her face. *"Yááteeh,* Kai." She held out her arms. *"Hágo."*

Kai set her bag down. Tolerating her mother's embrace, she said, "It's good to see you, Mother."

Secoya stepped back. Her eyes swept over Kai. "Is it?" she asked.

Kai's stomach knotted. Why was it always this way? The push and pull between the two of them. One minute, they were okay. The next, not so much.

"Please," Kai urged. "Just this once, can we not do this?"

Secoya's body stiffened. "Well, for someone who hasn't been home in quite some time, it makes me wonder why." She turned and beckoned over her shoulder. "Come inside."

Kai picked up her bag and followed. The house remained as she remembered it, with a living room open to an eat-in kitchen and a hallway leading to three small bedrooms and a bathroom.

"How long are you staying?" Secoya asked.

Kai braced herself. "I can stay a few days."

"*Doda!* After all this time, only a few days?"

"*Aoó.* Yes, I need to get back. I'm starting on a new task force in New York."

"Always work, always work," Secoya scolded.

"You should understand. I'm sure your job working for the Tribal Police is important to you, too."

Secoya turned away and prepared coffee for the two of them. Her mother's demeanor almost unbearable, Kai excused herself and went up the hallway to the bathroom. Inside, she huffed and splashed some cold water onto her face. "Stay calm," she admonished herself. "It's only a few days."

When she returned to the kitchen, two cups of coffee, cream, and sugar were on the table. "Are you hungry?" Secoya asked.

"No, thank you. Coffee is fine," Kai said. She removed her jacket and eased into a chair.

"Of course, my job is important, too," Secoya said. "But it never comes before family."

"Are you saying I don't value family?" Kai asked before taking a sip of coffee.

Secoya shrugged. "You aren't around often enough for me to know." She stared into her cup momentarily before meeting Kai's eyes. "I just want to be sure you remember where you came from and how meaningful your native culture is. There are too many of us who don't treasure Navajo beliefs once they leave the Reservation."

Kai's eyes started to water. Her body flushed under her mother's gaze. "You have no idea how wrong you are. I carry everything with me all the time."

"But I just want—"

"What?" Kai cut in. "What exactly is it you want, Mother? For me to remember some things and forget others. Forget what happened and how you did nothing to help me."

Kai shot up from her chair, her breath coming in spurts. Without a word, her mother rose, took both cups to the sink, and washed them.

"You'll never let it go," Secoya said, turning her back to Kai. "Every time you come here, you dig up the past."

Her tears flowing freely now, Kai grabbed her jacket. She tore out the front door and down the steps. A cold wind whipped around the side of the house, sending chills through her body. A light misty rain triggered a musky smell from the waxy leaves of the surrounding creosote bushes—a familiar scent, one that evoked fear.

Through misty eyes, she gazed at her grandmother's hogan. White smoke swirled up from the center of the roof like ghostly apparitions, easing her pain. She quickly headed toward it.

The six-sided conical structure constructed of logs, packed earth, and stone with a smoke hole in the center of the roof brought immediate comfort. The closer she came to the entrance, the more Kai's heartbeat regained its normal rhythm. Holding true to tradition, the entrance faced east to welcome the rising Father Sun, one of the most revered of the Navajo deities. She stopped at the front door and wiped her tears away.

"Yááteeh, Shimá sání," she called out as she opened it, the wooden hinges calling out a welcoming squeak. Stepping inside, the warm air hugged her body like a blanket. She almost sighed with pleasure at the familiar smell of fry bread. Keeping to tradition, Kai walked clockwise around the room until she reached her grandmother's outstretched arms.

"*Hágo*. Kai," her grandmother, Aponti, said, hugging her tight. She released her, and her hands cradled Kai's face. "Let me look at you. It has been too long."

"I know," Kai replied, feeling a flush sweep her cheeks. "I'm sorry. My job keeps me busy, but I know that is no excuse."

"Doda. No, your work is important. I understand." She ushered Kai across a large hand-woven rug, its rich black, turquoise, yellow, and white colors depicting the four spirit worlds. They sat together on a small couch, its back draped in an authentic Navajo Chief's red and black blanket handed down through the generations. It was one of Kai's favorite things. She could only guess at its worth.

She studied her grandmother in the firelight. Spun sheep's wool secured her silver hair in a tsiiyeel, where it is said the thoughts and prayers of the Navajo people are kept. The frown lines around her mouth had carved their own niche into her brown skin. Her body appeared frailer than Kai remembered, but her eyes remained alert and bright behind her wire-rim glasses.

"Tell me," Aponti asked. "How is life treating you?"

"Life is good," Kai said. "A few bumps here and there, but okay."

"Just okay? But I want my granddaughter to be more than just okay." She smiled, her frown lines deepening. "You know you can speak whatever it is you're hiding."

Ever since childhood, her grandmother could always sense when something was wrong. She stared into her eyes and knew she could never lie to her. So, she told her about Tony and how much she loved him even though he did some terrible things in the past.

After listening intently, Aponti said, "Háágoosh dini ya?"

"What do you mean by where am I going?"

"Yes. What path do you want to take in life? Which one will make you the happiest? To stay with this man you say you love, or go on without him?"

Kai pictured Tony's face. "I want to be with him, but I'm scared, Grandmother. Scared his past will collide with my present."

Aponti took both her hands. "*Hozho,* Kai. *Hozho.* You must be in peace, balance, beauty, and harmony. To be in *Hozho* is to be at one with, and part of, the world around you. That is the only thing you should seek in this life. Whether or not he can bring you these things, only you know the answer."

She let go of Kai's hands and got up. "Tomorrow, we do a smudging, clear away all the bad things." With a twinkle in her eye, she smiled down at Kai. "But first, tonight, we will eat fry bread just the way you like it, topped with honey."

As Kai sat watching her grandmother prepare the bread, her fear regarding Tony settled a bit. She sank back into the comfort of the warm blanket. She might be able to accept Tony's past, but she would never accept what happened to her here on the Rez all those years ago.

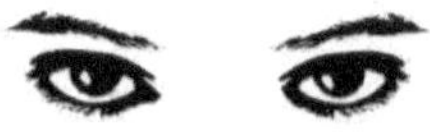

Chapter 10 — Alexei
The Meeting

Alexei and Leonid drove toward the New Jersey Seaport. Restless, Alexei fiddled with the radio before switching it off. "Whatever happened to good music?" he huffed.

Leonid chuckled. "They cater to the younger generation now. You know they spend money to download music."

"Sure, sure," Alexei said. "Mostly their parents' money."

"You heard about Artyom?" Leonid asked. "Poor guy. Shot dead in his own store."

"I know—such a terrible thing. No children, but he leaves a wife. I want you to make sure she is taken care of. Also, find out who is responsible. We can't have this in our neighborhood."

Leonid shrugged. "These things happen now. People here have guns, and they don't hesitate to use them. God bless America, as they say."

Alexei gave him a sideways glance. "Like I said. Ask around."

It was eerily quiet when they arrived at the warehouse not far from the Port Jersey Terminal. Too quiet for Alexei's comfort. Frosted glass laced with thin wire covered every window. Empty wooden pallets were stacked almost to the ceiling in one corner of the vast room. Oil stains dotted the cement floor. The scent of wet cardboard and another putrid smell, something Alexei failed to identify, wafted in the air. He glanced at his Rolex. Enzo Carbone was late. He turned to Leonid and shook his head.

"Ten more minutes, and we leave. I am so tired of all the drama with the Italians. It was easier dealing with the Ukrainians in Odessa. This damn war has made that even more difficult." Before Leonid could answer, they heard a vehicle pull up outside and car doors slamming shut.

A side door creaked open, and Enzo Carbone appeared with two bodyguards. They stationed themselves by the door. Enzo approached Alexei, an unlit cigar clamped between his teeth. His brown hair, slicked to one side, failed to hide his balding pate. An overcoat of dark wool covered his protruding belly.

He extended his hand. "Good to see you, Alexei."

"You're late," Alexei said, extending his own and making sure the inflection in his voice exhibited his annoyance. "I have another appointment, so let us make this quick."

Enzo arched an eyebrow. "Don't be miffed. I was held up with some other business."

"Then, I will get to the point, Enzo. I need your assurance that when the shipments arrive, they bypass customs without a problem."

"Of course. As long as we receive our cut, there won't be any problems."

"I thought Frank Uzelli controlled the seaport. There were never any issues when we dealt with him, so you can understand my hesitation."

Enzo visibly bristled, color rising in his fat cheeks. He removed the cigar, his eyes focused on Alexei. "Frank's old news. He only has a small part of the ports. As Under Boss, I took control of the rest after— you know—that little incident in Manhattan."

Alexei folded his arms as his stomach muscles tightened. "Little incident? I think it was much more than that. We lost a lot of money. I will never understand how those men of yours were able to pull something like that off. Everyone scattered and ceased doing business for a time."

"Yes, and we lost money, too," Enzo shot back. "Frank, Joey, and Sal's side operation went against everything the five families stand for. There has to be an equal split according to territory."

"When the FBI gets involved, it hurts all of us," Alexei said.

"Agreed. No one wants them snooping around. That's why we're being extra careful. I give you my word. You have nothing to worry about." He held out his hand.

The two men shook, and Enzo walked to the exit. He turned back toward Alexei. "Just keep your end of the bargain. There's plenty of room for everyone so long as we trust each other." He stepped through the doorway, his bodyguards following behind.

The door closed, and Leonid spoke for the first time. "Trust is no little thing."

Alexei paced, an unsettled feeling wrapped around him. "I am well aware. Were you not the one who convinced me to partner with them on this shipment?"

"*Da*. Because it is the only way. As long as the Italians control the ports, we have no other choice."

Alexei tried to read his face. Was this man being faithful to him? He wanted to believe he was. He chose to dismiss the rumors he heard from others. But maybe it was time to dig a little deeper and make sure.

Alexei jerked his head towards the door. "Come, let's go. Get in touch with Frank Uzelli. I need to get a feel for both sides before we continue to do business with Enzo. I must be sure we are not being taken for a ride."

They left the warehouse, and while Leonid drove, Alexei sat deep in thought. There could be no screw-ups this time. When the FBI raided the place in Manhattan, their tentacles reached far and wide, digging into every corner, searching for more illegal enterprises, and bringing a halt to all the other operations between his people and the Italians.

That could never happen again. It would mean disaster for him economically and all those who worked underneath him, maybe even jail time. He pictured his father, locked away in the Black Dolphin. To this day, Alexei had no idea if he was dead or alive.

Of course, the jails here in America were nothing like the ones in Russia, but losing his freedom might surely make him go mad.

He sighed and leaned back into the leather seat. Enzo Carbone better be right because trust was the only thing keeping them from tearing each other apart.

Chapter 11 — Monica
Settling In

Back in her townhome, with the renters gone, it took Monica a little over a week to have it re-painted and freshened up. It was late afternoon by the time she got Andrew bundled up and ready to go to Staten Island Hospital to pick up Cookie, who was scheduled to be discharged.

After a quick twenty-minute drive, she pulled into the parking lot. Grabbing Andrew from his car seat, she headed for Cookie's room. She was surprised to see her up, dressed, and walking back and forth on her crutches. A huge grin spread across her face when she saw them. She waved one of her crutches. "Six to eight weeks of this bullshit, then physical therapy."

Monica pointed at Andrew. "Careful with the cursing. He loves repeating things."

Cookie's cheeks flushed. "Oh, sorry."

"Listen," Monica said. "Things could be worse. Thank God you didn't hit your head and get knocked unconscious. Who knows what would have happened then?"

Cookie eased into one of the chairs, put her crutches aside, and held out her arms. "Give him up, Monica. I've missed my Godson."

To Monica's surprise, when she let go of Andrew's hand, he ran willingly to Cookie. His tiny arms hugged her neck.

"Aunt Cookie loves you, Andrew." She glanced up at Monica, her false eyelashes fluttering. "I was so afraid he wouldn't remember me."

"Well, with all the FaceTime calls, I'm not surprised," Monica said.

Cookie ran her hand through Andrew's dark hair. "God, he looks so much like..." her voice trailed off.

"I know," Monica said. "It's hard sometimes." Wanting to change the subject, she blurted out, "So how much longer should we keep the store closed?"

Cookie blinked. "Closed? I'll be there the day after tomorrow with bells on."

Monica shook her head. "Cookie, no. You need some more time off."

"To do what? Sit at home and watch reality TV. I'll use Uber until I start driving again." She glanced at the crutches. "I can get around pretty good on those things." She let out a long sigh. "I just wish they were prettier."

"Prettier?"

"Yeah, maybe I'll jazz them up a bit. Gotta match what I'm going to wear."

Monica burst out laughing. Same old Cookie, always looking to take things a step further. "But seriously, how are you feeling?"

"The pain is almost completely gone now. I'll admit, it was rough in the beginning. But I've got an excellent doctor."

Monica spotted the slight blush in Cookie's cheeks. "Do tell. What's the story?" She sat on the edge of the hospital bed across from Cookie. Andrew slid off Cookie's lap and headed straight to the window overlooking the parking lot. Standing on tiptoes, he peered out.

"Cars, Mommy. Look at all the cars," he chirped.

"Yes, there are lots of cars. See how many you can count." While Andrew counted, Monica turned her attention back to Cookie. "So, you're satisfied with this doctor?"

"Oh yeah. More than satisfied. He seems to know his stuff."

"I should hope so," Monica said.

"And he's easy on the eyes … if you know what I mean."

"Be careful, don't go jumping in headfirst."

"I know, I know," Cookie huffed. "I learned my lesson after Danny."

Monica checked the time on her cell phone. "So, when are you being discharged?"

"They said as soon as the doctor gives the okay."

Just then, a nurse in blue scrubs entered the room with a wheelchair. "So, Ms. Asante, the doctor has signed your discharge papers. You are free to go." She handed Cookie a sheaf of papers.

"I thought he would at least check on me before I leave," Cookie said, a note of disappointment in her voice.

"I'm sorry. He has an emergency surgery. Your follow-up appointment with him is written on your discharge papers."

Just like turning on a light switch, Monica saw Cookie's face brighten again. She's smitten, Monica thought. But at least he was an Orthopedic Surgeon. After Cookie was seated in the wheelchair, Monica grabbed the crutches and took Andrew by the hand.

"Over twenty cars," he piped, looking up at Monica.

"Wow, that's good, Andrew. Now, let's get Aunt Cookie home."

Later, after dropping Cookie off and getting her settled, Monica drove to Brides and Blooms to check on things. Once inside, with Andrew in tow, she assessed things and saw it was somewhat of a mess. She removed all the dead flowers from the refrigerated cases and straightened out some other arrangements. As she worked, she handed some of the flowers to Andrew, instructing him to throw them into a large trash bag by the door. She made a list of what needed to be purchased on her cell phone.

Heading to FBI Headquarters tomorrow, she would get Andrew settled in the Daycare Center. Although the twenty-four hundred dollars per month took a bite out of her paycheck, it was worth every penny knowing he was safe in the FBI building where onsite childcare was offered to Federal Employees.

Then, she looked forward to the trip to the Flower District on West 28th Street to buy fresh flowers. Coming back, she would work on rearranging the window and refrigerated cases. Things would be ready for Cookie's return.

* * * * *

She finished up, picked up Andrew, and drove toward home, slowing down as she passed Romano's restaurant. How many nights had she shared a meal with Eddie at their favorite table by the front window? A sinking feeling threatened to creep in, and she quickly pushed it away.

She needed to get used to all the things that evoked memories of them together. Otherwise, she might never heal. Next week would be her first briefing at FBI Headquarters and she wanted to focus and dive into her work again.

She glanced in the rearview mirror at Andrew, his head bobbed to one side, his eyes closed. Her sweet little boy gave her so much. Although he brought back memories of Eddie, he was also part of her healing process. Without him, things would be much worse.

Bob Acosta was right. She needed to let go and live her life, just as Eddie was out there living his.

Chapter 12 — Kai
Smudging

Kai woke early, dressed, and tiptoed past her mother's bedroom. She slipped on her jacket and hurried out the front door. The morning sky transformed into a watermelon red as the sun peeked over the horizon. She inhaled the earthy, arid scent of the desert.

Her grandmother emerged from her hogan and waved. *"Yá'át'ééh abiní,* Kai." Her traditional *Ké Ntsaaí* brown buckskin moccasins were wrapped with beige cloth halfway up her calves. Her black *Biil eeí* rug dress was trimmed around the middle with maroon and white wool, representing the universe. A silver and turquoise *Yoo'* or necklace hung from her neck.

Kai bent and kissed her on the cheek. "Good morning, Grandmother."

They both turned and faced the rising sun for the morning prayer.

"Be patient like the sun who waits and watches the four changes of the earth in loving each other," they chanted. "Be swift like the wind, be wise like the thunder clouds and lightning, be shining like the new morning dawn. Be proud like the tree and be brilliant like the rainbow colors."

"Come, we must start the smudging." She led Kai to the back of the hogan, where a wooden table was covered with a deep red and blue ceremonial cloth. On top of that lay a bowl filled with southwest cedar and white sage. A small cast iron pot, a box of matches, and an eagle feather rested beside it.

As they stood side by side, her grandmother placed some cedar along with sage into the pot. She struck a match, and Kai watched it form a slow burn. The sharp odor from the rising smoke stunned her senses, forcing them awake and evoking long-forgotten memories. She was a little girl again, her tiny hand wrapped inside the warmth of Aponti's own.

Her grandmother spoke a few prayer words in Navajo, then waved the eagle feather across the smoke to cleanse it. She proceeded to perform the same action, but this time with her hands. She passed them through the smoke, lifted them, and waved them across her eyes.

"This is so I will be able to see all the good things in front of me." She followed by gathering more smoke across her ears. "This is so I may hear what others speak to me." Then she smudged her mouth with the smoke. "This is where the sacred words will come from."

Kai dipped her hands into the smoke and repeated each motion and word precisely as her grandmother had done. Then, they both smudged their feet, and her grandmother declared, "This is so we walk with respect across Mother Earth."

Then, her grandmother picked up the bowl, took the eagle feather, passed it through the smoke, and moved it up and back down the front of Kai's body, saying, "I pray this will take all the negativity away from you, my granddaughter. May your heart lead you where you need to go."

A warmth spread through Kai, and a sudden calm engulfed her body. Her spirits lifted as if the weight she had been carrying dissipated with the last of the smoke.

When they finished, her grandmother lifted a string of juniper berry beads from the pocket of her *Biil eeí*. She pressed them into Kai's palm. "Ghost Beads, for you. They will protect you. I'm sorry I did not do more for you back then. *Ayóó ánóshní.*"

Her eyes growing moist, Kai ran her fingers over the polished beads, "Thank you," she said. "I love you, too." She hugged her grandmother and kissed her cheek again. "There's no need to feel sorry. You did what you could. I'll come back to see you soon. I promise." She placed the beads around her neck.

Aponti nodded in response but didn't speak. She turned and disappeared inside her hogan.

Kai returned to the house, where she found her mother sitting at the kitchen table, dressed in her Navajo Tribal Police Uniform, with a plate of eggs and a cup of coffee in front of her. She looked up and wrinkled her nose.

"Smudging?" Secoya asked.

"Yes," Kai said, helping herself to coffee and a plate of eggs from the stove. "Grandmother thought it would be a good idea. Besides, it makes me feel better. It helps to clear my head."

"Better change before you board your plane." She nodded her head towards Kai. "Ghost beads, too, I see. What's going on, Kai?"

"Does there have to be something going on? It's just a gift."

"But we both know what that gift means and why she gave it to you. Are you in some kind of trouble?"

Ignoring the question, Kai gulped some coffee and shoved a forkful of eggs into her mouth.

Secoya's palm slammed against the tabletop so hard Kai almost dropped her fork. She stared at her mother. "I'm not in any trouble. Just trying to figure some things out," she mumbled.

"Why can't you talk to *me* about these things instead of her?"

Kai pointed at her mother's palm, still lying in its rigid position on the table. "That's why. You always go losing your temper."

Secoya's face hardened. "And what about you? Your temper is far worse than mine. For the life of me, I can't comprehend—"

"What?" Kai interrupted. "What is it that you can't comprehend, Mother?"

She got up and took her plate over to the sink with thoughts of smashing it to pieces. Instead, she placed it down and redirected her attention towards her mother.

"You know why I'm the way I am. You just don't want to admit it."

Without waiting for an answer she knew would never come, Kai stomped down the hallway, packed her overnight bag, and rushed to the door. She would change at the airport. "I need to leave," she said, glancing at her mother.

"Sure, you go on. Run away like you always do," Secoya snapped. "That is your answer for everything."

"Maybe I wouldn't have to if you had taken care of things!" Kai shouted before slamming the door behind her. Tossing her bag into the back seat, she climbed into the car and tore off down the long driveway and out onto the main road.

As she drove toward the airport, Tony's face swam before her. Kai could almost feel his strong arms around her. She let out a cry so primal, so raw that her breath came in spurts, her chest heaving in and out. Hands shaking, she pulled to the side of the highway and stopped. All the comfort of the smudging ceremony dissipated like the whisps of smoke.

Taking several deep breaths, she tried to calm herself. She fingered the Ghost Beads. In her heart, she had already determined her future. No matter what, she couldn't give Tony up.

When she was with him, those awful memories from the past and the Rez seemed to dissolve, even if only for a time. He made her feel safe, something nobody else was able to do. Somehow, she would get him the information he needed to find Eddie Marconi. She could only hope it wouldn't lead to her downfall.

Chapter 13 — Damien
The Good Son

Damien Volkov blinked and rubbed his eyes. Tired from two longer-than-usual surgeries, he pulled out of the hospital parking lot in his BMW 740 I and headed for his apartment on the North Shore of Staten Island. Late afternoon sun beamed off the hood of the car. He reached overhead for his sunglasses clipped to the visor. Twenty minutes later, he parked and exited the vehicle.

Relatively new, the complex called Urby, short for Urban Farms, made his commute an easy one. With dining options on-site, communal kitchens, and outdoor terraced heated pools, it was the perfect place to relax after a hard day. The produce grown in a large center courtyard provided its own market with fresh vegetables. Damien loved the atmosphere there almost as much as the waterfront view from his two-bedroom apartment.

His stress evaporated as soon as he entered his home. He removed his shoes and put on slippers. The modern leather sofa, chrome, and glass end tables gave the living room a sparse look. A flat-screen television hung on one wall, and a small dining table and chairs sat at the other end.

His bedroom consisted of a simple bed and dresser. Moving in a couple of months ago, he purchased only the bare necessities, promising himself he would make it feel more like a home one day. But with so little free time, that hadn't happened yet.

He took a quick shower, dressed, and was about to go for a walk along the waterfront park when his phone rang.

"Hello, my *Pcholka*," Darya's voice swam in his ear. "How are you?"

"Fine, Mother. Just tired." He cringed every time she still called him her 'little bee,' a nickname from childhood.

"I know you are very busy, but please take care of yourself. Do not work so hard."

"I can't always pick and choose which surgeries I want to do when I'm on emergency room call."

"You should give that up," Darya said, a hint of annoyance in her voice. "Go completely into private practice. That is what most successful surgeons do."

"I plan to … eventually. But there is a terrible shortage in the E.R." With every minute of this conversation, Damien's stress threatened to return. Wanting to change the subject, he said, "So, tell me what's new."

"Oh, there is so much going on right now," she said, her tone brightening. "I'm planning Roman's twenty-first birthday party. You must come."

"Of course, I'll be there. Send me the date, and I'll make sure I'm not on call." He listened for the next ten minutes as his mother blurted out every single detail about the party she had arranged for his younger brother. After she finally finished and hung up, Damien sighed with relief and headed for a walk along the waterfront.

He loved his mother, but she could be overbearing at times, especially when it came to Roman. His brother was beyond spoiled. Not that it made any difference to him. His practice here in Staten Island kept him busy, so he didn't see Roman that often. But he did wish there was some direction to his half-brother's life instead of hanging out with his friends all the time and using his father as a cash cow.

Damien shrugged off the rest of these thoughts. He watched the late afternoon sun kiss the surface of the Verrazano Narrows waterway making it sparkle like pockets of diamonds. Easing onto one of the benches, he was thankful there was only a slight breeze. He inhaled the salty brine splashing up against the rocks near the seawall.

Two young women jogged by. One glanced at him and smiled. Damien nodded but did not attempt to take things further. Years of medical school, residency, and overcoming the obstacles of opening his practice left little time for dating. Of course, there were short-term dalliances here and there, but nothing serious. Thinking back over the last week, he pictured Carlotta Asante or Cookie as she insisted on being called. Damien had never met anyone like her before. He pulled out his cell phone and logged into her medical chart. Without giving it a second thought, he dialed her number. She answered on the third ring.

"Hello, this is Dr. Volkov. I was just checking in to see how you're doing."

"Wow, a doctor calling me at home. This is a first," she said.

Damien felt himself blush. "It's not unusual for me. I check up on my patients when I'm unable to see them prior to discharge."

"That's so nice. Usually, someone else from the doctor's office calls."

"So, how are you feeling? Any pain."

"A little, but it's easing."

A few seconds went by until Cookie blurted out. "When are you taking me to dinner?"

"I..." Her question threw him for a moment. "Dinner?"

"Yeah. Don't you remember I agreed to let you do the surgery as long as we have dinner together?"

"Sorry, I don't recall something like that." How easily she knocked him off balance.

"Something like that? No, as *I recall*, I said it plain and simple."

"I guess I didn't think you were serious. Drugs can make people say all kinds of stuff that they wouldn't ordinally mean."

"Okay, so let's be clear from the start so there are no misunderstandings. We don't know each other well except for a doctor-patient relationship, correct?" she teased.

"Yes," Damien said, wondering what prompted him to make the call in the first place.

"So, if there is one thing you should know about me, I don't say anything I don't mean. And I won't waste my time being with anyone who has no intention of being as honest as I am."

Damien bristled a bit. Cookie spoke her mind. Whatever she thought seemed to come right out of her mouth. Here was a woman you couldn't play games with. He suddenly found her quite refreshing. "Fair enough," Damien replied.

"Great. At least we agree. Now, how about that dinner you owe me?"

"Text me your address, and I'll pick you up on Friday evening at 7:00. I'm not on call, so that should work fine."

"See you then," Cookie said, ending the conversation.

Damien stared at his cell phone. He had broken his cardinal rule to never date one of his patients. Deciding to shrug it off, he told himself he would probably never see her again except professionally after that. But it could be uncomfortable for both of them. He rose and walked through the courtyard, stopping in the small restaurant to pick up a meal. While he waited, he thought about Cookie. It's just dinner, he told himself. Nothing more.

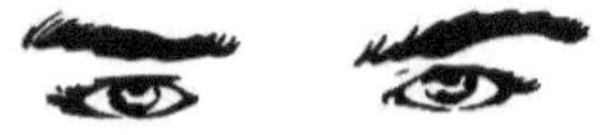

Chapter 14 — Bob
Monica

Bob scrolled through the names on his monitor. His new task force was shaping up nicely. Monica Cappelino would be his pick for Case Agent in charge of the operation. She was more than qualified for the position, and he trusted her instincts. Austin Faulkner, another one of his picks with a stellar background, would add immeasurably to the unit from his work with Drug Enforcement. Then there was Wanda Simmons. With her experience in forensics and homicide, her knowledge could come in handy. She had investigated several crimes here in New York.

He studied the last name on the screen. Kai Nez. Was he including her because he felt he owed her a favor? He sank into his chair and blew out a long breath.

When they were together, he made sure to clarify his position—no promises regarding her career. Their relationship needed to remain separate and apart from the Bureau. Everything went fine until he realized his feelings for her were waning. Not wanting to lead her on, he broke things off. He winced inside, recalling her angry reaction. But he didn't fault her for it. When the dust settled, they parted as friends.

He kept tabs on her and became increasingly impressed by her dedication to her job. She excelled in the Cyber Crimes Unit and worked with the Anti-Gang Task Force for a while. Unsure but pleased when she agreed to come to New York, his plan was for Monica to take her under her wing. Kai still had a lot to learn, and joining his task force could further her career.

As for Monica, he needed to exercise restraint. Drawn to her, he fantasized about a relationship between them. Knowing her feelings for Eddie Marconi, he never expressed his desires. Considering that she was coming back again to work directly under him, the whole thing would be improper anyway.

"Let it be, Bob," he mumbled. He glanced at the time. Monica would arrive for a briefing any minute. Things needed to stay professional between them.

His secretary buzzed, and a few seconds later, Monica, stunning in a navy pantsuit and pale pink blouse, sat across from him. "Good afternoon, sir," she said. "I'm prepared to review everything."

He studied her for a moment, her dark curls and green eyes a constant temptation.

A perplexed expression on her face, she repeated, "I'm ready to go over everything."

"Oh, sorry." Bob prayed she didn't notice the flush he felt creeping up his face. He turned away momentarily, focusing on his computer screen. "Yes, just give me a moment." He pretended to type something into his computer. How in the hell did he think this was going to work? He needed to get his act together. Monica more than deserved this chance.

He cleared his throat. "Settling in, okay?"

"Yes. I've moved back into my townhome, and Andrew is registered for daycare here, which makes everything so much smoother."

"Good," Bob said. "I wanted to inform you that you will be the Case Agent in charge of this task force." He noted the look on her face. "I can see you're quite surprised."

"Well, I wasn't expecting this, but I'm more than happy to be appointed to the position."

"I've chosen the rest of your team. I'll schedule for all of us to meet in the conference room on Friday at 3:00 pm. But I would like to review their files with you."

"Thank you, sir. I appreciate that."

He leaned forward and clasped his hands together on the desk. "Okay, first things first. We've known each other long enough. Let's drop the formalities. Please call me Bob."

"Of course. But it'll take getting used to."

He removed a folder from his desk drawer and handed it to her. "Here are the names and backgrounds of the agents you'll be working with."

Monica scanned each page. "Very impressive."

"Yes. There is one specific agent I want you to mentor. She could learn quite a bit from you."

"Who?"

"Kai Nez. She's done some top-notch work but is the youngest and could use some guidance." He saw a frown cross Monica's face. "Something wrong?"

"No. It's just that I don't want to have to babysit anyone. Are you sure she's up for the job?"

"I'm not expecting you to babysit her," Bob said. "Take an interest, that's all."

"Okay. I understand, sir. I mean, Bob." Her green eyes teased as she chuckled. "I'll do my best."

"Thanks. Is there anything else you require at this time?"

"No. I've been reviewing some of the case files on Alexei Volkov and a few of the others working for him. They're a rather nasty bunch who, if the information we have is correct, have done some despicable things.

"Yes. Things, up until this point, we've been unable to prove. We also believe Volkov is in bed with the Italian Mob. We have to determine who he is partnering with and why."

Monica's expression turned somber. "I may be jumping the gun, but I have a feeling we may need someone on the inside."

"Do you mean an asset?"

"Maybe. We both understand how challenging it is to get information any other way. We may need a UCA.

"That might be true. But I'm not sure someone on your team other than you could act as Under Cover Agent. And we both know you're going under is out of the question in light of the Marconi Case."

"Of course," Monica said, shaking her head. "Once we gather more intel, we'll see how things play out. If there is nothing else, I'll return to my desk and do more research." Monica got up and went to the door.

"Let me know what you need. I'll make sure those resources are available for you."

"Thanks, Bob. I appreciate that," she said, closing the door behind her. The light scent of her perfume lingered in the air, forcing him to inhale. He imagined kissing her neck and burying his face in her dark curls. This will never work, he told himself. He was obligated to put the task force under another person's supervision. But then he would have to admit why, which could lead to a lot of trouble for him. He cursed under his breath. For now, the best course of action would be to focus on getting the necessary evidence to prosecute Alexei Volkov and anyone else involved in his criminal acts. It might even involve pulling in some others in the Italian Mafia. His affection for Monica must not be acted upon until this whole thing was over. The question was, could he wait that long?

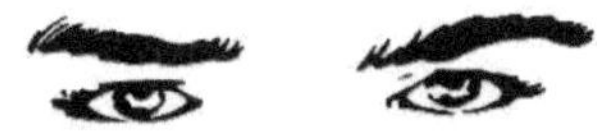

Chapter 15 — Cookie
The Date

Cookie glanced in the full-length mirror, her happy demeanor fading. She cursed under her breath. There was no way to show off her shapely legs with this lousy cast on her left ankle and one ballet flat on the other. She had mastered using the crutches, but they would detract from her usual sexy walk.

Smoothing the front of her red dress, she sighed, grabbed her crutches, and hobbled to the front closet. She removed her white wool winter coat. Leaning the crutches against the wall, she slipped it on.

Her doorbell rang promptly at 7:00. She opened it to see a handsome Damien Volkov dressed in jeans and a black leather jacket open at the front, revealing a simple pale blue shirt.

"Ready?" Damien asked.

"Absolutely," she said, grabbing her crutches and her purse. Once they were settled in his BMW, she studied his profile. Good looking to a fault. Why was he still single? "There must be a catch," she mumbled.

Damien gave her a sideways glance. "Did you say something?"

"Just wondering why you're still single."

"Well, I could ask the same thing of you."

She caught a hint of annoyance in his voice. She needed to rein herself in before she ruined things. "Sorry. I just meant you seem to have your life together. It's only logical that you would take the next step."

"Oh, I see," Damien said, his face relaxing as they drove away. "I didn't know there were steps I should be taking. What about you? Did you miss a step or what?"

Cookie laughed. She loved a guy who could keep up with her banter. "You got me on that one. To tell you the truth, I had what I thought was a serious relationship until the guy turned out to be a creep, among other things."

Twenty minutes later, Damien drove into the parking lot of The Stone House Restaurant at Clove Lakes. "I hope this is okay," he said.

It's only one of the pricier restaurants on Staten Island, she thought. "Sure, this is fine," she said.

Damien helped her out of the car, and they went inside. Nestled on the tranquil shores of the lake, the stone cottage was nothing short of spectacular. Massive wood beams formed an arch beneath the cathedral ceiling. Logs blazed in the fireplace while soft piano music played in the background. Damien gave the hostess his name, and they were led to a table overlooking the lake. The water shimmered under a full winter moon.

Damien asked her if it was okay before ordering a bottle of Sauvignon Blanc. After the waiter retreated, he asked, "So, this guy you were seeing turned out to be a creep?"

"Let's just say he wasn't very honest, and because of that, things didn't work out." She averted her eyes and studied the menu. The last person she wanted to talk about was Daniel Gage. The moment she thought of him, her muscles tensed up, the deep wounds threatening to resurface.

The waiter returned, poured each of them a glass of wine, and set the bottle in the ice bucket. "Are you ready to order?" he asked.

"Not just yet. Give us a few minutes," Damien said. He captured Cookie's gaze as she looked up from the menu. "Sorry. I didn't mean to upset you by asking about him."

She forced thoughts of Danny away. "No worries. At this stage, we all have some baggage from our past." She set the menu down. "You order for us, okay? I'm positive whatever it is, I'll enjoy it."

Damien's face relaxed, his eyes full of mischief, he said. "I like that you trust me so early on our date."

"Just with the food," she shot back. "The rest remains to be seen."

The waiter set down a basket of freshly baked roasted garlic bread and pecorino croissants with chive oil and truffle parmesan butter.

Damien ordered Blue Point Oysters Rockefeller for an appetizer and Chilean Sea Bass with forbidden rice, roasted tomato, and miso butter broth. "I'll leave dessert up to you," he said, winking at her.

As they dined, she noticed how he held his knife in his right hand and his fork in the left.

"What are you staring at?" he asked.

"I see you're left-handed."

He shook his head. "No. I'm right-handed." He glanced down at his hands. "Oh, you mean how I'm holding my utensils?"

"Yes."

"This is how I was raised. Russians always hold their knife in the right hand and their fork in the left."

"Seems strange," Cookie remarked. "I mean, if you're not left-handed."

Damien chuckled. "We manage."

She asked Damien about his work as a surgeon. He divulged the trials and tribulations of going through medical school.

"Did you always want to be a doctor?" Cookie asked, finishing off the last oyster. She spotted his hesitation before answering.

"Well, yes and no. It was expected of me."

The waiter set down the main course. Cookie's mouth watered at the sight and aroma of the Sea Bass.

"What do you mean? Did your parents force you to become a doctor?"

Damien shook his head. "No, no, not really. It's hard for me to explain. I could have chosen to be a lawyer, financier, or some other well-respected profession. I chose medicine because that is where my heart led me."

"Ah, I understand," Cookie said. "So long as it was something *they* could be proud of."

He set his fork down and stared at her for a second. "I never really thought about it like that, but I guess you're right. My parents do like to brag about their doctor son."

"You have any brothers or sisters?"

For a brief moment, his expression went dark. He shifted uncomfortably in his chair. "One half-brother, Roman. He's much younger than me. I was born in Russia. My mother gave birth to me when she was very young. She met my stepfather later, and they had Roman."

Cookie sipped her wine. A hunch told her that he and Roman didn't get along.

"But I have to say, my stepfather legally adopted me and always treated me as his own," he continued. "Only Roman and I are two different people. We're nothing alike. Don't get me wrong, I care about him, but I worry."

Cookie raised an eyebrow. "Worry?"

"To put it simply, he's still finding himself," Damien said, digging into his meal. "What about you?"

"Only child. Daddy's girl," she said, smiling. "My mother walked away when I was four. Haven't seen her since."

"I'm sorry," Damien said. "That must have been hard."

"Not really. I don't remember much about her. My father owns a restaurant. Nothing fancy. It's called The Hummingbird Bar & Grill, and I'm a partner in a florist shop with my best friend from high school.

"You enjoy it … the flower shop?"

"I love it. Brides and Blooms is like an oasis for me. Arranging flowers makes me happy. I love working with brides especially."

Cookie saw his expression soften. He reached across the table and covered her hand with his. "I'm glad you like what you do. It's important."

The waiter removed their empty plates and handed them menus for the second time. "Room for dessert?" he asked.

She hesitated as Damien pulled his hand away. "I don't know, I'm kinda full."

"Oh, come on," Damien said. "We can share something." He glanced at the menu. "I know I said I'd leave dessert up to you, but if you let me, I think you'll like my choice."

Cookie could tell that, for some reason, he was anxious to please her. "Okay, go ahead and order something."

"We'll have the white peach panna cotta with morello cherry coulis and crushed pistachio."

Almost squealing with delight, Cookie held herself back. The classic chilled Italian custard made of cream and flavored with vanilla was one of her favorites.

"Nice selection," the waiter chimed. "It's one of our specialties." He returned a short while later, placing the panna cotta in the center of the table with a flourish. He set two small plates and spoons in front of them and retreated.

Damien spooned some onto his plate and tasted it. Cookie followed suit. She savored the smooth, melt-in-your-mouth texture and the tartness of the cherry sauce. A hint of pistachio pulled it all together.

"Wow, this is fabulous," she said, dipping her spoon in again. They continued to converse while enjoying the rest of the meal.

Afterward, when they were settled in the BMW, Damien turned toward her. "I had a nice time."

"Me, too," she said softly. The streetlight above them made his amber eyes glisten. A familiar tingle swelled up inside her, just like with Danny.

Damien leaned in for a kiss. She jerked away, catching the hurt look on his face. He started the engine and backed out. "Damien, I'm … I'm sorry," she sputtered. "I'm not ready, yet."

He gunned the engine and sped off from the restaurant. "You don't need to explain. It's fine."

But she could tell it wasn't. "Please, pull over so we can talk."

He let out an audible exhale before coming to a stop. "Go on, Carlotta, say whatever you need to."

Did he just call her by her given name? A rigid profile dominated his face as he stared straight ahead. She didn't like this side of him and wasn't going to put up with it either.

Arms folded, she asked, "Do you always throw a tantrum when you don't get your way?"

He swiveled his head. "All I wanted was a simple kiss. You acted like I was about to attack you. I knew this was a bad idea. It was wrong for me to ask you out."

She shot him a venomous look. "First of all, I asked *you* out. Second, why did you agree if you thought this was such a bad idea?"

He dropped his hands from the steering wheel and leaned back into his seat. "I'm not sure," he said quietly.

"Not a good answer," Cookie said. "You agreed for a reason."

"I … I was attracted to you. However, it's important for you to know I broke my policy of never dating one of my patients."

Eyes wide, Cookie looked to the left, right, and over her shoulder.

Damien's brow creased. "What are you doing?"

"Making sure the world isn't coming to an end because you took me out on a date," she mocked.

"This is amusing to you, isn't it?"

"Look. I told you from the beginning I expect us to be honest with each other. If you have that much of a problem with it, then say so. And as for the attempted kiss, it's not that I don't want to kiss you, but I've been hurt before by moving too quickly. I am never going to find myself in that position a second time." Cookie shook her head and sighed. "If you can't deal with that, then I guess we don't need to see each other again, except on a professional level."

Damien's arm came around her. His eyes focused on her face. "I'm sorry. You're right. I shouldn't expect something you're not ready to give."

"So, where do we go from here?"

"I want to see you again, if that's okay?"

"It's fine by me, but what about your policy?"

Damien smiled, his face softening in the evening light. "Screw my policy."

"Oh, and one other thing," Cookie said. "Never call me Carlotta. Only my father calls me that."

Damien gave her a mischievous look. "Well, I like it. Maybe in the future, you'll make an exception."

Later that night, Cookie lay in bed, her mind spinning from her date with Damien. Her skin tingled as she recalled his attempt to kiss her. If only he knew how badly she wanted his kiss and more. Damien had broken his cardinal rule for her. Only time will tell if there would be any consequences.

Chapter 16 — Roman
Tatiana

Roman, Luka, and Emil strode past the people waiting in line outside Tatiana, his father's nightclub. The well-muscled bouncers never bothered to check their IDs. Right past the entrance, a young girl stamped hands with the club's logo and collected cover fees. She bobbed her head at the three young men as they sailed in the door.

Music blared and thumped from the speakers while colored lights bathed the packed dance floor. A few patrons were grouped around the DJ booth, beers in hand. A bar ran the length of one wall, with each stool occupied. Behind it, several bartenders mixed and poured drinks. Small round tables with chairs lined the perimeter. Skimpily clad waitresses snaked through the crowds while balancing trays of drinks. Several winked at Roman. None were ordinary looking. They were beautiful to a fault. A mixture of beer, whiskey, perfume, and sweat dominated the air.

They made their way to the roped-off VIP area by the front of the stage and sat at their usual table. This was Roman's safe place. The club made him feel respected. Everyone from the staff to the entertainers to the DJ knew he was the Wolf's son. Within seconds, one of the young waitresses approached. Her raven hair held streaks of bright purple. She locked eyes with Roman while addressing all three of them.

"Good seeing you again. What can I get you fellas?"

"The usual for me," Emil said, trying to catch her eye. "Vodka straight up."

"Gin and Tonic," Luka said, drumming his fingers on the table.

"I'll have a Firestarter, Amy," Roman said, his eyes traveling from her ample breasts to between her legs.

"Sure thing. I'll be right back."

"Roman, are you still going after these American girls?" Emil teased.

Roman's face pinched. *"Kraseevaia devushka.* What's wrong with that?"

"Yeah, she's beautiful," Luka chimed in. "But you know how our parents feel. They always say find a nice Russian girl."

Roman shrugged and laughed. "Maybe I'm not ready for a Russian girl."

Amy returned and set their drinks down, dipping especially low in front of Roman, her cleavage close to his face. He slipped her a hundred-dollar bill and beckoned her even closer.

"See you when you get off work?" he asked.

"Maybe." She turned and disappeared into the crowd on the dance floor.

"See, no respect," Luka said. "A Russian girl would jump at the chance to be with you."

Roman sipped his drink. "Yeah, but she wouldn't do the things Amy does for me."

The three burst out laughing. The music stopped, and the stage lit up, grabbing their attention. Three women came out in beaded gowns and sang. When they finished, the headliner, Pavel Obolensky, entered the stage, a handsome Russian with a long-standing contract at the club. He belted out one of his most popular songs. Roman glanced around. Most of the women in the club had their eyes fixed on the stage.

"I'll be right back," he said and threaded his way through the crowd until he spotted Amy at the rear of the club by the exit door. He grabbed her hand, pulled her outside into the alleyway, and let the door slam behind them.

Roman pushed her up against the hard cement wall beneath the soft light from the kitchen window. His hands cupped her breasts, and he kissed her long and deep. Her arms came up around his neck, and she buried her face against it.

"I need to tell you something important," she whispered.

Roman stopped his groping and stared into her almond-shaped eyes. "Can't it wait until we finish?"

Amy dropped her arms, one finger trailing down his chest, she said. "I'm afraid not."

Roman stepped back and sighed. "Go ahead. What is it?"

"I'm pregnant."

Her words hit him like a punch in the gut. He heard the thumping of the music coming from inside and then loud applause. Suddenly nauseated, he took a deep breath and tried to remain calm. "Are you sure?" he asked.

Amy nodded but didn't speak. He paced back and forth, his anger rising. "How could you let this happen?" He watched her eyes glisten as tears formed and slid down her cheeks.

"I … I don't know," she stuttered. "I thought we were being careful."

"We!" Roman spat. "You told me you were on birth control." He paced again, swear words coming out of his mouth in rapid succession. "Well," he said. "You know you can't have this baby. I'll make sure everything is taken care of."

"I won't have an abortion, Roman," she said, wiping at her tears.

"Too bad. I don't want to be a father yet. We're both too young for that."

Amy turned and walked to the door. "Like I said. I am not getting rid of the baby. But I will tell you one thing, Roman Volkov. You are not walking away from us. I refuse to raise this baby alone." She went inside, slamming the door behind her.

Roman stood in stark disbelief. "*Glupyy, Glupyy*!" he shouted. How could he be so stupid? This should never have happened. This girl trapped him on purpose. There was no other way to look at it. She probably lied about the birth control.

Roman stared at the exit door. Not wanting to return inside, he continued up the alleyway and onto the street. Ubers were still dropping people at the curb, and the line to the club entrance extended down the block even at this late hour.

Shoving his hands inside the pockets of his leather jacket, head down, he ambled up the street. He needed time to think. Besides this news from Amy, the incident with the grocer nagged at him. Artyom continually invaded his sleep. Waking up, his body wet with sweat, he would gasp for air before finally settling himself. Of course, he agreed with Emil. The man caused his demise by pulling out a weapon, but when would the nightmares stop? Would this old man haunt him for the rest of his life? Tugging the zipper of his jacket up against the cold draft sweeping across the back of his neck, he quickened his steps.

He needed to deal with Amy. No way was she going to have his kid. His life would be in ruins. Reduced to raising a family at barely twenty-one years old could not be in his future. He pictured his mother and father. Their reaction would be nothing short of catastrophic—especially his father. He had warned him numerous times about getting some girl pregnant. He must find a way to stop her from having this baby. No matter what it took.

Chapter 17 — Alexei
Catching Up with Frank

The back room of Tatiana, constructed to be soundproof, allowed Alexei to conduct business without the intrusion of noise from the club. It also had a side exit leading out to the back alley. His business associates could come and go without being seen from inside the club. Earlier that evening, upon his arrival, his eyes scanned the place for Roman. Observing Emil and Luka sitting in the VIP section but not his son, he asked his manager, Ivan Petrov, if he had seen the boy.

"*Da*, I saw him earlier with his friends," Ivan said. "He went outside to the back alley with Amy, one of the waitresses, but I did not see him after that."

Alexei sighed. Roman in the back alley with one of the waitresses could only mean one thing. "Is the girl still here?" he asked.

Ivan pointed to a young woman setting drinks down at one of the tables. "She is a good worker. No trouble, always comes in on time, and the customers like her."

Alexei eyed the young woman. She was pretty enough, but he always cautioned Roman about getting involved with any of the women who worked at his club. "Is she Russian?"

"No," Ivan said. "Definitely not Russian."

Alexei turned away and headed for his private room, where Leonid sat at a small bar against the far wall. He swiveled on the leather-topped stool and stared at Alexei. "You had me worried. I thought for a moment you were going to cancel the meeting."

Alexei poured himself a shot of vodka and swallowed it. "Why would you think that?"

Leonid shrugged. "I know you don't like dealing with both sides of the coin. Enzo Carbone on one and Frank Uzelli on the other."

Just then, the door opened. "Mr. Uzelli has arrived," Ivan said.

Frank stepped through the doorway. He nodded at Alexei and Leonid and then glanced around the room. After shaking hands with Alexei, he pronounced, "Nice digs."

"Thank you. But in the future, I would appreciate it if you would use the rear entrance. It keeps things private." He ignored Frank's frown. "Would you care for a drink?" Alexei asked. He took note of the expensive suit and short buzz cut Frank wore. How appropriate it went with his nickname, Frank 'The Razor' Uzelli. With his broad shoulders and tall stature, the new haircut made his hook nose even more prominent. Alexei wondered if he still carried his famous straight razor.

"Whiskey neat," Frank said, unbuttoning his coat. "By the way, one of my guys is outside. Precautionary measure."

Alexei held out the drink and motioned to him. "Come, sit. Let us talk about business." He pointed to two overstuffed chairs across from one another with small tables resting on either side.

They sat, and Frank swallowed his whiskey in one gulp and set the glass down. "I understand you met with Enzo Carbone."

Alexei raised an eyebrow. "I must check out all means of getting my goods into the country. I think if you were in my shoes, you would do the same."

"Be honest, how did you feel dealing with Enzo? Do you trust him?"

Here it was again, that word trust. A serious word so easily thrown around. "Do I have a choice? Enzo has assured me customs will not be a problem."

"I can guarantee that, too, and more."

"More?" Frank had piqued his curiosity.

"Look, the waterfront is split between me and Carbone. If your goods come into one of my ports, I can clear them and get them into the right hands."

"Meaning?"

"Come on, we both know the cartels in Mexico can't get the automatic weapons they need on their own."

"True." Alexei shifted uncomfortably in his chair. He didn't want the Italians involved in trafficking his weapons.

"So," Frank continued. "Let me help you out."

"Look," Alexei said. "I don't want any trouble with Carbone. So here is what I will do. The weapons will come through Carbone's territory, and then we will discuss your getting them into the right hands in Mexico. If your way is easier than mine, we have a deal."

Frank squinted at him, his menacing grey-green eyes sending a chill up Alexei's spine. He signaled to Leonid, who scooped up Frank's glass and quickly refilled it.

Frank downed the whiskey once more, the empty shot glass landing with an audible thunk on the side table. He cleared his throat and leaned forward. "I see you have more faith in Enzo than me."

Not one to be intimidated, Alexei stared back at him for a moment. "Let me, as they say, lay all my cards on the table. First, there was the incident in Manhattan. It cost everyone a lot of money."

Frank held up his hand. "Now, let's be real, Alexei, I never told the five families about the other side hustle we were doing together. I could have, but I didn't. I don't want to get into a pissing contest with Enzo Carbone. The commission agreed to grant me some grace so long as I paid them back the extra money that was made."

Frank took in an audible breath. "This was and still is a difficult task since one of my former made men, Tony Morello, took off with most of my cash. If I ever find the son of a bitch, I'll make sure my razor severs his head next time."

Alexei glanced over at Leonid. Frank definitely intended to keep using his razor. But could the information he had received about a contract be wrong? This was news to him.

"No, there is no contract, Alexei."

It was as if Frank could read his mind. "Well, there was talk of—"

"Yes," Frank interrupted. "I know. But since I didn't rat anyone out and am paying back the money, the contract was squashed. They let me keep part of my territory, so I can't complain. I could have ended up like Salvatore Marconi." Frank stood, a signal he was ready to leave.

Alexei rose also. "Listen, give me a little time. The shipment is not due yet. Come to my son's twenty-first birthday party and bring your wife. I can give you my answer then." Alexei followed Frank to the door. "It will be neutral territory where we can both relax." He glanced over his shoulder at Leonid. "Text him the details."

"See you then," Frank said, opening the door. Thumping music from the club flooded in. He gestured to his man to come into the office.

Alexei escorted them to the rear door. "Thank you for your consideration." The door swung shut behind the pair.

"So," Leonid said. "What do you think?"

Alexei eyed him. "I think we have to deal with the Italians one way or another. My major concern is getting the shipment and moving the weapons across the border. The only question is, who will I piss off, Enzo or Frank. That is all I need to decide."

He paced back and forth and poured another shot of vodka. "This thing that Frank said about the contract being canceled is bothering me."

"Do you feel he is not telling the truth?"

"He has no reason to lie to me, but there is a simple way to find out."

"What do you mean?"

"I have also invited Enzo Carbone to the party. We will see how they act around each other. I can find out the truth once and for all."

Leonid's eyes widened. He shook his head. "That may not be such a good idea, Alexei. These two men appear to have a mutual dislike for one another."

"That is not my problem. My business comes before any squabbling between the two. We will see what happens when they come face to face."

Chapter 18 — Kai
Making Up

Kai sat on the edge of the bed inside Tony's hotel room. She had called him the previous day upon returning from Arizona. He came and plopped down next to her, his arm wrapping around her shoulders, pulling her closer.

"I'm so glad you're here," Tony said, his voice low and laced with pain. "I don't want to lose you, baby."

Kai turned her head and studied his brown eyes. "I don't want to lose you, either. Why can't you give this thing up, whatever it is? Our life together should be more important."

He let out a sigh so deep his body shook. "I would do anything in this world for you but that. I can't let go of it. I'll never be okay until it's done."

She leaned her head against his shoulder and stared at the carpet. Anything for her, but that, he had said. There was no changing his mind. Her grandmother's words came back to her. 'You must be in peace, *Hozho*.' Would helping Tony bring her that? Deep inside, she knew the answer but refused to acknowledge it.

"It may take me a little time to get you the information." She clasped his hand. "But once I do, you can't tell me anything else."

"You're risking everything for me, Kai. It means more than you'll ever know." He cupped her chin and kissed her lips. "We won't talk about it anymore for now. I want to spend time with you before you leave for New York."

"When will we see each other again?" she asked.

"Don't worry. It might be a while, but I'll make it work."

He pushed her down onto the comforter, their hunger for each other consuming them. Long, deep kisses were followed by naked, passionate lovemaking. Her skin burned with desire for him. The feel of his hands along her body, his mouth on her breasts, and his teasing tongue drove her to new heights. Kai couldn't get enough. She wished they could stay right here in this hotel room forever.

It was late evening by the time they ordered room service. Kai insisted they spend more time together alone instead of going out. They dined on steak and champagne and a variety of pastries for dessert. They showered together, made love again, and fell asleep in each other's arms.

Kai woke to the morning sun streaking across the room. She inched toward a sleeping Tony and kissed his cheek. His eyes opened, and he smiled.

"Good morning, babe," he said, his voice husky and warm.

A single tear trickled from the corner of her eye and slid down her cheek. How could she love a man this much? He consumed her.

Tony leaned on one elbow and stared down at her. "Kai, what's wrong."

She shook her head. "I don't know. It's hard for me to explain. I love you so much it hurts. I'm afraid something will go wrong."

He brushed at her tear. "Nothing is going to go wrong. It will all be fine."

"How can you be so sure?"

"Because the love we have for each other is special, Kai. It's so strong, it can withstand anything. You don't have to worry about us. Promise me, please. I hate to think of you in New York in this state of mind."

He leaned back, and she snuggled into the crook of his arm. Her finger trailed along the faded scar running down the center of his chest. "I wish this never happened to you. I wish—"

He pressed his fingertip to her lips. "Shush," he soothed. "There is no wishing, only the reality of what is."

They made love again before Kai dressed to leave. Tony walked with her to the door. Wanting to remember this moment, she leaned against the frame for one last kiss. "I love you, Tony. Please be careful."

He grinned and found her lips one last time. As he closed the door behind her, she heard him say. "I love you, too."

That evening, Kai packed the last of her things for the move to New York. Giving up her apartment and renting a small place in Brooklyn Heights made sense. Not knowing how long she'd be assigned there, she opted for a month-to-month lease. All her belongings would be shipped, with the Bureau reimbursing her for moving expenses.

Exhausted, she showered and prepared for her last night sleeping here in Washington, D.C. She thought about Tony and the past twenty-four hours they spent together. All her doubts about him loving her receded because she knew that no matter what, they were meant to be together.

Somehow, she would get him Eddie Marconi's whereabouts. Then he would take care of whatever it was, and they could put the whole thing behind them. Kai fell back against the pillows, pulling the comforter around her. Tony was so sure everything would be fine. But why wasn't she as confident as him?

Chapter 19 — Monica
The Task Force

Monica entered the conference room at FBI headquarters in New York. While waiting for the others, she sat at the long mahogany table and opened her laptop. She pulled up the file on Alexei Volkov. Anyone seeing this man on the outside would never picture him as the head of one of the most dangerous Russian Cartels in the United States.

The door swung open. Monica recognized the tall young man who entered. Curly brown hair framed his angular face. She was impressed with his background and could see why Bob chose him for the task force.

He came toward her and extended his hand. "Special Agent, Austin Faulkner." His relaxed features immediately put her at ease. His file mentioned he was single. No children, either.

"Monica Cappelino. Nice to meet you, Austin." His handshake was firm, and his demeanor confident. "Glad you agreed to join our little group."

"Wouldn't have missed it," he said, pulling out a chair across from her and setting up his laptop. "I've always wanted to work Organized Crime."

"Yes, it can get very interesting," Monica said.

A minute later, Bob walked in, followed by an attractive woman in a business suit, her blonde hair pulled together at the nape of her neck. She shook hands with Monica first and then Austin.

"Special Agent, Wanda Simmons. Nice meeting you both." She eased into a chair next to Austin while Bob seated himself at the head of the table.

Bob glanced at his watch. "Well, we're only waiting for one more."

With that, the door opened, and Kai, breathless, rushed in. "So sorry," she said, color creeping up her face. "I took the wrong subway train."

Monica laughed. "It happens. Navigating the subway here in New York can be confusing. You'll get used to it." She took note of her beautiful raven hair and high cheekbones. *That one never has a problem getting a date, for sure.*

Kai glanced around the room at the others. "Kai Nez. Glad to be here."

"Okay then, let's get started," Bob said. "I'm appointing Monica as the Case Agent in Charge since she knows how the Mafia operates here in New York. She's done some spectacular casework that led to a number of RICO convictions."

"So I've heard," Austin said, giving Monica a sly wink.

Monica wasn't sure what to think at the moment. *Was he making fun of her?* Hopefully, he wasn't going to be a thorn in her side. She had high hopes for him going into this investigation. Deciding to brush it off, she said, "I grew up around a lot of mob-related people. I learned how they operate, what they tolerate, and how they worm their way into illegal activities."

"But what about the Russian mob?" Wanda asked, smoothing a whisp of blonde hair that had come loose from her chignon.

"Well, things seem to operate quite differently with them," Monica answered. "From studying our intel, I can assure you there is no loyalty among thieves where they're concerned. While the Italians are very structured, divided into families, and stick to a particular hierarchy, the Russians run a much looser operation. They appear to be more violent and unpredictable at times. There is no central leadership. It's more like a network of gangs. Some work together, and others work against each other. That being said, next to the Japanese Yakuza, the Russians are the second-largest organized crime group in the world."

"Then it seems like it's going to be even more difficult to pin down their illegal activities," Kai said.

"Somewhat," Monica replied. "You see, here's the catch. We want to focus on which gangs are working closely with the Italian mob. If we can do that, we can find out who the big fish are and what they are up to."

"I agree," Austin said. "If we can target all the players, we can get a step ahead."

Over the next two hours, they went through all the major people in Alexei Volkov's inner circle. Photographs of Alexei's family were also included in the files. Then, after reviewing pictures of the current known major players in the Mafia, they spoke about what they knew so far but couldn't prove and what their objectives would be. Monica closed her laptop and leaned back into the chrome and leather chair.

"First, we need to find out who Alexei's connection is in the Italian Mafia. It would be tough for him to do business in this city without their help."

"C.I.'s?" Bob asked.

"I think I might have one up my sleeve," Austin volunteered.

Everyone looked at him in surprise. For a newbie here in New York to have a Criminal Informant already would be invaluable.

"I found out one of my C.I. has moved here from Vegas recently," Austin continued. "He's pretty solid. No promises, but I can reach out and see if he knows anything."

"Great," Bob said. "In the meantime, let's start digging into the intel we have so far."

"What about putting a tail on Volkov?" Monica asked.

"That can be tricky," Bob said. "We need to be careful. I don't want him getting wind of our investigation. Let's wait and see what Austin's C.I. comes up with first."

The meeting ended, they gathered their laptops and left the conference room. Monica observed Wanda hanging back to talk to Bob Acosta. It shouldn't have bothered her, but it did.

Wanda Simmons rubbed her the wrong way. Not that she had done anything Monica could put her finger on. It was just a feeling. And her feelings were usually right.

She would do a little digging. Since her file showed she worked on a case in New York some time ago, maybe there was an answer as to why she felt the way she did about Wanda.

Chapter 20 — Kai
The U.S. Marshall

By the time Kai returned to her small apartment in Brooklyn Heights, exhaustion threatened to set in. Dealing with the move and settling into her new life here in New York had drained most of her energy. A quick shower and bed tempted her, but there was one other thing she needed to accomplish before she could rest.

Pulling out her cell phone, she scanned her contacts until she found the one she wanted. She pressed call and waited. She was about to hang up after ten rings when his voice came on the line.

"Hello. Kai?"

"Yes. How are you, Bret?" She had known Bret Summers before he left the FBI and became a U.S. Marshal. They worked together on the Anti-Gang Task Force and even dated briefly. Nothing too serious developed between them, but they remained good friends during the remainder of his time at the Bureau.

"Well, this is a surprise," Bret said. "I'm fine. What about you?"

Kai filled him in on her current assignment and move to New York. "Still out in Nevada?" she asked.

"Yeah. I'm stuck here for now, but it's not so bad. I'm getting used to it. But I'm curious, why the sudden phone call?"

"I thought you might be able to help me out with something. Since I'm on this new Organized Crime Task Force, I'm trying to get as much information as possible on a past operation that may be connected to a current situation we're investigating."

"And our agency was involved?"

"Yes. It seems several of the defendants were offered witness protection. Some of them declined, and some accepted. I was contacted by one of them who agreed to protection and is having second thoughts."

"Yeah, that happens sometimes," Bret said. "But once they make a deal, it's clear that if they decide to come out, we can't help them anymore unless they have some valuable information for law enforcement."

"Well, this particular person claims he can help out the task force I'm currently on," Kai said. "He sent me a few messages, but they're always from burner phones, and I can't seem to convince him to trust me."

"But what can I do?" Bret asked.

"Listen, Bret, I'll be honest with you. I might be over my head here in New York. I don't have half the amount of experience the rest of the task force does. I'm floundering a bit, and I thought if I could find out where this person is and convince him to tell me what else he knows, it would be a real godsend for me. Give me a leg up so the others respect me more. Right now, they're treating me like I just came out of Quantico."

"Look, New York is a tough place to be stationed, but this is a big ask, Kai."

"I know, I know," she said, adding just the right amount of anxiety to her voice. "I understand. I shouldn't have called you in the first place. I don't know what I was thinking. I'm glad you're doing okay. Just forget I said anything. It was great hearing your voice. Enjoy the rest of your night, and maybe we'll talk again soon."

"Wait, Kai. Please don't hang up. I didn't say I wouldn't help. When we worked together, I always had a ton of respect for you. And even after we dated a bit, I still felt the same way. You've always been a good person, and I know it must have taken a lot for you even to call me."

If he only knew, Kai thought, her hand trembling just a bit as she gripped the phone tighter. "No, really, Bret. I don't want to cause you any trouble."

"Well, let me sleep on it tonight. If I agree, you know what to do, right?"

"Yes, of course. I'll wait to hear from you."

"You get a grip," Bret said. "Show those New York agents what you're made of, okay?"

"I will. Thanks, Bret. Good night."

"Good night, Kai."

With the call ended, she tossed her phone onto the kitchen counter. "Damn you, Tony," she muttered, letting out a long breath. All she could do now was wait and see if Bret would help her. While Monica was out of the office earlier today, she studied the files on the Marconi case. Eddie Marconi's face had stared back at her on the computer screen, almost a foreboding of things to come.

Against her better judgment, she poured herself a glass of wine and opted for a bath instead of a shower. Her long hair gathered up and secured on top of her head, she nestled underneath shimmering bubbles. She contemplated her decision to call Bret. Telling him lies irritated her. She didn't like people who lied; now she had become one of them because of Tony. Reaching for the wine glass sitting on the tub's rim, she sipped and pictured his face.

"Only for you," she said aloud. Jeopardizing her job and possibly Bret's made her stomach muscles cinch. This whole thing could turn out to be a catastrophe. Being an FBI agent meant everything. No other career could satisfy her craving for recognition, self-esteem, and control over her life.

Strangely, both she and her mother ended up in law enforcement. Having tried to coax her into joining the Tribal Police, Kai had balked at the idea. No way could she live and work on the Rez. Keeping her culture and traditions close to her heart would be enough.

Kai finished bathing and stepped out of the tub. Grabbing a towel, she padded over to the full-length mirror hanging on the back of the bathroom door. After drying off, she let the towel drop to the floor. Her beautifully formed breasts sat high above a slim waist. She undid the clip, holding her hair, and let it cascade past her shoulder blades. Closing her eyes, she imagined Tony's hands fondling her breasts, then traveling across every inch of her body. She could almost feel his warm breath on her neck.

Then, without warning, she felt the shock of something else. The memories came so hard and fast her body shook. Opening her eyes, she grabbed the towel again and quickly wrapped it around her. Knees wobbling, she stumbled into the bedroom and dropped onto the bed, her mind hurling her back to that dark place on the Rez.

Would it never stop? This mind-numbing terror consumed her at times, causing her to retreat and then lash out at an unwanted intruder invading her thoughts at will. Her hands curled into fists, and she beat them against the pillows.

"How could you!" she cried, dissolving into tears. Breath heaving, she pounded away until complete exhaustion set in. Dizzy from her tirade, the towel still wrapped tightly around her, she pulled the comforter back and slipped beneath it.

Her breathing slowed as she willed herself to calm down. There was no other choice but to accept what happened to her. Maybe her mother was right.

She needed to leave things in the past where they belonged. But her mother could never understand. Those memories were like some savage animal clawing its way into her soul and refusing to let go.

Chapter 21 — Alexei
Happy Birthday, Roman

Located riverside, adjacent to the Brooklyn Bridge, The River Café held breathtaking views of New York City and the Statue of Liberty. Renowned for its world-class cuisine and award-winning wine list, it was one of the most exclusive restaurants. Outside, the massive Brooklyn Bridge spanned the Hudson, its lights glittering against the backdrop of the Manhattan skyline.

Inside, black and gold balloons lined the ceiling. Each long linen-topped table held fresh flowers with the number 21 stuck in the middle of the arrangement, their perfume filling the air.

Alexei sipped vodka and calculated the cost of the private Terrace Room Darya had booked. At a minimum of $250.00 per guest for dinner plus additional expenses for liquor, wine, and a DJ, Roman's party would end up costing close to forty-thousand dollars.

They would dine on oysters, wild shrimp, and sea scallops. Of course, there would be Siberian Sturgeon Caviar from Germany. When it came to the main course, the guests were offered two choices between Colorado rack of lamb, merguez sausage, stuffed baby eggplant, and English pea purée with natural lamb reduction or pan-roasted venison loin with King Trumpet mushrooms, glazed carrots, ramp spaetzle, with lingonberry jus.

Dessert was a made-to-order 6-tiered cake with fresh strawberry filling, which Darya had informed him would be wheeled out at just the right moment.

He silently thanked God they never produced a daughter together. With Darya at the helm, he couldn't imagine what the cost of her wedding might be.

As Darya scurried about making sure everything was just so, the absurdity of the evening struck him. All of this for a son turning twenty-one, and not the best of sons at that. On top of it all, parked outside was a brand-new BMW SUV, which cost him an additional $50,000.

"Roman must have a new car," Darya had insisted. "Something safe. No sports car."

"Why does Roman need a new car?" he had asked. "He has a perfectly good one."

"Because this is America, and every boy turning twenty-one should have a new car."

Alexei was growing tired of Darya's 'this is America sing song'. As much as he loved her, it grated on his nerves. She related almost everything to living here in America. But as always, he went along with it because, in his mind, he was not spoiling his son but keeping his wife happy. And that was the most important thing to him.

He checked his Rolex. Guests would be arriving any minute. He flagged Darya down. She came toward him in a red cocktail dress with a plunging neckline, something only she could pull off without looking like a whore.

"Everything looks wonderful," he said, kissing her on the cheek. "Where is Roman?"

"I received a text. He is on the way."

"He needs to be here to greet the guests," Alexei huffed. "That is the proper thing to do when people take time to celebrate your birthday."

"I know," Darya said, smoothing her blonde hair. "Don't worry, he was less than five minutes away." She looked past him at the door, her eyes lighting up. "See, here he is now."

Roman, handsome but looking uncomfortable in a custom-made dark blue suit, tugged at his tie. He greeted his mother first by kissing each of her cheeks. "Thank you for all of this," he said.

Darya took a step back. "Let me look at my handsome son. I can hardly believe you are turning twenty-one."

"Me, either," Roman replied, giving her a lopsided grin.

"Enjoy tonight and behave yourself. There will be many important people here besides your friends."

"Da," Roman said.

One of the servers signaled to Darya, and she rushed away. Alexei admired her from behind. She still gave him a rush to his loins. That thought made him turn to his son.

"Who is the girl at Tatiana?" he asked.

"What girl?" Roman said, shifting his feet and tugging at the knot in his tie.

"Do not take me for an idiot," Alexei said through clenched teeth. "Ivan told me about her."

"Oh, her," Roman said. "You mean Amy? It's nothing. We made out a few times, and that's all."

Alexei could always tell when Roman was lying, and he knew it for sure at this very moment. Not wanting to take things further here, he said, "We will discuss this later. You know how I feel about your dating anyone from the club."

"We're not dating," Roman protested. "I told you it's nothing."

"Like I said, we will talk later." Alexei strode to the bar and ordered another vodka. He did not tolerate lying from anyone, especially not his sons. His intuition told him there was more to him and this girl than Roman admitted.

One by one, the guests arrived, and he saw Darya grab Roman by the hand and station him beside her at the door. Alexei was about to return to the bar when he spotted Enzo Carbone enter with a pretty young woman on his arm. Alexei was certain she was not his wife since he had met her at another function with Darya. He watched as Darya greeted both of them, giving nothing away. He could always count on her to do the right thing.

Enzo, looking delighted, made a beeline toward him. Alexei wondered how long his good nature would last once Frank Uzelli arrived.

* * * * *

After greeting most of the guests, Roman excused himself. His eyes scanned the room for Emil and Luka. They had arrived earlier, Emil with his Russian girlfriend, Roksana, and Luka, solo as usual.

Roman signaled to them and headed for the men's room. Once the three were inside, he checked the stalls and locked the door.

"Wow, this is some party," Emil crowed. "Your parents must have paid a fortune for this."

Roman waved his hand at Emil. "Never mind that. My father knows about Amy. That stupid idiot Ivan told him."

"So," Luka said. "What's the big deal? Just break it off. It's not like you were actually dating her, more like fu—"

"She's pregnant," Roman blurted out, his words echoing off the tile walls.

"Are you sure?" Emil asked. "I mean, sometimes girls say things to get a reaction."

"Well, I believe her," Roman said. "She was serious and is insisting on having the baby."

"She can't do that," Emil said. "I mean, your parents would hit the ceiling."

Roman went to the sink and loosened his tie. He splashed cold water onto his face and then turned back toward his friends. "What am I going to do?"

"Make her get rid of it," Emil said. "Too bad for her. How can she expect you to raise a child with her?"

Roman leaned against the sink and stared at the terra cotta tiled floor. "I told you she's going to keep it."

"Then we need to have a talk with this girl," Emil argued. "Let her know what the deal is. She gets rid of the baby or else."

Roman's stomach coiled at his words. Heat flushed through his body, and for a moment, he thought he might be sick in front of his friends. He swallowed back the saliva gathering in his mouth. Though he would never admit it, he still hadn't gotten over Artyom's murder, and now Emil was making threats.

"Let me try to convince her to do the right thing," Roman said. "Maybe she'll agree."

There was a knock at the bathroom door. The three looked at each other. Roman motioned to Luka to open the door while he and Emil pretended to be washing their hands.

Leonid came through the doorway and stopped. "What's going on here?" Luka tried to walk past him. Leonid's bulk filled the doorway, preventing any exit. "Why was the door locked?"

"Nothing," Roman said, drying his hands and trying to act casual. "We were just talking."

"About what?"

The three boys glanced at each other. Roman knew better than to mess with Leonid. He was his godfather as well as his father's brigadier.

"I had an argument with my girlfriend," Emil blurted out. "They were just telling me how wrong I was and that I should apologize to her."

The two others nodded. "Yeah, he really should apologize. She's such a nice girl," Roman said. He gave Emil a playful punch in the arm. "Too nice for this *durachok*."

"Hey, who are you calling a dummy?" Emil asked.

"You," Roman said. "Now go make things right so we can enjoy my party."

Leonid let them pass, but the look on his face told Roman he didn't believe a word they said. The night went on with Roman half-heartedly enjoying himself. He couldn't get Amy off his mind. Plus, the dreaded conversation with his father about her would come later.

When his parents presented him with the BMW his spirits lifted until he envisioned a baby seat in the car. Later, on the dance floor, several girls tried in vain to be the one. All of them pined for him to ask them out on a date. But the pretty faces went by in a blur. Only Amy's face swam before him. Emil was right. If she didn't agree to get rid of the baby, they would have to deal with her.

* * * * *

Enzo sent his lady friend to converse with Darya, and his bodyguard went into the kitchen, as was the custom, while he sat at the bar with Alexei. From his vantage point at the very end, Alexei kept one eye on the door.

Enzo made a sweeping gesture with his hand. "This must be costing you a fortune. It's like a freaking wedding."

Alexei shrugged. No way would he let Enzo know the expensive party agitated him. "My son only turns twenty-one once. He will have his own responsibilities soon enough."

"True," Enzo said, downing a shot of whiskey. "My daughter is engaged. No date yet for the wedding, but I know it's gonna be over the top."

Alexei spotted Frank Uzelli walk in with his wife, a natural Italian beauty. He wondered what she saw in him besides his money. He signaled to Frank while Darya, with Enzo's girlfriend trailing behind, pulled her away. Thankfully, he could always count on Darya. She seemed to sense when he needed to talk business without the women around.

Frank headed toward Alexei and stopped when he spied Enzo. "We have company," Alexei said. "I hope you don't mind."

Enzo swiveled his head. He turned back to Alexei, his expression turning sour. "What the hell are you trying to pull?"

"Calm down," Alexei admonished him. "I'm tired of being caught in the middle of you two. It is time we three talked."

Alexei nodded and waved Frank over. He came and sat one stool away from Enzo. He reached inside his suit jacket, and for a moment, the image of a straight razor flashed in Alexei's mind.

Frank pulled out a pack of cigarettes. "If we're gonna do this thing. Let's go somewhere else so I can smoke."

The men got up and followed Alexei through a door leading to the rear of the building. Always watchful, Leonid followed close behind.

They ended up in a small break room off the kitchen where a placard read, 'Employees Only.' Alexei cracked a window and motioned to Frank. "You can smoke in here."

The room was sparse. Several wooden chairs, a small table, and a refrigerator were the only things visible. When they were seated, Frank lit up his cigarette and took a deep drag.

"Those things are gonna kill you one day," Enzo said, wrinkling his nose and waving the exhaled cloud of smoke away.

Frank grinned, his smile leaking acid. "Still chewing on those nasty cigars? Besides, we're all gonna die someday, Enzo. Some of us sooner than others."

Enzo leered at him. "Just remember who you're talking to. I rank higher than you, Frank." He pounded his fist on the table. "I deserve your respect. Especially after all your underhanded dealings."

Frank puffed on his cigarette and then exhaled, deliberately blowing smoke Enzo's way.

Enzo reared back. "No bodyguard, Frank?" he asked. "It would be a shame if something were to happen to you."

"Are you threatening me, Enzo?"

"Of course not. Just wondering, that's all."

"Wonder no more," Frank huffed. "You'll never see him coming."

"Okay," Alexei said, wanting to ease the tension. "Stop wasting time. Let us see if we can come to an agreement that will make everyone happy. I need my merchandise to pass through customs without any problems."

"And I promised you it would," spat Enzo. He nodded toward Frank, "So, why are you dealing with this clown?"

"Careful, Enzo," Frank said. "You know we each have territory sanctioned by the commission. We both have Customs Agents on the hook, so if Alexei wants to shop around, it's okay by me. I know I can offer him something you can't."

Enzo sucked in his protruding belly and let out a rush of air through his nose. "And what's that?"

"Once the goods arrive, I can transport them anywhere without a hitch."

Enzo slammed his fist on the table. "I don't give a rat's ass about what you can transport, but you better make sure the commission is aware. No more side hustle, Frank. You owe them big time already."

Frank flicked his ashes onto the floor before stubbing out his cigarette beneath his shoe. "I don't need you to remind me about the commission. We're fine. They know all about me transporting goods. I make them happy with the cut they get."

Alexei watched the sheen of sweat break out across Enzo's forehead, his chest heaving in and out. He needed to put a stop to all the bickering. "Look," Alexei said. "This is what I have decided. Enzo will handle the merchandise when it comes into port, and Frank will transport it where it needs to be. We must not fight among ourselves. It does no good and only elicits hard feelings.

He could feel the temperature in the room go down and see Enzo relax a bit. "When tempers flare, it never ends well. Let us agree on what I have said."

The two men nodded, and all three got up. "Next week," Alexei said to Enzo. "I will let you know the exact dates. Then I can get in touch with Frank." He gave them a false smile. "See, everything has worked out. Please go have something to eat and enjoy the party."

He watched the two men leave while he held back to speak with Leonid, who had stationed himself outside the door.

"It's all worked out," he said. "Enzo will clear, and Frank will transport."

Leonid shook his head. "Your trust in these men is much greater than mine."

Alexei clapped him on the back. "Who said anything about trust."

* * * * *

Damien glanced over at Cookie. The worried expression on her face made him almost change his mind about bringing her to Roman's party. They continued to date, and even though they hadn't slept together yet, Damien admitted he was falling for her hard. Hence his decision to bring her to meet his parents, knowing full well they would disapprove.

He refused to hide Cookie from them. He had never lied to them before, and he wasn't going to start now. His mother was thrilled when he told her he was dating someone. She insisted he bring her to the party, and Damien agreed.

"Are you okay?" he asked, reaching for her hand.

"I think so. Are you sure this is a good idea? I mean, we haven't been going out all that long."

Giving her hand a little squeeze, he said, "I care about you, and I want my family to meet you. Besides, it doesn't matter to me if they approve."

Cookie pulled her hand away. "Approve? Wait a minute. Are you telling me they might not like the idea of us dating … that I'm not good enough for you?"

Damien stopped at the side of the road and cut the ignition. "Listen, you have to understand my parents are very traditional. That being said, my life is my life, and I will date whomever I want. As a grown man, I'm giving them the courtesy of meeting you." He reached for her hand again. "I'm enjoying our dates and the time we spend together. Nothing is going to change what we have between us."

"Okay then," Cookie said. "But you know I won't put up with any funny business."

"Funny business?"

"If they're rude to me, I'm not staying at the party."

Damien leaned over and kissed her cheek. "And neither am I."

They reached the restaurant and went inside. Damien thought Cookie looked amazing in her black cocktail dress. A soft halo of auburn curls framed her face. She had graduated from a cast, to as she called it, 'a boot thingy.'

His mother came toward them smiling. "My *Pcholka.*" She stood on tiptoe and kissed him on each cheek.

Damien felt himself blush. He wished she would stop calling him that. He turned to Cookie, who squeezed his hand so tight he feared his circulation would be cut off.

"Mom, I would like you to meet Carlotta Asante." The squeeze became a vice. "But she prefers to be called Cookie," he said quickly.

Darya's eyes swept over her, the smile never leaving her face. "It is so nice to meet you, Cookie. You must be very special. Damien never brings anyone to meet us." She glanced down at Cookie's leg. "Oh my, I hope that doesn't hurt too much."

"It's nice meeting you, too," Cookie said. "Most of the pain is gone. Your son has taken very good care of my ankle fracture."

The pressure on Damien's hand lessened. "Where is Dad?" he asked.

Darya's eyes searched the room. "He was here a few moments ago. I think he stepped out when some business associates arrived. But he'll be back any minute. Go and have some food, maybe dance a little," she said, her eyes twinkling.

"Sure." After his mother drifted away, he found a place for himself and Cookie at one of the tables. "Hungry?" he asked.

"Starved," Cookie said. "This is some setup. Everything looks so nice. All this for your brother's birthday? Where is he, by the way? I'd like to meet him."

"I'm sure he's around somewhere." Damien signaled to a server, and they ordered drinks and food. While they were in the middle of eating, he felt a clap on his back. He glanced up and found Roman standing behind him.

Damien got up, and they hugged. "Happy birthday, Roman." He introduced him to Cookie, who grinned up at him.

Roman pulled Damien away from the table, calling over his shoulder, "Excuse us for a moment."

"You know that was rude," Damien said. "You could have said a few words to her before dragging me away."

Roman shook his head. "Sorry, you're right. It's just that you don't come around much anymore."

"I know. But you have to understand, as a doctor, I am a bit busy."

"Still, you used to come on Sundays for dinner. Now, you hardly ever do." He nodded toward Cookie. "Is she the one keeping you away from us?"

Damien bristled. "Look, I told you I've been busy. You think it's easy working as a trauma surgeon, being on call, and running a practice?" He studied Roman for a moment. "And what do you do all day? Run the streets with those friends of yours and hang out at Tatiana at night?"

Color swept Roman's cheeks, and for a moment, Damien was sorry for what he had said. It was Roman's birthday, and he didn't want to make him feel bad.

He reached and ruffled Roman's blond hair. "I'm sorry. I hope you appreciate everything our parents do for you."

"Of course I do," Roman huffed. "I just wish you would come around more often."

"I'll try," Damien said.

Roman's face brightened for a moment. "Did you know about the BMW?"

"What are you talking about?"

He pulled Damien toward one of the big windows overlooking the parking lot. "See there." Pointing at the brand new shiny black SUV with a big red bow on the hood," he said, "Can you believe it?"

"That's yours?" Damien asked.

"Yes. I love it."

A loud roar erupted throughout the room as Roman's cake, candles blazing, was wheeled out onto the middle of the dance floor.

"You better go," Damien said. He sat beside Cookie while the guests sang Happy Birthday to Roman, who strutted around the huge cake. A round of applause went up after he blew out the candles. Servers appeared and quickly cut and served pieces to all the guests.

"What's going on between you two?" Cookie asked.

"Nothing. He doesn't understand how busy I am."

"Who doesn't understand what?" Alexei said, hovering over Cookie and him.

Damien stood and kissed his father on each cheek. He reached for Cookie's hand, and she rose and faced Alexei. Introductions were made, and he scanned his father's face for a reaction but couldn't detect anything.

"Where have you been?" Damien asked. "I haven't seen you since we arrived a while ago."

"Business. You know how that is."

Of course. He remembered growing up and seeing his father with men in dark suits, their faces wooden, never giving anything away.

Alexei turned to Cookie. "Are you enjoying the party?"

"Yes. It's wonderful."

"Good. For what it is costing me, I hope everyone is having a great time." He pointed at Cookie's plate with a half-eaten piece of cake lying on it. "Please finish. Do you mind if I borrow my son for a moment?"

"Not at all," Cookie said.

"Come, walk outside with me, Damien."

They stepped out, a chill wind blowing at them from across the Hudson River. Alexei studied Damien for a moment. "This woman you brought to the party, is it serious?"

So here it comes, Damien thought. His mother must have said something to his father. "Maybe," he answered.

"Well, you have never brought anyone else around. Here it is Roman's birthday, a special occasion, and you are introducing this woman to us."

"Why are you making such a big deal? We're dating, that's all. I'm a grown man. I think I should be able to see whoever I want."

"Of course, I can't stop you. We want you to be happy, Damien. It is just that—"

"What?" Damien cut in. "She's not Russian?"

"Worse, still," Alexei said. "You said her last name is Asante. That is Italian, is it not?"

Damien threw up his hands. "Okay, so what? That doesn't matter to me."

"After all we have done for you. Putting you through medical school and helping you set up your practice should mean something. The least you could do is find a nice Russian woman."

Boiling inside, his stomach twisting into knots, Damien pointed across the parking lot at Roman's BMW. "And that?"

Alexei followed his gaze. "What about it?"

"Yes, you put me through school and helped with my practice. And I'm grateful for all of it. But I worked hard to graduate and become a surgeon. I still work hard every day, a son you could be proud of when I could have turned out like Roman."

He watched his father's face harden. "Roman has nothing to do with this."

"He has everything to do with *this*. You're upset with me because I brought a woman you disapprove of to the party. Yet, Roman has no direction in life. He's not in school, and he has no job. Still, you throw him this outrageous party and give him a brand-new car. It doesn't make any sense."

Alexei grew silent. He turned and stared at the moonlit water, the breeze rippling the waves. "I know," he said. "I know Roman is not like you. I try with the boy, but your mother coddles him."

"Look, all I'm saying is, I appreciate everything you've done for me, but I need to live my life the way I want. You and my mother should focus on Roman now. He still has a chance to become anything he wants to be if you'll stop spoiling him so much."

"Of course," Alexei said. "You are right. Let us forget about all this and go back inside. We hardly get to see you, so we should not fight on a night like this."

They walked together, his father's arm around his shoulders. His father said he was right, but Damien knew better. His parents were not going to overlook his relationship with Cookie. Not by a long shot.

Chapter 22 — Cookie
Damien

A week after Roman's party, Cookie, happy to finally be free from her boot, was dressed in tight black jeans and a white silk blouse. She perched on the edge of Damien's sofa. This was her first time seeing his apartment. Before this evening, they always ended up at her place. She took in her surroundings as Damien eased down beside her, a glass of wine in each hand.

"So, what do you think?" he said, handing her a glass.

She sipped her wine. What else could she say but the first thing that came to mind?

"Sparse. Very sparse. I might say, sterile even. But the view is fabulous."

"That bad, huh? I just haven't had the time to fix the place up yet. Maybe you could help me with that."

"Sure," Cookie said. "But my taste may not be the same as yours. I do love the apartment complex, though. It's so convenient having everything you need right here."

He set his wine on the end table and reached for hers. Cookie gladly gave up her glass. This would finally be the night. Keeping him and herself at bay from sleeping together was one of the hardest things she ever had to do.

Damien pulled her into his arms. He leaned in and kissed her, his tongue dipping between her lips. Cookie reciprocated, her own lashing his. Her fingers threaded through his hair while he unbuttoned her jeans, his hand sliding down inside them. She let out a soft moan. Her body quivered with desire, every muscle tensing with expectation. He removed his hand, traveling upward to unbutton her blouse. Her fingertips skated over the bulge in his pants.

"Come," he said as he rose and reached for her hand. Soon, they lay naked in his bed. His hand swept over her stomach before caressing her silky-smooth thigh. She melted into his warm body, feeling his skin's heat against hers. He cupped her breasts and teased her nipples with his tongue.

Cookie cried out with pleasure. He trailed open-mouthed kisses along her neck before finding her lips again. She traced the firm muscles running across his back. Her body ached with longing as he slipped inside her. Their hips thrust in a steady rhythm, bringing them closer to the breaking point. They rode waves of pleasure together until spent. After one final deep kiss, he laid down beside her.

Her rapid breathing slowed. Never in her life had she experienced feeling like this with anyone else. A true body and soul experience. Turning her head, she watched his chest rise and fall. She inched up on one elbow and stared down at him.

His amber eyes caught the evening light, and he grinned at her. "It was good, wasn't it?" he asked.

"More than good," she replied, kissing the tip of his nose. "I'm so glad we waited."

"Me, too. It meant so much more."

She caught the slight shadow sweeping across his face. "Something wrong?"

"No." He brought the bedsheet up around them and pulled her to him.

"Remember what I said, Damien. No lies between us. Whatever it is, you can tell me."

"Just thinking about my surgery schedule for this coming week."

His answer didn't feel right to her. There was something else brewing. Not wanting to spoil the evening, she let it drop. "So, have your parents said anything about me?"

Damien shook his head. "No, not really. They were too busy with the party to notice anything else."

"If you don't mind my asking, what did you speak to your father about when he pulled you away from the table?"

Damien turned away from her and sat up. "We talked about Roman. My brother is too spoiled."

Cookie let out a giggle. "Jealous, maybe?"

"Don't be ridiculous." He put on his underwear and pants. "I'll get the wine."

Was she imagining things, or was there a hint of annoyance in his voice? He returned a few moments later and handed her one of the glasses before sitting on the edge of the bed again, facing away from her. Cookie sipped and then set the glass aside. She went and snuggled against his warm back. "Please, don't be angry. Especially after we just had sex."

"Is that what you think it was?" he said with an edge to his voice.

For the first time, she didn't know what to say. Was there a right way or wrong way to answer that question? Cookie got up and gathered her clothes. Everything was fine between them a few minutes ago, and now he was trying to ruin things.

"Look," she said, buttoning her blouse. "I think it's time you drove me home."

Damien left the bed and came over to her. "I'm sorry," he said. "Please don't leave. Stay with me tonight."

"No, I don't think so. Suddenly, you're in a mood, and I can't figure out why."

"It has nothing to do with you. My father and I argued about Roman, so when you asked me what we talked about, I got upset. It seems we're always arguing about him." His eyes pleaded with her. "This was more than just sex for me, Cookie. My feelings for you go much deeper than you know."

Flashbacks of Daniel Gage touched the fringes of her mind. If Damien didn't really mean what he had just said, she wouldn't be able to bear another heartbreak.

Damien, I…"

He pressed his fingertip lightly to her lips. "You don't have to say anything. Just stay with me tonight."

She wanted to say yes, but the word stuck in her throat. Instead, she said, "No, not tonight. Please take me home."

Cookie studied his handsome face and became afraid. Afraid of how easy it would be to fall in love with him—to get her life torn apart again over another man. She couldn't take that risk with Damien or anyone else.

Chapter 23 — Monica
The Informant

Austin strode toward Monica's desk. "Gather the others," he said, his voice thrumming with excitement. "I'll meet you in the conference room."

All but Bob Acosta assembled and sat. As Case Agent, this was Monica's task force now. Austin, almost bouncing in his seat, exclaimed. "My C.I. came through with some intel. It seems he started frequenting a club in Brooklyn called Tatiana. The one owned by Alexei Volkov."

"I've heard of it," Wanda said. "Its popularity reaches farther than the local neighborhood."

"You've been there?" Monica asked, wondering how she knew about the club.

Wanda gave her a sideways glance. "No, I said I've heard of it."

Monica didn't believe her. There was this gut feeling again that something wasn't right regarding Wanda. "Go on, Austin," she said, keeping her suspicions in check.

"He says he saw Frank Uzelli there."

A chill swept over Monica. "Frank Uzelli? That's a surprise. Are you sure? Last we heard, there was a contract out on him."

"Apparently Frank spent some time in Vegas. My C.I. described him to a tee. He claims the contract was cancelled on the condition Frank pay back the commission. They gave him grace because he never ratted on anyone. He said he knows for a fact he still carries his straight razor and actually saw him almost use it on somebody. This guy was shaking when he talked about Frank."

"With good reason," Monica said. "I've seen some of his handiwork close up. He slit the throat of one of his own made men,

Tony Morello," Monica continued. "When we arrived on scene, I tore off my scarf to stem the bleeding until the ambulance arrived. That was the second hit for Tony. He had an old scar running down the center of his chest, courtesy of Frank.

"He should have gotten out after that," Austin mused. "Once should be enough."

"He could never do that," Monica said. "Once you're in, you can never walk away. But he did turn against him in the end, and I was lucky enough to place a round in Frank's arm right before he attempted to slit someone else's throat."

"Where is Morello now?" Austin asked.

"I have no idea," Monica said. "He refused to go into witness protection. He might be dead for all we know." She glanced at Kai, whose face paled. "Are you alright, Kai?"

"Um, fine. No worries. Just thinking how awful it must be when someone uses a straight razor on you."

Monica turned her attention back to Austin. "Was Frank with anyone?"

"According to my C.I., no. He saw him enter a back room at the far end of the club. But he never saw him leave. We can only assume there is another entrance, so if Frank was with someone, my C.I. might not have known."

"Well, we know Alexei Volkov owns that club," Monica said. "More than likely washes money through it. But it doesn't make sense for him to deal with someone who might still have a contract out on his head."

"But my C.I. swears that the contract was cancelled," Austin insisted.

Monica shook her head. "It's unusual for the mob to cancel a contract under any circumstances. In Frank's case, he went into business with Salvatore Marconi behind the commission's back. That's a major offense. What do you think, Wanda?" Monica asked, wanting to feel her out a bit more.

"I think there's a puzzle piece missing here. If the contract was cancelled, we need to find out who else in the mob knows Alexei Volkov is doing business with Frank Uzelli."

"Good point. I'm curious as to what Frank has to offer," Monica said. "Austin, do you think your C.I. can find out anything more? Like what Frank is into these days."

"He's a bit on edge, but I'll try."

"We do know that, at one time, Frank held control of the seaports in New Jersey. We need to know if that still holds true or if someone else has their finger in the pie," Monica said. "We need to dig further into Alexei Volkov's nightclub and the men working closely with him. One in particular I'm curious about is Leonid Rabinovich. He seems to be what the Russians call a brigadier, second in command under Alexei."

They rose to leave, and Monica remembered what Bob asked her to do concerning Kai Nez. "Please stay a minute, Kai." When the others were gone, she asked, "How are you settling in?"

"New York is very different from D.C., but I'm getting used to it."

"You've done some great work for the Bureau." She saw Kai blush.

"I love working for the FBI. There is nothing else I would rather be doing."

"I was a bit concerned earlier. Are you sure you're feeling okay?"

Kai shrugged. "I'm alright, just not one hundred percent today. I had a bad headache earlier, but it's easing now."

"Maybe you should take the rest of today off. You don't need to be here when you're not feeling well."

"No, that won't be necessary. I can work through it."

Monica wanted to get to know this woman better. Her background was stellar, and she could contribute much to the team. Maybe she's a bit homesick, Monica thought, remembering how she felt about her move to Washington. "Listen, if you're not doing anything later and feel up to it, how about dinner?"

Kai's face brightened a bit. "I would like that."

"Well, it will have to be at my place on Staten Island. I have a son, Andrew, downstairs in daycare. We can order in and relax."

"I sure appreciate you inviting me."

"I'll text you my address. Come over around seven. What kind of food would you prefer?"

"Oh, I'm easy," Kai said. "Order whatever you like."

When she was gone, Monica felt she had done the right thing in inviting Kai over for dinner. Things can get lonely quickly when you're in a new city. She was about to exit the conference room when Wanda stepped in.

"Need something?" Monica asked.

Wanda eyed her. "Look, I get the feeling you don't like me."

Heat swept through Monica's body. She didn't relish discussing this right now. "Honestly, I haven't had the time to get to know you. You were chosen for this task force because of your experience and excellent record."

"So then, am I imagining things?"

Monica wanted to say no but instead said, "Look, we need to work together as a cohesive team. I'm sure you're more than capable of doing that."

"Absolutely," Wanda replied. Her face softened a bit, and she held out her hand. "Let's start over then, shall we?"

Monica shook her hand and smiled. "When you have time, I would love to discuss the case you worked on here in New York. I heard it was quite a tough one."

"Serial killer," Wanda said. "A real bitch of a case."

"I can only imagine." Monica went to the door and held it open for Wanda. "Glad we cleared things up between us," she said. "I'm sure this task force is going to do some great work."

Wanda nodded and proceeded down the hall. Monica watched her walk away. That same uneasy feeling held on tight and wouldn't let go.

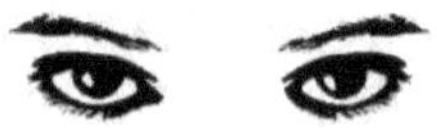

Chapter 24 — Frank
Pressure Cooker

Grey shadows draped the walls of Frank's study. With dusk fast approaching, he had yet to turn on any lights. He settled into the leather chair behind his desk. Most would say he was lucky the heads of the five families granted him a reprieve. Pay back the money he skimmed, or else die. It was as simple as that.

But his debt to them amounted to millions of dollars. Money he was hard-pressed to earn. If not for that prick, Tony Morello, his odds would be much better. The son of a bitch took almost every last dollar he stowed away. His biggest mistake was trusting Tony. He never dreamed he'd turn on him and help Sal's nephew rescue that girl.

So far, trying to find Tony proved to be an impossible task. No one heard a peep as to where the rat might have run. He wished the cut to Tony's throat had been deep enough to kill him. The punk still breathed the same air as everyone else.

Frank relished what he planned to do to Tony when he got his hands on him. Those first two cuts on his body would amount to nothing compared to the pain he intended to inflict on him.

Alexei Volkov, another thorn in his side, had not made the decision Frank was expecting. Splitting the deal between him and Enzo Carbone meant less money coming in. The commission knew what it was doing, dividing the seaport territory between them.

They wanted to make it difficult for him to make things right. Though smaller than before, his crew needed to work harder to bring in more cash.

His cell phone buzzed. He picked it up and glanced at the number. One of his made men and one of the few he could trust, Peter Bianchi, was calling.

"What's going on, Pete?" Frank asked.

"I got a bite on Tony Morello."

Frank sat straight up in his chair. "From who?"

"A buddy of mine in Palm Springs. Apparently, he spotted Tony with some broad a while back. He didn't realize at the time who Tony was until we spoke. I mentioned we were looking for someone and sent him a picture. He swears it was Tony."

"How long ago?"

"Couple of months, maybe."

Frank's chest muscles tightened. His fists clenched. Tony must be having the time of his life using his money.

"Do I need to take a trip?" Pete asked.

"He may not still be there, but I think it's worth checking into. Head that way and let me know if anything cooks."

"Will do," Pete said, ending the call.

Frank opened his desk drawer and pulled out a box. Almost salivating, he lifted the lid and took out the Dovo Bismark Cutthroat Razor. He rubbed his finger over the pearl-white handle. The ornate blade with 24-karat gold etching was made from the highest carbon steel. He had ordered the razor after his trial and release from prison with Tony in mind.

Someone he had helped to become a made man and treated almost like a son had turned on him and helped that bum Eddie Marconi destroy what he and others had built.

Frank pictured the blade cutting into Tony Morello's face. Maybe he'd take an eye, slice his nose, or cut off his ears first. He delighted in imagining all the things he would do when he caught up with him.

Yes, this razor was special, custom-made for the rat who stole his money.

Chapter 25 — Kai
Breaking The Law

On the Saturday after the last task force meeting, Kai rented a car and drove to Manassas, Virginia, to meet Tony. Bret Summers had come through with the information he wanted. Her eyes steady on the road, she tried not to think about the possible consequences of her decision. But when she passed Exit 148 off of I95 and saw the sign for Quantico, her breath caught, and her palms grew sweaty.

Agreeing to do this for Tony bordered on sheer madness. If anyone ever traced this back to her, she would lose everything she worked and trained so hard for, not to mention the ramifications Bret Summers could face. But she'd keep her promise never to reveal his involvement.

Her dinner with Monica only served to highlight the vast difference between the two of them. She could never picture Monica doing something like this. Her dedication to the FBI could never be breached. When she talked about some of the cases she solved, Kai caught the gleam of pride in her eyes.

Later that same night, back in her apartment in Brooklyn, her burner phone rang. Burners were the agreed upon form of communication if Bret was to give her information. After taking the call from Bret, Kai could barely look at herself in the mirror. She struggled to get a good night's sleep. But she couldn't block out the guilt hammering in her head.

Kai reached the hotel and swung into a parking spot. Sailing past the front desk clerk, she took the elevator to the fourth floor. Breathless, she reached Tony's room and pounded on the door. It cracked open, and she pushed her way in.

"Geez, Kai," Tony said. "I thought you were gonna break the door down." He closed and locked it behind her as she dropped down onto the bed. "Baby, are you okay?"

She shook her head. "Hell no, I'm not okay. I still can't believe I'm doing this." Her eyes focused on the gun in his hand.

"Oh, this," he said, tossing it into the bedside table drawer. "You know I can't be too careful." He sat next to her. His arm draped around her shoulders. "Your whole body's shaking." He stroked her back. "I can't stand seeing you like this."

"How else did you expect me to be? I could lose everything, Tony."

His hand dropped to her knee, giving it a gentle squeeze. "If this is too much for you, then you don't have to tell me anything regarding Eddie Marconi. I'll find another way."

"There's so many things going around in my head," she said, leaning into him. "Your name came up at a task force meeting."

Tony jumped up. He stared down at her, his face like iron. "What do you mean?"

"One of the agents mentioned how… how she stopped the bleeding from the gash across your neck."

"What agent?"

"You wouldn't know her."

"Try me," Tony said.

"Monica Cappelino," Kai responded. "Did you know she helped you?"

Tony took a step back. "Wow, Monica. I was totally out of it. No one ever told me." He went to the window. His back to her, he said. "She probably saved my life."

She got up and went to him. "Wait, you knew Monica?"

"She was Eddie's girl."

Confused, her head buzzed with questions. How could that be? Monica Cappelino and Eddie Marconi? She tugged at Tony's arm, pulling him around to face her. "You know she has a kid. A little boy about three years old."

"I don't know anything about a kid. But what I do know is that Eddie and Monica were together at one time. He came up to the hospital to see me before he went into witness protection. I was still a little drugged, but I do remember his biggest fear was that he would never see Monica again. But he never mentioned a son."

"Do you think her little boy could be his?"

"The math seems right, but I can't say for sure."

"Then tell me," she said. "Why do you want to find Eddie? He has nothing to do with you and Frank."

"Eddie and I are cut from the same cloth. His going into witness protection doesn't change that. Loyalty is everything in our culture. Just like I helped him, I need his help now."

"To get Frank?" she asked.

He ignored her question. "Was anything else mentioned about me?"

"No, but an informant says Frank is still working for the mob on the condition he pays back the money he made from an illegal operation. The contract on him was cancelled."

Tony's eyes flashed. "I knew it. I could feel the snake was still slithering around."

"But we don't have confirmation yet—sometimes we get bogus intel."

His eyes locked on hers. His arms wrapped around her, and he leaned in for a kiss. Their lips met, and Kai's resolve faltered. Her hunger for him never ceased—an empty well that could never be filled. Every time she saw him, she wanted more. This never-ceasing need scared her. It made her want to scream with fear and laugh with joy all at the same time.

Without another word between them, they stripped and made love. Wanting only to be consumed by Tony, she pushed thoughts of Frank and Eddie away. The safety she had sought all her life was right here in his arms. She couldn't chance losing that.

She snuggled closer, breathed in his scent, and knew what she was about to do.

"Scottsdale," she whispered. "Scottsdale, Arizona. He goes by the name of Jack Ricci at the Desert Sanctuary Resort."

Chapter 26 — Eddie
Eavesdropping

Eddie arrived at work early before the start of the next shift. Going over the latest reservations, he scrolled down the computer screen and stopped. Late last night, two new bookings were added. Names he recognized as belonging to one of the most powerful Mafia families on the East Coast. The family he and his Uncle Sal used to belong to. Due to arrive this afternoon, each one requested an expensive Mountain Suite Villa.

His shaking hands fumbled over the keyboard. Why the hell were these guys coming to Arizona? Just reading those names evoked memories he tried so hard to forget. It was not that long ago he had become a made man himself. Only these men were high-ranking Caporegime.

His Uncle Sal's face flashed before him. Everything from the past felt like a dream. Did all of it really happen? His Aunt Rita and Uncle Lorenzo remained incarcerated along with Jimmy Galante.

He read about Frank Uzelli getting off. Every time he remembered him slicing Tony Morello's throat, it sickened his stomach. Frank must be dead by now. The heads of the five families would have never let him live. Doing business behind their backs was major.

He guessed Tony Morello was probably dead, too. The last time he spoke with him at the hospital, he made it clear he was not going into witness protection. Poor Tony. Eddie still blamed himself for what happened to him.

He debated about whether or not to contact the U.S. Marshal's Office. His life would be in danger if any one of these men knew his whereabouts. But his old life crept in, attempting to sway his decision. Curiosity got the better of him. He wanted to know why these men were gathering.

At the moment, he had no idea how he would do this. The only thing he became sure of was keeping out of sight while they were here. He rechecked the reservations. Their booking was for a two-day stay. Short and sweet. This meant these particular men were here to discuss something others in the mob were not supposed to know anything about.

A few minutes from now Amelia would arrive. Eddie scribbled a note telling her he had tons of paperwork to catch up on and would spend the next few days working in his private office. He was not to be disturbed unless there was an emergency no one else could handle. He hoped she would follow his instructions.

Eddie crossed the lobby. This early in the morning only two guests sat drinking coffee. One read a newspaper while the other texted on his cell phone. Looking out of the floor-to-ceiling windows, he caught Amelia pulling into the parking lot. Assured the front desk would be covered, he waved and hurried to his office as she entered the automatic doors. Once inside, he collapsed into the chair behind his desk.

He lifted the telephone receiver and dialed the front desk. Amelia would be his lookout.

"Morning, Jack." Amelia's annoying sing-song voice grated at him more than usual.

"Morning. Did you get my message?"

"Yes. Boy, you must be way behind if you're going to stay in your office for—"

"Listen, Amelia," Eddie cut in. "I need you to let me know when all the guests scheduled to arrive today have checked in."

"As they check in?"

Eddie wanted to scream. "No, after *everyone* has checked in."

"Is there something going on?"

"Nothing is going on. We're booked full, so if anyone cancels or doesn't show, I want to be made aware."

"What if any issues come up?"

As much as he hated to say it, Eddie forced the words out. "Let Monty take care of it."

"Really? You know he's not very good at handling situations."

"Agreed, but I really need to catch up with things."

"Okey-dokey. You got it!"

The rest of the day dragged on until around 4 o'clock when Amelia informed him of the arrival of the two men who were the last to check-in.

"By the way," Amelia said. "They refused dinner seating in Elements. I tried telling them it's complementary on the first night you book a villa. They said they'll order room service later."

The news didn't surprise Eddie at all. They wouldn't want to discuss business in the restaurant. "That's fine. Make sure room service knows they're five-tier guests. Have them text me after the food is ordered." Five-tier meant the staff would go out of their way to accommodate them.

Eddie waited until dark before leaving his office by a rear exit. The hotel retained rooms where staff could stay if they worked a split shift. He made his way to the rear of the property and slipped inside an unoccupied unit. Driving home was out of the question. Returning at daylight might cause him to be seen by one of the men.

He needed time to think. Refusing to go to the restaurant meant they would either dine together in one of the villas or eat alone. Unable to sit still, he paced while checking his cell phone every other minute.

At 9:00 p.m., he received a text from room service. Food had just been delivered to only one of the villas. Eddie studied the suite number, picturing its location in his mind. Confident the men would be getting ready to eat, he stepped outside. With his senses heightened, he heard the throbbing of his heart inside his ears. His mind clouded with fear, and he froze. Unable to move forward, he tried to steady his breathing.

"You can do this," he whispered to himself. Continuing, he rounded the long row of villas. Light beamed out from several of the windows. He caught the scent of Spanish lavender, followed by lemon grass growing along the opposite side of the walkway. Across from them, a tall Japanese privet planted beneath the villa balconies would provide excellent cover for what he had in mind. The most secluded villa and the one to which the food was delivered stood at the end of the path.

With the Japanese privet for cover, Eddie ducked and positioned himself below. Hidden in the darkness by the tall shrubs, he waited. Muffled voices came from inside. He hoped they would open the sliding glass doors at some point. He didn't have to wait long before the sliders opened. Footsteps tapped against the tiled balcony floor. The acrid smell of cigarette smoke followed the sound of a match being struck. Eddie turned on his cell phone in hopes of recording their conversation.

"Look, Carmine, we can do this if we get the others on board," a man said.

"I agree, Martello has got to go," the second replied, his voice several octaves deeper than the first man. "He was the one that convinced the others to let Frank Uzelli off easy."

"Besides giving him half the Jersey Seaport to split with Carbone. You know Enzo isn't happy about that," the first one said. "We need to get Rocco Fischetti on this. He can take care of things easily. One, two, three—in and out."

Eddie's scalp prickled. Could they be talking about Paulie 'The Shiv' Martello, his Uncle Sal's old boss? Dread crept up from the pit of his stomach. Rocco Fischetti had murdered an FBI agent and then his Uncle Sal. As slippery as an eel, he had never been apprehended by the authorities.

"Look," the first man said. "The three of us are on board, and I'm sure we can get Enzo to agree. After all, as Under Boss, he's next in line. With Enzo on top, we can all do better than we're doing now."

Someone yelled from inside about the food getting cold, and then a third man stepped out onto the balcony. "Look, we all agree, right? So, let's just eat and relax. We'll get in touch with Rocco and get things moving. I need to get back to Staten Island tonight before I'm missed."

The hairs at the nape of Eddie's neck stood up. The third voice, all too familiar, made his pulse race at a dizzying speed. A cold sweat trickled down his back. He recalled the fear on Little Frankie's face, the sickening sound of a saw cutting through bones—the putrid smell of blood and guts. And then he remembered Domenico Conti's words. 'What can you do when the boss says someone has to get clipped?'

Apparently, Domenico now held the position that used to belong to his Uncle Lorenzo. Climbing up the ladder, he had become a Capo. His name didn't appear on the guest list because he never intended to stay the night. Eddie waited until he heard the men go back inside. With the slider still open, he crept along the wall and away from the bushes. Stepping out onto the path, he almost collided with Monty.

"What gives?" Monty yelled. "You almost knocked me down."

"Sorry," Eddie said in a hushed whisper.

"Hey, you," a voice called behind him. "Come here."

His back to the villa, Eddie saw Monty look up toward the balcony. He mustn't turn around. Panic threatened to set in. Fear snaked through his body.

"I think that guy is calling you," Monty said.

"Yeah, well, I've got something I need to take care of. Go see what he wants." Eddie forced his legs to move forward. "Don't run, don't run," he cautioned under his breath.

"By the way," Monty called out. "Some guy is waiting for you in the lobby. He said it's very important that he see you. He asked for you by name."

Eddie rounded the villas and broke into a fast trot. What the hell was Monty saying? Who could be calling for him at this time of night? If they asked for Jack Ricci, it must be one of the guests.

Taking several deep breaths to steady himself, he headed for the lobby. He would see whatever this person wanted and then drive home, far away from those guys in the villa.

Eddie stepped through the lobby doors. At first glance, it appeared deserted. Whoever it was must have left. Then, he observed a man sitting across the room, facing away from him. Just the back of his head could be seen. Next to him rested a large suitcase.

All he wanted to do was go home. After everything that transpired, his nerves were a jangled mess. He had heard made men plot the murder of one of the most powerful bosses in the Mafia. Now, he needed to figure out what, if anything, he should do with that information. Call the U.S. Marshal Service or, somehow, try to warn Paulie. All these things ran through his mind as he crossed the lobby.

Just as he reached the man, he got up and turned around. His heart almost stopped for the second time that night when he heard.

"Hey, Staten Island."

It was Tony Morello.

Chapter 27 — Bob
Monica

Bob leaned over and stared at Monica's laptop, his shoulder grazing hers. They were at her townhome discussing some new intel Monica obtained regarding Leonid Rabinovich. She had invited him to dinner, and after putting Andrew to bed, the two of them went over the information.

Working so closely together for a little over a month now hadn't been easy for Bob. In fact, it was driving him out of his mind. He needed to express his feelings, but he wasn't sure if Monica would even be open to hearing it.

"So, you see," Monica said, "There is a good chance he's playing both sides of the fence. I think he's going to try to push Alexei Volkov out. It looks like he's been having all these little side visits with another faction."

Bob stood back as Monica closed her laptop. "I think you're right. Maybe it's time we put surveillance on Rabinovich. See what he's up to."

"Austin might be a good pick for that," Monica said.

Unable to stand it any longer, Bob asked. "Could we talk for a moment?"

Monica grinned at him. "Sure."

He pointed to the sofa. "Let's sit."

They sat on opposite ends, with Bob keenly aware she always kept her distance. By no means did he want to be disrespectful in any way. During dinner, he caught the glint of gold in her green eyes, concentrated on the perfectly formed lips he longed to kiss and those long dark curls he wanted so badly to sweep his fingers through.

"I'm not sure how to begin," he said softly.

"Am I in some kind of trouble?"

"No, no. It's nothing like that."

"Then what is it? Someone on the task force do something?"

Bob heaved out a long sigh. "No, but maybe I'm about to. But I feel I need to say this."

"Now, I'm really confused," she said, quirking an eyebrow. "I've never seen you act this way."

"I'm probably about to make a fool of myself. I've developed feelings for you. I know I'm way out of line in telling you, and it isn't something I take lightly. We both know how the Bureau feels about colleagues dating."

Her green eyes blinked and searched his face. He couldn't tell whether she was upset or not.

"Bob, I …"

"Please, let me finish. I would like to ask if you'll consider going out with me sometime. We can keep it between us and see where it goes. But I'll understand if you don't feel you want to do that."

A dash of color swept her cheeks, but her eyes never left his face. "I can't say this comes as too much of a surprise," she said. "A woman has a certain intuition about these things. She can tell when a man is attracted to her. I've felt that from you for a long time now."

"And?" Nerves knotted in his stomach. Was she about to reject him? He thought he had prepared himself and would be able to accept it. Sitting at the opposite end of the sofa, he braced himself for the worst.

To his surprise, she said, "I think I, too, would like to see where this goes," her voice low and laden with emotion.

Bob moved closer. He swept her into his arms and took possession of her lips. His hands traveled down her back and then up toward the nape of her neck. Her soft moan tickled his ear.

Monica leaned away and then got up. She stretched out a beckoning hand and led him into her bedroom. Their undressing was deliberate and slow. Eyes feasting on one another's nakedness, they embraced and eased down onto the bed. His fingers ran through her ringlets of dark curls, and he let out a deep sigh.

Eager hands roamed over hot skin. Her fingertips traced the hard muscles on his chest and then drew a line along his chiseled jaw. They found each other's lips again and again. He teased the hard, rosy bud of her nipple with his fingers. He dipped his head, his mouth moving along the smooth skin of her stomach and down to her inner thighs before returning to her breasts. He whispered her name and then slipped inside of her. She let out a soft cry. A shudder rocked his body. Her legs came up and wrapped around his waist, her hunger for him revealed as she pulled him closer. They rode the wave of desire soaring through them until it crested and broke. When he sensed she was ready, he dropped down beside her. Monica snuggled up against him.

"That was nice," she said softly.

"Hmm, I'll take nice for now," he teased. He placed a finger beneath her chin and tilted her head up. Her green eyes shimmered. "You have no idea how long I've waited for this."

"The longer, the better," she teased back, easing up against the pillows. "I have to admit, I've thought about it too. I wondered when you would get around to telling me how you feel."

He pushed himself up next to her. "If only I would have known," he sighed.

Her face turned serious. "Let's take things slow. I can't think too far ahead right now."

"Agreed," he said. If only she knew just how far ahead his thoughts had gone, she would probably run the other way. He envisioned a long-term relationship with Monica, not some fling.

Monica swept her hand through his thick salt and pepper hair. "Can I ask you something?"

"Sure. Nothing is off the table unless it compromises the Bureau."

"Have you ever slept—I mean, been with anyone else who works for the FBI?"

Kai's face swam before him. They had made a deal. Neither one would ever talk about their past relationship under any circumstances, especially since he selected her to join the task force here in New York. He really muddied the waters with that one.

"No," he lied. "Although it goes on, the Bureau frowns on those types of dalliances. That's why we need to be careful. At least for now. If things become serious between us, then that's a different story."

"How serious are you talking?"

"Suppose we had other intentions. Like getting engaged, etc."

Monica sat straight up. "Whoa, wait a minute. I need to be clear about something. Marriage is nowhere in my future. Not now, not ever."

"Hold on," Bob said. "I was just giving you a scenario. No need to panic."

"I'm not panicking," she huffed. "Just being honest. Regardless of how we progress, I'm not hitching myself to anyone."

Deep down inside, he knew why she was so adamant about not getting married. Only one person was to blame for that. Eddie Marconi. Damn that guy. Would Monica ever get him out from under her skin?

Later that evening, as he lay in his bed thinking about the night, he wished Monica had been his all along—no ghosts from the past to come between them. He dated many women without ever finding the need to marry. But Monica scared him. Like a magnet, she kept pulling at him, the force too great for him to resist.

Bob recalled his lie about Kai Nez. No way could he break the promise he made. That little affair must stay hidden. If not for his and Kai's sake, then most of all for Monica's.

Why had he even dated Kai in the first place? As beautiful as she was, she had been way too young. Bob believed it was her intelligence that intrigued him the most. He admired intelligent women and enjoyed having meaningful conversations with them. But her temper when they parted was another thing to behold. It could be her blessing or a curse—a blessing when she needed to protect herself. It was a curse when some actions called for patience first.

Whenever he was around Kai lately, he noticed a difference in her. Maturity for sure, but there was something else. It made him wonder if she found someone who really understood her needs and treated her accordingly.

Kai never spoke too much about her past to him. Questions about her growing up on a Navajo Reservation appeared off-limits. Her eyes would cloud over, and she'd dissolve into herself. He often wondered what her life there was really like. Since she still had family there, it couldn't have been all bad. He knew for a fact that her mother worked with the Tribal Police.

But the past with Kai was behind him. He needed to help grow his relationship with Monica into something solid. In time, she'd see how much he cared for her. He had waited too long for his desires to be met to let anything or anyone come between them.

Chapter 28 — Leonid
The Basement

Leonid surveyed the unpainted drywall that covered the dark basement. Blood spatters marred a good portion of the surface. Behind them, acoustic panels nailed against foam insulation made the room soundproof. Damp, stale air mixed with urine and dried feces permeated his surroundings.

Lying on the outskirts of New York in the Catskill Mountains, surrounded by woods, it reeked of torture and death—the perfect place to kill and then dispose of a body. Overhead, a long chain led to a single light bulb dangling from a cord. It lit the room with an eerie yellowish glow. He set a metal case on a small table beside a wooden chair.

Impatient, he adjusted his black leather gloves and paced. The bottoms of his shoes scraped the cement floor. He should not have allowed things to go on as long as they did. Today, he would finish it.

The heavy basement door opened. Sergey Vassiliev tumbled down the stairs, blindfolded, gagged, and with his hands tied behind his back. Two men, their footsteps heavy on the treads, appeared. They yanked Sergey to his feet, removed the blindfold, and propelled him forward.

Sergey spotted Leonid. His eyes grew large, and he shook his head violently back and forth. One of the men ripped the duct tape from across his mouth while the other tore off his shirt and lowered his trousers down around his ankles. They tied his body to the wooden chair and then retreated to the far wall.

"So, here we are," Leonid said. He deposited a metal case on the floor then pulled on a white disposable coverall. He opened the metal case, revealing a drill and a hammer.

Sergey's eyes landed on the contents. His body trembled so violently that it caused the chair to move several inches. "Leonid, why are you doing this to me?"

"I think you know why. You are a dirty little spy. Giving Alexei information about me."

Beads of sweat broke out across Sergey's forehead. "No, no, you are wrong. I never told him anything about you. I would never do that!" he cried.

"Do not take me for a fool, Sergey. You should have known better than to conspire against me." Lifting out the drill, he inserted a long carbide drill bit into it. "Now, what I need to know from you is what you have told Alexei."

Sergey squeezed his eyes shut. "I have not said anything. I am telling you the truth."

"*Pravda!*" Leonid shouted. "What do you know about the truth? You have been telling lies behind my back for the past year. Whispering in Alexei's ear, trying to get him to distrust me."

Leonid turned on the drill. A loud, steady buzz filled the basement. Moving closer, he aimed it at Sergey's knee. "I guess you would rather be in pain than tell me what I want to know."

The drill bit tore into Sergey's kneecap. He let out a guttural howl. Blood spurted from the wound, dripped down his leg, and disappeared into the folds of his trousers.

"Please, please," he begged, gasping for breath.

Knowing going too deep would cause Sergey to pass out, he pulled the drill away. It was too soon for that. He needed to know what had transpired, if anything, between Sergey and Alexei. He turned to one of the men standing by the wall. "Nicolai, help Sergey remember. His memory doesn't seem to be so good."

Nicolai, a tall, barrel-shaped man with a thick mustache and ruddy complexion, lumbered over to Sergey. He hovered over him for a moment, and then, with a wicked gleam in his eyes, he drew back his fist and punched Sergey in the face. Bones crunched as Sergey's head flung backward. Blood poured from his broken nose as he let out a whimpering sob. Nicolai stepped away. He winked at Leonid, a look of satisfaction on his face.

Leonid beckoned to the other man. "Rurik, come and help Sergey remember."

"No, no," Sergey mumbled through tears. They rolled down his cheeks and dripped off his chin, his broken nose swelling to twice its normal size. "Stop, stop, please," he pleaded.

Rurik, slim with shaggy blond hair and quick as a fox, grabbed the hammer and swung. It landed with perfect accuracy on Sergey's other knee. He howled in pain like a wounded animal as Rurik resumed his place by the wall.

"Now," Leonid said. "For the last time, what have you told Alexei?"

"What does it matter!" Sergey shouted, his saliva mixed with blood spraying the air. "You intend to kill me anyway. So go ahead and do it."

Leonid rubbed his chin and stared at him for a moment. "Yes, that is true, but all that matters is whether you want a quick death or you would rather suffer some more."

"Okay, okay, I will tell you. Alexei said he suspected you were skimming off of the profits. He asked me to bring him proof."

"And." Leonid raised the drill.

"I told him I had not found anything. You must believe me."

"I do believe you, Sergey. I am delighted you have decided to tell me everything. But there is a slight problem. The fact that you even entertained Alexei's suspicions is very troublesome. It tells me you can no longer be trusted." He motioned to Nicolai, who stationed himself behind Sergey, his palms clamped tight to Sergey's head, right behind his ears.

Alexei placed the tip of the drill bit at Sergey's temple.

"Wait! You said if I told you, my death would be quick."

Leonid looked at the urine running down Sergey's shaking legs. "So sorry to tell you, but I lied." With that, he turned on the drill and proceeded to drill into Sergey's skull. He let out a high-pitched scream before passing out. Leonid continued to drill, the odor of tissue, blood, and brain matter wafting in the air. A few minutes later, he checked for a pulse, nodded at Nicolai, and stepped away.

Leonid pulled a rag from the metal box and wiped down the drill. Peeling off the coveralls, he kicked them aside. He motioned to Nicolai and Rurik. "Has either of you spoken about Sergey to anyone else?"

"*Nyet*," they said in unison.

"Good, then we proceed with our plan. I'm tired of Alexei Volkov thinking he can run things any way he wants. Have you checked into the grocer's murder?"

For a split second, the two men looked at each other. Leonid caught their hesitation. "Well, what is it? Do you have any idea who murdered the poor man?"

"There are rumors," Nicolai said.

Leonid shrugged. "What do I care about rumors? I want facts."

"It seems," Rurik said, "there is some kind of shakedown operation going on with the merchants in the neighborhood."

"Shakedown?" Leonid questioned. "That's impossible. I would know about something like that. Those merchants are good to us. They show us a lot of respect. No one gave any orders to harass them."

Rurik pushed strands of blond hair away from his eyes. "They say this shakedown is sanctioned by the Wolf."

Leonid folded his arms and stared at the two men. How could this be? Was Alexei shaking down these grocers behind his back—collecting extra money he knew nothing about?

"There's more," Nicolai said. "Several of them have said Roman Volkov and his two friends, Emil and Luka, are the ones collecting."

"Why haven't you come to me with this sooner?" Leonid growled.

Rurik spread out his hands. "Look, if this is true, it is a serious charge by these merchants. We wanted to dig a little deeper, make sure what they were telling us was true."

"Then dig, and dig fast," Leonid ordered. "You know what this means, don't you? If Alexei sanctioned this, then one of those boys is responsible for a murder." He took one last look at Sergey's body and ordered, "Get rid of him. And that." He pointed to the discarded coverall.

He picked up the metal case, climbed the basement stairs, and stepped out into the sunlight.

Chapter 29 — Austin
The Body

Austin's surveillance of Leonid Rabinovitch had not produced anything of interest thus far. Today, his tail led him out of the city to the Catskill Mountains. Everything went along fine until Rabinovitch turned down a long gravel drive surrounded by woods.

Austin cursed under his breath. There was no way he could turn up that drive. Continuing along the main road, he pulled off to one side and cut the ignition. Going in on foot would not be ideal, but he had no other choice. He hesitated a moment. Monica would never approve of this tactic without backup. But Rabinovitch might leave by the time other agents arrived.

Austin got out and headed for the woods. Mud stuck to the bottom of his shoes as he traversed the soggy, moss-covered terrain. A bramble bush caught at the hem of his jeans, making him appreciate not having worn a suit.

Ducking behind tree trunks, he made his way until he saw the outline of a two-story house. Gravel crunched, and he swiveled his head toward the sound. Crouching low, he spotted a second vehicle pull up to the house. Two men got out and glanced around. Austin removed his cell phone and snapped several pictures of the men before they opened the trunk and pulled a man out, his hands tied and his mouth duct taped. He snapped several more before all three disappeared inside. Then he took several pictures of the outside of the house.

Austin's heart thumped, his intuition and experience telling him something awful was about to happen. The man they brought inside was in for a rough time.

He crept along until he reached the side of the house. Blinds covered all the windows facing him on the first and second floors. Cement covered what used to be basement windows.

He confronted the same scenario after he made his way toward the back of the house. Whatever was going on in this place could not be good. Someone made sure that no one got a view of the inside.

He moved away from the house and back into the woods. Hidden by low-lying bushes and trees, he waited. A half-hour later, Rabinovitch came out carrying a metal case. He tossed it inside the trunk of his car and drove off.

His deciding between following Rabinovitch as instructed or waiting to see if the other men came out lasted less than a minute. He watched the red taillights of the car disappear down the driveway.

An hour passed, leaving Austin to wonder if he made the right decision. He was about to give up when the front door of the house swung open. Instinctively, his hand dipped inside his jacket. He removed his Glock 19M from the shoulder holster.

Each man held one end of a bulky rolled-up carpet. Austin put his gun away and took out his cell phone again. He snapped several pictures as they tossed the carpet down onto the ground. His flesh crawled, knowing what must be inside.

One of the men went to a small shed on the side of the house. He retrieved two shovels and handed one to the other man. They walked into the woods behind the house. Another forty-five minutes elapsed before they returned empty-handed. As Austin snapped away, they hoisted the carpet up again and carried it into the woods.

It was nearly dusk by the time they returned without the carpet and carrying the shovels which one man returned to the shed.

Tired and shivering from the cold, Austin hurried back through the woods and down the main road. Once inside the car, he made a U-turn and headed back to the city.

His mind buzzed. Could the Russians have their own burial ground behind that house? After what he witnessed today, everything inside him screamed yes. He could only imagine how many bodies might be buried there. He hoped the two other men might be identified from the pictures he took.

After a restless night, Austin arrived at FBI Headquarters pumped to inform the task force about yesterday's events. He sent Monica a text asking for an emergency meeting. Over the next 15 minutes, the task force assembled in one of the conference rooms.

"So, what's so urgent?" Monica asked, looking directly at Austin.

He repeated yesterday's events, ending with, "I've already sent the photos to Quantico's Facial Recognition Laboratory to see if we get a hit on any of these men."

"Austin, you know you broke protocol by not asking for backup first," Monica said, a hint of annoyance in her voice. "You were assigned to follow Leonid Rabinovitch, not go snooping around one of his properties alone."

Heat flashed through Austin's body. He rubbed his temples to ease the sudden throbbing in his head. Sure, he could tell Monica was miffed, but she should have appreciated what he had accomplished. His fingertips tapped against the tabletop. "I know what my assignment was, but I got this feeling something was going down, and I needed to stay right where I was."

Monica eyed him. "Look, I get hunches about things, too. I know it's hard not to follow through on them sometimes. The main thing I need you to hear is that you put yourself and the whole operation at risk by not calling in first. What if they had spotted you?"

Austin threw up his hands. "Okay, I get it."

"Monica's right," Wanda piped in. "You could have ended up buried behind that house, and we would never have known what happened to you."

"It's really great work," Monica said. "But next time, you let one of us know before you leap into something you might not be able to get out of."

"How much time elapsed between Rabinovitch leaving and the two men coming out?" Kai asked.

"Approximately an hour," Austin said. "What are you getting at?"

"Well, it goes to who actually committed the murder of the man you saw them take inside the house. It could have been Rabinovitch or one of the other men."

"Kai brings up a good point," Monica said. "Rabinovitch might have given the order but not done the actual killing."

Austin leaned forward, his hands clasped together. "True, but regardless, we do know someone was murdered in that house and buried in the woods."

"Well," Monica said. "It's too early for us to go digging up bodies. The Russians would know we were on to them, and our whole operation blows up before we nail Alexei Volkov. So, for now we wait and see what the lab at Quantico produces. Because if Volkov is making a deal with Uzelli, we need to know exactly what it is and who else is involved. There will be plenty of time to go digging up bodies after."

With the meeting ending, they dispersed, with Monica holding Austin back. Feeling like a scolded child, he waited for her to speak.

"Am I going to have a problem with you?" she asked, folding her arms and giving him a surly look.

"I know I went off the grid with what I did, but I'm not sorry."

"That's what worries me, Austin. As much as we hate following protocol, it was implemented for our safety. You're a great agent, but I need to know right now that you won't go against FBI policy in the future."

He couldn't promise her. When it came to his intuition, he relied on it whenever he worked on a case. "You have my word," he said, crossing his fingers under the table.

Chapter 30 — Alexei
Roman & The Girl

Alexei sat across from Roman in the back room of Tatiana. Only late afternoon, it was hours before opening time. He studied his son's face, the shaggy blond hair, and how he slouched in the chair.

"Can you not sit up straight like a man?" he barked.

"Yes, Father." Roman righted himself, his cheeks flushing a bright red.

"Now, let us talk about this girl. The one you have been fooling around with."

"But I told you, she's nothing to me. We kissed a couple of times, that's all."

"So, you are sticking to your story?" Adrenaline soared through Alexei's body. He could not tolerate lying, especially from his own flesh and blood. He inched his chair closer to Roman and leaned forward. "I am going to ask you one last time. What have you done with this girl besides kissing? I advise you not to lie to me again."

Roman's body visibly shook. His fingers grasped the arms of the chair, his knuckles turning pasty white from the pressure. "I … I mean, we did have sex a few times. But it didn't mean anything to either of us. That girl is very loose. I'm sure I'm not the only one she's been with."

"Ah," Alexei said. "Finally, the truth comes out of your mouth. You silly boy, you know there are cameras in the alley. You never had the decency to take her someplace else to put your pawing little hands all over her."

Roman's chin dipped, and he stared at the floor. "I'm sorry. She's a very pretty girl, and I—"

"Never mind that," Alexei snapped. "You are to stop this little fling you are having immediately before something happens. Or has it already happened?" Pressure built inside his chest. He forced himself to remain seated when all he wanted to do was leap out of it and throttle his son. Roman looked up. His face was all innocence. A look Alexei had witnessed dozens of times whenever he was in trouble.

"I don't know what you mean?"

"The last video from the camera showed the two of you arguing. You left the club without going back inside to say goodbye to your friends."

"Oh," Roman said, a slight grin on his face. "That is what I was trying to tell you. I broke things off, and she was upset. I didn't want her to make a scene if I went back into the club, so I left."

"So, I can be assured that this thing is over with the girl?"

"Absolutely," Roman said.

"Good. Then I better not find out you were with her again—no *Amerikanskiy*. If you are going to date, then find a nice Russian girl. Your mother and I would be very pleased."

"But what about Damien? He brought a woman to the party, and I don't think she was Russian."

"It is nothing serious. He told me so himself," Alexei lied. "You just worry about yourself. Damien is much older and wiser than you. He will not disappoint us. So, you will do as I told you?"

"*Da*, I promise you I will not see her anymore."

Alexei got up and motioned to Roman to do the same. He wrapped his arms around Roman and patted him on the back. "Good. This is all I am asking of you for now." He stepped away and regarded his son. "You are still young but not too young to start thinking about your future and what it is you want. You must know Tatiana from top to bottom and how it operates. In the meantime, I will let this girl go so you can start working here in the evenings next week."

"You're letting her go?"

"No, on second thought, as your first duty here, you will tell her."

Roman's eyes grew large. He opened his mouth and then quickly closed it.

"Is that a problem?" Alexei asked.

"No, no, not at all. I will tell her on her next shift."

"Good. All I want is for your mother and me to be proud of you, Roman. Even though you have done some bad things in the past, you must move forward now and become a man with responsibilities like your brother, Damien."

Alexei opened the door, his gaze following his son as he crossed the club floor. At least things were done now between him and the girl. He could only thank God Roman had not gotten into any real trouble lately. His mind settled, and his body relaxed. Yes, working here would make him grow up. After a while, he wouldn't have to worry about Roman anymore. The next thing he needed to do was convince Damien to rid himself of this Carlotta Asante.

Chapter 31 — Cookie
The Dinner

Cookie checked herself in the office mirror. A beige blouse complemented her short red and green plaid skirt. Longing to wear her black suede boots, she thought better of it. Since the surgery, she still had some swelling in her ankle, so she opted for ballet flats instead. Her long hair was gathered into a ponytail.

She went to the front of the shop to prepare the flowers she would take to Damien's parents' house. This sudden invitation to dinner rattled her. Even though they slept together regularly, she still hadn't spent an entire night at his place. She told herself it was her small way of guarding her heart. So far, Damien had accepted her limitations and stopped asking her to stay.

She pulled a bunch of yellow daisies from the refrigerated case just as Damien walked into the shop. He stretched out his arms toward her and then stopped.

"What are those?" he said, pointing to the flowers.

"They're for your mother."

Damien shook his head. "I don't think so. Not those, anyway."

Cookie studied the daisies, trying to decipher what was wrong. "Your mother doesn't like daisies?"

"Not necessarily." He held out his hand. "Put them down and come here a moment."

She set the flowers aside and took hold of his hand. He led her to the small round wooden table where brides and customers sat to go through the catalog of arrangements, and they sat across from each other.

"Okay, first I need to tell you all about Russian tradition when you're coming to dinner for the first time.

Cookie's eyebrow arched. "Oh boy, I can't wait."

"You want to make a good impression, don't you?"

"Go on, enlighten me."

"First, the flowers must always come in odd numbers unless you are going to a funeral. Yellow flowers are not a good choice. Yellow signifies mistrust or disloyalty in our culture. Red would be a better alternative."

She glanced at the daisies and then back at Damien. "Are you kidding me? They're freaking beautiful."

"Let me finish. There are some other things you should know. You must take your shoes off at the door. There will be slippers for you to use. Never shake hands across the threshold. It's considered impolite, and it brings bad luck into the home. Wait until you're inside. You can greet my mother with a slight kiss on each cheek three times quickly."

"Hold on a minute, buddy," Cookie interrupted. "I don't remember any of this when I came to your apartment that first time."

Damien cracked a smile. "I wanted to ease you into our culture."

"Is there anything else I should know?" she asked.

"Do not begin eating until my mother invites you to start. No elbows are allowed on the table, but your hands must always be visible. Rest your wrists on the table. Like me, hold your knife in the right hand and your fork in the left. Dishes are passed to the left. Leave a small amount of food on your plate and compliment the meal. When you are finished eating, place your fork and knife across the plate horizontally facing left."

Cookie's head swam. "I didn't realize I was going to visit the King and Queen."

Damien chuckled. "Almost. There's a little bit more."

She jumped up from the table. "We don't act like this in my culture. Everything is very relaxed and informal. Italians love to eat, and most manners fly out the window. We just want to have a good time and enjoy our food."

Damien sighed. "I know, but things are different with us. Please sit down. I have a few more things I want to tell you."

Cookie plopped into the chair and crossed her legs and arms. "Go on." He continued to stare at her without saying a word. "Well?"

He pointed to her legs. "It's impolite to show the soles of your feet."

Heat flushed through her body as she slowly uncrossed her legs. If Damien thought he was going to make some kind of Russian puppet out of her, he picked the wrong woman.

"I'm suggesting you make some kind of toast at dinner to honor my mother. My mother will serve tea after the meal. I bought a cake to go with it. And no one leaves the table before my mother suggests it.

Without a word, she got up, returned the daisies to the refrigerated case, and plucked nine red roses and some greenery from another. She placed them in a simple white vase and handed them to Damien.

"This will do," he said, grinning.

"It better."

An hour later, they arrived at Damien's parents' home in Brooklyn. Cookie kept going over all the customs in her mind. As predicted, after she presented Darya with the roses, she removed her shoes and was handed a pair of slippers by Darya. They greeted each other with the obligatory three kisses on the cheeks, after which she led her and Damien into the dining room.

Roman stepped forward and hugged his brother. A gleam shone in his eyes, and Cookie sensed that he loved Damien very much.

Damien ruffled his brother's hair. "See, I told you I would come for dinner."

The blue and white patterned Lomonosov China, imported from St. Petersburg, Russia, lined the dining room table. Five place settings of the delicate porcelain were arranged upon a white linen tablecloth. Crystal wine glasses with gold rims from Belarus gleamed alongside the embossed silverware. Cookie could only be impressed. Did they always dine like this?

They seated themselves, with Alexei at the head of the table. Darya sat to his left, and Cookie as the guest of honor to his right. Damien sat beside her, and Roman sat beside his mother. Before the food was served, everyone lifted their glasses, and Alexei made a toast.

"Vashe zrodovye. To our health," he said, smiling at Cookie.

Everyone sipped their wine, and before they could put down their glasses, Cookie said, "I would like to make a toast, too. Thank you for inviting me to your home and to Mrs. Volkov for preparing this wonderful meal."

"You are so welcome," Darya said. "Now, let us begin to eat."

The meal started with a simple salad of tomatoes, cucumbers, and radishes tossed in a sour cream dressing. Cookie surprised herself when she found it to be absolutely delicious.

This was followed by *piroshki,* baked puff pastries stuffed with potatoes and cheese. For the main dish, Darya presented beef stroganoff served over noodles.

The dinner conversation between her, Damien, and his parents remained casual. She felt surprisingly relaxed until she caught Roman staring at her. His eyes were on her every time she looked up from her plate.

"So, have you been dating my brother long?" he asked.

Wary of how much she should say, she waited for Damien to respond. When he didn't, she said, "A little while."

"You like him, then," he replied, a smirk on his face. "Have you been to his apartment?"

"Stop asking so many questions, Roman. It's not polite," Darya said. "Finish your dinner."

'It's okay," Cookie said. "Yes, I've been there. The complex is very nice."

Alexei cleared his throat and put his utensils down. "I understand you own some kind of flower establishment."

"Half own, actually," Cookie said. "I'm partners with my best friend from High School."

"That is so nice," Darya said. "You are lucky to be around beautiful flowers all day long."

"It's a nice place," Damien said. "Cookie does very well with it."

"Where is this store?" Roman asked.

"Staten Island, where I was born and raised."

"I can tell by your last name you're Italian, then," Alexei said as more of a statement than a question.

Cookie's newfound ease dissipated a bit. She caught the slight disapproval in the man's voice. First, Roman with all his questions, and now Damien's father was starting in. She would only let this go so far.

"Yes, my mother and father are both Italian. My father runs a small restaurant."

"And your mother?" Darya asked. "Does she help him run it?"

Cookie searched for an answer. It was as if the words got stuck in her throat. Not too many people ever asked about her mother—the woman who abandoned her and her father all those years ago.

Damien reached for her hand. "You don't have to talk about it," he said softly.

Collecting herself, she breathed in an audible breath. "No, it's okay." Looking straight at Darya, she blurted out, "My mother left when I was four. I haven't seen her since."

"Oh, I am so sorry," Darya said. "I should not have asked."

Cookie forced a smile. "Don't be. You had no way of knowing."

"Why did she leave?" Roman asked.

"Enough," Damien cautioned. "We are not going to talk about it anymore."

Cookie's fingers clenched the cloth napkin in her lap. She rose from the table. "Excuse me, I need to use the restroom."

Darya pointed to the doorway. "Of course. Make a left, and it is the first door on the right."

Though she could have run all the way, Cookie kept her steps slow and even. All she wanted was to get away from this place, from these people. She slipped inside the bathroom and closed the door. Taking measured breaths in and out, she tried to calm herself. Muffled voices came from the dining room.

She cracked the door open, her ear trained on the conversation. She heard Alexei and Damien arguing.

"I want you to stop seeing this woman," Alexei said.

"And I told you the night of the party, I will see whomever I please. I brought her here tonight so you could get to know her, so you could see what I see in her. She's a wonderful person, and she makes me happy. Doesn't that count for something?"

"Of course we want you to be happy," Darya cut in. "But wouldn't it be better with a Russian girl who knows our customs, our culture? I want my grandchildren to be Russian."

"No one is even talking about children. It's too early for that," Damien charged. "I can't believe this. I came here to have a nice dinner, and all of you are ruining it."

"I had to break things off with a girl I was seeing because she wasn't Russian," Roman piped in. "You need to do the same."

"You stay out of this," Damien said. "You've done enough damage with all your questions."

"I think it's best I leave now."

They all looked at Cookie standing in the doorway. Damien's face was red, his hands clenched and unclenched as he rose from the table. Without saying anything else, he took Cookie by the hand and led her to the front door. As they retrieved their shoes and coats, Darya came running.

"Please stay," she begged. "We are very sorry."

Alexei came up behind her. "Let them go, Darya. It is for the best. Damien and this woman need to know where we stand."

At his words, Cookie turned and looked him straight in the eye. "This woman has a name. It's Carlotta, Asante. You had best remember it."

She reached for Damien's hand, and they walked out the door together. They remained quiet until they crossed the Verrazano Narrows Bridge to Staten Island.

"I'm sorry," Damien said. "I feel so ashamed."

"What exactly are you sorry for?" Cookie asked.

"The way my family treated you tonight was awful. If I even thought anything like this would happen, I—"

"You would what? I heard everything. You lied to me when I asked what you and your father talked about at the party."

"I know, and I'm sorry," he said, reaching for her hand.

Cookie pulled hers away. "Remember what I told you from the very beginning. No lies. I've been down that road before."

"How can you blame me for trying to change their minds? I thought they could accept our relationship if they got to know you even a little bit." Damien pulled up in front of her apartment. He opened the car door.

"Don't," Cookie said, getting out of the car. "I'm good enough! Do you understand me? I don't want to have to win anybody over. Not even your parents. Please don't call me anymore. I'm done with your lying to me, and I'm done with us."

Leaving him no chance to see her tears, she hurried inside.

Chapter 32 — Monica
Finding Out About Wanda

Bob's lips brushed Monica's cheek before she closed the door behind him. Leaning her back against it, she let out a long sigh. They had slept together four times this past week. Despite her hunger for Bob, she still longed for Eddie. Will this yearning ever stop? Foolishly, she thought that by sleeping with Bob, her feelings for Eddie would dissipate.

Even though he never said anything, Bob was much too smart not to catch on. But she made no promises from the very beginning. Their relationship could not advance to anything serious. Her heart wouldn't let it progress.

The following day at work, she thought about Wanda Simmons. Sitting in her office, she pulled up Wanda's file. Her mood lifted when she learned the case she worked on was out of the 121st precinct on Staten Island. The same precinct Detective Richard Walsh had been assigned to. Walsh, the dirty snake who became a snitch for the Italian mob, got what he deserved when he was shot to death along with Salvatore Marconi.

Later that afternoon, she left work early and traveled to the 121st precinct. Luck was on her side when she learned Captain Thomas Toomey, Richie's old boss, had remained in charge.

Delighted when he agreed to see her, she rode the elevator to the second floor. His office lay in the far corner. Light poured in through the large floor-to-ceiling windows. Grey-haired and broad-shouldered, a smiling Captain Toomey rose from behind his desk. They shook hands, and Monica sat across from him.

"So, what brings the FBI to our neck of the woods, Special Agent Cappelino?"

"Well, I hope you can help me with a past case. It concerns one of your former detectives, a Richard Walsh."

At the mention of Walsh's name, Toomey grimaced and leaned back into his leather chair. "Now, that's one person I'd like to forget ever graced this building. I always took him as somewhat of a pain in the ass, but I never thought he was working with the mob. To be honest, I was glad to be rid of him."

"No doubt," Monica said. She needed to tread carefully in order to get the information she wanted. "I understand he worked a series of homicides, a serial killer case some time back with one of our agents."

Toomey nodded. "Yes, as I recall, the FBI was called in to help us with crime scene forensics. The guy was finally caught. Put away for life without parole. Should have gotten the death penalty for carving up women like that."

Arms folded, he stared at Monica, his once friendly eyes narrowing. "But you people would know all of this. So, why are you here?"

Monica shifted uncomfortably in the chair. "I'm going to be perfectly honest, Captain. I'm in charge of a new Organized Crime task force here in New York, and a member of my team, Wanda Simmons, was the agent who worked crime scene forensics for you."

"Oh, yeah, boy, do I remember her. If you'll excuse me saying so, a very attractive woman. She ended up working closely with Detective Walsh. Too close if you ask me."

"What do you mean?" Monica's adrenaline rose.

"Well, there was talk that the two were seeing each other on the side. Both of them were married, and it didn't sit well with me or the department. I called Richie in and told him as much. I ordered him to quit seeing her, or I would pull him off the case."

"And did he stop?"

Without answering her, Toomey picked up the telephone receiver on his desk. He punched a button and barked, "Reynolds, come into my office, please."

A moment later, a short man with a bushy mustache dressed in plain clothes appeared. Toomey introduced him as Detective Brian Reynolds. He pointed to a chair beside Monica. "Sit down, Reynolds. Special Agent Cappelino wants some information on Walsh."

Detective Reynolds' eyes widened. He turned toward Monica. "He sure was a piece of work. What can I help you with?"

Monica gave him an easy smile. "I was curious as to how long he was seeing Special Agent Wanda Simmons at the time they worked on the same case."

Color swept the detective's cheeks. He looked at Toomey as if asking permission.

Toomey waved his hand. "Go on, tell her what you know."

"As I recall," Reynolds said. "Richie told me they used to meet at a hotel in New Jersey. A couple of other times at a nightclub in Brooklyn called Tatiana. He was foolish enough to believe no one would ever find out what the two of them were doing. But as I'm sure you're aware, Agent Cappelino, office romances always come to light sooner or later."

At his last words, Monica pictured Bob Acosta's face. She could only hope their liaison never would. Focusing back, the mention of the nightclub confirmed Wanda lied about never having been there. "Do you know if he broke things off after Captain Toomey spoke to him?"

"Knowing Richie, probably not. I did ask him about it, but …" His eyes went to Toomey again.

"Spit it out, Reynolds," Toomey said, glaring at him.

"He said he didn't give a rat's ass what the captain said."

"Is that all?" Toomey asked with a stoic expression on his face.

"Basically," Reynolds said.

Toomey waved at the door. "Okay, you can go." He turned his attention to Monica. "Anything else I can do for you?"

A bit disappointed, Monica got up. "No, Captain. I appreciate your taking the time to see me."

Once outside in the parking lot, Monica couldn't help but think there was more to Richie and Wanda's relationship. She was about to get into her car when Detective Reynolds came sprinting across the lot, waving his hand.

When he reached her, he glanced around a moment before saying, "Can we go somewhere else and talk? There's a coffee shop right down the street."

Ten minutes later, each held Styrofoam cups of steaming coffee. Brian pointed to a small table in the corner. "Let's sit."

After they were settled, Monica spotted the nervous twitch below his right eye and the slight shake in his hand when he sipped his coffee. "So, what do you have to tell me, Detective?"

He leaned in, the twitch growing more visible. "Look, I didn't want to say anything in front of Captain Toomey about what I'm going to tell you. Richie bragged to me about it, but then again, Richie was always bragging, so I don't even know if it's true."

"What did he tell you?" Monica asked.

"Well, it was around the time one of your agents got killed, and the FBI came into our office to speak with the captain. Of course, everything was so hush hush, and it was driving Richie nuts. I didn't realize why at the time. But later, it made sense when we all learned he was snitching for the mob."

"Excuse me, detective," Monica said. "But so far, you haven't told me anything of value."

He gulped some coffee and then set the container aside. "Okay, so here's the thing. It was a little while after the Feds—I mean—the FBI guys came. Richie comes into the precinct and pulls me to the side. He says he got information that there is an FBI agent working undercover to try and nail Salvatore Marconi."

A tingle ran down the length of Monica's spine. Had Wanda given her up?

"So, I say, that's a good thing, isn't it?" he continued. "But Richie puffs out his chest, ignoring what I said. Instead, he goes on to say he knows who the agent is. That Wanda gave him the agent's name and so he tells me." Reynolds clasped his hands together and shook his head. "That is why when I heard your name today in the captain's office, I knew I had to tell you."

Monica looked him straight in the eye. "And you never reported this?"

"You gotta understand," Reynolds said. "Half the time, you couldn't believe anything Richie said. Besides, no one knew he was on the take. I asked him what he was going to do with the information. But he laughed in my face. He said I shouldn't be ridiculous … that he was only telling me because he thought I might get a kick out of him getting intel like that from Wanda. I think he wanted me to believe their relationship was still tight and that they were still seeing each other."

Monica grabbed her coffee and stood up. "I appreciate you telling me all this, Detective, but make no mistake, this doesn't sit well with me. I'm sure you're aware of how dangerous undercover work is. If that information had gotten out back then, we might not be sitting here having this conversation."

Reynolds's face flushed. He glanced up sheepishly at her. "Am I in trouble?"

"No, Detective, you're not in any trouble. You didn't have to tell me any of this, but I hope you won't take information of that nature lightly in the future. Someone's life could be on the line." Monica turned and strode out of the coffee shop without looking back.

On the drive into Manhattan, she debated whether or not to approach Wanda. She could only imagine Bob's reaction if he found out since he had handpicked her for the task force. However, the one thing Monica knew for sure was that her intuition was right all along. Wanda couldn't be trusted. For now, she would bide her time and keep the information she found out to herself. When the time was right, she'd ensure Wanda Simmons paid the consequences for her actions.

Chapter 33 — Eddie
Tony Morello

Eddie sat across from Tony at the kitchen table, their hands wrapped around cold beer bottles. The shock of seeing Tony still with him, he raised his beer and took two sips. On the drive home from the resort, they spoke little. But Eddie had lots of questions, and he wanted answers.

"How did you find me?" Eddie asked.

"That's quite a long story," Tony said, giving him a sly wink.

"You need to understand how nervous that makes me. No one outside the U.S. Marshals Office should be able to do that."

"Okay, Staten Island—or is it Jack? Take it easy, and I'll explain. You're not in any danger."

Tony told him about meeting Kai Nez and what had transpired between them. Eddie could tell by the way he spoke that his feelings for this woman ran deep. But loaded on top of the events earlier this evening, it was almost too much to take in.

"And now," Tony continued, "Kai is on a task force with Monica in New York." Tony took several swallows of his beer and set the bottle down. "By the way, you never told me that she saved my life. I would have liked to have had that information when you came to the hospital."

At the mention of Monica's name, Eddie's body throbbed with a familiar ache. He pictured her face, and with that, memories threatened to break through once again. Pushing them away, he tried to focus on the present.

"You okay?" Tony asked.

"Fine." Eddie finished off the last of his beer, rose, and grabbed two more from the fridge. He set one in front of Tony and then twisted the cap off the other. He eased down into the chair again. "Why are you here, Tony?"

Tony's face hardened. "I think you know."

"Look, I've always appreciated your helping me rescue Ann. I blame myself for what Frank Uzelli did to you that day."

"And rightly so," Tony said. "I helped you because we're cut from the same cloth. Both naïve enough to think we could leave that life behind just by rescuing a girl."

Eddie's jaw clenched. What the hell was he trying to say? "But I did leave it behind." He spread his arms. "Look around, Tony. *This* is my life now."

"Are you kidding me?" Tony said, laughing. "This is all a façade, a make-believe world. Eddie, you don't belong here."

"Then tell me, Tony. Where do I belong?"

Tony took a couple of draws on his beer. His eyes locked on Eddie's. "Let me ask you something. I noticed the picture on the fridge. Is the kid yours?"

Eddie's vision clouded. His fingertips glided over the condensation on the beer bottle. He wanted to reach across the table and grabbed Tony by the throat. Who did he think he was showing up here, talking about Monica and Andrew? He didn't need any of this. Every day without them was torture enough.

"I can see by the expression on your face I hit a nerve," Tony said, leaning away. "Look, I feel for you. I really do. I can't imagine being gone from a kid of mine for so long. Maybe even forever."

Eddie inhaled and tried to calm his anger. He got up, took the empty beer bottles, and chucked them into the trash. "I don't want to talk anymore tonight. I have an extra bedroom. You're welcome to stay as long as you like, but keep any mention of Monica or my son out of your mouth."

Tony grinned. "See, there it is. That's the Eddie I know." He rose and stretched. "As a matter of fact, I am a little tired. We can resume our conversation in the morning."

Eddie lay in bed, his mind churning, thoughts coming fast, tumbling over each other in a constant whirlwind. Not knowing what to do about the hit directed at Paulie Martello was foremost on his mind. Paulie was the one who had given the okay, the chance for him to become a made man. He had taken a blood oath that night with a cut to his finger, and sometimes, he could still feel the slice of the knife.

Eddie sat up and switched on the light. He studied his hands, almost able to feel the heat from the burning picture of the saint warm his flesh once again. He could still hear Paulie say, 'If you violate our code or betray our brothers, you will die and burn in hell just like the saint burned in your hands.' Loyalty meant everything back then. Did it mean the same now?

As for Tony's showing up, he should be glad to see an old friend who understood his past life. But Tony's presence made him uneasy. If Tony asked for something, would he be able to agree to whatever it was? Could he refuse after what Tony had done for him? Question after question came at him as he tossed about the bed, unable to fall asleep. As the sun rose over the horizon, exhausted, Eddie finally drifted off.

Stumbling into the kitchen at half past ten, still in pajama bottoms and a t-shirt, Eddie prepared a pot of coffee. While he waited for it to brew, he checked his cell phone for any messages from the resort. Thankfully, there were none. He called in to touch base with Amelia and let her know he would not be in today, but she could reach him at home if needed.

He poured himself a cup of coffee and inhaled the rich scent before taking a sip.

"Good morning. I see you're up and about."

Eddie whirled around to find Tony, fully dressed in jeans and a polo shirt, standing in the doorway.

"I've been up for hours. Nice view from your terrace, I might add."

"You could've made some coffee," Eddie grumbled. "Or maybe you don't know how."

Tony strolled past him and poured a cup. He turned, his eyes studying Eddie. "You don't like the fact that I showed up here, do you? It hurts my heart, Staten Island. I thought you missed me." He gave Eddie a mischievous grin. "Come, let's sit out on the terrace and talk. You can tell me what you think, and I'll explain why I came."

The two sat on the green and white striped cushioned Adirondack chairs. A slight breeze carried cool morning air across the terrace. A cloudless pale blue sky hovered above. In the distance, Eddie heard the tapping sound of a Gila Woodpecker.

"So," Eddie said, breaking the silence between them. "Why did you come?"

Tony shook his head. "Before I answer, tell me how you feel about my being here."

"I don't want you to think I'm unhappy to see you," Eddie said. "Being that you didn't go into witness protection, I actually thought you might be dead. You've been a good friend to me, Tony, but I've come a long way from being a made man. I feel uncomfortable visiting the past."

"I understand, but let me ask you something. Are you happy with this new life tucked away here in Arizona?"

Eddie gave him a sideways glance. "Happy is not a word I would use to describe my current state of mind. It's more like accepting my circumstances."

"Fair enough." Tony moved to the edge of the chair. He stared out into the distance, the mug of coffee still in his hand. "Eddie, I'm here because I need your help."

"With what?"

"I need to get Frank Uzelli and make things right for what he did to me."

"I had a feeling you were going to say that, but Frank's probably dead. You need to move on."

Tony set the mug down, rose, and wandered over to the terrace railing. Turning, he leaned his back against it. He raised his shirt. Fingers tracing the scars on his body, he said, "Could you let this go?" Eddie stared but didn't respond as Tony slowly lowered his shirt. "He's alive. Frank is still breathing."

"How do you know that?" Eddie asked.

"Because the FBI says so. The five families stopped the contract on the condition he pays back the money he made on the secret operation in New York. Since I took all his cash before he got free, he's probably a very busy man trying to make good."

"You have Frank's money?"

"Don't you think I deserve it and more after what he did? But now I need you because when I face him, I might need back-up."

"Back-up?"

"Yeah, if things don't go right, no matter what happens to me, I want you to make sure he's off this earth for good."

Eddie rubbed his temples, trying to stave off a pounding headache of monumental proportions. Tony was asking a lot. It meant leaving his life here in Arizona and putting it in danger. It also meant returning to a life Monica wanted him to leave behind.

Tony came toward him. "I asked you this question once a long time ago. Where does your loyalty lie?"

"That's not fair, Tony," Eddie said. "My head was in a different space."

"Nothing's fair, Staten Island. Now, I'm standing here as your friend and blood brother. We both took an oath. Are you with me or not?"

"Before I give you my answer, I need to tell you something," Eddie said. "If I decide to help you, it may work in our favor." He told him what had transpired at the resort the evening before. He went and got his cell phone and played the recording for Tony.

Tony's eyes widened. He sat in the Adirondack chair again and stared at Eddie. "Holy shit! This is incredible. What a stroke of luck. If we get to Paulie before this thing goes down, we can be golden again."

"For sure," Eddie said. "Bringing this to him will get us out of the hole." Without warning, those old familiar feelings of importance and notoriety came back. He was someone on Staten Island back then. No one messed with him. Money showed up regularly. He never did without. Even though he was well compensated at the resort, the self-satisfaction of being a made man wasn't there.

But those days also reminded him of the occasional panic attacks and nightmares he had suffered. Could it happen all over again? Torn, he got up and paced. If he stayed here, he would never see Monica or meet Andrew. Could he live the rest of his life with the reality of that?

Eddie looked at Tony. After what he had done for him, he owed this man. He held out his hand. "I'll help you. We'll do this thing together." Tony stood up, and the two shook.

"*La lealtà,* Loyalty," Tony said, smiling.

"Yes, *La lealtà,* " Eddie said, gripping Tony's hand tighter.

Chapter 34 — Roman
What About Amy?

On a chilly late afternoon, Roman, Luka, and Emil sat in the dimly lit corner of the Red Baron Bar on Brighton Beach Avenue. A half-finished bottle of vodka stood in the middle of the table. The small corner establishment was empty except for two other men drinking shots at the bar. A bartender, his sleeves rolled up, freshened their drinks while a football game played on a wall-mounted flat-screen television above the bar.

The boys had arrived here an hour ago when Roman sent a text asking them to meet him and discuss his problem with Amy. After talking with his father, Roman was determined to fix this thing with her. No baby, no way. This girl wasn't going to ruin his life. He could only imagine what his father might do if he found out about the pregnancy.

"I have two problems," Roman said. "First, I have to tell Amy that she can't have my baby." He knocked back a shot of vodka. "And second, that she's fired."

"Good," Emil chimed in. "You don't need her hanging around Tatiana if you're going to work there."

"I don't think she's going to be agreeable." Roman sputtered. "Especially where the baby is concerned. She insisted she is not going to get rid of it."

"Then, we'll make her do it," Emil said.

Roman and Luka exchanged looks. "Emil," Luka said. "You need to be careful. I mean, this is a delicate situation."

"Don't worry. There are ways," Emil said.

Roman stared into Emil's eyes, the menacing evil behind them almost making him shudder. He could tell Emil would be delighted to do something awful to Amy. "Hey, I just want to make sure she doesn't get hurt.

"She'll be here soon. What are you going to say?" Luka asked.

"Never mind. You two go wait by the bar."

A few minutes later, Amy came in and headed straight for Roman. Dressed in light denim jeans and a heavy cream-colored turtleneck, she removed her jacket and laid her purse on the table. She sat across from Roman, her eyes red-rimmed and her face pale. "Why have you been avoiding me, Roman?"

"It's not deliberate."

She reached across the table for his hand. Roman quickly pulled it away. He could not show any form of weakness. Amy needed to understand the urgency of the situation. What did he ever see in her anyway? He should listen to his father and find a Russian girl. A Russian girl would have more respect for him.

"Listen, Amy, I told you I don't want to be a father right now. Please be reasonable and let me help you take care of this. I'll pay for everything."

Pools of tears formed in her eyes. They spilled over, forming little rivers down her cheeks. She kept brushing them away, but they continued to fall.

"Enough," Roman said, annoyed. "Do you think by crying I'll change my mind?"

"I don't care whether you do or not. I'm not getting an abortion."

"How are you going to raise this baby? Babies cost money, Amy."

"I'll keep working. I'll even get a second job if I have to. My mother will help care for the baby while I'm gone."

Roman's stomach knotted. "You told your mother?"

"No, not yet. It's too soon, but I will when the time is right."

Roman smacked his palm on the table. "You see how stupid you sound. Work two jobs? That is no way to raise a baby."

"I wouldn't have to if you helped me," she hissed. "I may even have to go to court to get money if you refuse."

Roman let out a laugh. "Don't be ridiculous. We're not married. How do I even know the baby is mine."

Amy's arm came up, her open hand headed for Roman's face, just missing when he ducked and leaned back into the chair. "Are you crazy? Stop acting like a bitch."

"Then be a man, Roman. Be a man and take responsibility for our situation."

Beneath the table, Roman's hands curled into fists. He could see there was no changing her mind. "Let's see how you plan on raising a child without a job."

"What do you mean?"

"You're fired from Tatiana," Roman spat. "Those are my father's orders. I work there now, and you're out."

Amy grabbed her jacket and purse. She stood up and stared down at him. "We'll see what he has to say when he finds out I'm carrying his grandchild." She hurried away and out the front door.

Emil and Luka left the bar and came over to Roman. "What did she say?" Emil asked.

"She refused to get rid of the baby and said she is going to tell my father."

"Let's go," Emil said. "We need to stop her."

Roman dug in his pocket and tossed money onto the table. The three left the Red Baron. Outside, they spotted Amy turning the corner at the end of the street.

"I'll get the car," Luka cried, hurrying in the opposite direction.

Roman and Emil sprinted after her, ignoring the looks of passersby. Roman caught up to her first. His hand wrapped around her arm, and he pulled her toward him.

Amy's eyes went wide. She struggled and tried to break free. "Let go, Roman!"

Tires screeched, and Luka pulled to the curb just ahead of them. Emil gripped her other arm, and they forced her inside the backseat of the car, where he got in beside her.

Emil motioned at the front seat. "Come on, get in the car, Roman."

Roman stared into Amy's terrified eyes. Emil slammed the car door closed. The locks clicked, and Roman froze. What was happening? Were they going to kidnap Amy? He pounded on the passenger side window.

"Luka, unlock the doors and let her out!"

"Don't do it!" Emil shouted as he struggled to control Amy, who was kicking and screaming. His arm came around her neck, and he covered her mouth with his hand.

Luka floored the gas pedal, and they sped off, leaving Roman at the curb. He pulled out his cell phone and dialed Luka's number. It rang until his voicemail came on.

"Luka, you need to turn around and let Amy out," Roman pleaded. "Listen to me, Luka. Emil doesn't realize what he's doing. Please, turn around."

Roman scanned the street for any sign of the car returning, but there was none. He dialed Emil's number. His voice came on the line. Roman could hear Amy whimpering in the background. "Emil, let her go. This isn't right. I'll handle things."

"No way," Emil hissed. "I refuse to let this girl ruin your life. She'll get rid of the baby, or I'll get rid of it for her," he said, his voice full of venom.

The line went dead. Roman stared at his cell phone. His stomach wrenched, filling his mouth with saliva. He swallowed hard, forcing it down his throat. Emil, always the reckless one among them, was leading them down a disastrous path—first Artyom's murder and now this thing with Amy.

Roman turned and went toward the boardwalk, the only place he could clear his mind and think. A bitter wind followed behind him. He dug his hands deep into the pockets of his navy wool coat. Glancing up at a gravel-grey winter sky, he admonished himself for having Emil and Luka accompany him to the bar.

He should have known Emil would try to pull something. Stopping, he leaned against the railing. Ocean waves, roiling with foam, thundered as they crashed onto the shore. The strong scent of salt lingered in the air. He took out a pack of cigarettes and lit one. Taking two deep drags, he exhaled and pulled out his cell phone again.

Dialing Emil's number, he waited, listening to the continuous ring. When his voicemail came on, he pleaded again for Emil to let Amy go. "We'll work this out," he said, wanting to believe his own words.

Roman ended the call and flicked his unfinished cigarette away. He had no idea where Emil and Luka were taking Amy. Cursing against the cruel wind blasting in his face, he headed home, wishing they had taken his BMW instead of Luka's car today. He would have controlled the situation by having command of his vehicle.

Continuing off the boardwalk and onto Brighten Beach Avenue, he played out several scenarios in his head. Surely, Emil wouldn't kill Amy, just scare her enough to agree to abort the baby. Almost home, his cell phone buzzed. When he saw it was Emil, his pulse spiked.

"Emil, listen to me—"

"I…I need you to get help," Emil cut in, a tremor in his voice.

Roman's hand gripped the cell phone harder. "What did you do, Emil?"

"Call your brother now!" Emil shouted. "We're at the old terminal. Hurry, Amy is bleeding."

Adrenaline soared through Roman's body. What had Emil done to Amy? He should never have told him about the baby. His hands shaking, he ended the call and dialed Damien's number.

"Please answer, please answer," he said, pacing the sidewalk. Relief washed over him when he heard Damien's voice.

"I can't talk right now, Roman. I'm in the middle of something."

Tears welled up in Roman's eyes. "Wait, Damien, please. I need you. We're in trouble."

"Who, who's in trouble?"

"I can't explain over the phone. Come to the old Brooklyn terminal. I'll meet you there. Someone is bleeding, and we need your help."

"What did you do, Roman?"

"Nothing, I swear. It wasn't me. Please come." The absence of sound on the other end made Roman fear his brother had hung up.

"Okay, okay. Calm down. I'm leaving now."

Roman stared at his cell phone. What if Amy died? He hurried to the parking garage and got into his BMW. He charged out of the garage and headed for the terminal. Damien would know exactly what to do. Yes, he told himself. Damien will make everything alright.

Chapter 35 — Cookie
Best Friends

Cookie and Monica sat in a corner booth at Noodle Village on Mott Street in Manhattan. Dressed in jeans and a heavy blue hooded sweatshirt, Cookie had come into the city to go to the flower market. The aroma of meat sizzling filled the room. Cutlery scraped against the wok pans in the open kitchen. The small restaurant was full of lunchtime diners, and a line snaked from the door to the counter for takeout orders.

Within fifteen minutes, they had plates of Shao Mei Pork and Shrimp Dumplings, Braised Beef Brisket over rice, and a pot of hot tea before them.

"So, tell me," Monica said, loosening the buttons on the jacket of her black pantsuit. "How are things with the Doc?" Taking her chopsticks, she plucked a dumpling from a platter and slipped it into her mouth.

Cookie filled her plate with rice and brisket. Trying to sound casual, she said, "I'm not seeing him anymore."

Monica's eyebrow arched. "I thought you were getting serious about him?"

"I was, up until I met his folks. They don't approve."

"Are you kidding me?" Monica set her chopsticks down. "He's a grown man, a doctor, and he broke things off because of that?"

"I didn't say he broke things off." Cookie's stomach dipped a bit. Taking in a deep breath, she bit into a piece of brisket.

"Oh," Monica said. "I just assumed…"

Cookie eyed her. "Yeah, I get it, Monica. What man would want to stick up for me?"

"Come on, that's not what I meant. I'm sorry if I hurt your feelings. Tell me what happened."

"I had dinner at his parent's house." Cookie scrunched up her face. "There were all these rules I had to remember."

"Rules?"

"His parents are old school. They're very particular." Cookie told her about the party and how she had been lied to afterward. "I'm not gonna do that all over again. I told him from the beginning, no lies. I had enough of that with Danny."

"So, where do things stand now?"

"He's been calling and texting. You know the whole, I'm sorry, blah blah blah."

"Maybe you should give him another chance?" Monica said, pouring some tea for them.

Cookie shook her head. Despite her best efforts, her eyes watered, and her vision blurred momentarily. She missed Damien—missed him so much it hurt.

Monica eyed her. "I can tell you're not over him. Everyone deserves a second chance."

"What about Eddie? Did you give him a second chance after everything? Or was that just so you could get him to turn on his uncle?"

"You can't compare my situation to yours. Mine was much more complicated."

"I'm not so sure about that," Cookie said. "You could have forgiven him, gone away together. As much as Eddie and I had our differences, I hate to say this, but here you are raising Andrew, and he doesn't even know his father."

"No, Cookie, you're wrong. I didn't go with Eddie because he needed to find himself and a different way of living. Because of his uncle, all he ever knew was being a mobster. I couldn't do that for him. He had to do it himself."

"How will you ever know if he did?" Cookie asked, taking a sip of tea. "I mean, you don't have any contact with him, do you?"

"No. But I'm hoping without the mob, he's been forced to change. Maybe, someday, Andrew will know him."

Cookie threw up her hands. "Okay, enough. Let's not talk about all this stuff anymore. We're both getting on edge, and the last thing I want to do is get into a fight with you."

"Agreed," Monica said.

Later that afternoon, Cookie strolled along the rows of flowers at the Lexington Avenue Flower Market. The heady scents calmed her mind, easing the tension from her lunch with Monica. She placed orders for White Candlelight, Pale Toffee Colored Ecuador, and David Austin Red Tess Roses. She moved on to Hypericum Berries, which she would mix with a selection of Camelia Branches and Baby's Breath. And last, she ordered several varieties of orchids.

On the drive back to Staten Island, she thought about Damien. His handsome face and amber eyes swam before her. His smile alone could make her go weak inside. Her body craved the gentle touch of his hands on her naked skin.

But things would never work between them. How his family felt about her could only spell trouble for the future. Damien thinking he could change their minds about her was proof enough. If she meant so much to him, then their opinion wouldn't matter.

Cookie parked behind Brides and Blooms and carried in her purchases. She spent the rest of the afternoon rearranging flowers and creating new bouquets, which she placed in the refrigerated case.

As she finished the last arrangement, the bell over the shop door chimed. She whirled around to see Damien standing there wearing blue scrubs beneath his leather jacket, a forlorn look on his face.

"I couldn't stand you ending things between us," he said. "You won't answer my calls or texts, so I decided to come here."

"You shouldn't have," Cookie replied. "I meant what I said. I will not be with a man who lies."

He swiped a hand through his blond hair and stared at her, his eyes pleading. "I know we agreed from the beginning we would be honest with each other. I realize now how important that is in a relationship. You made me see that."

She came toward him, her eyes filling with tears. "You brought me to your parent's home knowing how they felt about me. How could you put me in a position like that, Damien?"

"I wanted them to see what I see. Cookie, I've never had strong feelings for any other woman. But you came into my life, and everything changed for me. You're who I want to be with. I don't care what anyone else thinks, including my parents."

"That's what you say now. But what about later on when you start feeling bad about them? It's going to affect our relationship, Damien, and I don't want to put you in a position where you regret choosing me."

He shook his head. "No, you're wrong. I will never regret choosing you. I love you, Carlotta Asante."

Cookie stood stock still. "What did you just say?"

Damien's eyes catching hers, he said, "I love you."

He held out his arms, and she came into them. She wrapped hers around his neck, forcing him closer. She stood on tiptoes and beamed up at him. "I love you, too, Damien Volkov," she whispered.

Their lips met, and he hugged her tighter, making the kiss go deeper. His cell phone buzzed, and he ended the kiss.

"Sorry. I'm on call."

Cookie grinned. "It's okay. I know you have to answer it."

Damien gave her a quick wink as he took the call. "I can't talk right now, Roman. I'm in the middle of something." He narrowed his eyes. "Who, who's in trouble?" He looked at Cookie and shook his head. "What did you do, Roman?"

Cookie caught the instant concern in Damien's voice. Something was going on with Roman, and it didn't sound too good.

"Okay, okay. Calm down. I'm leaving now." Damien ended the call, a perplexed look on his face.

"What's wrong?" Cookie asked.

"I'm not sure. My brother is in some kind of trouble. As usual. I need to go, but I'll call you later."

"Sure, go on." She ushered him to the door.

He leaned and gave her a quick kiss on the cheek. Cookie watched him hurry across the street and jump into his car. What did he mean when he said Roman was in trouble *as usual*? He must have asked Damien for help before this latest incident. She sighed as he drove away and out of sight.

Cookie gathered her purse and prepared to leave for home. She performed a momentary twirl and smiled. "He loves me," she whispered. "Finally, someone loves me."

Chapter 36 — Alexei
Where's Sergey

Alone in the back room at Tatiana, Alexei paced. He had heard nothing from Sergey for the past several weeks. Telling Leonid to get rid of him if he wasn't happy with his performance was all a ruse. Otherwise, he would have aroused suspicion.

The information Sergey had relayed indicated Leonid was plotting against him, recruiting several of his gang members to assist him. Alexei was no fool. These things happened all the time within the *Bratva*. One needs to be aware of what might be transpiring without one's knowledge.

Expecting Leonid at any moment, he poured himself a shot of vodka and swallowed it in a single gulp. There was a knock at the door. Alexei steeled himself before opening it.

Leonid crossed the threshold. "Sorry to be delayed."

"Nothing to worry about," Alexei said. "How are things going on your end?"

Leonid went to the bar and grabbed a shot glass. "The money is coming in at a steady pace. Everyone is doing their part."

Alexei watched as he filled the glass. Dare he ask about Sergey? Curiosity getting the better of him, he said, "I am wondering if you are happy with your men."

With a pained expression on his face, Leonid downed the shot of vodka. "For the most part, yes."

He seated himself on a stool by the bar. He unbuttoned his suit jacket and let out a sigh. "You know very well how it goes. Some work harder than others."

"What about Sergey? Not so long ago, you were complaining about him." He caught the uncomfortable shift in Leonid's posture and knew in that instant Sergey was dead.

Leonid waved an impatient hand. "He is doing better."

So, they were going to play this cat and mouse game, Alexei mused. The truth would come out sooner or later.

"The shipment is due next month," Alexei said. "We will meet here one last time with Enzo and Frank. I want to be sure that everything is in place. Moving the guns quickly is key. My contacts in Mexico expect a smooth transaction, the same as before."

"Yes, but last time, we used our contacts. I do not savor dealing with the Italians."

"Nor do I, but due to unforeseen circumstances, those contacts no longer exist. What other choice do we have?"

Leonid pounded his fist on the bar. A flush swept his face. "You know as well as I that is the fault of the Italians. Here we are doing business with the very people who got rid of them."

Alexei held up his hand. "I know, I know. But we have no other choice. They want their cut just like everyone else. To try and circumvent them was our mistake. We do this deal, and if all goes well, we will all make money. That is the goal, is it not?"

Leonid squared his shoulders. "I don't like it, but as you say, what other choice do we have but to use them."

"Is there anything else going on that I should know about?" He saw Leonid hesitate before downing another shot.

"Rurik and Nicolai told me something. But understand that none of this has been confirmed. They are still looking into it."

Alexei nodded his head. "Go on."

"Well, it concerns my godson."

A sudden sharp, throbbing spread across Alexei's forehead. What had the boy done now? How many more times would he have to clean up Roman's mess? He snapped his fingers at Leonid. "Come on, come on, tell me."

Leonid related what Rurik and Nicolai had told him. "Now remember, none of this has been confirmed. I must confess, it made me wonder if you were running some kind of operation with the grocers behind my back."

Alexei collapsed into one of the overstuffed chairs. The news could not have been worse. He leaned over, his head in his hands. Roman might have committed murder, plus the store owners believed he sanctioned the shakedown.

Looking up at Leonid, he said, "First, I would never do such a thing behind your back. It hurts me to think you even considered it, but I can see how it might look."

Alexei got up and reached for the vodka bottle. Pouring two fingers, he swallowed it down. "When will you know for sure?"

"Soon," Leonid said. "This hurts me, too, Alexei. For Roman to be involved in something like this is unconscionable. I know he has caused trouble before but …."

A sick feeling welled up inside Alexei. His stomach ached as if he had suffered a punch to his gut. His thoughts turned to Emil and Luka. If this news proved to be accurate, they, too, would pay.

Leonid rose and clapped Alexei on the back. "I will let you know as soon as I confirm his involvement, and I will set up the meeting with Enzo." He stepped out the door, closing it softly behind him.

Alexei tried to get his mind straight about what Leonid had told him. How could Roman even conceive of doing such a thing? He denied the boy nothing.

His mind drifted to the dinner with Damien and his girlfriend. They were unkind towards him by dismissing his feelings. Here was a son who had grown up to be independent and a successful surgeon. The contrast between him and Roman couldn't be more striking.

He left the back room, his eyes sweeping over the empty nightclub. Crowds would not arrive for several more hours at opening time.

He went into Ivan Petrov's small office on the other side of the club. Sitting behind his desk with a myriad of spreadsheets and a large computer screen, he looked up as Alexei came in.

"What can I do for you, boss?"

"Have you seen Roman today? His shift started an hour ago."

"No, I have not," Ivan said. "He has been coming in on time up until today."

"No call to say he would be late?" Alexei asked.

Ivan shook his head, "*Nyet*." He gathered the spreadsheets and clipped them together.

"I asked him to fire the girl, the waitress. Has he done it?"

"Hard to tell," Ivan said. "She worked her regular shift two days ago, and then she called in yesterday. I cannot say for sure until I speak with Roman."

Heat flushed through Alexei's body. Can this boy do anything right? He left Ivan's office and dialed Roman's cell phone. After seven rings, it went to voicemail.

"Call me as soon as you get this message," Alexei barked.

Having enough on his mind with Leonid, the impending shipment, and now Roman's newest caper, he exited the club. Leonid waited in the parking lot, smoking a cigarette.

"Let's go," Alexei said. "My head is about to burst. Be glad you never married or had children of your own."

"Did something happen?" Leonid asked. "I can tell you are upset. Can I be of help in any way?"

"Get me answers, Leonid," Alexei said. "If Roman is involved in this shakedown, I need to fix things. Someone is going to pay, but it won't only be Roman."

Chapter 37 — Eddie
Paulie 'The Shiv' Martello

Eddie glanced in the rearview mirror and watched as the Camelback Mountain Resort grew smaller and smaller. This morning, he packed a suitcase, cleaned out his bank account, and drove to the hotel with Tony to give his notice.

Despite giving up everything in Arizona, Eddie's excitement grew at the prospect of seeing his son for the first time. There was no way he could predict how it would happen, only that it would. He had a right to see Andrew. No one, not even Monica, was going to stop him.

Tony sat beside him in the passenger seat, dark sunglasses shielding his eyes, his long legs stretched out before him. They both agreed their main goal was to get to New York as soon as possible to warn Paulie about the hit.

"You good?" Tony asked.

"Sure. No worries," Eddie said. "I'm doing what I have to do. Leaving my place here in Arizona and resigning from my position wasn't easy, but I can live with it." He tried to sound casual but could almost hear Monica saying, 'Begin a new life … one you can be proud of.'

"Just think about the future now," Tony said. "You'll be straight again."

Eddie gave him a sideways glance. "And you?"

"Well, it all depends on how Paulie sees things regarding me. Remember, I was part of Frank's Jersey Crew. It's true I was just following orders, but that might not be enough."

"There is something you can offer," Eddie said.

"What's that?"

"Frank's money. I don't know how much you have, but it may be enough to get you right in the Commission's eyes."

Tony yawned. "We do think alike, Staten Island. The thought has already crossed my mind. When the time is right, I'll make an offer."

His eyes steady on the road ahead, Eddie asked, "If you don't mind my asking, just how much money do you have?"

"I'll give you a ballpark," Tony said. "This way, if anything comes up later on, you won't know the exact amount."

"Fair enough," Eddie said.

Tony removed his sunglasses and looked at Eddie. "Upwards of ten mil."

Eddie whistled. He never imagined Tony had taken that amount of money from Frank Uzelli. Which meant Frank was sure to be more than a bit pissed.

"I've been meaning to ask you," Tony said. "What about your uncle? Didn't he leave you anything?"

"It wouldn't matter if he had. The government confiscated the house and froze the bank accounts along with other assets he had. Besides, after what he did to my parents, I don't want any part of anything that belonged to him."

Tony arched an eyebrow. "Your parents?"

Eddie steeled himself. Anytime he thought about his parents dying at the hands of his Uncle Sal, Uncle Lorenzo, and Aunt Rita, a sickening tightness wrapped around his core. They had lied to him his whole life. Even telling him his nightmares after witnessing the murders at five years old were just bad dreams.

His hands gripped the steering wheel as he imagined them around his Uncle Sal's neck. But with Sal dead, there would never be any real closure for him. He inhaled, let out a slow breath, and told Tony what happened all those years ago.

"Geez, Eddie," Tony said. "I'm sorry you had to go through all that."

"Yeah, but I can't change the past. It's something I live with every day. It makes me wonder how different my life might have been without my uncle."

They drove for the next 19 hours, splitting time behind the wheel. They stopped halfway in Haseltine, Missouri, and checked into a hotel for the night. They planned to arrive in New York at around 3 A.M. the day after tomorrow.

They continued on early the following day, only taking time to grab something to eat. They exited the Holland Tunnel and reached Manhattan at sunrise.

Tony insisted on checking into the pricey Beekman Hotel. "It's Frank's money, after all," he quipped. "Let's enjoy ourselves after that long ride."

Set in the Financial District, each posh hotel room featured high ceilings, vintage furnishings, aged oak floors, luxury bedding with Sferra linens, a minibar, designer toiletries, rainfall showers, and plush robes. Beautifully appointed artwork adorned the walls.

They slept for the next eight hours. When Eddie woke famished, he dialed Tony's room. He answered on the fourth ring, his voice groggy.

"Hey, what is it, Staten Island?"

"Get up and get dressed. Even though it's past noon, I'm ordering breakfast."

A half-hour later, the two sat in Eddie's room, coffee, eggs, toast, and bacon on a table between them.

Eddie sipped his coffee and relished the warmth spreading through his body. Checking in last night, he had almost forgotten how cold the New York winters were. After devouring their meal, Eddie got up and pulled back the curtains. He took in the view from the 42nd floor.

One World Trade Center, City Hall Park, and the Woolworth Building were all within sight.

He thought again about Andrew and Monica and was struck by the momentary realization that they were here in New York. Tony had mentioned that Kai and Monica were working together. His gut told him they were near. He could feel their presence somehow.

Eddie turned away from the window to see Tony eating the last of the scrambled eggs.

"So, what's the plan?" Tony asked. "How do we get a hold of Paulie and warn him?"

"Paulie owns a restaurant in Little Italy. From what I remember, he goes there every Saturday night for dinner. I went once with my Uncle Sal. He has a private room in the back."

"Today's Saturday," Tony said, his eyes lighting up.

Eddie went and sat across from him. "But it won't be easy to get in to see him. You know as well as I do that you can't just walk into the place and ask for the Boss. Plus, my biggest worry is one of his Capos, Domenico Conti. He's in on the hit, and he knows me."

Tony leaned back and sipped his coffee. "Then we make sure before you do anything that this Domenico is not around."

"The only way to do that is to stake out the restaurant. That can be tricky because if any of the bodyguards taps us, things could go bad."

Tony got up. "Come on, Staten Island, let's take a ride to this restaurant and see if we can find a good vantage point. I'll get my coat and meet you in the lobby."

Just as Tony reached the door, Eddie called out to him. "And by the way, stop calling me Staten Island. It's Eddie from now on."

"Sure thing, Staten Island." Tony let out a chuckle and headed out the door.

With a frigid wind soaring between the skyscrapers, they drove to Little Italy. Bounded on the west by Tribeca and Soho, on the south by Chinatown, on the east by the Bowery and Lower East Side, and then north by Nolita, the neighborhood was known for its Italian restaurants, groceries, and the famous Ferrara's Bakery. Brick-front establishments lined the busy street. Dozens of people hustled in and out of the stores and restaurants.

Paulie's restaurant, La Vita Vino, stood in the middle of the block on Mulberry Street. Eddie slowly cruised along while Tony checked out possible surveillance places.

"There," he said, pointing to a coffee shop diagonally across from La Vita Vino. He pulled out his cell phone. "There open until 9:00. We can hold up there and wait to see who's with Paulie."

"I guess we can try," Eddie said. "But we need to be careful." He drove farther up the block and then over to Grand Street.

"What gives?" Tony asked. "Where are you going?"

Eddie couldn't help but smile. Back in his beloved New York City, he came alive again. His body thrummed with excitement as he parked in front of Ferrara's Bakery. He glanced at Tony. "Come on. You gotta taste these cannoli. They're world famous."

The two strode into the bakery. Eddie's eyes lit up at the sight of the long counter filled with rows of Rainbow Cookies, Sfogliatella, a flaky pastry filled with ricotta and candied fruit. There were soft Pignoli Cookies and his favorite Cannoli pastry shell filled with sweetened ricotta cream, studded with chocolate chips and candied citron.

Back in Arizona, he would dream about biting into the pastry, the richness of it bathing his tongue. He ordered six Cannoli, three dipped in Belgian Chocolate and three plain. Tony ordered some Rainbow Cookies, two slices of Italian Cheesecake, and Pignoli Cookies.

Later, back at the hotel, they feasted on their purchases with fresh, steaming hot cups of coffee.

Eddie patted his stomach and pushed away from the table. "Now that's some good stuff."

"Agreed," Tony said, taking a last bite of a Pignoli Cookie. He checked his watch. "What time does Paulie usually get to the restaurant?"

"Eight on the dot," Eddie said. "He's the most routine and punctual of all the Bosses."

"That means we need to leave here in a couple of hours. I'm going to shower and change. Meet you downstairs in the bar at 6:00 o'clock."

Promptly at 6:00, Eddie walked into the Bar Room at the Beekman. Light poured in from the pyramidal atrium skylight above and glanced off the Victorian wrought iron railings by the mirrored bar. Tony sat on one of the piped antique brass and emerald green stools, sipping a drink. Soft jazz music emanated from the speakers.

Eddie hoisted himself onto a stool beside him and ordered a scotch neat. They dined on Prime Grilled Hanger Steak with romesco, sweet peppers, and Bordelaise Sauce. After consuming another drink, they left the bar and arrived at the coffee shop on Mulberry Street at 7:30.

Lucky to grab a table by the window, they ordered two coffees and waited. They had a perfect view of the entrance to La Vita Vino. Eddie drummed his fingers on the table and glanced around. The few patrons in the shop were either busy on laptops or staring at cell phones. He turned back to the window and focused on the restaurant.

He had to believe that when he told Paulie what was happening, he would return to his good graces again. As for Tony, money talks, and it would be hard for Paulie to turn it down.

Paulie 'The Shiv' Martello, arrived at the predicted time with an entourage. There were two bodyguards who Eddie didn't recognize, along with two familiar Caporegime. His palms grew sweaty as his pulse raced so fast he heard the blood rush in his ears. One of the Capo's was Domenico Conti.

"What's wrong?" Tony asked. "Your face is pale."

Eddie pointed at the men who were still standing at the entrance, deep in conversation. "See that one there, in the black leather coat. That's Domenico, the guy I told you about. He's on the recording with the others." He watched as they all went inside the restaurant except for the other Capo who said something to Paulie and then got into a vehicle and left. One of the bodyguards came back out and stationed himself outside the door.

Tony swallowed the last of his coffee and got up.

"What are you doing?" Eddie asked. "We can't just barge into the restaurant."

Tony's body was rigid, his brow furrowed. He pulled his shoulders back. "It's now or never, Eddie. *You* need to do this thing. Show Paulie the proof. I'll wait in the car."

"Yeah, but …"

"But nothing. Go set things straight."

Eddie eased up and followed him out the door. Tony walked in the opposite direction while Eddie crossed the street. Paulie's bodyguard stubbed out his cigarette when he saw Eddie approach. His hand reached inside the lapel of his long winter coat. A burst of cold wind cut across the front entrance. A pile of trash sailed along the curb. Pieces of it swirled up into the air, landing a few feet from the man.

"What can I do for you, fella?" he asked. "You plan on going inside? If so, I gotta frisk you first."

"No," Eddie said. "I need to see Paulie. It's urgent."

The man, barrel-chested and over six feet tall, surveyed Eddie with an unsettled look. "Not tonight. Paulie doesn't like unexpected company."

"When he finds out who I am, he'll want to see me," Eddie said, stepping forward. "Please tell him Eddie Marconi is here, and it's urgent that I meet with him."

The man hesitated, a stunned expression on his face. "Marconi? I know that name. Everyone in the families knows your name."

"Yeah," Eddie said. "I'm sure they do. Now, tell Paulie I need to see him. But do me a favor. Don't let anyone else with him know I'm here. His life depends on it."

The man raised an eyebrow. "Is that so?" He motioned for Eddie to raise his arms and patted him down. "Wait here," he said. He opened the door to the restaurant and called out to the other bodyguard. "Keep an eye on this guy. I gotta talk to Paulie a minute."

The second bodyguard stepped out. He nodded but didn't speak. A few minutes passed before the first man returned. "Go around back. Someone will let you in."

Eddie shook his head. His gut was telling him not to do as the man said. "No, I need him to come out here."

"Boy, you're difficult," the man huffed. "Let me see what I can do."

He went back inside again while Eddie paced. The door swung open, and Paulie Martello came out. His face was pinched, his nostrils flared as he pointed his finger at Eddie. "You got some nerve coming here after what you did."

"And I wouldn't have," Eddie said, his confidence returning. Trying to protect Paulie was the right thing to do, and whether or not he agreed, he had to try. "I have a recording that you need to hear. There is a hit out on you."

Paulie's eyes bulged, and he stepped back. He jerked his head at his bodyguards and chuckled. "A hit? Are you fucking with me?"

"No," Eddie said. He held out his hands, nodded to the bodyguards, and pulled out his cell phone.

Just then, the door to the restaurant opened again. Domenico Conti stepped out. He looked at Paulie and then directly at Eddie. "You've got to be kidding me. What the hell is going on?"

Chapter 38 — Monica
Undercover Lovers

Frustrated with how much intel the Task Force had uncovered, Monica called Kai, Austin, and Wanda into the conference room. After they were all seated, she said, "The results on the photos Austin took came back from Quantico." She opened a folder, spread the pictures out on the table, and pointed to the first one. "This gentleman here is Rurik Bortnik. She pointed to the next photo. "And this one is Nicolai Galkin. They both work for Leonid Rabinovich, which means they are connected to Alexei Volkov.

"The house Austin saw them go into is listed under a corporation called Vested Enterprises. Now, the man they took inside the house and later out in a rolled-up carpet was harder to identify, but they believe he was Sergey Vassiliev, who also worked for Leonid Rabinovich.

"The question is why did they kill him? Was he skimming money? Did Alexei Volkov order the hit? Or did Leonid Rabinovich decide to get rid of him? We may never know, but one thing is for sure, the man was murdered in that house. Thanks to Austin, these photos have become evidence."

"Yeah," Austin said. "But I didn't like feeling helpless. I knew the minute they hauled him out of the trunk of that car he was as good as dead. I keep thinking I should have done something."

Monica shook her head. "Unfortunately, Sergey Vassiliev was collateral damage. If you tried to stop the killing, our whole operation would have blown wide open."

Austin fell silent for a moment. "I know you're right, but it's hard not to think otherwise."

"Look, we're not any closer to finding out who Alexei Volkov is dealing with besides Franki Uzelli," Monica said. "I've been thinking about changing tactics. I know you've done some surveillance, Austin, but I feel we need to do more."

"Like what?" Kai asked.

"I want to do an undercover operation at Volkov's club. I've been working with our Tactical Operations Unit. Bob helped to get a court order, and the TacOps team was able to place a bug at Tatiana in Alexei Volkov's private office. They're the best at using all sorts of diversion tactics. They cut one of the gas lines going to Volkov's nightclub, which made for a quick evacuation of staff until the problem was fixed.

"But I want eyes on the players to ensure we're headed in the right direction. I feel we've wasted enough time trying to figure out what Volkov and the rest of them are up to."

Austin's eyes lit up. "I'm in."

Monica eyed him. "I haven't decided who is going as of yet."

"I would love the opportunity," Kai said. "I did some undercover work when I was with the Anti-Gang Task Force."

Monica couldn't help but notice Wanda's stony expression. She turned to her and said, "What about you, Wanda? I'm considering sending two people in as just another couple enjoying the evening. Either you and Austin or Austin and Kai."

Wanda fiddled with one of her gold earrings. "I think it's risky."

"Not if it's played right," Monica said. "We make it look simple, a lover's tryst. A married couple is not going to spend as much time at Tatiana." She saw Wanda swallow hard and grow visibly uncomfortably in her seat. Memories of her and Richie at Tatiana must be surfacing.

"I like that idea," Austin said. He lifted up his left hand. "I'll put a wedding ring on. Makes it look more real."

"About that," Monica said. "If we decide to do this. No heroics of any kind. You call for backup."

Austin winked. "Of course."

"I still don't like this," Wanda said. "It's taking too much of a chance. Is Director Acosta in agreement with this?"

Monica gave her a sideways glance. "I'll take it up with him."

"So, how do you want to proceed?" Kai asked.

"I think it should be you and Austin. We don't know how long this will take before something jumps off. A couple having an affair would be regulars at the club versus a married couple. I think Austin's idea of wearing a wedding ring is good. Either way, you're together. It has to look authentic. I need to know if you're both up for that."

Kai caught Austin's eye. "I think we can be convincing."

"It's settled then. I want you two to become regulars at the club. Our main objective is to figure out the other players in Volkov's game. Tatiana seems to be one of his meeting places. Let's hope we get lucky."

"When do we start?" Austin asked.

"I'll fill Bob Acosta in and let you know, probably within the next few days. I'm going to have a surveillance van stationed a few blocks away as a precaution. If anything goes sideways, they'll be close by."

Later that afternoon, Monica sat across from Bob in his office. She had just finished telling him about the undercover operation.

"I can't say I agree," Bob said. "If anyone there gets an inkling that Kai and Austin are law enforcement, things could get rough."

"We need to do this, Bob. We're not getting anywhere. Things are moving too slowly."

Bob raised an eyebrow. "Too slow for whom? Listen, you've worked on enough cases to know that this type of investigation takes time. We need to use caution."

Monica folded her arms and leaned back into the chair. Was she in charge of this operation or not? She didn't like being talked down to. Of course, sometimes things move slow for various reasons, but not gaining ground is cause for action.

"Frank Uzelli was already fingered at Volkov's nightclub. That could only mean one thing. Something is in the works, and we must find out what it is. So far, all we know is that the Russians have a burial ground up in the Catskill Mountains, and somehow, they're also involved with Uzelli. We've got nothing yet on the bugs TacOps planted."

Bob sighed. He clasped his hands together and studied her. "Okay, I'll go along with it, but every precaution must be taken to ensure Austin and Kai's safety."

Monica's muscles relaxed. She lowered her arms and smiled at Bob. "Thanks for backing me up on this."

"Dinner later?" he asked.

"Sorry. My folks are in town. Living in Florida, they don't get to see their grandson that often." Monica took note of the disappointment on his face. "Don't worry, they're only staying a few days. Hold your thoughts until after they leave."

That night, Monica sat at the dinner table with Andrew and her parents. For the first time, she surveyed the lines around her mother's tanned face and how they had grown deeper. Her silver hair was still cut in a neat bob that swept her cheeks. Her father had most definitely put on a few pounds. She watched them both delight in their grandson.

"I'm so glad Andrew can be close by while you work," her mother said. "But maybe he can skip a few daycare days while we're here."

"Lillian," her father said, his eyes crinkling. "We don't want to ruin his routine."

Monica laughed. "I think at three years old, it's okay to disrupt his routine a bit while you're visiting."

Monica cleared the dinner plates and then lifted Andrew up and nuzzled his neck. "It's bath time for you."

Andrew clapped his hands. "Bath time," he repeated.

Her father got up. "You run the water, and I'll stay with him so you and your mother can have some alone time."

Fifteen minutes later, Andrew's squeals of delight, followed by her father's hearty laugh, could be heard throughout the house. Monica prepared two cups of coffee and handed one to her mother as they settled on the living room sofa.

"I'm so happy for you, Monica," Lillian said. "You're handling things so well as a single mother. I only wish we lived closer so we could be of more help."

"Don't worry," Monica said. "When he's a little older, I'll send him to Florida so you can spoil him rotten for a couple of weeks."

Lillian laughed. "I can't wait for that." She sipped her coffee, and then her face grew serious. "Have you heard anything about Eddie? I know you two aren't supposed to have contact, but I thought maybe…"

"What? That we've spoken? It's not possible since Eddie is in witness protection."

Lillian leaned forward and lowered her voice as if there was an audience in the living room. "Well, you told me about the picture you left."

"Yes, but that was a long time ago. I just wanted Eddie to know he had a son. I thought it would make him change his life for the better."

"I can't imagine how he must feel," Lillian said. "Not being able to watch Andrew grow up."

At her mother's words, a coldness swept Monica's core. To this day, she still questioned if she had done the right thing, leaving the photo of Andrew in Eddie's mailbox. All she ever wanted was for him to live a normal life away from the mob.

"Eddie made his choice, and it cost him," Monica said.

"And you?" Lillian said, her face softening. "Have you gotten over him, Monica?"

"I'm seeing someone. Nothing serious, but I've taken that step."

A grin spread across Lillian's face. "Good for you. That makes me happy. I don't want you sitting around moping over Eddie."

"I know you never liked him," Monica said.

"I had nothing personal against Eddie. He just wasn't what I wanted for you. Everything I told you that happened all those years ago with his Uncle Sal always plagued my mind. I was afraid that if you stayed with him, something might happen to you, too."

As a mother, Monica understood more than ever why she wanted to protect her from Eddie. But how could she sit here and pretend she didn't love him anymore? Andrew was a constant reminder of what they once shared.

"Mom, I—"

"Look at this little man now," her father said, coming into the room carrying Andrew dressed in pajamas. "He's squeaky clean."

"What is it you were going to say, Monica?" Lillian asked.

Monica stared at Andrew and then back at her mother. "Nothing. I just wanted you to know how happy I am that both of you are here."

Midnight blanketed the quiet of the house while Monica tossed and turned. With her parents and Andrew asleep, she got up, grabbed her robe, and stole out of the house. The air was frigid and crisp as she sat on the front steps and gazed at a full moon.

Eddie was under that same moon in Arizona. Did he still think about her? What were his dreams like? She let out a long breath as if trying to cleanse herself of thoughts of him.

To think she would never see him again, or that Andrew would never know his father, made her ache inside. Eddie was gone, but he left behind a longing, a fire deep inside whose embers she couldn't extinguish. Not now, not ever.

Chapter 39 — Damien
Saving Amy

Pulling up outside the old, deserted terminal, Damien spotted two cars. He recognized one as Roman's BMW. Popping the trunk, he took out a black leather bag he always kept for emergencies and hurried around the side of the building, searching for an entrance. He yanked open a grey, heavy metal door. Its rusted hinges squeaked and echoed across the empty terminal.

Shafts of light streamed in from the broken windows. The place was cold and dank, the cement floor laden with puddles of water from a hole in the roof. It smelled of rotted garbage and rat droppings. Huddled together at the far end were Emil and Luka. Roman crouched over a figure lying on the floor. He got up when he saw Damien coming towards him.

"Damien!" Roman's face was streaked with tears. "Please help her."

"What happened?" Damien set his bag down. He kneeled and began examining Amy. Her bottom lip was swollen and bruised. She moaned when he gently pressed her abdomen. He noted the blood stain between her legs. Her eyes fluttered open, and she gasped.

"It's okay," Damien said. "I'm here to help you. What's your name?"

"Amy," she croaked. "My name is Amy Walker."

"Nobody meant for her to get hurt," Roman sputtered. "They just wanted to scare her."

Damien shook his head. He opened his bag and pulled out a blood pressure cuff and a stethoscope. "Just stay still, Amy," he said, trying to soothe the young girl. After taking her vital signs, he rose and glared at the three boys. "What the hell went on here?"

The three glanced at each other, but no one spoke. "Is she going to be alright?" Roman asked, swiping his hands through his hair.

"I think so," Damien said. "But she needs a more thorough examination. She has to go to a hospital."

"Isn't there any other way?" Roman asked. "I mean, they'll ask questions. It was just a silly accident."

Damien gritted his teeth. Blood rushed to his head. He grabbed Roman by his shirt collar, twisting it and yanking him forward. His face inches from his brother, he said, "I want to know what went on here."

Emil stepped forward. "It's not Roman's fault. He wasn't even here when it happened. Me and Luka argued with the girl. I pushed her a bit, and she fell."

Damien let go of Roman and turned towards Emil. "Oh really! Is that how she got the split lip?"

"Well, I—"

"Shut up, Emil," Damien snapped. "I can tell every word coming out of your mouth is a lie." Damien moved away from them and pulled out his cell phone.

Roman came over to him. "Who are you calling? She's pregnant, you know, and it's mine. The baby is mine. But she refused to get rid of it, and we argued."

"Enough, Roman," Damien said, dialing his cell phone. "You're lucky someone owes me a favor." A woman's voice came on the line, and Damien moved away from Roman.

"Leticia? It's me, Damien Volkov. I have a young girl here who needs your help. Can I bring her to your office?" He nodded his head. "Sure, I'm coming right away. I'll see you there."

Ignoring the boys, he approached Amy and helped her stand. Tears collected in her eyes as she asked, "Did I lose the baby?"

"I can't say for sure, Amy. But a doctor friend of mine is going to help you. She is meeting us at her office in Manhattan. I'm going to drive you there."

Amy's eyes grew large. "Will you stay with me?"

"Of course." Damien collected his bag and steered Amy to the door and outside. He helped her into the backseat of his car. He deposited his bag into the trunk and removed a blanket. "You lay down and rest," he said to Amy. "It's only a twenty-minute ride." After he closed the door, Roman, Emil, and Luka came over to the car.

Damien pointed at Roman. "You go to my apartment and wait for me there. Do you understand me?"

Roman nodded his head. "I have the key you gave me."

Damien climbed behind the wheel and lowered the window. "Roman, you better be there when I get done." With that, he drove away from the terminal, the three boys fading in his rearview mirror.

Three hours later, Damien arrived home to find Roman asleep on his sofa. He tossed his keys aside and shoved at Roman's shoulder. "Wake up, Roman."

Roman rolled toward him and rubbed his eyes. He pushed himself up into a sitting position. "How is she?"

Damien eyed him. "You can't even say her name, can you?" He dropped down beside his brother and shook his head. "Now, you tell me all of it. If not, I'll call Dad, and you can tell him what happened."

Roman clutched his hands to his chest. "No, please don't call him. I'll tell you what I know. I wasn't at the terminal when Amy got hurt." Little by little, in a choking voice, he told Damien about the events leading up to the afternoon.

Damien leaned forward, his head in his hands. Once again, Roman had messed up. He had no clue as to what he was going to do about it yet. Of course, the right thing would be to call his father and tell him everything. But Damien knew from past experience that Alexei would stop at nothing to protect Roman.

He pictured Amy, her tears, and the swollen bottom lip. Absolutely terrified of Emil and Luka, she had told Damien she was leaving, going away somewhere to have her baby. She begged him not to tell Roman because she wanted nothing more to do with him. He could only imagine what his mother would say if she knew. 'I want my grandchildren to be Russian,' Darya had said that night at dinner. Would she have accepted this child of Romans?

Damien's head throbbed, a thunderstorm pounding inside. What should he tell Roman? He didn't deserve to know the truth, so he kept his promise to Amy.

"She lost the baby," Damien said, looking up at him. "So, that's one thing you need not worry about."

"Is she going to the police about Emil and Luka?" Roman asked.

"No. I talked her out of it. But none of you are to contact Amy ever again. Is that clear?"

Roman's shoulders relaxed, and he let out a deep sigh. "Thank you, Damien. I don't know what I would have done without your help."

Damien studied him for a moment. "Why do you hang out with those bums? One of these days, something is going to happen, and nobody will be able to help you."

"Well, I'm working at Tatiana now, so I won't be spending as much time with them anymore."

Damien wanted to throttle him. He could always tell when his little brother was lying. What's the use in trying to get him to change anyway? Roman was Roman. He stared into his brother's eyes. A sudden chill swept through Damien's body, and he got up. He didn't want to think about the day he might get a different call about Roman. Something that even he or his father couldn't fix.

Chapter 40 — Eddie
Proof

Domenico and Eddie's eyes met. A momentary silence fell over all the men. Domenico stepped forward and strode towards Eddie, his mouth set in a grim line. He squared his shoulders and pointed his finger.

"You bum. You got some nerve showing up here after hiding out like a rat."

A surge of adrenaline swept through Eddie. He stood stock still, clenching his fists. "This is none of your business, Domenico. I came to see Paulie."

Paulie looked at Eddie and then Domenico, a somber expression on his face. "You two, calm down," he snapped. "I don't want nothing going down out here in the street in front of my establishment." He nodded to one of his bodyguards. "Go get the car. We're all gonna take a little ride."

Eddie flinched. The last thing he wanted to do was get into an automobile with Domenico. He might try to weasel his way out of things, and Paulie might take his side. He gripped the cell phone in the pocket of his jacket. Here was proof. Paulie would either believe him or kill him.

While waiting for the car, Eddie turned away, his eyes sweeping the block. Surely, Tony had a full view of them from wherever he decided to wait. If anything were to happen, he believed Tony would come to his aid.

A silver Cadillac Escalade Sedan pulled up to the curb. Paulie ordered Domenico and Eddie into the rear. "You two behave. I don't want no funny business. Not a word between here and the club."

As the car sped away, Eddie hoped Tony was not too far behind. The direction they were traveling in led him to believe they were headed for the private social club in Manhattan that Paulie owned. He had visited the place in the past with his Uncle Sal.

The tension in the backseat was palpable. Eddie avoided looking at Domenico. Trying to calm his jangling nerves, he leaned against the door and stared out the window. He had left everything he had built these past years, and now, more than ever, he wanted to return to his former life. Tony was right. They were the same. The mob had embedded itself inside his DNA, becoming an integral part of who he was as a man.

The car turned a corner and drove up an alley behind a red brick building. Paulie ordered them out of the vehicle. He ushered them into a rear entrance and down a small set of stairs with the bodyguards following behind.

The dimly lit bottom level was vacant except for a sectional sofa in the middle of the room, a long coffee table, fully stocked bar, and an area rug. Voices could be heard coming from above them. Upstairs was where the usual high-stakes card games were played by made men. The odor of cigarettes and cigars, mixed with whiskey, stung Eddie's nose.

Paulie pointed to the sofa. "Both of you sit."

Domenico gave Paulie a sideways glance. "I can't believe you're taking this so lightly after what Marconi here did."

Paulie's face flushed a deep red. "What did you think I was going to do? Gun him down in the middle of the street? If he came out of protection, there must be a good reason. After I hear it, I'll decide how I want to handle things." He turned to Eddie. "So, start talking. This better be good, or you know what happens next."

Eddie glanced over at the two bodyguards leaning against the bar, their eyes fixed on him. "First, I need to get my cell phone out," he said. Easing his hand into his pocket, he removed it, swiped his finger to the recording, and laid it on the coffee table.

"What the hell is that for?" Domenico asked. "Just start talking, rat."

Eddies heart pumped faster. Adrenaline surged through his body, and he narrowed his eyes at Domenico. "I'm going to let this do the talking for me." He leaned over, put the cell phone on speaker, and hit play.

The voices of Domenico and the other men came through loud and clear. Eddie watched as Paulie's facial expression went from impatience to incredulous. His eyes bulged, and he focused on Domenico. "So, you, Bruno, and Willie were going to have me clipped?" His voice cut through the room like a blade of steel.

"No!" Domenico shouted. "That recording is doctored. I swear, I would never try to do something like that."

"Oh, really?" Paulie towered over him. "So, what I'm hearing with my own ears is all bullshit?"

Domenico rubbed his palms down the front of his jeans. Beads of sweat broke out across his brow. "Listen, Paulie. I was there as a spy. I needed to find out what Bruno and Willie were planning."

Paulie tilted his head. "But didn't you just claim the recording was doctored?"

Domenico shot Eddie a look. "You better tell him. Tell him I was only there to spy."

For the first time that night, some of the tension eased from Eddie's body. "So, who's the rat now? Remember Little Frankie?" he asked.

"What's that got to do with anything?" Domenico snapped. "That happened a long time ago."

"Right," Eddie said. "But I always remembered what you told me that night we dumped his body in the ocean."

"So, I say a lot of things."

"Yeah, but this kinda stuck with me. As I recall, you said, "Someday, it might be our turn. All it takes is one mistake, or someone higher up gets pissed at something you did or said." Eddie nodded toward Paulie. "I think he's pretty pissed right now."

At Eddie's words, he sprang up. He vaulted over the back of the sectional and ran for the stairs. Eddie and the two bodyguards raced after him. Domenico reached the top of the stairs and flung open the door. Eddie reached out to grab the back of his leather jacket and missed. The next thing he knew, Domenico let out a yell and then lay sprawled face down on the ground outside. Eddie stepped through the doorway after him. Tony Morello stood there, grinning, his foot planted firmly on the small of Domenico's back.

"I think he tripped," Tony said, giving Eddie a wink.

Tony moved away as the bodyguards grabbed Domenico and dragged him towards the SUV, yelling and still proclaiming his innocence.

Paulie, slightly out of breath, caught up to them. He blinked and then stared at Tony. "I thought *you* were dead."

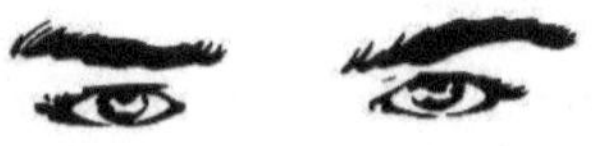

Chapter 41 — Alexei
The Tell

Alexei pulled into the lot and cut the engine. He had driven over an hour in traffic to Flushing Meadows Corona Park in Queens. One of the city's most iconic parks and the site of two twentieth-century World Fairs was nearly deserted. Weather forecasters had predicted a winter snowstorm. Biting wind staggered across the parking lot, rocking his Mercedes momentarily. Its high-pitched whistle a foreboding of the coming onslaught. Thick, heavy, low-hanging clouds stationed themselves above. Within minutes, they burst, releasing a shower of snowflakes.

Alexei reached into the glove box and removed his 9mm. He released the safety, his body tense as he fingered the trigger. A black sedan with tinted windows and tires screeching swerved into the lot, stopping inches from Alexei's car.

The door opened, and Rurik Bortnik climbed out and strode toward him. Keeping his finger on the trigger, Alexei lowered the weapon out of sight beside him. He released the door locks, and Rurik dropped into the passenger seat.

Sweeping his long fingers through his shaggy blond hair, he said. "Sorry for the delay. I had to make sure Leonid did not tail me."

"I understand," Alexei said. "We must use caution. This has been a terrible few weeks. First, a gas leak at Tatiana and a million other annoying little things have cemented my mood. Now, tell me about Sergey."

Rurik released a long, ragged breath. "It was not good. Leonid used a drill."

"And you?" Alexei asked. "What was your participation in the torture?"

Rurik spread out his hands. "What was I to do? If I didn't go along with things, Nicolai and Leonid would have turned on me next."

"I'm waiting," Alexei said.

"A…a hammer," Rurik said. "But it was Leonid who made Sergey suffer before he finished him. Nicolai and I buried him behind the house."

"There are many unmarked graves there," Alexei said. His insides twisted. Poor Sergey. All because he had asked him to spy on Leonid. The last report only confirmed what he suspected all along. Leonid was skimming some of the profits.

"What is he planning?" Alexei asked.

Rurik rubbed his hands together and glanced out the passenger window. "He wants to take over. Leonid doesn't like taking orders from anyone, especially you."

"Go on," Alexei said.

"Well, he has Nicolai in his pocket, and the men under him will do whatever Nicolai tells them to do." Rurik shrugged. "They follow him like sheep, not realizing he cares nothing about them. All Nicolai wants to do is please Leonid. He thinks this will get him a higher position in the *Bratva*."

"And you? What do you think, Rurik?"

"Of course, you must know by now how I feel about Leonid. The man is like a dog who wants to lead the pack." He fell silent and stared at Alexei.

"So, I have your loyalty then?"

"Of course, Alexei. You have always been good to me. From the time I first came to this country, you have made sure that my family and I have everything we need."

Alexei patted his shoulder. "I care for those who watch out for me. I ensure they are rewarded just as you will be when we finish Leonid for good."

Rurik nodded. "I will always be loyal to the Wolf. Always."

"There is one other thing I need to know," Alexei said. "Is my Roman and his friends involved in the shooting of Artyom the grocer?"

Rurik's expression changed. Alexei took note of his frightened eyes. "It's alright. You can tell me whatever it is that you have found out."

Rurik told him about the sting operation Roman and his friends were pulling. He shook his head. "The worst thing besides the killing of that poor man is all the merchants' on those blocks think this was sanctioned by you."

Alexei stared at the snowflakes swirling outside. Blood rushed to his head. Of all the things Roman had done, this was by far the worst. He eyed Rurik a moment and then asked the question he needed to know. "Who pulled the trigger?"

"The word is Emil Kutuzov was the one who shot the grocer."

"Are you sure?"

"Yes. It was not Roman who pulled the trigger. Yes, he was there and took part in all of it but not the shooting."

Alexei fell silent, trying to come to grips with what Rurik told him. Artyom's wife was already being taken care of. Now, the responsibility fell on him to make things right with the rest of the merchants. "How long has this shakedown been going on?"

"From what I was able to find out, approximately two years."

Hearing this, Alexei felt like a fool. Roman was doing this right under his nose, and he had no idea. He recalled Roman's party and all they had done for him. His head throbbed while the pit of his stomach burned. Such an ungrateful boy, his Roman was.

"Is there anything I can do?" Rurik asked.

"No. I must handle this myself. But if I need to, I will reach out."

Rurik opened the passenger side door. Cold air burst in, bringing a rush of snowflakes with it. "Just like back home," he said before slipping out and getting into his car. He drove away, his red taillights disappearing from view behind a heavy veil of snow.

Alexei waited a few moments, then engaged the safety on the 9mm and placed it into the glovebox before driving toward home. His mind had a battery of thoughts about Roman. How had he and Darya raised such a deceitful boy?

The wipers slapped at the falling snow. If not for the highway lights, visibility would have been nearly impossible. He concentrated on the slippery road ahead. Pressing the touchscreen on the dash, he tapped Damien's number. All he wanted at this moment was to make things right with his other son.

"Hello." Damien's voice was strained. An evident weariness Alexei had never heard before. Could he still be upset about the argument at dinner that night? The two had not spoken since.

"How are you, my son?" Alexei said.

"Okay, and you?"

"Well, I was thinking about that night at dinner. I believe your mother and I treated you unfairly."

"Just me?" Damien asked. "What about Cookie?"

"It's … only that we weren't expecting—"

"Stop," Damien said. "You met her at Roman's party and I made it clear that night how I felt. I believed bringing her to dinner might clear things up."

Alexei blew out a long breath. "Yes, you are right. We never gave her a chance."

"Listen, I'm glad you called, but unless things are going to change with my choice of a girlfriend, I prefer to end this conversation."

"Damien, that is the main reason I wanted to speak to you. Will you give us, your mother and me, another chance? Maybe we could meet for dinner with the two of you. Pick a restaurant, day, and time, and I will make sure we are there."

"I would need to speak to Cookie first."

"Of course. Take whatever time you need and let me know." Alexei hesitated before saying, "You sound strange. Is it work? Are you doing too much?"

"No. But I need to go. I'll talk to you soon."

The call ended, and Alexei stared at the touchscreen. Something told him there was more than just the dinner bothering Damien.

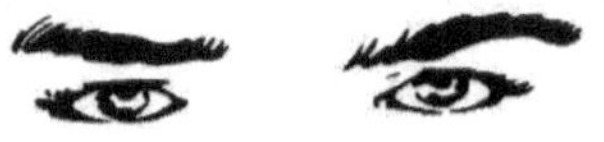

Chapter 42 — Monica
Eddie's Out

Stunned by the news Bob Acosta had just delivered, Monica sat frozen in a chair across from his desk. A slight tremor traveled through her body. It couldn't be true. Eddie leaving witness protection was the last thing she wanted to hear. Her stomach twisted into knots.

"Are you okay?" Bob asked. "I know this is somewhat of a shock. The U.S. Marshals Office informed me early this morning. He left witness protection over a week ago."

Monica stared at him. "Over a week ago? And we're just being informed about it now?"

"You know how things work, Monica. When someone goes into the program, a lot of secrecy is involved. They're given a new identity. Eddie's been in protection for a good while, and from what I learned, he appeared to be doing well. He never asked to leave, so the Marshal's office was unaware until they did their usual discreet checking. The resort in Arizona no longer employs him, and he broke the lease on his apartment."

"I just can't understand why he would leave if, as you say, he was doing so well," Monica said. "I know him better than anyone, and there has to be something or someone who made him leave."

Bob leaned forward, his elbows planted firmly on the desk. "Are you trying to say he was forced to leave?"

Without answering, Monica got up and walked to the tall floor to ceiling windows overlooking Lower Manhattan. Yesterday's snowstorm left its mark on the streets below. Working through the night, plows had pushed heavy snow piles to either side of the roads.

New York was more than prepared for the inclement weather. Salting before the storm's arrival always helped to make the clearing easier. As she observed the busy street below, everything familiar appeared different somehow to her now. Eddie was out there, and there was no doubt in her mind that he would do anything to see his son. She twisted one of her long dark curls around her finger and sucked in her bottom lip.

"Look, I can't say for sure he was forced, but him not informing the U.S. Marshal's office worries me," she finally said.

"Monica," Bob said. "I need to know in light of this news that you're still up for leading the task force."

She whirled around and stared at him. "Of course I am," she declared. "You should know by now that outside circumstances have never affected my work at the Bureau."

Bob held up his hands. "Okay. But you do understand I had to ask."

Monica kept her eyes focused on him. "Go on, ask your next question. The one we both know you're thinking."

A slight blush crept across his cheeks. He gave her a sheepish look. "Of course, I'm worried how Eddie's leaving the program will affect our relationship."

"It won't. You'll just have to trust me." She hurried to the door. "I need to get back to work. I have two agents about to go undercover tonight."

Back in her office down the hall, she quickly dialed her mother's cell number. Her parents had decided to stay an extra week so they could spend more time with Andrew. As soon as Lillian answered, Monica said, "Mom, listen, I have something to ask you. How would you like to take Andrew to Florida for a few weeks? I know you're anxious to escape all this snowy weather."

"Really? Can we?" Lillian said. "I thought you felt he wasn't old enough yet."

Despite her mother being right, she said. "Maybe I'm just being overprotective."

"Monica, is there something we should know?"

"Of course not. If you feel you can't take Andrew with you this time—"

"I didn't say that," Lillian cut in. "When you get home later, you can pack his things. We're leaving early in the morning for the drive back."

After ending the call, Monica inhaled several deep breaths. Andrew would be safe in Florida. But safe from what? His own father? She cringed inside, ashamed of sending their son away. Eddie had a right to see Andrew. But what if he was mixed up in something sinister or mob-related again? Her mind shooting off in several different directions, she refused to think about it anymore right now.

She picked up the phone on her desk and asked Austin and Kai to come into her office. When they were seated across from her, she said, "Tonight will be your first time going to Volkov's club. Your fake identification is all set.

"I need the both of you to be careful. I'm not expecting anything off-kilter. Just be vigilant. Volkov may not even be there this evening."

Austin lifted his left hand. A shiny gold wedding band encircled his ring finger. "Bought it yesterday. Feels a bit odd." He grinned and winked at Kai who shifted uncomfortably in her chair. "Look," Austin continued. "I need to tell you that I did a bit of surveillance on Volkov."

Monica drummed her fingers on the desk. "I thought I told you to stop."

"It was only for a few days. Something interesting happened yesterday. Volkov met with Rurik Bortnik last evening."

"So," Monica said. "What's so unusual about that? He works under Leonid Rabinovich, who is Volkov's Brigadier."

Austin looked at Kai. "Go on, tell her," Kai said. "I think you're on to something."

"Spill it, Austin," Monica said.

He leaned forward, his eyes earnest. "This didn't look like an ordinary meeting. They came in separate cars and met in Flushing

Meadows Corona Park at night. And if you remember, Bortnik was one of the men I saw at that house up in the Catskills. I'm thinking he was letting Volkov know what happened up there, which might mean he didn't sanction that murder."

"Maybe," Monica said. "Or he could have been confirming that the job got done."

Austin shook his head. "I disagree with that. This meeting was too secretive. A simple phone call would have taken care of it. I believe they were meeting behind Rabinovich's back."

"If you're right," Monica said. "Then that means a power struggle is going on within the *Bratva*." She pushed back her chair and got up. "It pains me to say, nice work, but I think you've brought in some good intel. Is there any chance you can reach out to your C.I. again?"

"I can try," Austin said, cracking a smile.

"Okay then. You two remember to stay alert."

Later that night, Monica packed a small suitcase for Andrew. The thought of him going to Florida made her ache, but she didn't dare show her true feelings. This must be the best decision for now. Until she knew what made Eddie leave Arizona, she'd keep Andrew far away.

Chapter 43 — Tony
A Way In

Tony grinned at Paulie Martello. "No," he said. "It's me in the flesh, alive and well." The swift zipping sound from a silencer charged the air as a flash of light from a gun muzzle lit the interior of the SUV. All three stared at the vehicle before it sped out of the parking lot.

"One down, two to go," Paulie said. He motioned for Eddie and Tony to come back inside. The three descended the steps and went over to the bar.

"Pour me a shot of whiskey," Paulie said to Eddie.

Eddie got behind the bar, poured a shot of Johnny Walker Blue Label, and handed it to Paulie. He downed the shot in one gulp. "Now pour one for each of you, and come sit down. We need to talk."

Tony and Eddie carried their drinks over to the sofa and sat at the opposite end of the sectional from Paulie.

"You," Paulie said, pointing to Tony. "From the beginning. Don't leave anything out."

Tony swallowed some whiskey, and then he explained how he refused to go into witness protection and that he was forced to work the side hustle with Frank Uzelli and Salvatore Marconi. Last, he removed his wool coat, unbuttoned his shirt, and revealed his scars.

Paulie scowled as Tony buttoned his shirt up and then finished off his drink. "I knew about the last cut Frank gave you, but not the one running down the center of your chest," Paulie said. "But I don't want to dwell on the whys or hows of past things. I'm only interested in now."

He went to the bar and poured a second shot. Returning to the sofa, he eased down and stared at Tony. "So, what is it you want from me?"

Tony looked him squarely in the eye. "I want back in, Paulie. I need to belong again."

Paulie shook his head. "That's all well and good, but what are you bringing to the table? I mean, Eddie here actually saved me from a hit."

"Money. Lots of money," Tony said. "The money Frank cheated you out of." Knowing how critical this moment was, he added, "And the chance to take care of Frank once and for all. You won't have to lift a finger."

Paulie smirked. "So that's it. You want revenge. I can't blame you in a way. But let's talk about the money. Give me a figure."

"A little over six million," Tony said. "I knew all the places Frank hid his money, even the offshore accounts."

"So, Frank knows you took it then?"

"Absolutely. I was the only one he trusted with that information."

"What a mistake," Paulie said. "Now, of course, I'm not going to turn down that kind of money. And to be fair, the rest of the families will get their cut."

"Of course," Tony said. "All that is up to you." He had expected this answer. If it were discovered that Paulie kept all the money to himself, his life would be worth nothing to the mob.

"Both of you have done well in showing your loyalty," Paulie said. "But I need to meet with the other heads of the families before I let the two of you back in. Frank isn't high up enough anymore to be aware." He stared at Tony. "Right now, it's hands off Frank until we figure all this out. Give me your cell numbers so I can stay in touch. And Eddie, send me a copy of that recording."

Eddie and Tony did as they were told. Paulie jerked his head towards the stairs. "Time to go. I'll reach out soon."

Once they were outside and away from the club, Tony said. "I think that went well."

"Seems so," Eddie said, hunkering down against the cold as they searched for a cab.

Later that night, back at the hotel, they ordered room service and ate in Eddie's room. Dining on roast chicken, mashed potatoes and seasoned green beans, Tony relaxed for the first time in months. In light of everything that happened, he believed Paulie would do the right thing by them.

To be back in the good graces of the mob meant everything. But if they didn't let him whack Frank Uzelli, it could turn out to be a big problem. That part was a deal breaker for him.

"What a night," Eddie said. "You showed up in the nick of time."

"Since Paulie made you and Domenico get in the car together, I figured something was going to go down. But I knew you had the upper hand with the recording," Tony said.

"Even with that, Domenico tried to weasel his way out of things." Eddie set his fork down and pushed away from the small table. His eyes held a faraway look.

"What gives?" Tony asked. "You don't look so happy."

"Just thinking about my kid. I need to see him. I can't stand being here in New York and not meeting him for the first time."

"So, why don't you try calling Monica?"

Eddie's face drooped. "She changed her number after I left."

"Then you need to do what I did in order to meet Kai. Stake out the building where she works. You might get lucky. You got nothing to lose. Either she turns up or not."

"I'm worried what will happen when she sees me. Maybe she'll try and keep my boy from me."

"You can't allow that to happen," Tony said. "You have every right to see your son."

"I know. But I don't have any legal avenues. With my record, forcing the issue won't fly with the courts."

"Look, try doing what I said. She might soften when she sees you."

Eddie shook his head. "I already know she's gonna be angry when I approach her. She wanted me to stay in witness protection."

"But you weren't happy in Arizona. What's the point of all that if you can't be a father to your son? You need to be firm with her, not let her control the situation." Tony got up. "Look, I'm exhausted. Let's sleep on things tonight. See how you feel in the morning. We'll figure things out. Right now, our priority is Paulie and what his intentions are."

Eddie walked with him to the door. "You're right. Everything hinges on Paulie. If we're not made good, we need to make other plans."

Back in his room, Tony lay across the bed, cell phone in his hand. He pulled up a picture of Kai. How could he miss a woman so much? Not seeing her was driving him crazy. He sent her a quick text. Once everything was settled, he'd make it his business to see her. All he wanted at this very moment was to look into her beautiful eyes and tell her how much he loved her. Regardless of Paulie's decision, one thing was certain. He would never give up Kai Nez.

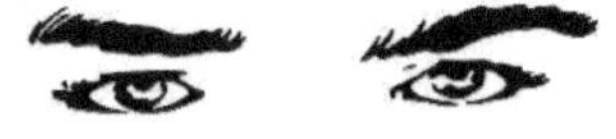

Chapter 44 — Kai
Tatiana

Kai pulled up the collar of her white winter coat against the frigid night's weather. She looped her arm through Austin's as they approached the entrance to the Tatiana Nightclub. To avoid the reported long lines, they arrived early.

They stopped in front of a bouncer, a tall, heavyset man, swaying back and forth, trying to keep warm. He rubbed his bare hands together and blew on them.

"Not a night to be outside, is it?" Kai said, giving him her best smile.

The man's eyes swept over the two, his expression rigid. "No, it is not."

"Can we go in?" Austin asked.

"I have never seen you here before," the man said.

Austin nodded and removed his black leather gloves. "Nope, this is our first time. I heard so much about it that I wanted to bring my lady to see what all the fuss was about."

Kai caught the man checking out Austin's wedding band. "So, you are a nice married couple then?"

"Do we have to be to get in?" Kai asked, wanting the man to believe she and Austin were having a clandestine love affair."

He fell silent and continued to stare while a line formed behind them. Austin dug into his coat pocket and pulled out his wallet. He removed a twenty-dollar bill and attempted to slip it to the man. When he made no move to accept the money, he took out a second one, folded it together with the first, and held it out. The man reached, grabbed the money, and stepped aside. "Have a nice evening."

Inside, a young lady stamped their wrists. Austin led Kai into the dimly lit club, where music pulsed in the background. They made their way to a table near the stage and he helped Kai remove her coat. He let out a long whistle. "Wow. You look fabulous."

"Thanks." She smoothed the front of her silver-beaded cocktail dress and sat down. Austin draped both their coats on the backs of the chairs. "Not so bad yourself," Kai said, observing his dark navy suit.

Crowds streamed in, jockeying for tables. Kai glanced at the stage in front of them. "Looks like we might have some entertainment." The music thumped and grew louder. Colored lights flashed as people moved onto the dance floor.

Austin got up. "I'm going to head toward the other side where the restrooms are. I need to be comfortable with the lay of the land just in case."

"Sure." Kai watched as he disappeared into the crowd of people. She bobbed her head to the music while keeping alert for any sign of Volkov. A young waitress came and she ordered a bottle of wine for their table. The music stopped, and the crowd on the dance floor dispersed. The stage lit up, and an announcer came out. Her eyes swept the club again. She recognized the young man standing across the room. It was Roman Volkov. Dressed in a suit and tie, he turned and focused on her, then strode in her direction.

Kai kept a smile firmly planted on her face. Where the hell was Austin?

He made a slight bow and held out his hand. "Roman Volkov. I'm the owner's son."

"Elizabeth Williams … Beth for short. It's nice to meet you."

"I'm told this is your first time at the club. I hope you're enjoying it."

"Yes," Kai said, still wondering where Austin went off to. "I think it's very nice."

Just then, Austin came toward them. He nodded at Roman. "Jake. Jake Turner."

Kai saw Roman glance at Austin's wedding band. "I'm Roman Volkov. I was just asking Eliza…I mean, Beth if everything is okay since it's your first time at the club."

Austin nudged Roman's shoulder. "I hope things are kept discreet here. We drove all the way from Queens. Have to be far away from home, if you know what I mean."

Roman's face flushed. "Oh, absolutely. Your privacy is important to the management here. Have a good night."

After Roman stepped away, the waitress brought the bottle of wine and two glasses. When they were alone, Kai asked, "Where the hell did you go?"

"The restroom and to scope some things out. Train your eyes on the door marked private across the dance floor to the far right. It's the one my C.I. described. It's where he saw Frank Uzelli go in." He poured them each a glass of wine, then moved his chair closer to Kai. His arm draped around her shoulders. "Gotta make the cheating husband thing look good."

Kai gave him a look and then sipped some wine. "Do you think we should have told Monica about our plan?"

"Not necessary," Austin said. "This is only our first night here. Who knows if we'll even put it into play."

They took in the show, and Kai had to admit it was pretty good. Even the atmosphere in the club lent itself to relaxation and enjoyment. She could understand why it became so popular.

Leaving the club just after midnight, Austin dropped her off in Brooklyn Heights while he headed for home on the Upper West Side of Manhattan.

Kai undressed and showered. Lying alone in bed every night only made her miss Tony that much more. Where was he now? Kai hoped he was okay. Her mood soured as thoughts of him subsided and drifted to her last visit home.

The relationship between herself and her mother appeared to worsen whenever they were together. She truly wanted them to heal. But Kai couldn't see a way forward anytime soon, with the past gripping her like a vise.

About to drift off, her cell dinged. She grabbed it off the nightstand and sat straight up. It was a message from Tony.

Missing you so much. Hope to see you soon. Several heart emojis followed it. Did this mean he wasn't that far away after all? Had he located Eddie Marconi? Questions continued to swirl inside her head. Am I mad to think I can continue this relationship? Things wouldn't go well if anyone at the Bureau found out she was seeing a former mobster.

She considered Monica and how Andrew was more than likely Eddie's son. The few times they had gotten together after work, it was on the tip of her tongue to inquire who the boy's father was. But she backed off at the last minute. It must be hard for Monica knowing her son could never have a relationship with his father. That is unless he happened to turn up.

Kai had never wanted to know Tony's intentions after he found Eddie. She had already divulged too much information to Tony from the task force meeting. Maybe it would help him get whatever this thing was over with quicker.

She fell into a restless sleep, her dreams switching back and forth from nightmare memories of the Rez and Tony and the scars embedded in his skin.

Chapter 45 — Monica
Eddie Reappears

Monica trudged from the Jacob K. Javits Federal Building, her face numb from the blasts of wind blowing across Federal Plaza. All she wanted was a nice, quiet spot at the Brickyard Craft Kitchen and Bar to eat a late lunch. It was after 2:00 PM when she arrived. Meetings with her task force had run over. Bob offered to go with her, but she put him off. She needed time to think.

Monica entered through the heavy glass doors into the darkened interior. Televisions lined one wall, with all the stations tuned to sports. The high gloss wood floors beamed against the dark rows of long high-top tables. Approximately 15 people were scattered about. Some worked on laptops while they sipped beer and ate.

Monica found a quiet spot near the rear. In the mood for pizza, she ordered a small Veggie Pie, and since she was still on the clock, a Non-Alcoholic Brew called Athletic Run Wild. The shock of Eddie leaving witness protection had still not worn off. She was finding it hard not to show how much it affected her in front of Bob. Lying about it not messing with their relationship pained her. He was a good man, a really good man, and she didn't want to do anything to hurt him.

The waitress came and set her pie and beer down. Monica inhaled the scent of the mushroom, onion, black olives, artichoke, and tomato toppings. Famished, she reached for a piece and took a bite.

"Got a slice for me?"

Monica froze. She raised her eyes, and there he was. Her breath caught. Hands shaking, she set the piece of pizza down.

Eddie slid onto a seat across from her. "Aren't you happy to see me?" he said, his voice as smooth as she remembered.

She could hardly believe he was sitting in front of her. Collecting herself, she asked, "Should I be?"

"Come on, Monica. I know you missed me as much as I missed you."

She squeezed her eyes shut. Maybe he wasn't really here. Opening them again, she saw that smile on the face she loved so much, his nautical blue eyes and thick black hair. He reached across the table. His hand rested on top of hers, his touch like electricity thrumming through her body.

Monica looked down and quickly pulled her hand away. "Please don't do that, Eddie."

His eyes swept over her. He frowned and shook his head. "I want much more than that."

What was she doing? She needed to get up and walk away. Her legs failed to obey, while her whole body became weak. "Why are you here?" she asked.

"I came to see you and our son," he said, placing his hands flat on the table.

"No. You know what I mean. Why did you leave witness protection? I thought you were doing okay."

"And how would you know that?"

"The U.S. Marshal's office informed us of your leaving. They couldn't understand why you never contacted them."

"Oh, that. Well, it's a long story."

"Try me," she said.

"I will, but first, we need to talk about Andrew." The softness in his voice disappeared. "I want to see him, Monica. All you left me was a picture with his name on the back.

Like a knee-jerk reaction, she shook her head. Hearing Eddie say Andrew's name for the first time made her insides tremble. It was not that he said it, but how it was tinged with anger. At this moment, she needed to be stronger than him. Make herself clear about him seeing their son.

"No, Eddie. Besides, Andrew isn't here in New York."

"What do you mean? Where is he?"

"Never mind Andrew, for now. I need to know why you left Arizona."

"Not until I see him, Monica. It's only fair. I've been away from him long enough." His eyes hardened, and he leaned in. "How could you leave me that photograph and then expect me not to come looking for him one day?"

Her foot tapped nervously beneath the table. For the first time, her strength failing and at a loss for words, she hesitated. He was right. Her intentions were good, but she never realized how it would affect him in the long run. "I … I probably shouldn't have done that. It's just—"

Eddie slapped his palm on the table. "Just what, Monica! So you could have the upper hand as usual."

"No. Please don't think that. I wanted you to know about Andrew so you could change your life for the better. Be someone he could be proud of."

"Funny," Eddie sneered. "I did everything to change. I got my degree, a good job. and I stayed out of trouble, but all I thought about every single stinking day was you and Andrew."

Her eyes filled, and she looked away. All of this was her fault. If she had never left that photo, maybe Eddie would still be in witness protection.

"What?" Eddie said. "You got nothing more to say to me?"

Monica got up and gathered her coat and purse. "I can't do this with you."

"Sit down, Monica."

She captured the thunder behind his eyes. Her body tensed. This was an Eddie she had never witnessed before. He was not the same man who left three years ago. What he had experienced hardened him somehow. The naivety was gone.

"I need to get back to work."

"I said sit down, Monica." He pointed to her chair. "You're not going to just walk away."

She glanced around. People were starting to stare. She didn't want to cause a scene, so she eased back onto the chair. "Okay," she said. "I can see how upset you are."

"Yeah, just a bit," he said. His eyes softened, and he reached for a slice of pizza. He took a bite and made a face. "Veggie?" He set the slice down and wiped his hands on a napkin. "Now, I promise to tell you everything after I see Andrew, not before."

"I told you he's not here. He's with my parents in Florida."

"Do I need to go there, or will you bring him to me?"

"No. You wouldn't. I mean you can't go there. Please, I understand how much you want to see him, but…"

"Two days, Monica. You have forty-eight hours starting tomorrow to bring him to see me. Otherwise, I go to Florida and surprise your parents."

"Why are you doing this, Eddie? I've never seen you act this way."

"I don't like acting this way. I love you and our son, but I won't stand for you trying to keep him from me. He has a right to know who his father is." This time, Eddie got up. He reached into his coat pocket and tossed a piece of paper on the table. "Here's my number. Two days," he repeated. "We meet by the carousel at The Battery. Or else I go to Florida. I know where your parents live." He leaned down, his hand sweeping through her dark curls. Without another word, he turned and headed for the door.

Monica removed her wallet and threw more than enough on the table to cover the bill. She slipped on her coat and rushed after him. Her head swung left and then right, her eyes scanning the street. Eddie was nowhere to be seen. Her heart pumped at a dizzying pace—so fast she thought it might burst from her chest.

Monica hurried toward the Federal Building, her mind in turmoil. There was no doubt in her mind that Eddie meant every word he said. If he went to Florida and demanded to see his son, her parents wouldn't know what to do. She never told them he left witness protection.

Trying to keep her wits about her, she retreated to her office and dialed her mother's number. The truth would come out sooner or later. It might as well be sooner.

When Lillian answered, she said, "Mom, I'm catching a flight. I need to bring Andrew back home. I'll explain everything when I get there."

"But I thought you wanted him to stay for a while."

"I do. I mean, I did."

"What happened?"

"I said I'll explain when I get there. I'll text you the flight information." Monica ended the call. She had never been afraid of Eddie. But this was an Eddie she didn't recognize. Her eyes filled, and the room blurred. Had she caused this change in him by not going into witness protection with him like he wanted? She'd never forget the look on his face that last day when he realized she had chosen the Bureau over him.

He mentioned getting a degree. Wasn't that a good thing? And if he planned on staying here in New York, he would want to see Andrew that much more. Over the last two years she had shown Andrew pictures of Eddie, trying to make him understand that this man was his father. But he was still too young to comprehend or ask questions.

Elbows perched on the desk, she placed her head in her hands. From the moment she saw him again, there was no denying how much she still loved him. Eddie was so right about that part.

Only she needed to know why he left Arizona. The only way to find out would be to let him see Andrew. There was no other choice. For now, she'd keep their meeting to herself. Whether she liked it or not, Eddie was back in her life.

Chapter 46 — Cookie
Convincing Cookie

Damien and Cookie lay facing each other on her bed. After an hour of fierce lovemaking, they were both satisfied and spent. Cookie snuggled closer. She brushed the back of her hand against Damien's cheek and sighed.

"I'm so glad you're not on call at the hospital tonight."

"Me, too," Damien said. "But there is something I need to talk to you about."

"Does it have anything to do with Roman? I mean the way you bolted out of the shop that day—"

"I don't want to talk about Roman. He's a real thorn in my side." Damien inched up against the pillows, pulling Cookie with him. He kissed the top of her head.

Cookie giggled. "A thorn, huh? Why don't you just say he's a pain in the ass?"

"That, too," Damien said, laughing with her. "No, there is something I've been meaning to tell you. My father called me the other night. He wanted to apologize for the way he and my mother treated you. They would like to meet us for dinner."

Cookie moved away and sat on the edge of the bed, her back to him. "I'm not sure I want to do that." She got up, grabbed her robe from the pink velvet tufted bench at the foot of the bed, and slipped it on.

"I told him I would see how you felt about it. It's okay if you want to decline their invitation," Damien said. "I mean that, Cookie."

She turned towards him as she sinched her robe. "It's just I don't think they're going to suddenly change how they feel about me."

"Cookie, I've made myself very clear to them. I am not giving you up. Instead of dinner we can have drinks at my father's club in Brooklyn. Makes things easier if a fast exit becomes necessary."

"Well, I guess if we're going to be together, I can't avoid them forever. So tell them okay." She wagged her finger at him. "But I'm warning you, Doctor Volkov, if anything goes wrong, I won't be polite."

Damien stretched out his arm. "Now, take off that robe and come back to bed."

* * * * *

Two days later, in order to avoid the evening crowd, the four met at 4:00 p.m. Damien escorted Cookie to a VIP table near the stage where Darya and Alexei sat. Except for the waitstaff and a few customers seated at the bar, the place was empty. Not caring whether or not she made a good impression, Cookie had dressed casually in jeans, a sweater, and a leather jacket.

Alexei rose, smiled, and pulled out a chair for Cookie. "I am so glad you agreed to come."

"Yes," Darya said, smiling up at them as Damien bent and kissed her on both cheeks.

No kissing for me, Cookie thought as she settled into the chair.

After Cookie and Damien were seated, Alexei ordered a bottle of expensive wine and poured them each a glass. "I just want to tell you how sorry we are for the way we acted at dinner," he said. "It was not a nice thing to do. Especially since we invited you to our home. We were caught off guard a bit. Damien has not brought anyone to meet us for a very long time."

"And now?" Cookie asked. She wasn't going to pull any punches with them tonight. People don't change at the drop of a hat. Something must have happened.

Darya smoothed her blonde hair and sipped her wine. She set the glass down, her eyes focused on Cookie, she said, "And now we realize what a mistake we made. For us to judge you before getting to know you was wrong."

Cookie liked what she was hearing, but could she believe them? "I appreciate your apology. But the thing is, I'm not Russian. I'm never going to be Russian. I'm not ashamed of my heritage. I can respect your customs and even honor them, but if we are going to have any kind of relationship, then you need to do the same."

Alexei and Darya each cast a glance at Damien. "Cookie's right," he said. "We need to put any differences or opinions of each other aside. I love her and intend to be with her regardless of anyone else's thoughts."

Cookie beamed inside. Damien had told them he loved her, something she never expected him to do. "And I love your son," she blurted out. "So, I hope we can all get along."

Darya reached out and touched Cookie's hand. "Of course. If you make my Damien happy, then that is all we want." She turned towards Alexei. "Right?"

"Yes, yes. We want both of you to be happy," Alexei said. He raised his wine glass. "*Za nashikh.* To love."

Later that evening, Cookie, more than satisfied with the night's events, sat snuggled against Damien on his sofa. Relaxed and content, she thought about the nightclub Alexei owned. "Is Tatiana the only business your father has?" she asked.

"Among other things," Damien said.

"Like what?" She sensed Damien growing uncomfortable. She eased away and sat up straight. "I don't mean to be nosey. I'm just curious."

"He's a businessman. I don't keep track of everything he's involved in."

Cookie mulled over his answer. Involved was an unusual word to use. She hesitated and tried to decide whether or not to take things further. "Well," Cookie said. "You must know what else he does besides manage the nightclub."

Damien's brow furrowed. "Where is all this coming from?"

"Look, you know my father owns a restaurant. That's how he makes his living. When you say your father is involved in other things, it makes sense for me to ask about it."

Damien shot up from the sofa. "I'm not going to discuss my father's business with you. It has nothing to do with us." He went to the window and stared out, his back turned to her.

Caught off guard by his reaction, she grew silent for a moment. Damien getting this upset about his father was a huge red flag. What if Alexei dealt in some illegal enterprise? Cookie got up and walked over to him. He stared down at her, his amber eyes glassy. Something was very wrong.

"Why are you getting so upset?" she asked. "Whatever it is, you can tell me. It won't make me love you any less."

"I … I'm not sure what else he does," Damien said, a hint of hurt in his voice. "To be honest, I don't want to know. Even though he's not my biological father, he adopted me and gave me his name. He has always been there for me and my mother."

"I'm not doubting that. I can tell how much he cares about you," Cookie said.

Damien pulled her close, the warmth of his body wrapped around hers. "I promised I would be honest with you. My father may deal with some undesirable people. But I don't know firsthand who they are or what they do. I can't wrap my head around it. It would be too painful if I did find out the truth. So, I don't ask any questions."

His body trembled, and she pulled him closer. "It's alright. We won't talk about it anymore. All that matters is that we have each other no matter what."

Damien kissed her lightly on the lips. "Thank you," he said.

"For what?"

"Understanding how I feel. That means a lot to me."

Bathed in moonlight, they held on to each other while Cookie tried to push away thoughts of Alexei Volkov and who he might really be.

Chapter 47 — Eddie
Moving Backwards

Eddie glanced over at Tony as he climbed into the BMW. Paulie Martello had called and asked to meet with them. It was decision day. Eddie surmised that Paulie had met with the heads of the other families. They would either be in or out. Or maybe only one of them had been chosen to be let back in.

"So, how did things go with Monica?" Tony asked.

The two had not had a chance to talk since his meeting with Monica yesterday. Eddie needed time alone. After seeing Monica again, his heart was torn between wanting to hold her in his arms and tell her how much he loved her and screaming at the top of his lungs. As smart as she was, did it not ever occur to her how much he would miss their son?

"It was rough," Eddie said. "I still love her, but I'm angry."

Tony leaned against the headrest. A pair of Ray-Ban Aviator sunglasses shielded his dark eyes. "I can't blame you one bit."

"My son is in Florida with her parents. I told her she has 48 hours to bring him to New York."

"How'd she take that?" Tony asked, moving the sunglasses down to the tip of his nose and peering at Eddie.

"Not well, but she understood I meant it. I have no doubt I will meet my son for the first time real soon."

They pulled into the lot behind Paulie's social club. Memories of Domenico flashed through Eddie's mind. He wondered where they had dumped his body. They exited the car and went inside, going down the same stairs as before.

The lights were dimmed. Paulie sat on the sectional waiting. In the far corner by the bar, a man was sitting facing away from them, the collar of his wool coat pulled all the way up. Something about him made Eddie flinch inside.

Paulie motioned for them to sit. "Now, I have talked with the others, and we are all in agreement that the two of you should be let back in. You both work under me now as made men."

Tony smiled and removed his sunglasses. "Thanks, Paulie."

"Don't thank me yet. There are conditions." He leaned forward, clasping his hands together. "First, of course, is the money Tony offered. This stays between us and the heads of the families. We don't want Frank Uzelli getting wind of anything. He still needs to make good for as long as we see fit."

Tony nodded. "Sure, no problem."

"Second, there is to be no retaliation from you against him until we give the okay. Right now, we have a big deal going on with the Russians at the seaport. I don't want anything to get in the way. Once that is finished, Frank is yours. I need you to lay low until that time."

"I can live with that," Tony said.

Paulie turned his eyes on Eddie. "I need you in on the seaport deal. In a few days, you'll attend a meeting with Enzo Carbone and the Russians. You are going to be my eyes and ears."

"Sure thing," Eddie said, still unsettled by the dark figure at the bar. There was something familiar about his size and how he was hunched over while holding a drink.

"After hearing Enzo mentioned on that recording, I'm not sure I can trust him," Paulie continued. "Right now, I still need him, but his time may come." He handed Eddie a sealed envelope. "The details are inside. Burn it after you finish reading it. So, we're all clear on everything."

"Absolutely," Eddie said.

Paulie studied Eddie a moment. "If you do as good as your Uncle Sal before he decided to cut us out of the action, you could be a

Capo someday." He went to a small side table and pulled open a drawer. Lifting out a 9mm, he handed it to Eddie. "In case you ever need one."

"Thanks, Paulie," Eddie said, tucking the weapon behind him in his waistband.

He turned and nodded at Tony. "Are you good?"

Tony produced his gun and then returned it to his waistband. "I'm good, Paulie."

"We'll talk about the transfer of the money tomorrow. You meet me here at the same time as today."

Paulie got up and turned towards the man at the bar. He motioned for Eddie and Tony to follow him. "I want you guys to meet someone."

The man swiveled around to face them. He rose, his dark hooded eyes focused on them. He approached the group and stuck out his hand. Eddie's stomach sinched. He would know this man anywhere. There was no one in the Mafia more feared than him.

"Rocco Fischetti," he said in a deep, gravelly voice.

Showing not a hint of fear, Tony shook his hand first. "Tony Morello. Nice meeting you."

Rocco turned to Eddie. "I believe we met once before. Eddie, isn't it? Eddie Marconi. Sal's nephew."

Having no choice, Eddie reciprocated the handshake, Rocco's huge palm swallowing his. How could this man even mention his uncle's name after shooting him to death?

"Of course," Paulie said. "You met him that time up in the Pocono Mountains. I wanted you two to know that Rocco took care of everything with Willie and Bruno." He clapped Eddie on the back. "Thanks to Eddie here, I'm still alive and breathing."

Despite Paulie's compliment, Eddie's stomach turned sour, the bile almost rising in his throat. All he wanted was to be far away from Rocco.

"Now that business is out of the way, stay and have a drink," Paulie said, pointing to the bar.

"I don't want to be rude," Eddie said. "I have some things I need to take care of."

Paulie's eyes flashed. "One drink won't hurt, will it?"

Seeing he had no choice, Eddie said, "Sure. One drink."

The three men sat at the bar while Paulie went behind it and poured each of them a shot.

Paulie raised his glass, "*Salute.*"

They all polished off their whiskey, the liquor doing a slow burn inside Eddie's chest. Thoughts of his Uncle Sal came roaring through. All those years he had admired and loved him disintegrated when he discovered the truth. How complicit he was in murdering his parents. Rocco was bringing all of it back.

He discovered his anger toward Rocco lay in the fact that he never got to confront his uncle. Rocco put an end to him too soon.

A half-hour later, Eddie and Tony left the social club. Behind the wheel, Eddie charged out of the lot.

"Whoa!" Tony said, gripping the dashboard. "Who put a fire under your ass?"

Eddie eased up on the gas. "To tell you the truth, I couldn't wait to get away from Rocco Fischetti."

"Yeah, that's one bad dude. But you can't show fear, Eddie. You just got to roll with things as they come up. A man like him can smell fear a mile away."

"I know. It's just … he's the one who killed my Uncle Sal. It brought up too many memories. I never had any closure."

"I get it," Tony said. "But maybe that was for the best. Your uncle probably would have tried to justify what happened."

"Yeah, I guess. But I'll never know, will I?"

That night in his hotel room with Tony, Eddie opened the envelope from Paulie. He memorized the time and meeting place.

"Hey, you still got that lighter from Frank?" Eddie asked.

"Yeah, it's a real keepsake, if you know what I mean."

He tossed it to Eddie, who held the note over the toilet, set it on fire, and flushed it away. They ordered room service, and in the middle of eating, Eddie received a text from Monica.

I'm bringing Andrew home tomorrow. Let me know what time you want to meet on Saturday. He couldn't help but smile. Finally, he was going to see his son.

Chapter 48 — Alexei
Dissolution

Alexei glanced over at Rurik behind the wheel, his eyes steady on the road ahead. This ride to the Catskills felt so different from the others before. Leonid had been his Brigadier for the last ten years. How did he not see the falsehoods, the lies, the betrayal before now?

Three of Alexei's most loyal men followed in a car behind. "Today, the truth will no longer be hidden," Alexei said. "We put an end to this disloyalty and move on."

They turned onto the gravel drive and pulled up to the front of the house. Alexei got out and signaled for the others to park around the back out of sight. A slight breeze fanned through the bare tree limbs under an overcast sky. Crows squawked in the distance as Alexei and Rurik entered the house.

"Do you think he will come?" Rurik asked.

"Oh yes, he will come. I have told Leonid that it is you I suspect of planning to overthrow me. He will realize you are about to tell me the truth about him." Alexei let out a low chuckle. "I imagine he might have the same plans for me today as I do for him." They entered the sparse living room, and Alexei sat on an old, worn sofa.

Rurik seated himself across from him. He wrung his hands and tapped his brown booted foot rapidly up and down.

"Relax," Alexei said. "Everything will be fine. The men know what to do after Leonid's car arrives."

"It's just that Nicolai and some others are on Leonid's side."

"Not for long, my Rurik. Not for long. They will gladly come back under my rule again when they realize the consequences of deceiving me and also what they might gain by being loyal."

"What do you mean?" Rurik asked.

"As a reward for today, you shall be my new Brigadier and live in my building in Leonid's apartment. You only need to clear out his things, as I own it anyway."

Rurik's mouth dropped open. "I never imagined…"

"What?" Alexei smiled. "I know you are someone I can trust."

Rurik dipped his head. "Thank you. I will never forget this."

A car cruised up the drive, the sound making Rurik rise out of his seat. He went to one of the front windows. "It is Leonid and Nicolai. I don't see anyone else."

"You must cease your jittering," Alexei said, his face flushed. "Take your weapon out and go wait in the other room." Giving Alexei one last glance, Rurik did as he was told.

The front door opened, and Leonid appeared in the living room doorway, Nicolai at his side. "What is going on? Why the rush to meet all the way up here?" he grumbled.

Alexei pointed to a chair. "Stop being so dramatic and sit down. I want to make sure that nothing goes wrong with our upcoming deal at the seaport."

Leonid hesitated before seating himself while Nicolai remained stationed by the doorway. "But you know that Enzo and Frank have agreed to everything. Are you having second thoughts?" Leonid said.

Alexei checked his watch and then got up from the sofa. "As a matter of fact, I am." He blew out a low whistle, and Rurik appeared, his gun drawn and aimed at Leonid. Alexei's other men, Dimitri, Maxim, and Boris, rushed in the front door, guns drawn. Boris slammed a shocked Nicolai up against the doorway. His gun pressed into the small of his back.

The color drained from Leonid's face. He rose from his seat. "What the hell is this, Alexei?"

"I think you know, Leonid, my so-called trusted Brigadier." He nodded towards Rurik. "He has informed me of your plans to take over in the *Bratva*. You made a big mistake thinking you could overthrow me, the Wolf!" Alexei shouted.

Leonid's cold, dark eyes swept over Rurik. "You snake, you devil!" he shouted. "After all that I promised you."

Rurik shook his head. "My loyalty will always be with Alexei. It is you who should be ashamed of plotting against him. He has always been good to everyone."

Leonid's fists clenched. "Is that how you see things now? What about all you agreed to do for me?"

"That meant nothing," Rurik spat. "You are the one who is the devil, not me."

"Enough of this chatter," Alexei said. He pointed to the hallway. "Take them to the basement." Alexei followed behind as the men took Leonid and Nicolai down the stairs.

At the bottom, Alexei found the putrid smell of torture and death at once invigorating and disgusting. Except for poor Sergey, this place where so many died had never haunted his dreams.

"Down on your knees!" Alexei shouted, pointing to Leonid and Nicolai.

Nicolai clasped his hands together. "Please, Alexei, I had no choice. He forced me to do it."

Alexei's chest heaved. His pulse beat a steady rhythm. Nothing would dissuade him from executing these two men. He stared at Nicolai. "Do you expect me to believe that? Now, do as I say."

The two men dropped to their knees, Leonid maintaining a defiant look on his face. Alexei quickly drew his 9mm and shot Nicolai dead center in the forehead. Nicolai toppled over onto the floor and lay still.

"Go on, go on!" Leonid screamed. "Get it over with."

But Alexei lowered his weapon, tucking it back behind him. He stepped closer and looked down at Leonid. "Oh no, my dear friend. I have other plans for you." He nodded at Rurik. "Go get my things from the trunk."

Rurik took off up the stairs, returning moments later with a black case and several lengths of rope, and set it all on the small table.

Alexei opened the case and put on a pair of brown leather gloves. Pulling a pair of disposable coveralls from the large box, he smiled at Leonid. "You are prepared for anything, aren't you?" He studied Leonid's face, finally finding the fear in his eyes. He turned to the others. "Get him up and tie him to the chair."

With Leonid now secured, Alexei lifted a drill out of the case and turned it on. He aimed for Leonid's kneecaps. "This is for Sergey," he said. Seconds later, Leonid's screams filled the basement.

Chapter 49 — Monica
Florida

Monica sat at her mother's kitchen table. Getting in late last night, she had not told her why she needed to bring Andrew home. With her father gone to the park with Andrew, there was no other choice but to talk to her about Eddie.

With morning cups of coffee between them, Monica said, "Listen, I need to tell you the real reason I came to get Andrew."

Lillian took a sip from her cup. "Were you going to lie to me?"

"If I'm being honest, I did think about it," Monica said, shame washing over her. The thing is … I mean, Eddie's back."

A pained expression crossed Lillian's face. "What do you mean he's back? I thought he was in witness protection."

"He was, but he left, and now he's in New York, and wants to see Andrew."

Lilian's brow arched. "Monica, I'm a bit confused. Isn't it dangerous for him to be out of witness protection?"

Monica stared into her coffee cup, not sure how much to say. "I think it is."

"Well, then, if he wants to see Andrew, you can't let him do that."

"Oh, Mom, things are not that simple. Besides, I know he would never let anything happen to his son." Her eyes filled, and her mother's face blurred. "This is all my fault. He might have stayed where he was if I never left that photo."

"No, Monica. Don't do that. Don't go blaming yourself. You did what you thought was right."

"But now, I'm not sure what he might be involved in," Monica said, wiping her eyes. "He wasn't acting the same."

"What do you mean?"

"He … he was very clear on what he wanted."

"Monica, you're scaring me," Lillian said. "Do you mean he threatened you?"

"Kind of."

"For God's sake, Monica. You're an FBI agent. He can't do that."

"I know, I know. I was caught off guard. I never expected to see him. I was having lunch and he just walked in the door of the restaurant. He must have been waiting and watching for me by the Federal Building."

Lilian reached her hand across the table and placed it on top of Monica's. "Honey, listen to me. You cannot let that man intimidate you in any way. He's starting to remind me of his Uncle Sal."

Monica pulled her hand away and sat straight up. "Please don't say that. Eddie is nothing like his uncle."

"Are you sure?" Lilian asked. "I mean you don't even know why he came back. It might have something to do with the mob."

"That's just it. He won't give me any details until he sees Andrew. So, you can see how I need to do this. Once I find out why he left the program, I'll know what to do from there."

"The next time you're with him, you need to be very careful," Lillian said. "I'm worried he'll try and snatch my grandson away."

Monica shook her head. "No. He would never do that. I'm sure of it. Not with the job I have. He'd have the whole Bureau come down on him all across the globe. There would be nowhere he could hide."

Lillian let out a soft sigh. "I guess you're right about that. Just be careful, Monica."

Later that evening after returning home, and with Andrew settled in for the night, Monica poured a glass of wine and retreated to the bedroom. She set the glass on the nightstand and lay back against the pillows. Her cell buzzed and she picked it up. It was Bob calling for the second time that evening. He knew about her trip to Florida but she hadn't told him anything else.

"Hi," she said, trying to sound casual.

"Just checking to see you arrived home okay. I could have met you at the airport."

"No, that wasn't necessary. We're home safe and sound."

There was an audible breath on the other end, a pronounced frustration. "Monica, what's going on? I mean, you said Andrew was staying with your folks for several weeks and then you abruptly got on a flight to bring him home."

Her head swam. She didn't need this right now, but she couldn't give anything away either. "My father wasn't feeling too well," she lied. "He had to have some tests done. I didn't want my mom to have to take care of Andrew while all that is going on."

"Oh. I guess that makes sense."

"You guess?" she asked, the fingertips of her free hand digging into the quilt. "What are you trying to say?"

"Come on, don't get annoyed," Bob said, easing his tone. "I didn't mean anything by it."

"Sorry. I'm just a bit tired."

"No worries. Besides, tomorrow is Saturday and we're both off. Feel like spending the day together?"

Why did she even think to start this relationship in the first place? With Eddie back, she couldn't imagine being with Bob and acting like everything was great. "Listen," she said. "I've got a bunch of personal things to catch up on. Plus, Andrew needs a haircut, and I have to grocery shop. Maybe, Sunday afternoon?"

"Sure. I understand. See you then. Have a goodnight."

"You, too." Monica set her cell down. Why did he have to be so damn nice? Now, she felt guilty lying to him. There were no personal things, and Andrew didn't need a haircut. Tomorrow she was taking Andrew to meet Eddie by the Sea Glass Carousel.

The thought of seeing him again made her go weak inside. A strange flutter hit the pit of her stomach. Being in his presence again had awakened all those old feelings. But she desperately needed to push all that aside. Things could never work between them. They were too different from one another. Opposite in every way.

Trying to calm her nerves, she reached for her glass of wine and sipped. She needed to stay focused. Tomorrow she would find out the real reason he left Arizona. Then, she could decide what, if anything, to do with that information.

Chapter 50 — Kai
Who She Saw

Kai sat snuggled against Austin while the performers at Tatiana danced across the stage. The two had become regulars at the club these past weeks. So far, they had not gathered any new intel. Alexei Volkov had not even shown his face.

She knew from previous undercover work that these things either sprung quickly or took more time to pan out. Her mind drifted to the text from Tony. What did he mean by hope to see you soon? Could he be closer than she thought? For sure he must have made his way to Arizona after she gave him Eddie Marconi's whereabouts.

"Kai. Did you hear what I said?"

Jolted out of her thoughts by Austin, she turned her attention back to him. "Sorry. I think I'm just bored."

"Well, I think something is about to jump off."

"What are you talking about?"

"I saw the manager, that Petrov guy, go into that private room with several bottles of liquor. Alexei Volkov was right behind him. Petrov came out a few minutes ago."

Kai scanned the room. "Look," she said. "I think you're right. There he goes again with a tray of food. I guess Alexei Volkov is about to have company."

The stage show ended and the room filled with applause. Dance music blared from the speakers again and soon the club floor was packed with patrons gyrating to the beat.

"Kai, Volkov's standing outside that door, probably waiting for someone. His eyes are fixed on the crowd. So, what do you think?" Austin said. "Is now the time?"

Kai grinned. "Yeah, this is perfect … that is, if it works." She waited for the next song to end and then jumped up from the table, her face enraged. She threw her drink right into Austin's face. "You son of a bitch," she screamed. "How could you do that to me?"

The room fell silent as everyone gawked at her and Austin. Kai grabbed her purse and coat. She tore across the dance floor, forcing tears into her eyes. She caught a glimpse of Alexei Volkov coming toward her.

Before she knew what was happening, he had blocked her path. "What is wrong?" he asked. "Is there something I can do?"

In the background, the music started up again, a slow paced, love song forcing people to return to the dance floor.

Kai wiped her eyes. "I'm sorry. I didn't mean to cause a scene. We love coming here, and now he's ruined everything."

Alexei nodded toward Austin, who was still sitting at their table, dabbing at the liquor running down his suit. "You mean that man over there?"

"Yes," Kai said, bringing more tears to her eyes. She started for the door but then felt a hand on her arm.

"Come with me for a moment," Alexei said. "You must not leave like this. You are too upset."

"Before she knew it, he ushered her into his private room and closed the door. The lack of noise coming from outside shocked her. The room must be soundproofed.

Leading her over to a chair, he said, "Please sit for a moment. You must collect yourself." Alexei sat across from her.

Kai reached into her purse and pulled out a tissue. "I'm so sorry."

Alexei put up his hand. "Stop saying you are sorry. There is no need. Petrov has told me you are a regular customer here. Tell me what happened. What did your husband do? Maybe, there is something I can do to help."

Kai shook her head and lowered her eyes. "I don't think so. I'm too ashamed to tell you."

"Come now," Alexei said. "It is probably nothing I have not heard before."

Kai raised her head. If Volkov was expecting someone, she needed to keep this thing going. "Well … he's not my husband. Actually, he's married to someone else."

"Oh, I see," Alexei said. "Why is such a beautiful woman like you seeing a married man? For sure you could find someone else."

"I guess. But I do really love him and he promised to leave his wife. But tonight…" She wiped her eyes again.

"Go on," Alexei said.

"Tonight, he told me, he decided not to leave her. After all the promises he made to me. I just can't believe it."

Alexei let out a chuckle. "That explains the drink ending up in his face."

"Yes. I couldn't help it."

"So, now that you know this, what will you do?"

"I'm not sure," Kai said, just as there was a knock on the door.

Alexei got up. "Are you sure there is nothing I can do?"

"No. You've been very kind and I appreciate your trying to help. I'll figure things out." Kai stuffed the tissue inside her purse and eased up from the chair.

"Well, you are always welcome in my club. I hope you make the right decision."

"Thank you," Kai said.

A side door at the rear of the room opened. Three men entered. One of them nodded at Alexei. He ushered Kai to the other door leading to the club and opened it. It immediately closed behind her. The music boomed and the room filled with flashing lights. Kai made her way through the stuffy club as a chill threaded through her body. She recognized every single one of those men meeting with Alexei.

Kai scanned the room. The table where she and Austin had sat was empty. She slipped on her coat and hurried to the exit. Up the street, Austin waited in the car.

Kai got in, and they drove away. After they were a reasonable distance from the club, he pulled over to the curb and parked.

"Well, how did things go?"

"Everything went great," she said. "I know who he's meeting with."

Austin leaned toward her, his eyes lit with excitement. "What's the intel?"

"He's meeting with Enzo Carbone, and Frank Uzelli. I recognized them from the photographs in our files at the Bureau."

"Wow. We did good tonight, didn't we?"

"Yeah, but I'm not so sure Monica will agree with our little stunt. Things could have gone either way."

"We'll just have to convince her otherwise," Austin said. "This has been so great working with you, Kai."

"Same here," she said, giving him a sideways glance and a smile. Before she knew what was happening, Austin's arm came around her shoulders. "What are you doing?"

"I really like you a lot, Kai. I … mean."

"Austin, stop. We can't."

"Why not?"

The hurt look on his face tugged at her heart. She knew firsthand what rejection was like. But her feelings for Tony outweighed anything that might happen between her and Austin.

"We just shouldn't, that's all," she said. "Things could get complicated."

"How complicated? We're both single … unless maybe you're not telling me something."

"No. I'm not ready for another relationship. I got out of one not that long ago."

Austin removed his arm from around her shoulders. His face sagged. "Oh, I get it."

Inside, Kai knew she would be better off with someone like Austin. He was a really nice guy—a guy whose past could never compare with Tony's turbulent one.

"Can't blame me for trying," Austin said. "But if you ever change your mind, I'll be around."

"Thanks for understanding," Kai said.

They drove toward Kai's apartment in silence. Glad for the respite, she thought about what she didn't mention to Austin. How was she going to handle what she had seen earlier that evening at Tatiana.

Yes, she did see Enzo Carbone and Frank Uzelli. But she also saw someone she never expected to see. Not two feet from her, in between the two men, stood Eddie Marconi.

Chapter 51 — Eddie
My Son

Eddie arrived at The Battery a few minutes early. Traces of snow still marked the patterned walkways. The park lay almost empty on this cold winter afternoon. A brisk winter breeze caught the back of his neck. Pulling up the collar of his leather jacket he headed for the SeaGlass Carousel. The aroma of a street vendor's buttery, sweet roasted chestnuts brought back memories of the last time he was here.

He had come to this very spot only to climb into a van to be wired by the FBI. All of it appeared like a scene from a movie in the back of his mind. But he never forgot this carousel and how he told Monica he hoped one day their children would ride it.

Then, that photograph of Andrew came. His little boy, riding this very carousel. He viewed the thirty massive fiberglass fish with color changing LED lights as they sped past the window. A few children perched inside each fish as it rotated, while the lights created a beautiful undersea effect.

"Eddie."

He turned at the sound of her voice. Monica stood holding Andrew's hand. Dressed in a small navy peacoat and tan corduroy pants, his dark curls peeking out from under a wool cap, his blue eyes searched Eddie's face.

Eddie froze. He couldn't move, couldn't breathe. It was like looking in a mirror. His little boy was the spitting image of him. Monica bent down beside him and pointed at Eddie.

"Andrew, this is your daddy. Say hello."

Andrew gave Eddie a curious look as Monica pushed him forward. "Go on, say hello."

Eddie's knees almost gave way as he crouched down and held out his arms. The lump growing in his throat swelled and tears stung the corners of his eyes. Never in his life had he experienced love like this. Not even the love he felt for Monica could compare to it.

"Hi, Andrew," he said softly. "Can I have a hug?" Andrew took a few furtive steps until he reached Eddie. His arms wrapped around his son as tears streamed down his cheeks. He hugged him closer and repeated his name over and over. When he finally looked up at Monica, she was crying, too.

Eddie brushed his tears away and lifted his son up. He went over to the carousel. "Do you want to ride?" he asked.

Andrew bobbed his head up and down. He pointed at the window. "Yes. I want to go for a ride." He quickly swiveled his head to make sure Monica was following behind them. "Come, Mommy," he said. "Come see me ride."

A few minutes later, Monica and Eddie watched as Andrew glided past inside a blue Angelfish. Eddie's arm wrapped around Monica. "Thank you," he said, his voice breaking.

"Some feeling, isn't it?" Monica said. "A love there are no real words for."

Eddie shook his head. "I never could have imagined it. Not in a million years."

When the ride ended, they hurried from the park and into a small restaurant up the street. They settled into a booth at the very rear with Andrew in a booster seat next to Monica. They ordered coffee for themselves and hot chocolate for Andrew with a side of mac and cheese.

"It's his favorite," Monica explained, loosening his coat and pulling the wool cap off his head.

Andrew swiped at the dark curls falling across his forehead while shoving some mac and cheese into his tiny mouth.

Eddie couldn't stop staring at his son. His head buzzed and his body felt lighter than it had in years. His eyes filled again.

"So," Monica said. "I brought him to you but we still need to talk."

"I know." Eddie tore his eyes away from Andrew. "I'm going to be honest and say, there are things I will tell you and things that I can't."

"Eddie, that wasn't the deal. I need to know why you left witness protection. I want the truth."

This was going to be more difficult than he thought. No way could he tell Monica about him and Tony, and the hit he overheard causing Paulie to let him back in. She might never let him see Andrew again.

"Look. I wasn't happy in Arizona. Yes, I got my degree and I'm still proud of that but…"

"But what?"

He could tell she was getting annoyed. "I just kept thinking about you and Andrew."

Monica shook her head. "You know how dangerous it is for you to be out. Certain people will be looking for you."

"Okay, Monica. Enough said." His body went rigid. There was no getting around things with her. He might as well tell her some things.

"I don't want anything to happen to you, Eddie." Her hand trembled as she reached for a napkin to wipe Andrew's mouth.

"You don't have to worry about me because I've settled things. No one's after me."

Her green eyes bore into him. "What are you talking about?"

Eddie told her he had overheard some sensitive information regarding Paulie. "I felt obligated to come to New York and let Paulie know." He completely left Tony out of the picture.

"What kind of information?" Monica asked.

"I don't want to put you in an awkward position. It's best I leave that part out. But don't you see," he continued. "It was the only way I could ever see you and Andrew again."

The last traces of softness drained from her face. "How could you do this? Going back into the mob is the last thing I expected from you. After everything that went on before, and even with your panic attacks."

"Well, maybe if you had given up your precious Bureau and come with me, none of this what have happened," he huffed. "Look, you wanted the truth so I told you. I could have sat here and lied."

"Oh, how big of you, Eddie. I hope you're real proud of yourself." She turned to Andrew and after wiping his face and hands she buttoned his coat.

"What are you doing?" Eddie asked, a jolt hitting the pit of his stomach.

"I'm taking Andrew home. I can't do this with you."

"Meaning?"

"Meaning, I don't want our son involved with a mobster."

Eddie pounded his fist on the table. Andrew jumped and then looked first at him and then at Monica. "I'm sorry, buddy," Eddie said.

Andrew pointed his finger at Eddie. "No more, Daddy."

Eddie wanted to melt at the sound of his son calling him daddy. "Okay, no more." He took a deep breath and focused on Monica. "Look, let's all calm down and talk things through."

"Are you kidding?" Monica said. "There is nothing to talk through. I guess you're back where you want to be. But until you somehow get out, I can't have Andrew anywhere near you."

"I was afraid you would say that. Please don't write me off, Monica. I love you and I love Andrew. I just want to be able to see both of you again."

Monica placed Andrew's wool cap on his head, then stood and took him out of the booster seat. "You just can't see it, can you?" A tear trailed down her cheek. "It amazes me how you manage to ruin everything all the time."

"Monica, wait. Don't go."

She grabbed her purse and took Andrew by the hand. "Do not contact me again, Eddie. I mean it."

Eddie's vision clouded. His jaw clenched tight, he got up, paid the check and followed Monica out of the restaurant.

Outside, the wind had picked up while flurries fell from a grey sky. He caught Monica's arm. "You can't keep my son from me, Monica. You know I'll always keep him safe. But he needs to know me and I need to know him, too."

She pulled her arm away and gave him a scathing look. "Say goodbye, Andrew."

Andrew stared up at Eddie. "Bye, Daddy."

Eddie crouched down before him. "I love you, Andrew," Eddie said. "Remember your Daddy loves you." He watched them walk away, his heart exploding inside his chest. No matter what, he would see his son again. And no one, not even Monica, was going to stop him.

Chapter 52 — Alexei
Roman & Emil

Alexei arrived at Tatiana with Rurik behind the wheel of the Chevy Suburban. The sun played hide-and-seek against a ghost-grey sky. He nodded to Rurik as the two climbed out of the car and went inside the club.

Several employees mopped floors while others wiped down tables and polished the brass railings near the stage. Voices came from the kitchen amid pots and silverware clanging. Alexei pushed open the swinging door, his eyes searching.

Ivan Petrov hurried over. "Is there something you need?"

"No," Alexei said. "I have called Roman to come here now. We will be in my private room. I do not wish to be disturbed."

"Of course," Ivan said. "I will make sure."

Alexei and Rurik settled themselves by the bar. Rurik poured a shot of vodka and handed it to Alexei. "I am sorry this needs to be taken care of. Young boys are often wild."

"Yes, and they need to be tamed," Alexei said. He downed the shot and set the glass aside. Focusing on the shipment coming in was priority now. Therefore, the matter at hand needed to be stricken off his list.

A knock sounded on the door. "Come," Alexei called.

Roman strode in all smiles. His jeans were neatly pressed, and he sported a new black wool winter coat, which Alexei was certain had been bought by Darya. He pointed to one of the chairs. "Sit down, Roman." His body stiff from trying to control his rage, Alexei dropped down into a chair across from his son while Rurik stood behind Roman's chair.

"Now, I want you to tell me all about this little shakedown you have going with your friends."

The smile vanishing from Roman's face, he tried to rise but Rurik pushed him back down onto the chair. "I don't know what you're talking about," Roman sputtered.

In a flash, Alexei rose. He towered over Roman and raised his arm. His open palm tore across Roman's left cheek.

Roman's head rolled to one side and he cried out. A large red blotch appeared where Alexei's blow had landed.

"Now, let's begin again," Alexei said, a false softness in his voice. "Tell me about the merchants you have been stealing from in my name."

Roman rubbed his cheek and his eyes watered. A shudder appeared to pass through him. He put up his hands defensively. "Okay, okay. I'll tell you," he cried.

Alexei lowered himself back into his chair. "Go on. Leave nothing out, or I will know you are lying again." He listened as Roman told him how he and his friends had threatened the store owners in exchange for money and how they used Alexei's name to sanction what they were doing.

"And?" Alexei said. He started to rise up again. "Is there anything else you are leaving out?"

Roman reared back. Tears rolling down his cheeks, he spoke about the day Artyom died. "We didn't mean for it to happen. He pulled a gun and he was going to shoot me, so Emil shot him first."

"So, are you trying to justify this man's murder by saying Emil saved your life?"

"Well … I … guess so," Roman stammered. "I mean he could've shot me first."

"Of all the things you have ever done, this by far is the worst. I am ashamed to call you my son. Using my name to back your treacherous dealings. Making people in this neighborhood think less of me. Do I not give you everything you want?"

Roman nodded. "Yes, of course. But we didn't mean to hurt anyone."

"Unfortunately, you did. My son, when those of you decide to play grown-up games then you will pay a grown-up price."

"What are you going to do?"

"Text your friend, Emil, and tell him to come and meet you here."

"But…"

"Do as I say. I will let Ivan know he is coming." Alexei got up and poured himself another shot of vodka. He needed to make sure Roman understood how serious the whole situation was.

Twenty minutes later, Ivan escorted Emil Kutuzov into Alexei's room, left and then closed the door.

Emil looked at Roman, then Alexei and Rurik. He started for the door but Rurik blocked his way. His face blanched a pasty white. "What's going on?"

"We are all going to take a little ride," Alexei said.

"Where to?" Emil asked.

Rurik grabbed his arm and pushed him out the side door and into the alley. "Never mind. Keep your mouth shut."

Alexei followed with Roman. They settled the young men in the rear of the SUV. With Rurik behind the wheel and Alexei in the passenger seat, they drove off. To ensure there would be no attempt to escape, Rurik hit the child door locks.

Without turning his head, Alexei said, "You need to settle in. We have a long ride ahead of us."

"But … I need to go home," Emil said. "My mother will be worried."

"Do not upset yourself, Emil," Alexei chided. "Your mother will be fine. I promise you."

Silence engulfed the long ride up to the Catskill Mountains. Alexei was glad for the peace and quiet, managing to close his eyes for part of the way.

By the time the car drove up the long gravel drive, a hazy winter sun prepared to dip below the horizon. Alexei ordered the boys out of the car and into the house.

"Where are we?" Emil asked Roman.

Roman shook his head. "I don't know. Just do as my father says."

In the sparse living room, they seated the boys in chairs across from one another. Rurik stood behind Emil's chair. Waiting for further instructions, he kept his eyes focused on Alexei.

"You know what this is about, Emil," Alexei said. "Do you remember the grocer, Artyom?"

"Oh, that," Emil said, looking relieved. "I saved your son's life, you know."

Blood rushed to Alexei's head. His vision blurred as adrenaline soared through his body. What was wrong with this boy? Thinking he could pull off an unsanctioned murder of an innocent man like it was nothing. Alexei went and stood behind Roman. His hands pressing down on the top of his shoulders, he nodded at Rurik.

Rurik pulled a length of wire from inside his coat pocket and quickly wrapped it around Emil's neck.

Emil's hands flew up. He grabbed at the wire, his eyes bulging, he choked out, "Please … I'm … I'm sorry." His feet kicked against the floor and then the bottom of the chair.

Roman gasped. He tried to get up but was pushed back down by Alexei. "*Tikhiy*," Alexei whispered in his ear. "Stay quiet. Not a word. You will sit and you will watch."

Rurik pulled the wire tighter. Emil continued to try and tear it from around his neck. It cut into his fingertips, causing them to bleed. Strange sounds emanated from his mouth as his struggling weakened. Urine stained the crotch of his pants. He let out one last breath. His body went still.

Rurik removed the wire. Emil's head flopped to one side. His eyes remained open in a death stare.

Alexei kept his hands pressed on Roman's trembling body. He leaned down and kissed the top of Roman's head. "There, there. Calm yourself. It is all over now. Rurik will take care of everything." He came from behind Roman's chair and helped him stand. He wiped the tears streaming down his son's face and pulled him close.

"We will never speak of this again," he said.

He led Roman out of the house, leaving Rurik with Emil's body. Roman remained stiff and silent by his father's side.

"Let us take a little walk down the drive while we wait for Rurik."

An hour later, he helped Roman into the SUV. After Rurik was seated behind the wheel, Alexei said, "Now, we must go home."

Chapter 53 — Kai
Keeping Secrets

While Tony ordered room service, Kai languished in the king size bed in his hotel room. She marveled at the opulence of her surroundings. Leave it to Tony, he never spared any expense. When she arrived late last night, their hunger for each other needed no words between them. Their bodies entwined, hands traveling over familiar territory, they tried to quiet the desperate longing inside them.

Tony set the receiver down and rolled over to face her. "I missed you so much," he said, pulling her closer. "I need you, Kai."

She stared into his dark eyes. "I need you, too," she whispered, planting a kiss on his lips. "I was so worried about you."

"I told you that wasn't necessary. I can take care of myself." His fingers swept over her necklace "What are these?"

"They're called Ghost Beads. My grandmother gave them to me."

"Hmm, sounds serious. What do they mean?"

"They're a form of protection."

"Oh, I get it. Like a good luck charm," Tony said.

"Something like that. They protect me from evil."

"I hope that doesn't include me."

"Stop. Don't say things like that." Kai threaded her fingers through his dark hair. "What happens now that you found Eddie?"

"Nothing immediate," Tony said. "But things will get settled sooner or later."

"Did you ask Eddie about the boy … Andrew? Is it his son?"

"Yes. Andrew is his. As a matter of fact, he had a little meeting with Monica. It didn't go too well. He's still mad about her leaving that photograph and then not expecting him to come looking for his son."

Kai's head swam. So, Monica knows Eddie is back. But of course, she didn't mention anything at the task force meetings. That can only mean one thing. She must be protecting Eddie because she is still in love with him.

"Hey," Tony said. "Where did you go?"

"What?"

"I was saying maybe we can go out tomorrow night. I'll take you someplace nice for dinner."

Kai pushed up against the pillows. "You know I can't do that, Tony. I need to be careful."

"I understand. But you would tell me if anything were going to jump off with the task force, right?"

"Don't ask me about anything related to my job." Kai got up from the bed. She grabbed Tony's dress shirt hanging on the back of a chair and slipped it on.

"But if you love me, you won't want anything bad to happen to me."

"If you don't do anything illegal then nothing will," Kai said, training her eyes on him. Adrenaline coursed through her. How could he put that kind of weight on her? She turned away and began gathering her things. "I think it's time for me to leave."

Tony jumped up from the bed. "Hey, slow down."

Ignoring him, Kai dressed, secured her Glock, and then picked up her purse. Things were getting too real between them. How foolish she had been to think falling in love with someone like Tony wouldn't jeopardize her job with the FBI. She walked to the door with Tony padding behind her.

"Why do you always run away, Kai?"

"I'm not running away. You knew before we even met that I worked for the Bureau. You admitted you planned everything. I made it clear I would not compromise my job any further for you. Giving you Eddie's whereabouts was enough."

Tony grabbed her arm. "I'm sorry. You're right. I shouldn't even ask you to do something like that."

"But you did," Kai said. "And you meant it. If I agree to give you intel, then it makes me…"

"What?" Tony's face reddened. A vein pulsed on the side of his forehead. "A criminal like me. Is that all you think I am?"

"Tell me, Tony, what else have you shown me so far? Your searching for Eddie, talking about Frank Uzelli, all of this can't be good."

Tony's hand dropped and he backed away. "Look, I love you more than anything in this world but I can't change who I am. You're going to have to decide whether you can accept that or not."

A million thoughts swirled inside her head at his words. Could she stand to lose him? What about her job at the Bureau which she had already risked once for him? "I need time to think," she said. Without looking back, she hurried out the door.

Later that evening, alone at home, Kai dialed Monica's number.

"Kai? Is something wrong," Monica's worried tone came through the line.

"I'm sorry to call you so late, but I need to talk to you. Can we meet somewhere tomorrow?"

"Meet somewhere? Why not at the Bureau?"

"No. I prefer not to meet there. Please, Monica."

"Sure, okay. Urban Backyard is close by. I'll see you there at 8:30 after I drop Andrew at day care."

"Thanks, Monica."

After nearly no sleep, Kai walked into Urban Backyard. The aroma of freshly roasted coffee hung in the air. Various plants lined the dark barn wood walls on both sides of the café, giving it an outdoor feel. Kai stepped up to the counter, where glass shelves showed off a variety of various pastries and fancy cupcakes. Slices of Banana Bread, Blueberry Lemon Loaf, and Almond Coconut loaf tempted her, but she opted for a plain buttered bagel and a Spiced Chai Latte.

Finding a quiet place in a corner, she sat and waited for Monica, while eating her bagel. Her decision to talk about seeing Eddie at Alexei Volkov's club hadn't come easy. But Tony telling her they had already met about Andrew cemented her decision.

Monica strode into the café, her black curls were bound up and tied at the nape of her neck. A red and green plaid scarf hung down the front of her woolen coat. She ordered an Americano coffee and then sat across from Kai.

"Why the urgency to meet?" she asked.

"Okay," Kai said. "I may get into trouble for this but I need to tell you there was someone else at Tatiana that I left out of the intel I reported."

Monica's eyebrow arched. "By the way, as I said before, you and Austin did outstanding undercover work. But why would you leave someone out?"

"Because the person I saw was Eddie Marconi." Kai waited for Monica's reaction. What must be going through her head after hearing this?

Monica sipped her Americano, her eyes studying Kai's face. "Leaving out information like that is wrong. We need to know who all the players are."

She's trying to steady herself, Kai thought. But the slight shake in her hand when she lifted her coffee cup gave things away. "Okay, Monica, let's be real. You knew Eddie was back in New York and out of witness protection, yet you never informed the task force. Why?"

Monica fell silent. She set her coffee down and stared at her. "What do you want from me Kai? Eddie is Andrew's father."

"I know," Kai said.

Color swarmed Monica's cheeks. "What do you mean, you know?"

"Let's just say I got the information from a good source."

"Who, Kai? Who gave you that information?"

"Tony Morello," Kai said.

Monica leaned back into the chair and shook her head. "Tony Morello is alive?"

"Yes. He's alive and well. He also told me about the photograph you left Eddie in Arizona. How were you able to do that, Monica? I mean, Eddie was in witness protection."

Monica grabbed her coffee and got up. "Don't think for one minute you can threaten me, Kai."

"Please sit down," Kai said. "I like you, Monica. You've been very good to me. I'm not threatening you. Let me tell you my side of things, and then if you still want to leave, then go."

Monica dropped down into the seat, an incredulous expression on her face.

Kai told her about Tony, how they met, what she found out after he confessed everything to her, and even the information she gave him about Eddie's whereabouts. "I know what I did was wrong, but what you did amounted to the same thing."

"But Kai, do you realize Eddie might still be in witness protection if you hadn't given Tony what he needed to find him?"

"I'm not so sure about that," Kai said. "According to Tony, Eddie was miserable in Arizona, missing you, and missing his son. It was only a matter of time before he returned to New York."

Monica stared down into her coffee cup. "Maybe," she said, her voice laced with sadness. "But now, he's all tangled up with the mob again. And probably Tony, too. That isn't the kind of life I want for my son's father."

"I know," Kai said. "But I wanted to bring this information to you first."

"And what about you and Tony?"

"I know the right thing to do, but I can't seem to let go of him, Monica. I thought you, more than anyone, would understand how I feel. But you must believe me when I say I will never give Tony any intel regarding our operations. I've made that clear to him. I won't jeopardize the Bureau. I gave him Eddie, and that's all I'm giving him."

"After everything you've told me, how can I trust you, Kai?"

"I promise, you can. If anything gets crazy, I'll come to you first. Who else knows Eddie is out of witness protection?"

"Bob Acosta, of course," Monica said. "The Marshall's Office informed him, and then he told me."

"Yeah, good old Bob," Kai snapped.

"What do you mean by that?"

"Oh, nothing much. It's just that after we broke up—"

"Broke up? Do you mean you and Bob had a relationship?" Monica said, her face stiff as iron.

"Yeah, but that's old news. He broke things off, and in the long run, I'm glad he did."

"But how, when?" Monica asked.

"Back in D.C. We got together whenever he flew in from New York. We lasted just over a year."

Monica got up. "I need to get to the office and take time to think about everything you've told me, Kai."

"I understand. I'm sure you know more than anyone what it is like when you love someone. I can't imagine having a kid thrown into the mix. I really am sorry, Monica."

Kai stared after her as she rushed to the door. Everything was out now. So, if Monica decided to come clean and tell Bob Acosta everything, she would deal with it head on.

Only Moncia would face her own consequences if she did.

Chapter 54 — Roman
Reality Settles In

Roman sat on the bench and waited for Damien. His nightmares were getting worse and worse. He couldn't erase the image of Emil's face as Rurik slowly choked the life out of him, the wire cutting deeper and deeper into his neck. The fear in Emil's eyes as he struggled to break free was almost more than he could bear. Not knowing what to do with it all, he had called Damien. They agreed to meet by the waterfront near Damien's apartment.

Roman observed the cars and trucks lumbering across the Verrazano Narrows Bridge, wishing he could climb into one and be whisked far away. A fishing boat passed with a flock of gulls squawking above it, hoping for scraps. The frigid wind raced across the water where foamy whitecaps swelled.

All those things people said about his father and how much they feared him were true. Roman now knew for sure it was the reason he and his friends had so easily persuaded the merchants to cooperate with their sting operation.

For as long as he could remember, his father had many businesses to run. The coming and going of men dressed in expensive suits, the closed-door meetings, who would have thought murder was included in all of it?

He got up as Damien approached. "So, why the urgent call to see me?" Damien's eyes swept over him. "You don't look so well. Sit down and talk to me."

Roman eased onto the bench again. He leaned forward, his head in his hands. "Something terrible has happened," he croaked. Tears flooded his eyes as Damien's arm came around his shoulders.

"What did you do now, Roman?"

Roman wiped his face and peered up at Damien. "No, not me. I didn't do anything. It was him. He had Emil killed right in front of me."

Damien drew back. "What are you talking about? You're not making any sense. Who had Emil killed?"

"Our … father. He had Rurik choke him with a wire, and now I can't sleep, I can't eat. Damien, please help me. I don't know what to do."

"Why would he do something like that? What aren't you telling me, Roman?"

Roman's chest heaved. He wiped his face again and then proceeded to tell Damien what he and his friends had been up to and how Artyom ended up dead at Emil's hand.

"My God, Roman! How could you be so stupid? Why would you even conceive of doing something like that?"

Roman shook his head back and forth, his tears coming again. "We never meant to hurt anyone."

"Our parents give you everything. Isn't it enough?"

"Please don't be mad at me, Damien."

Damien got up and went to the railing overlooking the water. Roman came and stood next to him. "Did you know?" he asked.

"Know what?"

"That our father did things like that?"

Damien shrugged. "There was always talk about him. Years ago, I used to hear it in school. Some of the kids wouldn't even be friends with me. They said their parents wouldn't allow it."

Roman fell silent for a moment. Damien knew more than he was willing to say. It showed in his demeanor, the way he avoided looking directly at him. "There is something else."

"What?" Damien's eyes remained focused on the water.

"Leonid. You know he's my godfather."

"Of course, I know that," Damien huffed. "What about him?"

"He's gone."

Damien's head whirled around, his eyes now focused on Roman's. "What do you mean gone?"

"He hasn't been around, and Rurik lives in his old apartment. He drives our father everywhere just like Leonid used to do."

"Look, Roman. You need to keep your head down. Go back to school and get a career so you can get out like I did. Otherwise…"

"Otherwise, what?"

"You will become just like him." Damien draped his arm around Roman. "You can change things for yourself if you really want to."

"But what do I do right now? I mean Emil's mother is looking for him. She keeps calling and asking me questions."

"You can't tell her anything. Just say you haven't seen him. Make up a story. The two of you had a falling out and don't hang around each other anymore."

"But—"

"But nothing, Roman. Be smart for once, and listen to everything I'm saying. I know this is hard. Probably the hardest thing you'll ever do."

Roman dipped his head and stared at the ground. Damien was right. If he didn't make a change, he would be trapped inside his father's web. He needed to find a way to accept what his father was capable of but also plan for a different future for himself. He admired his big brother and wanted nothing more than to show him he could do it.

The two stayed by the railing and stared out at the rough water. Whitecaps showed no mercy as they formed huge swells and crashed against the slick rocks below.

"I promise you I'll try, Damien," Roman said, knowing that just like those waves slamming against the rocks, the nightmare of Emil's death would stay with him forever.

272 | MOBBED UP II: RETURN TO NEW YORK

Chapter 55 — Bob
A Bad Mistake

Bob paced the length of his office. Something was very wrong with Monica, but he couldn't put his finger on it. She had put him off these past few nights, making all sorts of excuses as to why she couldn't see him. Always one to keep her feelings to herself, he was afraid to push lest it caused a rift between them. So, he decided to go the patient route, but his patience was waning. He cared for her more than she could ever imagine.

Under Monica's supervision the task force was making real progress. Her decision to press him on the court order and have TacOps place a listening device in Volkov's club could prove to be invaluable. That unit was the best at finding ways to get inside a place. Monica would have the transcripts from Quantico soon, and he was anxious to hear what intel might help them determine their next course of action.

Unable to concentrate, he decided to take a little walk down to Monica's office. He found her sitting behind her desk, green eyes focused on the computer screen. Her long dark curls framed her face while the white silk blouse flattered her complexion.

He tapped on the open door. "May I?" he asked. The light scent of her perfume drifted by.

Without looking away from the computer, she said, "Sure."

Bob closed the door and seated himself across from her desk. "How are things going? Any word from Quantico?"

"No, nothing yet," she said, studying the screen.

"Monica, can we talk?"

"About what?"

"Please stop whatever it is you're doing and look at me."

Monica turned away from the computer and rolled her chair back. "Okay, go ahead, talk," she said.

He was right all along. Something was terribly wrong. "Did I do something … I mean, these past few days, you seem so distant."

She folded her arms, her face a mask. "Aren't you the innocent one," she said, batting her eyelashes at him. "For starters, let's talk about how you lied to me."

His stomach tightened. Inside his head, a slight pounding presented itself. What was she talking about? "I don't know what you mean. I wouldn't—"

"Careful," she cut in. "Think really hard before you finish that sentence."

It came to him in a flash. How had she found out? Did Kai say something? They had both agreed never to discuss their relationship with anyone at the Bureau.

"Very quiet now, aren't we?" Monica snapped. "Kai Nez? Really?"

Bob got up and attempted to come around the other side of the desk.

"Don't even think about it." She pointed to the chair. "If I were you, I would sit back down."

His head swam. He had never experienced this side of Monica before. He retreated to the chair. "Can you at least let me explain a few things?"

"What is there to explain, Bob?" Her eyes bore into him. "I asked if you had ever dated anyone at the Bureau, and you explicitly told me no. Then I find out you not only dated someone at the Bureau, but you also picked that person to be on my task force. How could you do that?"

"Kai was picked on her own merits," Bob said. "You know she's good at her job, and her case work with the Bureau speaks for itself."

"So, your past relationship had nothing to do with selecting her?"

Bob shook his head. "I swear to you that had nothing to do with my choosing Kai. We had a brief relationship before I broke things off."

"How brief?"

"What?"

"You heard me. How brief a relationship? A couple of months?"

"Why are you pushing this thing so hard, Monica? It's not like I fell madly in love with her. Things just didn't click anymore between us. At least not for me."

"Just over a year. Am I correct? That's what you call a brief relationship?"

Every bone in his body told him she was slipping away. "Monica, please don't let this come between us."

"From now on, our relationship is strictly professional."

"Monica, come on. You're taking this too seriously."

"I don't think so. Who knows what else you'll lie about."

"Please, let me try and make it up to you."

"No, thanks. I'm too old for hide and seek. I don't want to be with someone who keeps me guessing. Now, I need to get back to work." She rolled her chair in and turned to her computer screen again.

"I know what's at the core of your anger," Bob said. "Eddie Marconi on the loose again has you not thinking clearly."

Monica stood up so abruptly her chair sailed back and hit the wall. "How dare you! Your lying has nothing to do with him. The least you can do is take responsibility for what you did and not blame it on Eddie."

His body flushed with shame. Why did he bring up Eddie Marconi? "I'm sorry. You're right. I shouldn't have said that."

Monica swept a hand through her hair and sighed. "Look, we still need to work together, but right now, I would appreciate you leaving my office. This whole thing between us was a bad idea to begin with."

Bob eased up and went to the door. "I'm sorry, Monica. Truly, I am." He stepped out and shut the door behind him. Why did he try to hide this thing between him and Kai? With her joining the task force, it was bound to come out. Women have different relationships with each other than men.

The best thing to do would be to back away. Give Monica time to sort out her feelings. Bob could tell there was no use in pursuing their relationship right now. He lumbered down the hallway and into his office. Standing by the floor to ceiling windows, he stared at the moving traffic below.

Would he ever be able to get her back? Only time would tell.

Chapter 56 — Monica
Hearing Eddie

Monica let out a long breath. Would anything in her life ever go right again? Her nerves were spent between finding out about Wanda Simmons, Eddie coming back, Kai and Tony Morello, and Bob's past relationship.

An alert flashed on her computer screen. There was a message coming in for her from Quantico over a secure server. She grabbed her cell phone and hurried out of the office. She took the elevator to the massive server room, where sensitive data was kept and backed up. Using her cell phone, she pulled up her QR code check-in to unlock the door.

Relieved when she found the room empty, she went to the appropriate server, punched in a code, and waited. With her information verified, the server would now send the encrypted documents to her computer where they would be run through a software program and be deciphered.

Palms sweaty, she rode the elevator back up to her office. What intel had the bug planted in Alexei Volkov's club produced? It was especially urgent that she read the transcripts before anyone else. According to Kai, Eddie had attended a meeting at Tatiana.

At Urban Backyard, she had been torn between leaping across the table and strangling Kai or thanking her for keeping Eddie out of the last briefing session. She reached her office, closed the door, and turned the lock. Back behind her desk, she pulled up the transcripts and ran the software. Her fingernails tapped the desktop while she anticipated what she might hear. How did Eddie end up in bed with Russian Bratva?

The software finished and she searched the transcripts for the appropriate date. She would listen to that one first. Opening her desk drawer, she pulled out a set of headphones and plugged them into her computer. She listened while following the transcript on the screen.

"Come in, gentlemen, and take a seat." (Voice believed to be that of Alexei Volkov) (A.V.)

"We're not gonna be staying long." (Voice believed to be that of Enzo Carbone) (E.C.)

"Why are you always in such a hurry?" (Voice believed to be that of Frank Uzelli) (F.U.)

"Unlike you, I have other business to attend to. By the way, where is Leonid?" (E.C.)

"Urgent family matters. He flew back to Russia for a time." (A.V.)

"That's too bad." (E.C.)

"Enzo, are you going to introduce me to your friend here?" (A.V.)

"Oh, sure thing. Paulie insisted I bring him in. This is Eddie Marconi." (E.C.)

"Good to meet you, Mr. Volkov." (Voice believed to be that of Edward Marconi) (E.M.)

Monica's breath caught. She clicked pause and sat back in her chair. Eddie was involved with some big players. But none of this made sense. He comes out of witness protection, tells Paul Martello some information and just like that, he's back in. If she was sure of anything, it was that Eddie would have to prove himself all over again somewhere down the line.

She resumed listening to the transcript. It appeared they had finally hit the jackpot. A shipment of some kind was due to come into the Jersey Seaport soon. Whatever was in that shipment had made partners of the Russians and the Italians. Several things came to her mind. Drugs, weapons, or stolen goods, like high-priced jewelry or art. Whatever it was, both sides found it necessary to use each other's resources. Since the Ukrainian War, the Russians were having a harder time transporting goods.

Monica listened to the rest of that evening's transcript and then went back and started from when TacOps had first placed the listening device. Almost two hours later, her heart lurched. She hit pause again and checked the date.

In this portion of the transcript, Alexei Volkov was reprimanding his son, Roman. Something about a shakedown he had going with his friends. At the sound of a loud crack, Monica shuddered. There was no mistaking that Volkov had hit the boy.

By the time Roman's friend Emil came into the mix, Monica's fears grew. Surely, Volkov wouldn't kill his son's friend. They were going for a ride. But to where?

She thought about Austin and what he had witnessed at the house in the Catskills. Monica hit stop this time and removed her headphones. Volkov was probably going to put a scare into those boys. She made some notes and stared at the name Artyom. This whole thing needed looking into. Picking up her phone, she asked Austin to come to her office.

Monica got up and unlocked her door just as he arrived. "Come in. I need you to look into something for me. I just got some of the transcripts from Alexei Volkov's club. In one of them, he reprimanded his son and one of his friends … something about a shakedown with the local merchants." Monica handed him her notes. Find out what you can. I only have a first name.

Austin read over her notes. "All this took place in the nightclub?"

"Yeah," Monica said. "But then Volkov and Rurik Bortnik took the boys and left. I have no idea what happened after that. All I know is Roman's friend Emil shot this person named Artyom. He claimed he did it to save Roman's life. See what you can dig up on all of this. Volkov was all fired up because the boys used his name."

"Sure," Austin said. "No worries." His brows drew together, and he shook his head. "I hope he didn't take those boys to the Catskill Mountains."

"I don't think Volkov would kill his own son," Monica said.

"It's not his son that worries me."

"You mean the other boy, Emil?"

"After what I saw that day, these people are capable of anything. It kinda fits in with something I've been following up on. You're telling me Rurik and not Leonid, the supposed Brigadier, was not involved in any of this?"

"Leonid was never mentioned on that transcript," Monica said. "But later, on another one, Volkov claims he left the country. Something about family. Only we have nothing from Homeland Security showing Leonid left the country."

"Remember the meeting I told you about. I'm positive a power play was going on, and I think Rurik Bortnik won."

"So, then," Monica said, her mind racing. "After all this time, Leonid is out."

Austin nodded. "Think Catskills, Monica. It's the only explanation for his sudden disappearance."

A chill marched down Monica's spine. "That graveyard is getting bigger by the day. Let me know what you find out as far as Volkov's son is concerned."

"Sure thing," Austin said. He got up and strode to the door. "Keeps me up at night thinking about that place." He gave her a quick wink and left.

Monica logged out of her computer. A throbbing ache clung to her forehead. The meeting Eddie attended was now official FBI evidence. She didn't dare conceal it and would make that perfectly clear to Kai.

But there was one thing she needed to do before letting the others on the task force have access to the transcripts. She picked up her cell phone and sent Eddie a text. '*If you want to see Andrew again, come to my place around 7:00 tonight.*'

Chapter 57 — Damien
My Father

Several hours before opening time, Damien strode into Tatiana. As Ivan Petrov rushed toward him, he plastered a fake smile on his face. He wasn't in any mood for pleasantries.

"It is so good to see you, Dr. Volkov," Ivan said. "How can I be of help?"

"Is my father here?"

"Yes, yes. Come with me. He is in his private room."

Ivan appeared to have little wings on the back of his shoes. Damien struggled to keep up with him as he followed behind. He tapped on the door and called out. "Dr. Volkov is here to see you."

The door swung open, and Alexei stepped aside. "Come, come. I am always happy to see you, my son."

Damien turned to thank Ivan, but the man had somehow disappeared.

"He is very quick, my Ivan," Alexei chuckled. His arm came around Damien's shoulders. "I cannot tell you enough how much this unexpected visit means to me." He went to the bar and held up a vodka bottle. "Drink?"

"Nyet, ni nada," Damien said before realizing he had slipped into his native tongue, something he hardly ever used.

Alexei poured himself a drink and pointed to the chairs. "Come sit. To what do I owe this visit from you? Is there something you need? Not on call on tonight, then?"

Damien shook his head. "No, I'm not." He studied his father as he swallowed the vodka in one gulp. Memories came flooding back when, as a child, Alexei would tell him he could not wait until Damien was old enough to drink a shot of vodka with him. All those cold, snowy nights, he would sit and tell stories of his boyhood. All of it false, of course. It didn't take long for Damien to realize how easily Alexei lied about certain things.

The comings and goings of certain men. The shouting behind a closed door. Someone pleading with Alexei about one thing or another. And yet, he owed this man so much. If his mother had not met Alexei, they would still be back in Russia.

He pictured Roman. His brother was not to blame for his behavior. He had learned from the best, from this man sitting right here across from him.

"Why are you so quiet?" Alexei asked. "Tell me what is going on?"

"Roman came to see me." Damien could not help but notice his father's expression turn sour.

Alexei waved his hand. "That boy is going to be the death of me."

"He told me what you had Rurik do. He told me about his friend Emil—"

"Enough!" Alexei's face flushed a deep red. "You do not know the whole story. This friend of his, this Emil, murdered one of the merchants. He talked your brother into doing terrible things. Roman needed—"

"Needed what?" Damien cut in. "To be taught a lesson? Hasn't he learned enough from you already? Why do you think Roman is the way he is?"

Alexei set his drink aside. He wagged his finger at Damien. "Careful, my son. You better tread lightly. Think before you speak any more of your ugly words to me."

Alexei got up. He picked up his glass and slammed it down on the bar. His back turned to Damien, he said. "Do you have any idea what kind of life you would be living right now if it hadn't been for me?"

"I'll always be grateful for everything you did for me and my mother, but forcing Roman to watch Rurik murder someone … I just can't wrap my head around it."

Alexei spun around to face him. "Then leave it alone, Damien. It is not for you to dissect. I have my own way of dealing with Roman. And yes, it is unfortunate your brother learns only the hard way. And this, right now, is a perfect example."

Damien shuddered inside. "What do you mean?"

"I told him not to speak of what happened ever again. What does the boy do? He goes running to you and spills his guts."

Damien stood up. "Roman is having nightmares over what you did. He will carry what he witnessed inside him forever."

"And so he should," Alexei said. "You see, my son, that is the whole point."

Damien went to the door. "I can't do this with you. I should have never come. Please don't tell Roman I was here. Leave him be. He's been through enough." Damien opened the door and stepped out.

"Wait. Before you leave," Alexei said. "Please do not hate me for what I did."

Damien turned and stared into his father's eyes. "Hate you? I could never hate you. From the time I was a child, and up until today, all I ever did was fear you." He hurried toward the exit without looking back.

Chapter 58 — Frank
Fallen

Frank drummed his fingers on the console between himself and Carlo, his driver. The meeting with Alexei Volkov had gone well last week, but he couldn't figure out how Sal's nephew was back in. The son of a bitch had ruined their whole operation. The bum was supposed to be in witness protection. Given strict orders by Paulie to keep his hands off Eddie, it took everything he had not to whip out his razor and slice him good.

"What's up, Frank?" Carlo asked. "You've been stewing for days."

"I just can't believe Paulie. He let Eddie Marconi back in? Why?"

"Well, I did some snooping on that very matter. It seems he uncovered a hit on Paulie and brought it to him. I heard three people got whacked."

"Who"

"Domenico, Willie, and Bruno. Seems they were going to push Domenico to the top."

Frank shook his head and let out a low whistle. "I never liked Domenico. I'm glad he's gone. As for Willie and Bruno, I guess they bet on the wrong horse."

"Pete ever find out anything about Tony Morello?"

"Naw," Frank huffed. "Seems he vanished off the face of the earth after Palm Springs. It just kills me to know the rat is out there spending my money."

"Do you think this thing with the Russians will put you in the black with the Commission?"

"No, but it helps. I'll have to pull in a lot more cash in order to make things right with them. It'll take time." Frank rubbed the dark stubble on his chin. "Now, if I could find Tony and get my money back…"

"Let me do some digging, boss. You never know what might turn up."

"Dig all you want," Frank said. "But I don't think you'll find him. I've had some of the best people looking for him."

The car swung into Frank's driveway in Jersey. He climbed out and went inside to his office. A few moments later, there was a light tap on his door. His wife, Antonia, stuck her head in.

"You're home early for once," she said.

"Yeah, home and a little hungry."

"Come into the kitchen. I'll fix you something."

Frank got up and followed her. He sat at the kitchen table and watched her prepare a heaping plate of sausage and peppers. She set it down along with two plates and chunks of bread.

He glanced around the small kitchen. Instead of a huge marble island, a small peninsula jutted out from under the dark wood cabinets. White appliances screamed at him. No stainless steel anywhere. How far he had fallen from their palatial home in Franklin Lakes. No longer able to afford the luxuries he once had, he downsized to this simple two-story frame house in a decent neighborhood.

He stared at Antonia sitting across from him. Her long raven hair was pulled into a ponytail. A simple white sweater cut low at the neck showed off her ample breasts. She had stuck by him, even when the money was gone.

"I'm sorry," he said.

She looked up from her plate. "For what?"

His appetite gone, Frank leaned back in his chair and spread out his arms. "All this. You deserve so much more."

"Don't be silly, she said, spearing a piece of sausage with her fork and placing it into her mouth. "We're fine, Frank."

"I promise you we will have everything again. I just need a little more time. You deserve to be in a big, beautiful house."

Antonia shook her head. "You worry too much about what we don't have. Concentrate on what we do have, Frank. At least you're not in jail. Where would me and the kids be then?"

He pictured his twins, Maria and Joseph. At age ten, they only needed video games, toys, and friends to play with. They had no idea how far down he'd fallen.

"Where are they?" Frank asked.

"Playing next door. They'll be home in a bit."

He leaned forward and reached for her hand. "Then we have time for something else?"

Antonia smiled and pointed to his plate. "Sure, eat first."

Later that night, Frank padded from the bedroom and down to his office. He plopped down behind his desk, took his cell phone out of his pajama pocket, and hit a number.

"Find that prick, Carlo. Find Tony Morello. My razor's getting rusty."

Chapter 59 — Monica
Eddie

Eddie kneeled by the bathtub as Andrew splashed in the water. Monica observed the joy on their faces as they played back and forth. Her son's laughter echoed through the room as Eddie poured water from a small bucket over Andrew's shoulders.

"Okay, you two," Monica said. "Time to get out, Andrew. Your fingertips are wrinkled like prunes." She lifted Andrew and wrapped a towel around him. "Come on, time for bed."

Eddie followed her into Andrew's room. A pale green covered the walls lined with train tracks, and small red locomotives wrapped around the space.

"I see he loves trains," Eddie said.

"Yeah, it's kind of his thing right now," Monica said as she slipped Andrew's pajamas on him. "Say goodnight, Andrew."

Eddie bent down to meet his eyes. He held out his arms. "Come here," he said. "Give me a hug and a kiss."

Andrew snuggled against him and kissed Eddie's cheek. "Good night, Daddy." He rubbed his eyes and asked, "Are you staying?"

"We'll see," Eddie said, glancing up at Monica who shook her head no.

After Andrew had settled in bed, Monica put the nightlight on and led Eddie out of the room, leaving the door ajar.

Back in the living room, she poured them each a glass of wine and dropped onto the sofa. "I love him to death," she said. "But sometimes he exhausts me."

"I get it," Eddie said, sitting on the opposite end of the sofa. "Having a kid is a lot of work, especially when you do it alone." He winked at her and sipped some wine. "So, why the sudden change of heart, Monica?"

"Who said anything about a change of heart?"

"The last time we saw each other, you were pretty upset."

"Listen, you know part of my job is to gather intelligence on the cases I work."

"Of course." Eddie's brow wrinkled, and he set the wine glass on the end table. "Are you asking me to be an asset again? Cause if so, the answer is a flat no."

"Eddie, you can't live the life you're living and get out alive. Eventually—"

"Don't go there, Monica. Just like you chose the Bureau over me, I'm choosing the mob." He got up and stood over her. "You're going to have to deal with it one way or the other."

She turned her head away. "I'd like you to leave now, Eddie. If that's your decision, we have nothing further to discuss."

"No. I'm not going anywhere." He reached down and pulled her to her feet. "His hand swept through her dark curls. "Do you have any idea how much I've missed you?"

Monica stared into his eyes. Her knees went weak, and she swayed a bit before he caught her and pulled her close. Eddie … I …"

His lips found hers, his tongue dipping deep inside. She melted into him and returned the kiss with the same urgency. His fingers skated down the nape of her neck. She uttered a breathless whisper, her heart commanding her not to stop.

Taking her hand, he led her into the bedroom. Silently, they stripped. He pushed her down onto the comforter. She arched her back as he trailed open-mouthed kisses from her lips and then along her breasts. He teased her nipples and then continued down to her navel. His hand dipped between her thighs, searching. Monica gasped. Her fingers raked through his hair, urging him on. When she was satisfied, he worked his way back up again. Her stomach quivered while her heart thumped hard and steady against his chest. She took pleasure in the warmth of his skin against her own. Her thighs parted, and he slipped inside her.

Their hips found a familiar rhythm. Her body filled with an overpowering desire. He drove deeper still until his body shuddered, and he called out her name. Monica held onto him, afraid to let go, before he finally let out a breath and dropped down beside her.

"Baby," he whispered. "You're amazing."

Monica inched up against the pillows, her hand resting lightly on his forehead. She wanted, no needed, this to happen between them. Her love and desire for him had lain sleeping for so long. But how could they continue? Knowing his voice was on those recordings was eating away at her.

Eddie turned his head and stared up at her. "So, now what?"

She moved away, got out of bed, and grabbed a robe from a hook on the back of the bedroom door. "I don't know, Eddie. I can't think straight."

'No worries, I won't push you." He proceeded to put on his clothes. "When can I see Andrew again? I mean, everything is good between us, right?" He reached into his back pocket and pulled out his wallet. Removing a stack of bills, he said, "Here, this is for Andrew. Use it towards his daycare or whatever else you need. I'll be giving you money each week."

"You don't need to do that," Monica said.

"Yes, I do. He's my son. So, like I said, when can I see Andrew again?"

Monica squeezed her eyes shut and then opened them. "Of course, I'll let you see him. You're his father. But I need to be careful. After all, I'm consorting with a known criminal."

"Is that what you think of me?"

"Oh, Eddie. Why do you have to make everything so hard? I mean … you waltz back into our lives, and I'm just supposed to accept what you're about to do?"

He crossed his arms and stepped back. "What do you mean by that? I haven't done anything."

"Yet," she said.

"Is there something you aren't telling me?"

Knowing she had almost blown it, she quickly shook her head. "No. It's just I know it's only a matter of time before you do." Her head ached, and she pressed her fingers to her temples. "By the way, how come you never mentioned Tony Morello?"

"Why would I mention him?"

"Because I know he went to Arizona to find you. Is he the one who convinced you to leave?"

Eddie's eyes widened. "Wait a minute. How do you know about Tony Morello?"

"We do get intel, you know," Monica huffed.

"This is getting quite interesting. Might I ask if you got your intel from someone named Kai Nez?"

She grabbed his hand and led him to the front door. "Let's call it a night. I'm tired and Andrew gets up early."

Eddie stopped short and pulled his hand away. "No, I don't think so. Answer the question, Monica."

"Yes, I know Kai. We're on the task force together."

"This gets better by the minute. Then, of course, you know, she gave Tony my information."

"Yes … but I …"

"Wow. She gave Tony information on how to find me, but I'm curious as to how you were able to leave that picture of Andrew in my mailbox. You don't work for the U.S. Marshals Service."

"I'm not discussing any of this with you."

"I'm not the one who brought it up. You mentioned Tony Morello first."

At this point, her head was pounding so hard she wanted to scream. She should have kept her mouth shut about Tony. Things were starting to go sideways. "Please leave, Eddie."

"Sure," he said, flashing her a smile. "We don't have to talk about all this tonight. I love you, Monica." He opened the door and went down the front steps whistling a tune. "Call me when you're ready for me to see Andrew."

She closed the door and leaned her back against it. What had she done? Tears stung her eyes as she slid down onto the floor. She let him into her life for the second time—only this time, he was squarely on the side of the mob. She could tell there was no way he would become an asset again. But no matter what, she couldn't let her feelings stand in the way of her job at the Bureau. Eddie made his decision, and in the long run he would have to suffer the consequences.

Chapter 60 — Kai
Grandmother

Kai rummaged through her purse in search of her keys. Wanting to get a head start on finishing the transcripts from Quantico, she decided to go into the office early. Just as her fingers struck gold and she pulled them out, her cell phone rang. Without glancing at the number, she answered.

"Kai." Secoya's voice had an unfamiliar urgency to it. "You need to come home now, today."

Kai set her purse on the counter. "What is it, Mother?"

"Your *shimá sání,* Aponti, is very sick. She began failing a few days ago."

"I'll catch a flight," Kai said and hung up. She immediately booked an airline ticket for a flight leaving in a couple of hours from JFK. Grabbing her overnight bag, she threw in basic necessities and several changes of clothes and headed for the airport. On the way, she texted Monica, letting her know where she would be.

Later, settled on the plane, she found it almost impossible to sit still. She ran a shaky hand through her hair and stared out the window. Please don't let her die before I get there, she silently begged. Remembering her broken promise to return soon, tears stung the corners of her eyes. Maybe her mother was right. It was always her work that she put before everything else.

It was early evening by the time she reached home. Her grandmother's brightly lit hogan spewed white smoke from its center. There were several cars parked beside it. Kai got out of her rental car and hurried over.

Inside, her grandmother lay on her bed in the corner of the room, surrounded by Secoya and two of Kai's aunts, Chepi and Ewa. Kai assessed the tiny, fragile figure. Her silver hair hung loose and fanned out across the pillow. Her grandmother had always appeared so strong until now. The apparent weight loss had hollowed her cheeks, making the bones appear more prominent, while her skin had become sallow.

They all looked up as Kai came toward the bed. After quick hugs with Chepi and Ewa, she asked, "How is she?"

"Fading," Ewa said. "She will leave us soon."

Kai shook her head. "What does the doctor say?"

"The cancer has been here for a long time, Kai," Secoya said. "She made me promise to let her die here in her hogan. She's on medicine to keep her comfortable."

Kai moved closer and knelt by the bed, her hand reaching for Aponti's. "Cancer? What are you talking about? She never said anything the last time I was here."

"Knowing your grandmother, she wouldn't," Chepi said, her silver and turquoise earrings catching the firelight.

"Grandmother," Kai said, gently squeezing her hand. "I'm here with you."

Aponti's eyes fluttered open, and a slow smile crossed her lips. "*Hágo.* Kai."

She swept her hand across Aponti's cheek and tried to smile back. "*Ayóó ánóshní.* I love you."

Aponti gave a slight nod. "Me, too, granddaughter," she whispered, her eyes closing again. Tears blurred Kai's vision as she felt the one person who meant everything to her slip away.

Early the next morning, with her aunts gone and her mother asleep, still dressed in pajamas, Kai went to her grandmother's hogan. She stepped through the doorway, the emptiness inside filling her soul. The body had been taken away to be prepared for burial in one of the small Navajo cemeteries. Memories flooding her mind, she went and sat down on the sofa. She could still smell the remnants of the fry bread her grandmother used to bake for her. Lowering her head, she wept for this loss that cut her so deeply. There were no words for how much her grandmother had affected her life. She turned and fingered the Navajo Chief's red and black blanket covering the back of the sofa.

"Beautiful, isn't it?"

Kai froze. That voice … his voice. She would know it anywhere. Slowly, she turned her head towards the door. He was almost the same as she remembered him. Much older but with the same evil glint in his eyes.

"Aren't you going to say hello to your Uncle Tokala?"

Kai eased up off the sofa. "I have nothing to say to you. You spoil my grandmother's memory and this hogan just by coming inside it."

His face grew sour, and he stepped closer. "She was my mother!" he snapped. "You think she loved you more than her own children?"

Wishing for a weapon, Kai's eyes searched the room. How could this be happening? Her monster was back once again. "Don't come any closer," she warned.

"Why not?" He took another step forward. "What are you going to do? You know you liked what I did to you all those years ago. Come," he beckoned. "Let's see if we can have some more fun, Kai." Beads of sweat formed on his forehead as he leered at her. His tongue darted in and out from between his lips.

Kai's body shook. Her heart thundered inside her chest and roared in her ears. A weight pressed against her chest, and she struggled to take in air. Before she could react, he sprung forward, pushing her down onto the sofa. He grabbed her wrists in one hand and held her arms over her head. His entire body weight came down on top of her.

"Get off of me, you son of a bitch!" Kai screamed. She could smell the alcohol on his breath and heard his heavy grunting sounds in her ear. His free hand tore at her pajama top, searching for her breasts.

"No, no, no," she cried. It was happening all over again. She felt her mind drifting away like it used to all those years ago when she was a child. Away from him, away from the pain.

Chapter 61 — Austin
Missing

Austin parked in front of the two-story brick home, proceeded up the front steps and rang the bell. The door swung open, and a woman who appeared to be in her mid to late forties appeared. Her eyes were red and puffy as if she had been crying. Her dark hair, streaked with grey, was pulled back away from her face.

"Can I help you?" she asked in a thick Russian accent.

Austin pulled out his badge. "Special Agent, Austin Faulkner. Are you Mrs. Kutuzov?"

She gave a slight nod. "Yes. What do you want?"

"Are you Emil Kutuzov's mother?"

Her hand flew to her chest, and she reared back. "Yes. Has something happened to Emil? Do you know where he is?"

"I'm not sure," Austin said. "May I come in?"

"Yes, yes, please come in." She stepped away from the door, and Austin followed her inside to a small living room. She pointed to a grey sectional. "Please sit."

It hadn't taken Austin long to find where Emil lived. Everyone in the neighborhood seemed to know him. Some of them spoke with disdain about the young man who was a known troublemaker.

"When was the last time you saw Emil?" Austin asked, pulling out a small pad and pen.

Tears flooding her eyes, she reached for a box of tissues standing on an end table. "I'm sorry," she said, wiping her eyes.

"It's okay. Take your time."

"It has been more than a week since he has come home. I have asked his friends and no one seems to know where he is. You are from the FBI?"

"Yes."

"I do not understand. Why is the FBI asking about my son?"

Austin drew in a breath. He couldn't reveal too much at this point. This woman could reach out to Alexei Volkov if he told her everything they knew so far.

"Well, I was handling another investigation in the area and someone mentioned that you were looking for your son. I thought maybe I could help."

"That is very kind of you. His absence worries me because one of his best friends is Roman Volkov, the son of Alexei Volkov. The father has a reputation in the neighborhood." She wiped her eyes again and fell silent a moment.

"What kind of reputation?" Austin asked.

"He has a nickname. They call him, The Volk."

"The Volk? What does that mean?"

"The Wolf," she said, her bottom lip trembling. "I've heard things about him. Not very nice things."

"Who else did Emil hang out with?"

Her face softened for a moment. "Luka Nikitin. He is a nice boy. Always polite when he comes into my home."

"Do you know where he lives?"

"Sure, sure, just two houses down the street. The house with the red door. But I have already spoken to him. He claims he does not know anything about where Emil might be."

Austin rose from the sofa and pulled out one of his cards and handed it to her. "If you hear from Emil, please let me know. In the meantime, if I find out anything, I'll contact you."

She got up and followed him to the door. "Thank you for coming to see me. I feel better knowing the FBI has taken an interest."

Outside, Austin walked up the street to Luka Nikitin's house. He rang the bell and waited. Heavy footsteps could be heard on the other side of the door before it swung open. A young man, broad shouldered and well over six feet tall with shaggy brown hair appeared. His heavy brows formed a perfect arch across his forehead.

"Can I help you?" he asked.

"Are you, Luka Nikitin?"

The young man eyed him a moment and then shook his head. "Yes."

Austin pulled out his badge again and introduced himself. "I would like to talk to you about Emil Kutuzov."

"What about him?"

"May I come in a moment?"

"My parents are not at home. I'm not sure if I should be talking to you without them here."

"Look, you're not in any trouble. I just talked to Emil's mother and she mentioned that you're a good friend of Emil's. You know he's missing, right?"

"Missing? I'm not sure about that. I just haven't seen him lately." He stepped aside and led Austin into a dining room to the left of the foyer. He pointed to a chair and then sat opposite of Austin. "What do you want to know?"

"Would there be any reason for Emil to be in trouble with Alexei Volkov?" Austin watched him grow visibly uncomfortable, swiping a hand through his hair and shifting his body slightly.

"What makes you think that?" Luka asked, staring down at the table, his finger rubbing a small spot.

"I'm not going to assume anything, Luka. I need you to tell me what you think might have happened to Emil."

"I … I don't know. Maybe he went away somewhere."

Austin appraised the fear in Luka's eyes. He definitely knew something. Deciding to take a stab at what the transcripts had revealed he said, "We know about your little sting operation, Luka."

Luka's head jerked up. "You said I wasn't in any trouble."

"You're not. I just need you to tell me what happened. Tell me about Artyom."

Luka squeezed his eyes shut. "It should not have happened. Emil took things too far. He shot the grocer because he aimed a gun at Roman Volkov. He probably did it to scare us. I don't think Artyom would have killed Roman."

"Did Alexei Volkov have any part in all of this?"

Luka shook his head. "No. We used his name to scare the store owners and we kept the money for ourselves."

"So, if he found out, what do you think he would do?"

Beads of sweat broke out across Luka's forehead. He stared at Austin. "Do you think that's why Emil is missing?"

"I'm not sure. But if I were you, Luka, I would be very careful. From what I understand Alexei Volkov is not a person you want to mess with." Austin got up. "You take care, Luka."

Back outside, Austin headed for his car. He was sure more than ever that Emil Kutuzov was dead—his grave behind a house in the Catskills.

Chapter 62 — Kai
The Rez

Kai's chest heaved. Suffocating under his weight, she struggled to break free. Tokala tore at her pajama top, until the buttons gave way. His dark eyes trained on hers, his face full of fury. She shifted, her knee aiming for his groin. He let out a howl but refused to get off of her. His hand traveled down while the other one held her wrists together. Panting, he pulled at her pajama bottoms and tried to force her legs apart.

"Get off of her, you son of a bitch!" The sound of a shotgun racking filled the hogan. "I said, get off of her!"

Tokala's heavy breath fanned her face. He let go of Kai's wrists and eased up. Hands in the air, he turned and faced Secoya. He let out a laugh and pointed his finger. "What do you think you're gonna do with that, little sister?"

"What I should have done years ago," Secoya spat.

Tokala took a step forward. "Why would you say that. You liked it when I use to crawl into your bed."

"No, you're wrong. I was too young and too afraid to stop you. Then you did to my daughter what you used to do to me. I held everything inside. I couldn't face the shame of having a predator for a brother. Neither could our parents. Mother tried, but Father always stopped her. He didn't want our tribe to know, so he shielded you until Mother made him take you and leave. He beat her that day, but she never gave in. By then, the damage was done to all of us."

Kai sat up. She could hardly believe what she was hearing. This man, this monster had done things to her mother. She had always wondered why Aponti never spoke of her grandfather after he left. He too, knew all along and only wanted to save face.

Tears traveled down Secoya's cheeks. "I'm sorry, Kai. I should have protected you from him."

Tokala took another step. "Come on, put down the gun, Secoya. Let's talk this out. We're family after all. Kai is fine, and you're fine. There's no need to be angry."

"Fine!" Secoya screamed, her face filled with rage, the gun still trained on her brother. "Nobody is fine, Tokala. I've suffered along with my sisters and Kai has suffered way too long. You tried to ruin me and then you went after my daughter. I was too afraid to help her back then, but not anymore."

"Sister, please. Let's sit and talk."

"There is nothing to talk about." Secoya stepped back and pulled the trigger. Tokala's body jerked, the blast from the shotgun lifting him up and sending him backward where he fell to the floor. Bright red seeped from the center of his chest. His eyes were wide open in a death stare.

Kai froze. She looked from her mother to her dead uncle lying on the floor. How many times had she wished for him to die? Too many. Now, he lay still. Her monster was finally dead.

No questions were asked later that day when they held Aponti's funeral. The man who had caused so much pain was buried behind the hogan with the blessing of Chepi and Ewa. Kai could only imagine how her mother and her sisters had suffered.

She thought about Aponti, held in check for years by her grandfather until she finally stood up to him and made him take her uncle and leave.

It was early evening by the time she packed her overnight bag and got ready to go. This place where she had endured such abuse could never really be called home. But the Rez no longer threatened her sanity. She would try to remember only the places that made her happy. Memories of days spent playing on its grasslands, walking through its forests, mesas, and canyons with its domes of red and orange rocks helped replace the terror that had consumed her.

Her memories of Aponti would always be with her. The grandmother who loved her and nurtured her. Who taught her so much about herself and the peace she still needed to find out there, away from the Rez.

She took her overnight bag and stepped outside. Smoke poured out from the roof of her grandmother's hogan. A single lantern stood lit in one of the windows. Kai set her bag down and walked toward it. She inhaled the scent of the creosote and found comfort instead of fear.

Secoya came out of the hogan. She held out the Navajo Chief's red and black blanket.

"She would want you to have this."

Kai took the blanket and pressed it close to her chest. "I'll always cherish it. Thank you, Mother."

"*Ayóó ánóshní*, Kai, Secoya whispered. "Always remember that."

"I love you, too," Kai said.

Chapter 63 — Monica
Fixing Wanda

With the task force gathered in the conference room, Monica wanted to be sure they had listened to the transcripts. If anyone was surprised about hearing Eddie, so far, no one let on. The date for the shipment was near and she wanted to be sure the task force would be ready to act. They had received another transcript from a meeting between Frank Uzelli and Alexei Volkov. They now knew what was in the shipment and where it was going.

"We know weapons are in this shipment," Monica said. "The partnership between the Russians and the Italian Mafia means the Russians are using them to get it to the Mexican Cartels. They're transporting the weapons to the border between El Paso and Ciudad Juarez. We want them for not only obtaining illegal weapons but trafficking, too."

"Yeah," Austin said. "I think this is going to prove to be a big bust."

"Would you update everyone on your assessment of some of the other things we learned from the transcripts?" Monica asked.

"Sure." Austin proceeded to tell them about his meeting with Emil Kutuzov's mother and Luka Nikitin. "I'm pretty certain Volkov had Emil killed."

"And once the arrests are over, we'll get a court order to dig up the place in the Catskills," Monica said. "There should be enough evidence there to bring Volkov up on murder charges."

"There are some interesting players," Bob said. "We got Frank Uzelli and Eddie Marconi back in the mix."

"My C.I. was right," Austin said. "Guess the contract on Uzelli did get canceled."

"For now," Monica said trying not to flinch at the mention of Eddie's name. "You'd be surprised at how fast that could change."

"Didn't Eddie Marconi leave witness protection?" Wanda asked.

"Yes," Bob said. "We just can't figure out why the mob would let him back in."

Monica avoided looking at Bob. Truth be told, even she didn't know the real reason they let Eddie in. Seeing how good Eddie was with Andrew and making love with him again was clouding her judgement. She didn't want anything to happen to him. The love she still felt for him was permanent. It would never go away. The only question now was how much she was willing to sacrifice to protect him.

With a blueprint of the seaport spread out on the table, they went over their positions and explored different scenarios in case things didn't go according to plan.

"When the shipment comes in, we need to wait to see who it's handed off to," Monica said. "Let them feel safe. Later, we arrest the remaining suspects and then follow the shipment to the Mexican Border. Are there any questions?"

"I think that's it," Bob said. "We'll meet one last time the day before the shipments due."

As the group dispersed, Bob nodded at Monica. "Wanda," Monica said. "Could you stay back please."

"Sure," Wanda said, dropping back down into her seat.

With the room cleared, Monica closed the door and sat across from Wanda. "Remember when I asked you about Tatiana, Volkov's club?"

A slight blush crept up Wanda's face. "Sure, I told you I had never been there but that I had heard of it."

"Are you sure you don't want to change that story?" Monica asked.

Wanda folded her arms and leaned back into her chair. "Why would I?"

"Does the name Richard Walsh mean anything to you?" Bob asked.

"Of course. We worked together on a case here in New York. I was really surprised when I found out he was in with the mob."

"I bet you were," Monica said rising out of her seat. "Wanda, I think it's time you came clean."

Wanda dropped her arms. She looked at Bob. "What the hell is going on here?"

Monica reached down into a folder and pulled out a sheet of paper. "Were you and Detective Walsh having an affair?"

Wanda's face went from pink to bright red. "So, what if we did. People have affairs all the time. Besides, it didn't last very long. It's not like it's a crime."

"Yeah, you're right," Monica said. "It's not a crime. But what is a crime is putting the life of an FBI agent in jeopardy."

Wanda's eyes bore into Monica's. "I have no idea what you're talking about."

Monica set the sheet of paper down in front of her. "This is a statement from one Detective Brian Reynolds from the 121st Precinct on Staten Island. He claims that Detective Walsh told him you gave him my name when I was working on the Salvatore Marconi case."

Wanda pushed her chair back and got up. "That's ridiculous. Besides it's his word against mine."

"Oh, I don't think so," Bob said. "We matched his phone records with yours and so we know you were still in communication with him back in Washington."

The door to the conference room opened and two male agents stepped inside. "I believe you need to go with these gentlemen, Wanda. I hope you find a good lawyer," Monica said.

"You haven't got a case against me. Just because I was talking to Richie doesn't mean I gave him any information about you, Monica."

"Well, that's where you're wrong," Monica said. "You made one mistake. Calls from the forensics lab are recorded on a periodic basis. It just so happens we got you giving Richie my last name. You put my life in jeopardy, Wanda. Things could have turned out very badly."

"But I didn't know he was working with Salvatore Marconi," Wanda said, her voice breaking. "I would have never given him your name if I had known that."

"But you did. Like I said, I hope you find a good lawyer. You're going to need one."

Monica watched the agents lead Wanda away. She turned to Bob. "Thanks for helping me out on this one."

"Any time," Bob said. "Look, I hope you'll reconsider our relationship. Give me a chance to make it up to you."

Monica shook her head. "You're a decent guy. I'm way past being angry with you. But right now, I just need to be by myself."

"Are you sure about that?"

"Perfectly. Is there something else you want to say?"

"Look, I know Eddie was at your place."

Monica shot him a look. "Are you spying on me?"

"No. Not on purpose. I came by your place because I was upset about how things ended between us. I saw Eddie go inside." Bob frowned. "Monica, are you willing to risk your career for him?"

"Of course not. You have to understand. He's Andrew's father and he has the right to see him. So far, Eddie hasn't done anything wrong. If he took me to court, he would win visitation."

"So far, being the operative word," Bob said. "Be careful, Monica. We know Eddie is involved with the mob again. Don't put yourself between them and him. It won't end well for either of you. If you ever reconsider your feelings, I'll be around." Bob got up and left the room.

Monica eased down into a chair. She meant what she said to Bob. Right now, more than anything else, she needed space. Being with Eddie had been a mistake. It only made her more confused and hurt. Soon, he would be swept up in a raid. He would probably never forgive her but he chose his path and now she would choose hers.

Chapter 64 — Eddie
Tony Gets the Green Light

Just after noon, Eddie and Tony entered La Vito Vino, Paulie's restaurant in Little Italy. The aroma of red gravy hung in the air. Waiters hurried from table to table setting down drinks on white tablecloths along with plates of pasta for the lunch crowd. Sinatra tunes emanated from the speakers. They proceeded to a private dining room in the rear. Paulie, already seated, beckoned to them. "Come, sit. We need to talk about a few things."

Eddie sat across from Paulie while Tony took a seat to his right. "Nice place," Tony said. "The food smells good."

Paulie puffed out his chest and grinned. "Everything here is top notch. I make sure of that." He nodded at one of the waiters who hustled into the kitchen and returned with plates of clams oreganata. He set them down in the center of the table. He hurried away again only to return with a bottle of red wine. Pouring them each a glass, he bowed and said, "Let me know when you're ready for the next course."

The three men each placed clams on their plates and dug in. Eddie savored the texture and taste of the rubbery clams. The seasoning was just right. "These are great, Paulie. I haven't had any in a very long time."

"*Mangiare,*" Paulie said, smiling. "Eat up while we talk some business." He slipped a clam into his mouth and swallowed. "Look, the deal we have with the Russians is about to go down."

"I'm aware," Eddie said. "After the shipment comes in, Frank is supposed to get it to the Mexican Border."

"That's what I want to talk to you two about. Eddie will accompany Frank to the border to make sure the goods and the money change hands." He nodded at Tony. "That's where you come in. Once that deal is done, Frank is yours. You do whatever you want with him."

Eddie stared at Tony who pumped his fist and slapped the table. "Finally. I've been waiting a long time for this, Paulie."

"I know. Just make sure you do the job right. I don't want to hear Frank got the better of you." He wagged his finger at Tony. "No slip ups. I don't want to have to call Rocco Fischetti in on this."

"You don't have to worry. Frank will be out of the picture for good."

Paulie signaled the waiter, who disappeared into the kitchen again. When he returned to the table, he set down plates of Veal Milanese and sides of pasta before retreating again.

"When all of this is over, there's gonna be major changes. If you both do good, you'll be rewarded. The Commission is on board. They expect things to go smooth," Paulie said.

"Sure, Paulie," Eddie said. "Everything will go the way it's supposed to."

Later, back in Eddie's hotel room, he and Tony sat sipping beers. Paulie's last words on his mind, Eddie said, "What do you think he meant by major changes?"

"Not sure," Tony said taking a swig of beer. "But once you start eliminating people, others get the chance to move up the ranks."

"With Domenico and two others out, plus Frank, this could be good for us," Eddie said.

"Yeah. I've been thinking about you accompanying Frank to sell the guns. That will be the perfect time to get rid of him."

Eddie eyed him. "What do you mean?"

"You have all the information for the cartel, right?"

"Yeah, Paulie insisted just in case."

Well, let's say I lag behind a bit and then catch up. You're bound to make a stop somewhere."

"Probably. It's a long way to the border, a day and a half at least."

"I just need to know the route you're taking."

"So, you're gonna finish him after he finishes the deal?"

"Frank's not going to get rid of the guns, we are."

"Wait a minute. Are you saying we meet with the cartel?"

"Why not? Where I kill Frank doesn't matter so long as I get to do it."

"That could be dangerous. Frank's connection doesn't know us."

"All the cartel is interested in is getting the weapons. We'll be honest with them. Let them know Frank is no longer in the game. They understand things like that. Frank's gone, Paulie gets his money and everybody is happy."

"Sounds okay," Eddie said. "You work out the details and let me know."

Eddie sipped his beer and fell silent. His thoughts turned to Monica and Andrew. He had wanted to go back in, couldn't deal much longer with his life in Arizona, but could all of this cause him to lose his son? Monica would never be happy with him so long as he was a part of the mob.

"How are things going with Monica?" Tony asked. "You must be over the moon after seeing your son again."

"Yeah, I was just thinking about that. Things are okay right now, but Monica made it pretty clear that my leaving witness protection is not sitting well with her."

"Regardless. Andrew's your son and he should always be a part of your life, no matter what."

Eddie finished the last of his beer and set the bottle aside. "By the way, she mentioned you and wanted to know why I haven't."

Tony grinned. "Must have been Kai that told her about me."

"But why would she do that?"

"I think it's tit for tat, if you know what I mean. Kai gave me information I should never have had and she knows about Monica leaving that picture in your mailbox. They both could be in hot water if anyone at the Bureau finds out."

"I don't like the idea of Kai holding that over Monica's head."

"Nothing to be done about it. Kai knows what she's doing. Basically, now they have to protect each other." Tony got up and went to the window. His back to Eddie," he said, "We need them in that position. It makes their relationship stronger and protects us."

"I guess," Eddie said. "But I know for sure, Monica isn't happy about that."

After Tony left, Eddie lay on the bed, hands resting behind his head. Everything seemed to happen so fast once they arrived in New York. He pictured Monica as they made love the other night. He ached to be with her all the time. Ached to be with Andrew. But deep in his heart, he had to accept the knowledge Monica would always choose the Bureau over him. Their lives remained separate from one another so long as she valued that more than making them a family. Eddie sighed. His eyes heavy and his heart in turmoil he drifted off to sleep, hoping that nothing went wrong these next few days with Frank and Tony."

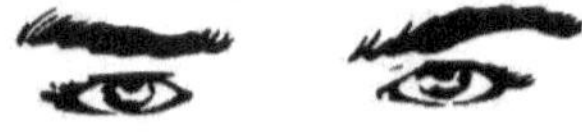

Chapter 65 — Roman
Luka

Roman checked his cell phone again. Besides texting, Luka had left several messages to call him. Ever since Emil's murder, he had been avoiding Luka. Deciding not to put it off any longer he made the call.

"Luka, why are you calling and texting like crazy?"

"Where have you been?" Luka yelled. "Why are you avoiding me?"

"I'm not avoiding you. I just wanted a little break."

"Do you know Emil is missing?"

Roman gripped the phone. The last thing he wanted to do was talk about Emil. "I heard. But you know how he his. Emil always likes to do his own thing."

"I want you to meet me, Roman."

"What for?"

"There are things we need to talk about. There was an FBI agent at my house today."

Something in the pit of Roman's stomach told him that couldn't be good. Why was an FBI agent snooping around? "What did he want?"

"He knew, Roman. He … knew about our little operation."

"But how could he know anything?"

"Look, meet me at the old terminal and I'll tell you what he said."

Roman hesitated. He really didn't want to see Luka, but if he refused, Luka would only push harder. "No, not there. It reminds me of Amy." Wanting to get it over with, he said, "Meet me down by the waterfront, near the Verrazzano-Narrows Bridge. See you there in an hour."

Roman drove to the waterfront and parked. A bitter wind blasted across the water leaving the parking lot deserted on such a cold day. Memories of his talk with Damien flooded his mind. He stopped short of walking over to one of the benches. Instead, he leaned against the BMW and waited for Luka's car to arrive. An uneasy feeling shook him to his core. Luka had mentioned the FBI. If they knew so much about what the three of them had done, why didn't they arrest them?

None of it made sense. With Emil gone that left him and Luka holding the bag. What if the FBI came looking for him, too? He would fall apart if they asked him about Emil. His nightmares had not ceased to haunt him.

He turned at the sound of a car pulling into the lot. Luka got out and lumbered toward him. "Let's go down by the water."

"*Nyet*," Roman said. "It's too cold."

Luka glanced around. "Okay, we can stay here."

"So, what is this about an FBI agent?"

Luka let out a breath and paced. "He said he knew about Artyom and our little operation."

"And what did you tell him, Luka?"

Luka's face turned ashen. He stopped pacing and spread out his hands. "I was honest. I didn't want to get into trouble. I told him Emil protected you."

Roman stared at him in disbelief. "You idiot!" he shouted. "Why would you admit to anything? You should have told him you didn't know what he was talking about."

"I was scared. He mentioned your father and wanted to know if he knew."

"My father?" Roman's gut twisted. If any of this got back to him regarding the FBI, he couldn't imagine what he might do.

"Yes," Luka said. "But I told him your father didn't know what we were doing … that we only used his name."

Roman crossed his arms and leaned against the BMW again. This conversation with Luka was making him sick inside. All he wanted to do was forget everything he had done in the past. Start over like he promised Damien he would.

"What happened to Emil?" Luka asked. "I'm sure you know something."

Roman shook his head. "Why do you think I know anything about Emil?"

Luka moved closer, his hand retrieving a gun from his jacket pocket. He pointed it at Roman. "You stop lying, Roman," Luka said between clenched teeth. "You tell me right now what happened to Emil."

Roman tried to smile. "Come on, put that thing away. Don't be stupid Luka. You're not going to shoot me."

"If you don't tell me right now what happened to Emil, I will use this," Luka said waving the gun at Roman.

Roman broke out in a cold sweat. He had never seen Luka like this before. At this very moment, he believed Luka would use the gun on him. "Okay, okay. First you put the gun away and I'll tell you."

Luka lowered the gun and slipped it back into his pocket. "Start talking, Roman."

Little by little, forcing the words out, Roman told him about Emil and how he died at Rurik's hands. "There was nothing I could do!" Roman shouted. "It was awful. I can hardly sleep or eat. I dream about it constantly."

Tears poured down Luka's face. "How could you not save him? Why did you let him die?"

"You don't understand. There was nothing I could do."

"You could have begged your father for his life." Luka pulled out the gun again.

"No," Roman said, his eyes trained on the gun. "You don't know my father. I was helpless. I couldn't stop it."

"And what about me?" Luka shouted. "Am I next? Will your father come after me now?"

"It's over and done with. He won't come after you. I promise. Please put the gun away, Luka."

"You'll be the only one standing when he finishes with me. Of course, the son of the Wolf will get away with everything while his friends die."

"That's not true, Luka. I wouldn't lie to you."

"I'm sorry, Roman."

Luka pulled the trigger twice. White hot heat seared Roman's insides. Blood seeped through his shirt. Roman grabbed his chest. His knees buckled and he sank to the ground. The image of Luka standing over him faded as he heard a third shot and then lay still.

Chapter 66 — Monica
The Raid

With the shipment in port and awaiting possession, Monica, Bob, and Kai, plus a swat team of FBI agents, took their positions inside a shipping container on the perimeter. Radio contact with Austin, who lay on top of a container stacked three stories high, allowed them to know when to strike. He had spotted Alexei Volkov, Rurik Bortnik, and Enzo Carbone earlier. Now, they waited to see who else would arrive.

Monica prayed Eddie would not appear. But after listening to the transcripts, her hope was futile. Eddie was definitely involved in this crime. To have to arrest the father of her child would be devastating. Even worse was how to tell Andrew when he was older.

There had been no further discussion between her and Kai about Tony or Eddie. It was as if both understood the consequences of what was about to take place.

Austin's voice burst into her earpiece. "Frank Uzelli is approaching driving a white van."

"Okay, we wait to see who they hand off to," Monica replied into her two-way radio. "If he takes the goods, we leave him alone and arrest the others after he's gone. Make sure you get clear pictures."

"Will do," Austin said.

Minutes ticked by. Monica's heart ramped up, beating wildly against her chest. She wiped her brow and adjusted her heavy bullet proof vest. No sign of Eddie? It didn't make sense. He should be here with the rest of them.

Austin's voice came over the radio again. "Cargo being removed from the container. Several heavy crates loaded into the van. Pictures taken and sent to you with license plate number."

"Let me know when Uzelli leaves," Monica said. "Keep eyes on him."

"Okay, the van is pulling out," Austin said. Minutes ticked by before Monica heard him say, "Uzelli is a good distance away. But … holy shit! Where did he come from?"

"Austin, what's going on? Who are you talking about?" Monica snapped.

"Tell swat to go," Austin said. "There's a fourth suspect on the scene. He's aiming a gun at Enzo Carbone."

Monica gave the order as gunfire erupted outside. The container flew open and they all poured out with their weapons drawn. They surrounded Alexei Volkov who stood stock still with his hands in the air, a look of shock on his face. Rurik Bortnik immediately dropped his weapon and also raised his hands in surrender. Enzo Carbone lay dead on the ground. Another body lay a foot from his.

"Austin, where are you!" Monica shouted into her radio.

"Coming to you now," Austin said.

Monica turned and watched Austin climb down from the containers. He hurried over to her, his face pale and sweaty. "It seems Enzo here was destined for a bullet," Austin said. "The mob must have sent the other guy lying over there to take him out. He has a bullet wound to the head, courtesy of me."

Monica and Bob bent over the other man. "Well, look who we have here," Bob said. "He's on the FBI's most wanted list. It's none other than Roco Fischetti, hitman for the mob."

Bob nodded at Austin. "Do you know how long we've been looking for this guy? He killed an undercover FBI agent and many others who worked for the mob."

Austin shook his head. "Only problem is I couldn't get to him before he got to Enzo Carbone."

"Although we would have liked to see him and Enzo on trial, it's no great loss," Monica said. "Great work today, Austin."

"At least we have Alexei Volkov and his sidekick," Kai said. "I'll call in forensics."

Monica gestured to the swat team. "Take those two clowns away." She turned to Austin. "You'll need to be debriefed and stay on scene until forensics arrives."

"No problem," Austin said.

Alexei Volkov, hands cuffed, and pushed forward by a member of the swat team, eyed her. "You will be sorry for this. I have done nothing wrong."

"We'll see," Monica said. "You'll have your day in court. And by the way, we know about your burial ground up in the Catskills." She caught the slight twitch beneath his right eye.

"I have no idea what you are talking about," he spat.

"I think you know all too well. Get him out of here," Monica said.

An hour later, with the crime scene secured, Monica, Kai, and Bob settled themselves on a jet at Newark Airport. They would fly to El Paso and meet up with FBI and Border Agents awaiting Frank Uzelli's arrival with the weapons.

While Bob made phone calls to update his superiors at the rear of the plane, Monica seated at the other end, sipped coffee, her mind still alert after today's events. Eddie was nowhere to be found at the seaport. She couldn't wrap her head around that. Could the mob have pulled him out at the last minute?

"Monica, I think we need to talk," Kai said, sitting across from her. "I was sure Eddie and maybe even Tony would be there at the seaport."

"Eddie, yes," Monica said. "But Tony and Frank don't mix. I can't see them working together on this."

Kai stared out of the window. "I guess so. But…"

Monica let out a deep sigh. She really didn't feel like talking about Eddie or Tony right now. There could be a hundred reasons why neither one was at the seaport. "But what? Do you know something you're not telling me?"

"Of course not," Kai said quickly. "I told you I wouldn't jeopardize the Bureau and I meant it. I made it clear to Tony, too. Things didn't end well the last time I saw him."

"I don't know if I should say I'm sorry about that," Monica said. "You need to break away from him, Kai. My situation is a bit different from yours. Eddie and I have a child together. As long as he's out there, free, I know he'll be in Andrew's life."

"And if he ends up in jail?" Kai asked.

"I'll have to deal with that. But just like you, I won't jeopardize my career for him. Now, I suggest we both catch some sleep. It's been a long day and we have a lot ahead of us when Frank Uzelli arrives at the border some time tomorrow."

Kai nodded and closed her eyes. A few minutes later, Monica watched the rise and fall of her chest. Her beautiful face so serene and relaxed. If only she would listen and stay away from Tony Morello. A feeling of shame washed over. She was no one to give Kai advice when, in her heart, she had no idea how to give up Eddie Marconi.

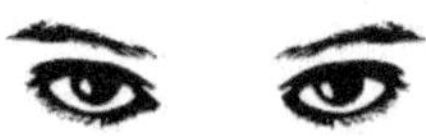

Chapter 67 — Damien
Roman

Having just finished his last surgery for the day, Damien prepared to leave the hospital. Down the corridor from the Emergency Room, he heard the wailing of ambulance sirens. Tired, but always dedicated, he hurried to the triage area to see if he could help.

Damien nodded at Dr. Wallace. "What's coming in?" he asked.

"Gunshot wound to the chest. Another one has a gunshot wound to the head. I think that one is already gone."

Within minutes, the ambulance arrived and the EMT's removed a stretcher, while a second ambulance pulled in alongside and did the same.

Damien hurried over as the first gunshot victim was removed from the stretcher and onto a bed. Nurses and E.R. doctors took vital signs and assessed the wounds.

"This one is crashing," Dr. Wallace said.

Damien stood in the doorway watching as Dr. Wallace and another doctor tried to revive the patient. The ding of a flat line could be heard on the heart monitor machine. He couldn't get a clear view of the face until one of the nurses moved away from the bed.

Damien surged forward. It couldn't be. He pushed one of the nurses out of the way.

"That's my brother," Damien said, his voice breaking. "That's my brother."

"Dr Volkov!" Dr. Wallace shouted. "What are you doing. Stand back."

"You need to leave now," Dr. Wallace said. "We're doing everything we can to try and save him. He has two bullet wounds in his chest. You're well aware of hospital policy. Please step away!"

One of the male nurses grabbed Damien's arm in an attempt to remove him from the room. He shook loose and came toward the bed again. "Please let me help. That's my brother."

"Do I have to call security?" Dr. Wallace said. "I understand, but you know what the protocol is. I'm asking you for the last time, leave now." He turned away as the second doctor prepared to shock Roman's heart again.

"We have a pulse," Dr. Wallace said. "Let's get him to the O.R."

Damien watched helplessly as they sailed past him toward a bank of elevators. He rushed to keep up with them catching only glimpses of Roman's pale face. The elevator doors opened and Roman was wheeled inside.

Damien went to step into the elevator. Dr. Wallace shook his head as the elevator doors closed leaving Damien, tears streaming down his face, standing all alone. His stomach twisting into knots, he pulled out his cell phone.

"Mother, you need to come to the hospital right away. Roman's been hurt."

"What do you mean? Is he alright? What happened?"

"There is no time to explain. Come right now." Damien hung up the phone and made his way up to the waiting room. Thankful it was empty, he plopped down into one of the chairs. Head in his hands, he stared down at the floor, the agony of not being able to help save Roman killing him inside.

Thoughts of their last conversation played in his head. Was Roman a victim or did he get himself involved in something more sinister?

"Dr. Volkov?"

Damien raised his head. A man in a suit and tie stood before him holding out a badge. "Yes, that's me."

"I'm Detective Martin from the 110th Precinct. I understand from one of the nurses that Roman Volkov is your brother?"

Damien nodded. "Do you know what happened?"

"It appears to be an attempted murder suicide. We believe the second man shot himself in the head after shooting your brother."

"Why would anyone do such a thing. Who is this other man?"

"His name is Luka Nikitin."

Damien rose from the chair. "That's impossible. They were good friends."

"Apparently something happened between them. We're certain Luka was the shooter in this case. Do you have any idea why they might have had a falling out?"

Of course he knew. This all went back to his father. Either Luka found out about Emil's murder somehow or Roman told him. There was no other explanation for this sudden rage. But he couldn't tell this police officer any of that.

"No," he said. "I have no idea. All I ever knew was that they were friends."

"I know this is a terrible time. I may need to talk to you again. I'll be in touch."

Damien sank back down into the chair as the detective stepped inside the elevator. He kept his eyes trained on the long hallway leading to the O.R. Roman must not die. He had so much life ahead of him.

The doors swung open. Dr. Wallace came toward him. Even from here, Damien could see his brother's blood on his scrubs.

"I'm sorry," Dr. Volkov. We did everything we could. He lost a lot of blood and the bullets did too much damage."

Damien's comprehension stopped at the words, I'm sorry. The rest was just gibberish. He got up and faced Dr. Wallace. "I need to see him."

"Of course. But wait until we prepare the body. You don't want to see him like this." Dr. Wallace sighed. "You do know, since this is now a homicide, the coroner will have to take custody of the body."

Damien nodded. "Yes. I'll wait here. I just need to see him one last time."

Dr. Wallace turned and trekked back up the hallway just as the elevator doors opened and Darya rushed out.

"Where is he?" she cried. "Where is my Roman?"

Damien held out his arms. "I'm sorry, Roman is gone. There is nothing more to be done."

Darya backed away. "No … no … do not say that. You were supposed to save him. You're a doctor after all. Why didn't you save him?" she screamed.

Damien reached and grabbed her shoulders, forcing her into his arms as she wept. His fingertip lifting her chin, he stared into his mother's tear-filled eyes. "He couldn't be saved. Roman was past saving a long time ago. We will go and see him together."

His cell phone buzzed. He led Darya over to a chair before answering.

His father's voice came through the line. "Damien, I need you to do something for me. I've been arrested. Nothing serious but I am going to need you to call my lawyer. His name is Michael Powers. Can you take down his number?"

Damien couldn't believe what he was hearing. He glanced at Darya, still weeping, her chest heaving in and out. Dare he tell his father about Roman now? He wouldn't be of any use, locked up in jail. No, this was not the right time—something like this needed to be done in person.

"Okay, give me the number," Damien said and entered it into his cell phone.

"Please do not say anything to your mother or Roman. I will handle things."

The call ended and Damien stared at his mother. Their family now in ruins. Roman dead, his father arrested. His body trembled as he eased down beside Darya. Where would all of this lead them? How could anything so broken ever be put back together again?

Chapter 68 — Monica
The Border

Restless from hours of waiting in a vehicle by her station near the border, Monica got out and paced with a radio transmitter in her hand. There had been no sightings of Frank's van by the many agents on watch, which made her question the intel they had received. The transcripts were clear about the time and location, and yet her gut was telling her something had changed. She checked the time again and was thankful Cookie agreed to pick Andrew up from daycare and keep him overnight.

"What do you think happened?" Kai asked, exiting the car and coming toward her. "Frank should be here by now. There's no sign of any of the cartel, either."

"Maybe the mob got tipped off somehow." Monica tried to silence the warning inside her. "Kai … you didn't—"

"Don't even go there, Monica. I told you I would never do anything to jeopardize the work the task force is doing. Besides, just like you, I only know what was said on the transcripts. I haven't even spoken to Tony in a good while and even if I did, he would never reveal anything to me."

"Sorry, but I had to ask," Monica said. "Eddie never said anything, either." Monica dropped down onto a flat rock on top of the desert sand. It was late afternoon, at the height of the day's heat. Her eyes scanned the sparsely vegetated surroundings. "This whole situation is crazy," she said. "Here we are two FBI agents with lousy intel, both of us not wanting to admit we're worried about the criminals we fell in love with."

Kai plopped down next to her. "I know," she said quietly. "What are we going to do? I mean neither of us is willing to give up the FBI. How can we make any of this work?"

Monica shook her head. "We can't. It comes down to deciding. The FBI or the man."

Bob Acosta's voice came over the radio. "Monica, there's been a development. Drive up to the meeting point and I'll fill you in."

"Leaving now," Monica said.

She returned to the car with Kai and they sped off. Neither one spoke as clouds of dust flew up behind them obscuring the rear view. Hands gripping the wheel, her mind spun off in several different directions. Was this about Eddie or Tony? Did they spot Frank somewhere miles down along the border?

When they reached Bob standing with several other agents, she couldn't get out of the car fast enough. "What's going on?" she asked.

Kai came up behind her. "Is there any word on Frank Uzelli?"

"Well," Bob said. "I'm not sure what's going on but Frank's empty van was found in a diner parking lot about 50 miles from here. Frank's cell phone was found inside. It could tell us what his last communication was. One of the waitresses at the diner gave a good description of Frank and another man. Eddie Marconi appears to have been with him."

Monica went weak inside. An empty van, no sign of either one. Had the mob gone through with their contracts on Frank and Eddie?

"There's something else," Bob said, his eyes focused on Monica. "Blood stains were found on the blacktop near the van. Forensics is there doing what they can, but with all this heat, I'm not sure how much we're going to get."

"No sign of anyone else?" Kai asked.

"No. I wish that rinky dink diner would have had cameras in the lot," Bob said. "At least this tells us why Frank never showed up."

"It may also tell us something about the cartel," Monica said. "They either changed the plan and did away with Frank and Eddie, or the mob stepped in."

"Unfortunately, I was thinking the same thing. Sometimes contracts never go away. We need to head back to New York and wait for forensics."

The group of agents dispersed. Kai took the keys from Monica and got into the car while Monica stayed with Bob. "I guess we'll find out what happened eventually," she said.

Bob reached out and touched her arm. "Are you going to be alright?"

"I'm fine. I warned Eddie about getting back in bed with the mob. Nothing good could come of it. I'll see you back at headquarters in New York." She made her way over to the car. Of course she wasn't alright. Frank and Eddie missing. Bloodstains near the van. It could only mean one thing.

With Kai now behind the wheel, they drove toward the airport. Monica leaned back against the headrest and closed her eyes. How could she continue to live in this world knowing Eddie was probably dead? Andrew had just started to bond with him. The pure joy on his face when he looked at Eddie almost made up for his long absence. And then there was the night she finally gave in to what her heart wanted and needed. Wrapping her arms around Eddie again, and making love, only proved to show their connection was still so strong.

"Monica," Kai said. "Is there anything I can do?"

"No. But I appreciate your asking."

Kai pulled to the side of the highway and stopped. "Look, if you say it's okay, I can reach out to Tony. Maybe he knows something."

Monica opened her eyes and stared at Kai. "Even if he knew, he wouldn't tell you. That's how things work in the mob. If a contract goes through, it's over and done. And since we haven't any clue as to what is going on, we can't reach out to Eddie or Tony. It could put the Bureau in an awkward position if anyone higher up in the mob found out about us."

"Do you really think they had Frank and Eddie killed?"

"Things are looking that way. Now, please, no more talk about this. Let's get to the airport."

"There is one thing I haven't told you regarding Tony. You know about his history with Frank Uzelli."

"Boy do I," Monica said. "That man sliced Tony up good. Twice."

"I believe Tony was out for revenge. The way he talked about the past and all the things Frank made him do, besides cutting him so badly."

"But Tony isn't even mentioned anywhere in the transcripts."

"Exactly," Kai said. "Maybe he wasn't mentioned because Frank Uzelli was unaware he was even around."

Monica sat straight up. She peered out at the sun's rays as they glanced off the hood of the car. Her eyes burned and her head ached from the day's events. "That means," she said. "Frank had no idea about a possible hit on him with regards to Tony."

"I mean the empty van, the blood stains, all point to something awful," Kai said. "But that doesn't mean anything happened to Eddie."

"I don't know, Kai. It's a stretch. Right now, there's no sign of either one of them."

Kai swung the car back out onto the highway. "It was just a thought."

Later, back in New York, they stopped by headquarters. Bob Acosta rushed toward them as they stepped out of the elevator.

"I got the warrants to search Volkov's place in the Catskills. Tomorrow, the four of us will be taking a ride up there. It should be interesting to see what we find. I've already let Austin know. He's been debriefed. His kill shot was justified with regards to Rocco Fischetti. Let's meet here in the morning and we'll helicopter out and meet the forensics team at the property.

It was well after 10 o'clock when Monica reached home. After shedding her clothes, laden with desert dust, she showered and fell into bed. Just the thought of food made her stomach cinch. She lay awake unable to turn off the day's events.

Reaching for her cell phone, she checked her messages. Nothing from Eddie. "Damn it, where the heck are you?" she blurted out. If she didn't hear something soon, she might go mad. She needed to know for sure if Eddie was still alive.

Monica switched on the light and sat up against the pillows. Against her better judgement, she grabbed her cell again and typed. *'Are you okay?'*

Her eyes focused on the screen, waiting for the little ghost bubble to appear before a response. Minutes ticked by, but the screen remained empty. She stayed that way, dozing on and off for the rest of the night.

Chapter 69 — Alexei
Locked Up

Alexei cursed and paced in his cell at the Metropolitan Correctional Center in Lower Manhattan. Everything had happened so fast. One minute they were loading the weapons into Frank's van and the next, all hell broke loose. Enzo was killed by some man Alexei had never encountered before and then the man himself was shot by an FBI agent.

At first, he couldn't comprehend how all of this had come about. Where was the leak? Certainly, none of his people would have had the nerve to work with the FBI. But then, his lawyer, Michael Powers, had come to the jail during the initial arrest and interrogation. They were told the FBI had planted a bug inside his office. But how, and when? The whole matter was so unbelievable. Still, he denied knowing what was inside the crates at the seaport. He surmised the FBI could more than likely prove otherwise.

Alexei stopped his pacing, his eyes focused on his surroundings. Three sides of concrete walls stared back at him, one with a small window that barely let in any decent amount of light. There was a metal cot, sink, and toilet. The fourth wall held a metal door with a tiny window for the guards to see in and a slot for meal trays. An overhead fluorescent light emitted a constant buzzing noise. The pungent odor of some type of antiseptic filled his nostrils.

His eyes dropped to the uncomfortable orange jumpsuit he was forced to wear, another thing used to humiliate him.

For the first time in his life, he had been caged like an animal. Like his father all those years ago, if convicted, he now faced the possibility of life in prison. His thoughts turned to Rurik. He made sure to have his attorney defend him also. Leaving Rurik out in the cold could cause him to strike a deal with the government.

Alexei jumped at the sudden loud rap on the metal door. A bolt turned, the door opened and one of the guards appeared.

"You have a visitor," he said. He anchored a waist chain around Alexei and then cuffed his hands to it. Outside, he led him down to a corridor and into a large room with a line of windows. He directed Alexei to one of the chairs. His heart thumped when he saw Damien on the other side. His eyes were puffy and red. For sure he had been crying.

Alexei sat and picked up the receiver from the phone hanging by the wall while Damien did the same on the other side of the glass.

"You did not have to come here," Alexei said. "My lawyer is taking care of things. I have a hearing tomorrow. I will get bail and then be home soon."

"No, I had to come," Damien said. "There is something you need to know. It wouldn't be right if I didn't come here to tell you myself."

"If you came here to chastise me, then I would rather go back to my cell." He watched a tear erupt from Damien's eye and travel down his cheek. Had his being arrested upset him so much that it made him cry?

"It's … it's about Roman," Damien said, his voice cracking. "He's dead."

He must have heard Damien wrong. "Dead? What are you talking about. How can he be dead?"

"He was shot earlier today. They brought him to my hospital. But the bullet wounds had done too much damage."

The air around Alexei thinned. His body broke out in a sweat. A sick feeling welled up inside him. His heart rate accelerated while his pulse slammed in his ears. "How did this happen?"

"Luka Nikitin. He shot Roman and then killed himself."

Alexei bowed his head, his shoulders shook and his chest heaved as he tried not to lose control in front of Damien. "Why would Luka do such a thing?"

"All this is because of you," Damien spat, wiping his face. "You know very well how upset Roman was. I told you when I came to see you. But you insisted your way was the only way. I hope you're happy."

"Damien, please understand I was only trying to—"

"What!" Damien yelled. "Teach him a lesson. Well, guess what? Your lesson time is over and done for good. I hope you rot in here for the rest of your life." Damien slammed the phone back into the cradle and got up.

"Wait, please tell me about your mother. How is Darya?"

Damien shook his head, and turned and walked out of the visitor's room.

Alexei slowly hung up the phone. He rose as the guard came to return him to his cell. His eyes blurred, the long corridor appearing to swallow up everything around him.

Alone again, he dropped down onto his cot. The pain over the news he had received almost too much to bear, he wrapped his arms around his body and rocked back and forth. "Roman, Roman, Roman, my poor boy, my poor boy," he cried. "I am so sorry." Tears burst forth and dripped down onto his lap. He had no memory of when or if he had ever cried before today.

His thoughts turned to Darya, all alone and hurting without him. He had no idea how much Damien would tell her. If she knew what he had done to Roman, she would never forgive him.

Alexei pictured Roman's face, the fright in his eyes as he watched Emil die. This was to be part of his last thoughts at the end of his life. And then, to die so violently himself. Yes, Damien was right to hate him. He did not deserve his love anymore.

Alexei raised his head and stared at the far wall. Like his father before him, he was destined to remain incarcerated for the rest of his life.

A sudden calm washed over him. "I will do it for Roman," he whispered. Tomorrow, he would let his lawyer know he intended to plead guilty.

Chapter 70 — Eddie
Time's Up

Eddie kept alert as he drove the van down the highway. Careful to stay within the speed limit and not draw any attention, he anticipated what was up ahead. It had taken Tony a long time to catch up with Frank. He remembered how this man sitting next to him had sliced Tony's neck. His skin crawled just thinking about it. Eddie didn't blame Tony one bit for what he was about to do.

Adjusting his sunglasses, he checked the time, while Frank dozed beside him in the passenger seat. Leaving New York at noon after Frank picked him up at the hotel, they had traveled through the night only stopping for gas and quick snacks before resuming the drive. Eddie hoped they would reach Texas by nightfall. The plan as Tony told him was to get Frank to stop a couple of hours from the border for a regular meal.

He thought about Monica. They hadn't spoken since the night they made love. He longed to see her and Andrew again, hold her in his arms and promise to be a good father to his son.

Knowing Tony wasn't far behind them in a dark blue van, he glanced in the rearview mirror. This thing between these two men needed to end and soon.

Frank opened his eyes and stretched. "I can't wait to get rid of this load. It always makes me a little nervous. Too bad we can't fly back. No way we could get through the airport with all the cash."

"Right, Frank," Eddie said. The man had no clue as to what was about to happen.

"Look, I hate to harbor any bad feelings but I'll never understand why you turned on your Uncle Sal like you did. I mean, him being a blood relative and all."

"It was easy once I found out he and my Uncle Lorenzo killed my parents."

"You're joking, right?"

"No, Frank. That's nothing to joke about. It happened."

Frank let out a low whistle. "I never took Sal to be that way. That's a shame. Maybe I would have done the same thing if it happened to me."

They continued on for hours, sharing the driving, with Frank now behind the wheel. It was just after 8:00 p.m. when they crossed over into Texas.

"Look," Eddie said. "I'm tired of eating gas station food. Can we pull over for a real meal?"

"I don't like stopping at restaurants when I have a load in the van."

"There's a sign blinking off the main road up ahead. It must be a diner. Come on, Frank, I need to eat."

"Okay, stop yapping. We have hours to go before the meeting. I guess it'll be okay."

Frank exited off the highway and down a single-lane road. A red neon sign flashed announcing Sally's Diner. He pulled into the lot where a couple of other cars were parked. They got out, went inside, and slipped into a booth facing the parking lot. Eddie glanced around. This far out on the highway and with the late hour, only two other people perched on stools at the long counter. The smell of meat sizzling on a grill made Eddie's stomach growl. He actually could go for a burger.

"I gotta take a piss," Frank said, getting up. "Order me that ribeye special they got posted. Medium rare."

"Sure, Frank," Eddie said. He waited until Frank disappeared into the men's room. A slim, red-headed waitress came and took the order, her big brown eyes sending signals Eddie had no interest in. After she left, he pulled out his cell phone and called Tony.

"How far away are you?"

"I see a red sign up ahead."

"Yeah. We're sitting in a diner. Frank's in the bathroom."

"Perfect. I'll be waiting."

Eddie ended the call just as Frank slid back into the booth. "You talking to someone?"

"Yeah. Just saying goodnight to my little boy. I haven't seen him in a while."

"That's too bad," Frank said. "I know how it feels to miss them. They grow up fast, though."

The waitress set their meals down. Eddie stared at the burger, his gut turning sour. Of course, Frank would have to mention his kids.

"I thought you were hungry," Frank growled as he cut into his steak. "Eat up because we're not staying long."

Eddie bit into his burger. He couldn't let on how he was feeling. With each swallow, his stomach grew tighter. This whole thing had to work the way Tony said it would. Once Frank was out of the picture, they would deliver the guns, collect the money, and head back to New York.

Frank's cell phone buzzed. He set his knife and fork down and retrieved the phone from inside his jacket.

"Hey, Carlo. What's going on?"

Eddie took note of the strange look on Frank's face. He leaned back into the booth. His eyes appeared to glaze over—a sure sign of temper. Eddie sensed something was wrong.

"Sure, I get it," Frank said. "No, it's okay. I'll take care of it."

With Frank's clipped responses, Eddie could only imagine what the call was about. Maybe someone in Frank's crew had done something wrong.

As Frank ended the call, the waitress appeared. By this time, they were the only customers left in the place. "Sorry, gentlemen. Closing time in ten minutes."

"No problem," Frank said, picking up his utensils again. "We're almost done." He gestured at Eddie with his knife. "Eat up. We got to get going anyway."

Eddie finished the last of his burger and then swallowed down his coke. They rose at the same time and exited the diner. The night air, muggy and thicker than New York, engulfed them. Texas was about to head into spring. In the unlit parking lot, the night sky blanketed with stars seemed to go on forever. A pale moon moved between a few passing clouds. Before they reached the van, Frank pulled out a pack of cigarettes and lit one.

"Give me a minute," he said. "I just need a smoke."

Eddie turned as the lit diner sign went black, followed by the lights inside. The waitress and cook appeared, got into their respective vehicles, and pulled away. With no other cars in sight, Eddie grew wary. Where the hell was Tony?

Frank finished his cigarette, tossed it onto the ground, and crushed it with his shoe. He moved closer to Eddie. His arm came around and rested on his shoulders. "So, I just got some news, and I'm in shock."

"You mean the phone call?" Eddie asked, gooseflesh breaking out on his arms. He didn't like the feel of Frank's arm pressing down on his shoulders.

"Yeah, a little birdy told me that you and Tony Morello have been hanging out together back in New York."

Caught off guard, Eddie's heart beat at a dizzying pace. His hands clenched and unclenched at his sides. "I have no idea who told you that, but the last time I saw Tony, he was lying in a hospital bed with his throat cut."

"No," Frank said, his arm squeezing Eddie's shoulders hard. "You're lying. I think you know exactly where Tony is, and you're going to tell me right now or else—"

"I'm right here, Frank." Tony stepped out of the shadows from behind the van.

At the sound of Tony's voice, Eddie elbowed Frank in the chest and broke free. Frank stumbled backward against the van. His hand dove inside his jacket and reappeared, holding the Dovo Bismarck Razor. His nostrils flared, air pumping in and out. He turned and faced Tony. "I got this one especially for you." He waved his arm, the blade glinting in the moonlight. "You think you can steal from me and get away with it!" Frank screamed. "No one takes what is mine, you little prick."

Tony's hand came up. He aimed his 9mm with a silencer attached at Frank. A wicked gleam in his eye, he said, "Oh, but I did take your money, Frank. I took every last bit of it."

Frank stared at Tony's face and then at the gun. "You're nothing but a punk."

To Eddie's horror, Tony tossed the gun aside. He watched it slide across the asphalt and land a few feet away.

"There," Tony said. "Now we can fight fair. That ought to make you feel better. Only there's no one here to hold me down while you slice into me like that first time."

Frank growled. He rushed at Tony, the blade held high in his hand. Tony took a quick sidestep. Frank wobbled past him, almost losing his balance. Tony grinned, removed his jacket, and tossed it down.

"Come on, Frank," Tony said, waving his hands. "Come and get me."

Frank rushed at him again, the blade held high above his head. "You son of a bitch!"

Tony pivoted. His leg sprang upwards. The heel of his shoe slammed into Frank's chest, sending him sprawling backward onto the asphalt. The razor flew from Frank's hand, landing a few feet away. Eddie scooped it up.

"Give it here," Tony said between clenched teeth.

"Just do it quick," Eddie said. "Use your gun."

Tony shook his head. "No. I waited too long for this. Give me the razor."

Frank tried to scramble to his feet, but not quick enough. Tony kicked him in the chest again. Frank yelled and fell back down.

Eddie tossed the razor to Tony and then retrieved the gun. After what Frank had done to him, he couldn't really blame Tony. He couldn't imagine the agony of having someone slice you open.

With the razor in his hand, Tony stood over Frank, who lay almost breathless on the ground. His chest heaved. Sweat gleamed across his forehead. He raised his arms in a defensive mode. "Okay, enough," Frank whimpered. "You can keep the money. I don't care about it anymore."

Tony shook his head. "How sweet, Frank. You're giving me permission. Did you think I was going to give it back?"

Tony's hand came down, the razor glinting in the moonlight. It tore first across Frank's left arm, slicing through his jacket. He howled and grabbed his arm, leaving his face exposed. Tony drove the razor down the center of Frank's face, splitting his nose and lips wide open. Blood poured from his forehead and down the length of his face. His screams echoed across the lot as he grabbed at his face, blood pouring down his hands.

Tony turned to Eddie. Frank's blood stained the front of his shirt. "I'll take that gun now."

Eddie tossed him the 9mm. His stomach threatened to rid him of the hamburger as he watched Frank, covered in blood, writhing on the ground.

Tony stood over Frank and aimed the 9mm at his forehead. "Now you know how it feels, Frank. All those times, you cut into people without thinking twice. But the thing I hate you most for is how much pleasure you got out of it. You're a sick fuck, Frank. And now you're done."

Tony aimed and pulled the trigger, putting two shots into Frank's forehead. Frank's body jerked and then went still.

Eddie grabbed Tony's arm. "Look, we gotta get out of here. Where did you park the van?"

Tony picked up his jacket and put it on. "I parked around back. I'll go get it. We need to transfer the goods and get rid of him." Tony hurried across the lot and disappeared around the side of the building. He returned a few minutes later with the dark blue van.

"First," Tony said. "We transfer the weapons, then we wipe down the van. Your prints can't be found anywhere on it."

Eddie nodded. "Let's hurry."

They spent the next fifteen minutes moving the crates into Tony's van and wiping everything down. "What about Frank?" Eddie asked.

Tony grinned. "Not to worry. I came prepared." He pulled a role of heavy plastic from inside the van. "Help me get him wrapped. Leave his cell phone in the white van. Make sure you wipe it clean."

After securing Frank's body in the plastic, they placed it inside the van on top of one of the crates. "We'll find a nice place to bury him along the way."

"Bury him?"

"Yeah, I got two shovels in the back. Remember, Paulie said no slip-ups. We gotta make it so he can't be found anytime soon, if at all." He looked Eddie up and down. "Listen, thanks for being there for me. I'll never forget it."

"I'll always stand by you, Tony," Eddie said. "Now, let's get the hell out of here. After we bury Frank, we need to finish getting the guns to the cartel."

As Eddie drove out of the lot, he had no more doubts about his decision to return to his old life. Tony was right. They were cut from the same cloth. As far as Frank Uzelli goes, he got what he deserved. This is how the game is played, and you either win or lose.

After tonight, Eddie was more determined than ever to stay on the winning side.

Chapter 71 — Cookie
Damien's Loss

Cookie's heart ached watching Damien make calls to arrange for Roman's funeral. It was hard to believe the young man was gone—shot to death in a senseless killing by one of his friends. Now, she understood Damien's concern for his only brother.

"No, I'm not sure when the body is going to be released from the Coroner's Office," Damien said, his cell phone plastered to his ear while he paced her living room. He had arrived late last night after Monica picked up Andrew. He ended the call and sat next to her on the sofa. He threaded his hands through his hair and sighed.

"What can I do?" Cookie asked.

He placed his hand on her thigh. "Just your being here helps."

"What about your mother?"

"She will never get over Roman dying. Her friends have gathered around her, which might bring her some comfort."

"And your father?"

"Yes, my dear father. There is something I haven't told you."

Cookie set her hand on top of his. "You can tell me anything, Damien. You need to trust me."

"My father's been arrested. They are holding him in the Federal Prison in Manhattan."

Cookie's breath hitched in her throat. This was the last thing she expected him to say. "Arrested for what?"

"According to his lawyer, for trafficking weapons. I'm sure there will be other charges against him. The FBI raided the New Jersey Seaport. I think he was caught in the act."

The minute he said FBI, Cookie thought of Monica. Was she involved in the raid? This was all too much at once. Roman dead, and his father in jail. Poor Darya. "I want you to take me to see your mother."

"I don't think that's a good idea right now."

Cookie got up. "No, it's only right that I go and see her." She grabbed a jacket from the closet by the front door. "Come on, Damien. Please take me to your mother's house."

A half-hour later, they stepped off the elevator and stood in front of Darya's door. "Are you sure about this?" Damien said, his fingers inches from pushing the doorbell.

"Yes. If she asks me to leave, that's okay, too. But she needs to know I care about what happened."

Damien pressed the buzzer. Footsteps could be heard padding to the door. It opened to a puffy-eyed Darya. Her always neatly done hair now hung in limp blonde strands. All color had receded from her cheeks, making her appear ghostly. She wore simple pale blue pajamas.

"May we come in?" Cookie said.

Darya nodded and then stepped away from the door. Cookie and Damien entered, exchanging their shoes for slippers by the door. They proceeded into the living room, where Darya sat on one end of the sofa, her knees pressed to her chest, a forlorn look on her face. Everything around her was in disarray. End table drawers hung open, pillows were tossed about, and artwork had been removed from their place on the walls.

"What happened here?" Damien asked.

"The authorities came and searched the house," Darya said. "I kept telling them they would not find anything. They showed me a court order, so I had no choice."

"Don't worry," Damien said. "Cookie and I will help put things back together."

Cookie went and sat beside her while Damien took a seat across from them. "I want you to know how terribly sorry I am about Roman," Cookie said. "Is there anything I can do for you?"

Darya's eyes filled with tears. "Bring my boy back," she said. "I want my Roman back."

"Mother, you know we can't do that," Damien said.

Without warning, Darya sprung up from the sofa. She pointed her finger at Damien. "Why did you let him die? If you were in the room, you could have saved him. But you let your brother die." She tore off down the hall and into the bedroom, slamming the door behind her.

"She doesn't mean that," Cookie said to a stricken Damien. "She's just grieving." Cookie left the living room and went down the hall.

"What are you doing?" Damien said. "I think it's best to leave her alone right now."

Cookie shook her head. "No. The last thing she needs right now is to be alone." Cookie tapped lightly on the bedroom door while Damien threw up his hands and retreated toward the kitchen. "I'll make her some tea," he said.

Cookie tapped again and then turned the knob. She stepped inside, where Darya lay in a fetal position on the bed facing the windows. Her shoulders shook as she whimpered and cried. Around her, dresser drawers lay empty, their contents spilled out onto the floor.

Cookie surveyed the mess and then eased down beside her. She touched Darya's shoulder. "You go ahead and cry. You need to mourn for the son you lost, but please remember, you still have another son who loves you. Damien would do anything to bring Roman back. He told me the doctors tried everything, but his wounds were too severe."

Darya wiped her eyes and peered up at Cookie. "Why wasn't Damien the one to operate?"

"The hospital has certain policies against doctors working on relatives. They wouldn't let Damien in the operating room."

"He should have insisted," Darya said, pushing herself up against the pillows.

"Things don't work that way. Damien would have gotten in trouble." Cookie studied Darya's face, the unconvinced look in her eyes. This woman had been sheltered from the real world for a long time. Her life with her husband was something out of the ordinary. Roman's birthday party was testament to that. Now, the real world had intruded on her once-perfect life. She would have a hard time handling the sudden shift.

"And Alexei?" Darya asked. "Why have they put him in prison? I am sure he has done nothing wrong. He should be here with me. I want him to come home."

"That's for the lawyer to work out," Cookie said. "In the meantime, you need to build up your strength for what is ahead."

"You mean … Roman's funeral?" Darya asked pitifully. "I do not want to think about that."

"Damien is taking care of everything. But I'm sure he needs your help with this. I know you would want things a certain way."

"Of course. Yes, you are right. With Alexei gone, we need to take care of things."

There was a light tap on the door, and Damien entered with a tray. Cookie got up and moved away as he set it on top of the dresser and then poured tea from a porcelain pot. His hand shook slightly as he lifted the cup and handed it to Darya. "Here, drink some of this."

Darya accepted the cup and swallowed several sips before setting it on the nightstand. She patted the comforter. "Come, sit. We need to talk about Roman's funeral. I do not want you to have to make all the decisions. I know what he would have wanted."

Cookie backed away and left the room, her heart breaking for Damien and Darya. Their lives ripped apart by a man who chose to break the law and a son who couldn't find his way.

Chapter 72 — Monica
The Burial Ground

Monica surveyed the army of forensics personnel behind Alexei Volkov's house in the Catskills. They had already uncovered over ten graves, including Leonid Rabinovich and the most recent one, the body of Emil Kutuzov. Her stomach turned when she observed the basement torture chamber. From the rancid odor and blood and urine spatters, she could only imagine what horrific acts had taken place there.

Last night, she retrieved Andrew from Cookie's and this morning, dropped him off at daycare. Cookie's strange behavior had her guessing what might be going on with her friend. She seemed in a rush to have Monica gone. She said she was expecting her doctor boyfriend.

Outside, she stepped away from the house and checked her cell phone again. Nothing from Eddie and no news on finding Frank Uzelli. He seemed to have disappeared off the face of the earth, a sure sign of the mob at work.

"I'm wondering just how many more bodies we're going to uncover," Kai said, coming up behind her. "Austin sure hit the jackpot with this. Alexei Volkov will be spending the rest of his life behind bars for sure."

Bob Acosta appeared from the side of the house. "I just got some news."

Monica steeled herself. If it was about Eddie, she didn't want to hear it. Right now, not knowing was the better choice.

"Alexei Volkov plans on pleading guilty."

Monica's body relaxed. "I hope he's not going to try and make a deal."

Bob spread out his arms. "With all this, I don't think there's a deal to be made. His younger son, Roman, was shot dead yesterday. A murder-suicide is the information I got. I think that might have been the reason for the guilty plea. People make sudden changes in times of grief. A team searched his club, Tatiana, and his residence. They confiscated the computers from the club. More than likely, our Digital Forensic team will probably find two sets of books. There was nothing of significance found at his home."

It was early evening by the time Monica and Kai headed back to the city. Forensics would continue to work on the scene over the next few months. Kai, in the passenger seat, kept checking her cell phone.

"Expecting a call or text?" Monica asked, her hands steady on the wheel.

"I thought I would hear something from Tony by now. It's kind of eerie. He has never gone silent for this long a time."

"I'm sure you'll hear something sooner or later," Monica said. "I keep thinking about Frank Uzelli, disappearing like that. I'm convinced it was a mob hit. There is no other explanation."

"I guess," Kai said. She fell silent and stared out the passenger side window. "Monica, what am I going to do if he does reach out? I'm tangled up with a mobster. A man with whom I'm so in love, it scares me."

"That's for you to decide, Kai. But if the Bureau found out you were associating with a known criminal, you could lose everything."

"I only wish I could get him to see he's on the wrong side," Kai said.

Monica chuckled. "Mobsters don't see it that way. They believe in the lifestyle. It's ingrained in them. They don't want to live any other way."

After picking up Andrew and dropping Kai off in Brooklyn, she headed over to Cookie's place. When she arrived, she hauled Andrew, who was fast asleep, out of his car seat. After ringing the bell several times, she was about to call Cookie on her cell when the door opened.

"Finally," Monica said, shifting Andrew to her other hip. "This kid is no light weight." She sailed past Cookie and into the living room where she laid Andrew on the chaise. Taking note of Cookie's silence and, suddenly embarrassed, she asked, "Am I interrupting something?"

Cookie gave her a crooked smile. "No, it's fine. I do have company though. He's in the bedroom."

"Oh, now I really feel stupid," Monica said.

"No, he's resting. There was a death in his family among other things."

"I'm sorry to hear that," Monica said. "Who died?"

"His younger brother, Roman."

Monica's jaw dropped. She stared at Cookie. "What did you say his brother's name was?"

"Roman, and before you say anything, I have something to ask you. Were you involved in a raid at the New Jersey Seaport?"

Monica frowned. "How do you know about that?"

"From Damien. It seems his father was arrested in the raid."

Monica sank down onto the sofa. She rubbed her temples and tried to control herself. Cookie was dating Damien Volkov. What were the odds? Out of all the eligible men on Staten Island, she ends up with him. "First of all, I can't discuss anything with regards to the raid with you. Second, you never told me you were dating a man whose father is a known criminal. One of the most feared in the Russian *Bratva*. His nickname is the 'Wolf' for God's sake."

"Yes, I've heard what they call my father." Damien leaned against the bedroom door frame, his hands shoved into his pants pockets.

Monica eased up from the sofa. She stared at Damien while he returned an equal gaze.

"You two haven't met, yet," Cookie said, breaking the silence. "Monica, this is Dr. Damien Volkov. Damien, this is my best friend, Monica Cappelino."

Damien walked over to Monica. He stretched out his hand. "Nice to finally meet you."

Monica's palm slid into his. "Same here," she said.

"So, you seem to know a lot about my father. Why is that?"

"I'm an FBI agent. We've been investigating your father for months."

"And now you have him locked up tight," Damien said. "I'm not surprised. I knew the day would come sooner or later."

Monica was rapidly changing her opinion of this man. "You knew how your father made his living?" she asked.

"No. Nor did I want to. He married my mother many years ago when I was a child. He brought us here to the United States. He raised me, paid for my education and yes, even loved me. But for the most part, he kept the darker side of his life from his family."

"I'm sorry about Roman," Monica said. "How did he end up so different from you?"

"Alexei was strict with me, but Roman was spoiled. I understand it because I know how long they waited to have a child between them. Roman feared my father, just like me, but he also idolized him. He tried in many ways to emulate him. But Roman didn't understand the consequences of doing so."

"Listen," Monica said. "I need to say one other thing before I go."

"What's that?" Damien asked.

"I hope you realize how special Cookie is. Don't ever hurt her or I'll come looking for you, Dr. Volkov."

For the first time, Damien smiled. "Believe me, I already know how special Carlotta is. You can rest easy. She's in good hands."

Happy Cookie had found someone who genuinely cared for her, Monica collected Andrew. Cookie followed her to the door. She turned, looked at Cookie and said, "Carlotta, huh? I think I like this guy."

Monica drove home glad Cookie didn't know anything about Eddie being back. She'd keep that to herself for a while. Those two were like oil and water.

Tired from a full day, she fed Andrew dinner, bathed him and prepared to put him down for the night. She reached for one of his favorite books about trains and settled with him on her lap in the rocker.

"Where is Daddy?" Andrew asked. "When is he coming back?"

Monica studied the face before her. It was the spitting image of Eddie's down to his nautical blue eyes. "I'm not sure, Andrew."

"But I want to see him." He snuggled against her, his head on her chest.

Her heart grew heavy at his words. A lump formed in her throat and she swallowed hard.

"Me, too, Andrew," she whispered. "Me, too."

Chapter 73 — Tony
Moving Up

Tony and Eddie waited for Paulie at his restaurant. Even with Eddie insisting on changing the meeting place not far from the Mexican Border in Arizona, everything had gone smoothly with the cartels. Tony had relished shoveling the last mound of dirt onto Frank's grave. His body felt lighter somehow, years of resentment washed away with the flick of a razor and a gun.

"Feels good to be back in New York," Eddie said. "But I gotta find a place on Staten Island, near my kid."

"Yeah," Tony said. "You should do that."

The waiter set down steaming plates of pasta and a basket filled with garlic rolls. He poured each of them a glass of red wine, smiled and retreated.

Tony raised his glass. "To us and the future."

"To the future," Eddie said, swallowing some wine.

"Hey, what's this?" Paulie asked, sitting down at the table. "Starting without me?"

"The past few days were rough," Tony said. "We need a taste of something good."

Paulie laughed and signaled the waiter for a glass of wine. "I ain't got time to eat. I have another meeting, but you two did good. Real good. The commission is very, very happy." He caught Eddie's eye. "Really smart changing the meet after what happened at the seaport. We lost Alexei Volkov, but someone else will take his place. That's the way it always goes."

"Glad everyone's satisfied," Eddie said.

Paulie leaned forward and lowered his voice. "I have it on good authority you two will be moving up the ranks."

Tony set his fork down. "For sure?" he asked.

Paulie slapped his arm. "Yes, for sure. Seems we're light since some others had to depart this life."

"How high?" Eddie asked.

"Capo's. Both of you. You'll have your own crew of earners. But remember, it's not an easy position. A lot will be expected of both of you. We'll meet with the commission next week and set everything up."

Tony couldn't stop grinning. He had waited so long for this. To be Caporegime with his own crew. A position once held by his old boss, Frank Uzelli. Having Eddie in the same position truly put things over the top.

Paulie rubbed the dark stubble on his chin. "You took care of the other thing, right?"

"Absolutely," Tony said.

"Nothing's gonna pop up. If you know what I mean."

"Not a chance," Tony said.

Paulie finished his wine and got up. "You two enjoy. I'll be in touch."

After he left, they finished up their pasta and wine and then ordered two expressos. Tony leaned back in his chair and sighed. "How sweet is this?" he asked.

Eddie sipped his expresso. "Yeah, real sweet but Paulie doesn't realize we knew nothing about what happened at the seaport before I changed the meeting place. Talk about luck."

"As long as things keep going our way, we'll be fine," Tony said. He pulled out his cell phone and checked his messages. Still nothing from Kai. The need to see her gnawed at him.

"Have you heard from Monica?" Tony asked.

Eddie's face flushed. "One message asking if I was okay. I didn't answer it. I'm not even sure why."

"Have your feelings for her changed?"

"No. That ain't gonna happen. I can barely breathe without her. I feel like I'm living half a life. Know what I mean?"

"I sure do. I haven't heard from Kai at all. I think she's finished with me."

Eddie fingered his napkin, a faraway expression on his face. "You know it's hard for them with the careers they have. They love what they do as much as us. Here we are back in the mob, happy about the future while they work to tear it all apart."

"Crazy, isn't it," Tony said. "I guess we'll just have to see how it all plays out. At least you have one up on me?"

"What's that?"

"Your son. Monica is not going to put the father of her son in jail."

Eddie let out a chuckle. "You don't know Monica. I never take anything for granted with her. Her dedication to the Bureau surpasses all else, even me."

Later, in his hotel room, Tony stretched out on the bed, unable to get Kai off of his mind. He picked up his cell and called her number. About to hang up after it rang ten times, her voice came over the line.

"Tony?"

"Yeah, baby it's me. Kai, listen. I need to see you. Please come to the hotel. We need to talk things out."

"I was so worried about you. I'm glad you're alright but I don't think that's a good idea."

"Please, baby. Just for a little while. I can't stand being apart. Don't I mean anything to you?"

"You know how I feel, Tony. That will never change. Stay safe."

Tony held onto the phone and listened to the silence at the other end. He was right. Kai did not intend to continue their relationship. Why couldn't he have the one woman he wanted? Easing up, he undressed, showered and returned to bed. He turned on the television in an effort to distract himself.

A light tap on the door startled him. It couldn't be Eddie. He would have called first. Reaching into the nightstand, he pulled out his 9mm and padded to the door. The tapping sounded again. He peered through the peephole but saw nothing but the empty hallway. His pulse raced and he backed away from the door. Had Paulie changed his mind and sent someone to straighten him out?

There was a third knock on the door. Angry now, gun in his hand he flung it open. Kai stood there smiling. "You ought to be more careful."

Tony's body relaxed and with his free hand, he pulled her inside and closed the door. "Not funny, Kai. Not funny at all."

"I was testing you," she said, moving over to the bed.

Tony followed and placed the gun back into the nightstand. He turned and took in this gorgeous creature standing in front of him. Reaching out, he cradled her face in his hands and peered into her dark eyes.

"God, how I've missed you," he said, his voice was low-pitched, almost crooning. He attempted to pull her to him, but she pushed him away.

"Before any of that," she said. "I need to tell you something. You were honest with me about your past and I need to do the same."

"Sure, whatever you want," he said, dropping down onto the bed.

Kai sat beside him. "You deserve to know where my anger was coming from and what happened to me on the Rez. I couldn't talk about any of it before."

Tony sat and listened as she poured the words out. How she suffered sexual abuse at the hands of her uncle from the time she was a child all the way up to her teenage years. His body burned, his muscles twisting tight inside him, he vowed to find this man and kill him.

"Then, when my grandmother was dying, I returned home," she said, her voice breaking. She finished with his attack on her again and her mother putting an end to it all. "So, you see, I had so much built up inside of me and no way to get rid of it."

"You could have told me, Kai," Tony said. "I would have helped you through it."

"I couldn't. I always blamed myself. I thought something was wrong with me. But now I know I was just one of his many victims, as was my mother and her sisters."

"Your mother should have protected you."

"But then she would have to admit things to herself that she just couldn't face. Like me, she buried it away. Now, we have a rebirth of sorts between us. We understand each other much better."

"Well, I'm happy things turned out the way they did. Lucky your uncle is gone or he would have to deal with me."

"Is that right?" Kai said, pushing him down onto the comforter. Her lips found his.

The hunger inside of him rose. He wrapped his arms around her and pulled her close. "What are we going to do?" he whispered. "I can't live fully in this world without you."

"Let's not decide that tonight," she said. "For now, as my people say, we will be in *Hozho*.

"*Hozho*?" Tony questioned.

"To be in *Hozho*, is to be at one with and part of the world around you," Kai said, stroking his cheek. "Right now, at this moment, you're my world, Tony Morello."

"And you're mine," Tony whispered.

Chapter 74 — Eddie
Monica

Signs of spring were evident at The Battery on a Saturday afternoon. Sitting on a bench waiting for Monica and Andrew, Eddie caught glimpses of yellow and white daffodils fanning out across the grass. The cold crisp air, had been replaced by a tepid breeze. Rays of sun reflected off the windows of the Sea Glass Carousel. Crowds of people meandered about enjoying the weather. Eddie had sent Monica a text the previous night asking to meet. Things needed to be settled between them for Andrew's sake.

Eddie rose at the sight of his son galloping toward him with Monica trailing behind. He knelt and held out his arms. Andrew slammed into him with such force he almost fell backward.

"Daddy, Daddy," Andrew cried, hugging his neck. "Where have you been?"

"I missed you so much," Eddie said. "I was away on business."

Andrew dropped his arms and pointed at the carousel. "I want to go for a ride."

"Sure, come on." Eddie took Andrew by the hand, bought a ticket, and settled him in a bright purple glass fish. He stepped away as the motorized fish spun and turned. Andrew joined in the chorus of children who squealed with delight.

Monica, dressed in jeans, a white turtleneck sweater, and a navy jacket, waved and smiled at Andrew.

"We need to talk," Eddie said. "I'm sorry I haven't been in touch. There was a lot going on." Her eyes caught his, and he could see the fire behind them.

"Do you have any idea how worried I was? I thought you were dead."

Eddie gave her a quirky smile. "So, you do still care about me."

"Of course, I care about you. You're Andrew's father."

"Is that all I am? Just Andrew's father," Eddie said. "I was hoping I meant something more than that to you."

"It's a little more complicated than that now you've decided to switch careers," she said, her voice dripping with sarcasm.

"Come on, Monica. I don't want us to keep going down that road. For Andrew's sake, if nothing else, we need to come to an agreement."

Monica laughed. "An agreement? How about you agree to quit the mob and go back into witness protection?"

Eddie reached for her hand. Glad when she didn't pull away, he said, "You know that's not going to happen. The sooner you realize it, the better. This is my choice, Monica."

"No, your Uncle Sal made the choice for you a long time ago. I wish you could see things from my side. If only you had stayed in Arizona—"

"And what?" Eddie cut in. "Stay there knowing I could never be with you and Andrew. You have no idea how hard it was for me. I thought about the two of you every single day. My little boy was growing up without me."

"I'm sorry," Monica said. "I only wanted for you to be safe."

"I am safe," Eddie said.

"For now. What about when they decide to change things or the law catches up to you? Let's face it, Eddie, you'll never *really* be safe."

Eddie squeezed her hand. "None of us are, Monica." He turned and pulled her close, his arms wrapped around her body. He kissed the top of her head, her dark curls soft against his lips.

"All I need to know is I have you and Andrew. Nothing else matters to me. My love for the two of you will never change, no matter what happens."

The carousel ride ended, and Andrew came running over to them, his cheeks flushed a deep red. Monica stepped away from Eddie. "Did you have fun?" she asked.

He nodded his head up and down. "Can I ride again?"

"No," Monica said. "I think it's time to go."

Eddie looked at her, his eyes pleading. "Why go so soon? You just got here. I want to spend time with the two of you."

Her eyes misted over. She blinked and turned away. Grabbing Andrew's hand, she said, "Come on, we need to catch the ferry." Andrew pulled away and folded his arms.

"Don't do this, Monica," Eddie said.

"I need time to think. You know I won't stop you from seeing Andrew. We'll work something out."

Eddie knelt. He hugged and kissed his son. "Daddy will see you again real soon."

Andrew pursed his lips. "No. I want you to come with us now. Come home, Daddy." His eyes filled with tears and coursed down his cheeks. He let out a low wailing sound.

Eddie's heart filled with a sadness that he could barely comprehend. He had never seen his little boy cry. He looked up at Monica. "Is this what you want?"

"Don't blame this on me," she said. "You made a choice, and that choice is putting me in an awkward position." Monica took Andrew's hand. "Come on. You'll see Daddy again soon."

Eddie ached inside as they walked away, his heart breaking with each step they took. Andrew turned his head, tears flowing freely down his face. He waved at Eddie.

Eddie waved back and stared after them. They receded into the distance, becoming smaller and smaller until the throngs of people swallowed them up. He left The Battery and headed for the hotel. Tomorrow, he would find a place on Staten Island and make sure there was a room for Andrew.

If it took him the rest of his life, somehow, he would convince Monica that they belonged together. They were a family. The only family he had left, and families stayed together.

Chapter 75 — Darya
Guess Who's Coming to Dinner

Darya checked the contents of the large pot on the stove. Damien and Carlotta were expected to come for dinner later this evening. She decided to make Pelmeni, one of her specialties. The pasta-like dough wrapped around minced meat originated in Siberia.

Her set of Lomonosov China once again graced the dining room table. With Roman gone a little over nine months and Alexei in prison, she felt it was time to concentrate on the present. The past, at times too awful to even comprehend, left her drained and craving a life that no longer existed.

Never in a million years had she dreamed she would lose a son and a husband at the same time. Going to visit Alexei in prison was painful but not as cruel and agonizing as visiting Roman's grave, which she did faithfully once a week.

She no longer blamed Damien for Roman's death, nor did she blame Alexei, even though he blamed himself. There was no use in putting blame anywhere. It would never bring Roman back. On those nights when she missed him the most, she would have a good cry and then try to remember the good times when both her boys were young and innocent.

As for Alexei and what they had accused him of, she decided to dwell only on his love for her and she for him. Sentenced to spend the rest of his life in prison was punishment enough for the man who had saved her and her little boy from poverty all those years ago in Russia.

Now, she no longer had the luxury of spending money so freely. The government had returned the money in the regular bank accounts to her when they couldn't tie it to Alexei's illegal activities as they had with his earnings from Tatiana.

Without anyone's knowledge, Alexei had transferred the penthouse apartment into Damien's name many years ago. How telling that he had the foresight to do so. Darya knew he was only protecting her.

Darya finished preparing several side dishes and checked the table setting once again. She showered and changed into a simple pair of black pants and a pale blue sweater. Finished with her hair just as the doorbell rang, she hurried to answer it.

Damien and Carlotta stepped through the doorway, all smiles. Darya had grown an attachment to her son's girlfriend. She proved to be a caring and loving person not only toward Damien but also toward her, staying by her side during Roman's funeral and even afterward.

It no longer mattered she was not Russian, only that she made Damien happy. And when Darya insisted on calling her by her given name, which she found so much nicer than Cookie, she graciously accepted.

"Come," Darya said as they set their shoes by the door and put on slippers. "I have made something special."

"Your Pelmeni comes to mind," Damien said, laughing.

"Sounds interesting," Cookie said. She handed Darya a box of Italian Pastries. "For dessert," she said.

They seated themselves at the table, still following all the traditional customs. Damien poured each of them a glass of wine. Cookie insisted on making a toast and thanking Darya for the wonderful meal. Their conversation remained light, always staying away from the topic of Roman or Alexei.

They finished the meal, and Darya set about plating the pastries while Cookie set the teapot and cups on the table. They all looked startled when the doorbell rang.

"Are you expecting someone," Damien asked.

Darya shook her head. "No. I cannot imagine who it might be. Let me go see."

She padded to the door and opened it. A pretty young woman stood in the hallway with an infant in her arms, wrapped in a blue blanket. Darya immediately thought she must have the wrong apartment.

"Can I help you?" she asked.

"Mrs. Volkov?" she asked.

"Yes."

"My name is Amy. Amy Walker." Slowly, she pushed back the blanket covering the baby's face. "This is Alexander Roman Walker. We call him Alex," she said. "He's your grandson."

Epilogue
Monica & Kai

Monica and Kai strolled along the Brooklyn Heights Promenade. People paraded up and down the cobblestone path. Spring and summer had quickly progressed into late fall. A popular place, it offered unmatched views of the Manhattan skyline and several landmarks. Sun glinted off the East River as tugboats and cargo ships passed by. A few stray clouds dotted an otherwise pale blue sky.

They stopped for a moment and took in the massive Brooklyn Bridge spanning the East River. "Everything seems so peaceful," Kai said.

"It sure does," Monica said. Her eyes rested on the vast expanse of the bridge. "If people only knew how hard we work to try and keep it that way." Her cell phone buzzed, and she retrieved it from her coat pocket. It was Bob Acosta.

"Everything okay?" she asked.

"I just thought there was something you needed to know. We got some new intel."

This couldn't be good. For Bob to call and not wait for her to return to the office made her pulse spike. "Regarding what?" she asked.

"It seems Eddie Marconi and Tony Morello have moved up in the world. They were both reported to be Caporegime, each with their own crew of soldiers."

Monica's gut clenched. Eddie a Capo? He was way more connected than even she thought he could be. That was a bold move on the mob's part. "Thanks for letting me know, Bob. I guess we'll have to see how things progress."

"It means more work for the task force," Bob said. "Just be careful, Monica."

She ended the call and turned to Kai. "It seems Eddie and Tony are Caporegime now."

"Did Eddie say anything to you about this?"

"No. We leave that kind of stuff alone. He comes to pick up Andrew or I drop him off at his place. We don't talk much unless it pertains to Andrew, though every once in a while, he tries to get me to change my mind by guilting me about family."

"That must be so hard," Kai said.

"I'm learning to live with it. What about you and Tony?"

"I haven't seen Tony in a while. We speak on occasion." Kai stopped and went over to the railing. Monica joined her and listened to the sound of the waves crashing against the rocks below—a reminder of how turbulent her life had become these past few years.

"Truthfully," Kai said. "I miss him so much at times it hurts to breathe."

"I know what you mean. I still love Eddie, but I can't condone what he has chosen to do with his life. I wanted so much more for him."

"It's almost funny," Kai said. "I can't picture Tony doing anything else with his. It's like the mob is ingrained in his soul."

Monica leaned against the railing and stared out over the water. "I just hope they both know what they're doing and what it might cost them in the end."

"Do you think we made the right decision?" Kai asked. "I mean, we traded our happiness for the Bureau."

Monica focused her eyes on Kai. "I'm sure I did. But if you have any doubts, then you need to come to grips with them right now. It will be too late once we continue our work with the task force."

Kai turned her face away. "I believe in my heart that I did the right thing. But why doesn't it feel that way?"

"Oh, Kai. You can't have it both ways. Life just doesn't work like that."

They moved away from the railing and continued to walk down the promenade. Memories of Eddie swirled through Monica's mind. She thought about the time before she agreed to rejoin the Bureau. If Daniel Gage hadn't shown up at her store that day, where would she and Eddie be now?

Monica stole glances at some of the passersby, ordinary people with everyday lives. She couldn't help but wonder what the future held for her and Eddie. Who would win in the end? The Bureau or the Mob?

Nominated for Georgia Author of the Year for Redemption, the first book in her Sicario Files Trilogy, Stephanie is dedicated to giving her reader's fast-paced, high-stakes, page-turning stories that keep you on the edge of your seat and are full of surprising twists! Stephanie's second novel, Retribution, the thrilling sequel to Redemption, was released in 2019 and was followed by Reckoning in 2021. Her fourth novel, Mobbed Up, was released in February 2023; the sequel, Mobbed Up 2, Return to New York, is set to be released in September 2024. She is hard at work on the last book in the Mobbed Up Trilogy. You can find her online at www.stephaniebaldi2.com or follow her on Facebook and Twitter at sbauthor7.

The Sicario Files
REDEMPTION

Murder is the catalyst pushing Carrie Overton headlong into the arms of the hitman sent to kill her.

Determined to escape her alcoholic and drug-addicted mother and distance herself from the memory of the son she lost, Carrie leaves home with Travis Montgomery, a man twenty years her senior who harbors shocking secrets connected to her past.

After Travis forces her to help him steal two million dollars from a drug lord, leaving two people dead, Carrie decides to add a third victim to her list, and Travis is left lying on the floor.

Eager to start over, she takes the stolen money and travels to the small mountain town of Laurel, Pennsylvania. Carrie lies about her past and relaxes into her new life. Before long, Carrie's lies are piling up, and her crimes are about to catch up to her.

Nicholas D'Angelo is known as a ghost, a contract killer for one of the biggest drug lords in Miami. His assignment is simple. Find the people, who stole the two million dollars, recover the money and eliminate them.

With a hitman on her trail, Carrie is forced to make a choice. Trust the hitman who vows to disobey his orders and protect her. Or stay in Laurel and face the drug lord determined to end her life. Either one might kill her.

RETRIBUTION

Almost six long years have passed since Carmela Santiago witnessed the hitman she loved assassinate her father. Now she is ready to exact her plan of revenge against him and the people he loves. Carmela will stop at nothing to tear his family apart. Running her father's drug smuggling empire, she will use every resource at her disposal, including money, sex, the men in her life, and her very own cold-blooded sicario, to help her carry out her deeds.

Nicholas D'Angelo, the contract killer, once employed by Carmela's father has his family safely tucked away in a compound in Tuscany, Italy. Many times, he has regretted his decision to let Carmela live. Forced by the government to return to the United States and resume the life of a killer, Nick knows will put his family in jeopardy.

Carmela Santiago has the means to destroy him and all those he holds dear. Carmela moves forward with her plan of revenge, but her closest allies are fast becoming her enemies. As she pushes things to the limit, Carmela gets caught in her own web of lies, murder, and deceit. With the stakes rising higher, she is determined to win. Nick will use everything at his disposal to stop her.

RECKONING

One terrible night in Tahoe left Carmela Santiago dead and a visible scar on Miguel Medina's face. After three long years, a still open wound lies hidden inside his cold heart.

Once Carmela's trusted Sicario and lover, he is determined to exact vengeance on the man responsible for her death. Miguel knows going up against such a man as Nicholas D'Angelo, will not be easy.

Both ghosts, hitmen at the top of their game, their past confrontation in Tahoe has proven they possess the skills to eliminate one another. Only Miguel's plans run much deeper.

Vowing to reclaim Carmela's daughter, Natalia, and raise her as his own, Miguel has struck at the heart of Nick's family by stealing away something they love.

With pressure mounting and time running out, Nick must find a way to take back what rightfully belongs to him and destroy Miguel Medina once and for all.

Available in paperback and eBook
And on Audible

And the first volume in the **Mobbed Up Series**

Mobbed Up

Former FBI agent, Monica Cappelino wants nothing more than to forget about her time at the Bureau. Returning to her hometown of Staten Island, New York to start over, she believes she has left all the ghosts from the past behind her … that is until Eddie Marconi, the man she once loved and who broke her heart, comes back into her life unexpectaedly.

His return causes the FBI to come calling. Only this time, they want Monica back on the the condition she convinces Eddie, who is connected to Organized Crime, to become an asset. Monica must get Eddie to turn against his uncle, Salvatore Marconi, a powerful and feared Under Boss in the Mafia.

Monica is caught between her loyalty to the FBI and her love for Eddie. Will she agree to help the Bureau putting both thei lives in jeopardy?

Available in paperback and eBook